# ALANA KAY

# DARKEST VALLEY

## RADIANT LEGACY BOOK ONE

ISBN: 979-8-9912918-6-6 (Ebook edition)
ISBN: 979-8-9912918-7-3 (Paperback edition)

Library of Congress Control Number: 2025915855

First edition 2025



Cover by Miblart

Edited by EJL Editing

Published by Fate Unbound Publishing LLC
Los Angeles, CA

Visit the author's website at www.alanakayauthor.com for content details.

# DARKEST VALLEY

RADIANT LEGACY BOOK ONE

# ONE

## CELINE

A shiver rolls down my spine as I wrap my calf around the pole and arch my back until the tips of my hair and wings graze the stage. Dozens of eyes on me. Leering. They rake across my exposed skin hungrily, like ghostly fingers.

My audience pays the bills. That earns them the right to look to their hearts' content. But if they try to touch me, I'll torch them . . . and I'll have a great time doing it.

Humming along with the music, I throw my hips back and smile.

There's a wild energy hovering around the Naked Fang tonight. The tips are better than usual, and—something hard pings off my forehead. I slide a foot down the pole before I catch myself, palms prickling from the unexpected friction. The sharp sting is followed by a dull, painful throb that syncs up with the beat of the drums and my pounding heart.

Adrenaline pumping, my eyes follow the object as it hits the stage, rolling around and wobbling before falling flat. A quarter. Someone threw a fucking quarter. And with the supernatural clientele in here, there's zero chance it was an accident, the collective senses and reflexes are too advanced.

The urge to touch my skin to see if I'm bleeding is hard to ignore, but I focus on my dance instead. I won't give the jackass who tried to humiliate me the satisfaction of seeing me hurt.

With my teeth gritted so tightly my jaw aches, I feel heat rolling off my wings in waves. It brings the temperature on the stage up several degrees, a warning for me to chill out or release some of my rage before I accidentally burn the club to the ground. I choose release.

Flipping back off the pole, I drop into a full split and scan the audience until I spot the dick who threw the coin. Legs spread wide, he's grinning, the oscillating stage lights illuminating exactly how pleased he is with himself. He winks when he sees me staring, saluting me with . . . another coin. It's clenched in his meaty fingers, and he lifts it higher in a toasting motion. He's taunting me.

The temperature rises around me again.

I roll my bottom lip between my teeth and look him up and down deliberately. He trembles with excitement. *Loser.* It's easy to memorize his blockish face as I crawl across the stage, dipping my pelvis in rhythmic rolls and collecting fallen cash as I go.

The quarter winks at me from its landing spot, tangerine-colored strobe lights reflecting off the shiny surface. I grab it, rolling it between my knuckles like a magician as the crowd roars with delight.

As the song ends, I glance back at the coin-throwing dick, blow a kiss, and flick his change back at him with a hint of my full strength. It shoots directly into his slack-jawed, gaping mouth, and I hear a tooth crack. *Bullseye.*

He falls back in his seat, visibly choking, hands wrapped around his throat. I watch with satisfaction as he struggles to breathe. When he gags, dislodging the quarter in the process, my lips curl into an obvious pout.

More cash hits the stage. They love it when I'm mean. I gather it up, heat rolling down my wings as I work to control what's left of my anger.

"Better luck next time, babe," Imani says, her husky tone tickling my ears and giving me goosebumps. I shiver, even though she's not trying to ensnare me.

My best friend does everything she can to keep a lid on her magnetism, but there's only so much she can do about the magic she was born with.

"Maybe he'll want payback for the tooth," I whisper, hearing the hopeful note in my own voice. I'm spoiling for a fight, and a meathead with a pocket full of coins is the perfect target for my frustration.

Imani laughs, the beautiful sound carrying into our audience. A man in the front row moans, squirming uncomfortably in his chair. I shake my head and pull Imani into a dirty dance, grinding against her in a patented move that never fails to make the audience go crazy.

Bills hit the stage in a frenzied flurry as I wrap my wings around the both of us, grazing her lower back in a teasing caress. An angry angel dancing with a sexy siren—that shit sells itself. They can't get enough of us.

"Knock them dead," I say as the song reaches our transition point, raising my voice to be heard over the music and cheers.

"If only I were that lucky." Imani sighs, and I spin her away from me with a controlled move that appears more reckless than it is. We've practiced a thousand times, and I know exactly how much force to use.

Imani goes up on the toe of one chunky platform heel, spinning dozens of times, faster and faster, until she's a whirl of tightly coiled curls and gleaming umber skin. Only when it seems the spin has escaped her control, and the crowd holds its collective breath does she catch the pole with her right hand and allow the momentum to carry her into a one-armed backbend.

Satisfied every eye is where it belongs—on my ride or die—I strut off the stage, my good mood returning as the stunned silence erupts into raucous cheers. Like every other night, Imani will end this set by dancing away with their valuable cash while discarding their worthless, drunken promises of eternal devotion. I'll cheer her on for every sensual eight-count, then help her count every crumpled single.

Air conditioning hits my flushed skin as I walk into the dressing room, sighing with relief. Holding my wings out wide so the cool air can do its job, I take a deep breath, then narrow my eyes as I notice the room is suspiciously empty of other dancers.

"You know you're not supposed to use magic against the paying customers." Luca leans back in *my* chair, his hazel eyes sparking.

The wooden floor here and in the main room is scratched, scuffed, and dented, battered by a million beatings from a thousand different stilettos. The air is laced with the comforting scent of perfume and hairspray, capped with a faint whiff of burned product from the curling irons and straighteners leeching power from every available outlet. If I close my eyes, I catch notes of latex, assorted magic, and cash—that unmistakable trace of a dozen strangers' sweaty palms.

"Are we really calling a quarter payment? In this economy?" I keep my tone light and playful. Luca hands me a cool water bottle, folding his arms over his chest in a silent demand for me to try again. I huff. "Would you believe me if I said it slipped?"

Luca groans. "You're developing a reputation, Celine."

"Yeah? We both know that's why they line up around the

block," I remind him, annoyed that he's questioning my judgment, and even more annoyed that he might be right.

Brushing past Luca, I lean forward to examine the mark on my forehead in the mirror. Shit, the thing is almost as red as my hair. With my pale skin, it's especially obvious. Sighing, I shove body glitter to the side to reach for my concealer.

"Let me see it," Luca says. His voice is tight, and if I didn't know better, I would think my ass in his face was affecting him.

Ignoring his demand, I bend over further to test my theory and soothe my wounded pride while I'm at it. The fabric of my lingerie shifts to reveal more of my bare skin, but Luca's eyes never leave mine in the mirror. It's oddly disappointing. I'm supposed to have one of the best bodies in Las Vegas, but Luca never notices. Some perverse part of my mind hates that.

"Are you playing manager?" I tease, dabbing product on my forehead.

He rolls his eyes. "I am your manager."

"And you know I hate to be managed," I say casually, blending the concealer in until the mark and the makeup are practically invisible. "I don't know why you keep trying."

"What happens if he comes back with friends when you're leaving work?"

I picture breaking more of the blockhead's teeth and grin. "Don't threaten me with a good time."

"This isn't a joke, Celine!" Luca's hands curl around the armrests of the chair, his knuckles whiting out from the pressure. "Some of these guys are frothing at the bit to take an angel down a notch, and you're feeding into it."

My amusement vanishes. I'm not wearing a sign that tells guys to behave like animals, so why is it my fault when they do? Luca should know better than to press me about this.

"What exactly do you want me to do?" I snap, my voice sharp as my anger surges back to life. "Because the day I start living my life to appease every horny, supernatural pig in this dusty ass valley is the day my life is no longer worth living."

"Don't say that," Luca hisses, sitting up straighter in my chair.

I spin, looming over him from my standing position between his knees. "I don't have a death wish, but I won't back down. Not to those creeps." Not to anyone, but there's no reason to tell Luca that. It would make his blood pressure spike, and it's way too early in our shift to get him that riled up.

He groans and throws his head back. I watch his Adam's apple bob with interest, then shove the unwanted fantasy of licking my way up the column of his throat out of my head. I need to get laid. If I'm having nasty thoughts about a good friend, it's been way too long since I scratched the itch.

"The coin was a test," Luca insists, and I roll my eyes. *Duh.*

"A test I made him choke on." The anger inside me surges, then spills over, and I groan as the excess unfurls along each feather of my wings as bright orange, dancing flames. We'll be sweltering in seconds; the air conditioning in this building is older than me.

Luca shoves to his feet. Instead of retreating from my obvious rage, he steps closer to me instead. "You're going to set off the smoke alarm again."

"Yeah, well, you pissed me off," I grunt, trying my best to shove the excess anger back inside myself where it belongs. I hate when my emotions are on display. It makes me feel far more exposed than stripping in front of strangers.

Luca's hands cradle my face, one painted black fingernail grazing my bottom lip as he sighs. "I'm not sorry."

"You're also not helping."

A drop of sweat rolls down from his hairline to his cheek, before finally dripping off the edge of his chiseled jaw. My flames climb higher. He doesn't let me go.

"Luca," I hiss. "You'll get burned."

He shakes his head, ignoring my warning. "You won't hurt me," he says. "Even if I piss you off."

Luca's solid confidence in me breaks my anger's hold, because he's right. Even the thought of making his beautiful face twist with pain turns my stomach.

The flames die abruptly around us, and Luca smiles. I roll my eyes and shove him back into the chair, reclaiming my personal space and severing this odd tension between us at the same time.

His face is damp with sweat from my flaming wings, his normally milk chocolate brown hair melting to a darker shade at the roots. "I think you're the one with a death wish," I mutter, using my thumbs to fix his smudged eyeliner.

The disheveled, messy, rockstar style somehow makes him better looking. Sexier. Like he just spent a handful of hours bending someone over the nearest flat surface and making them scream.

I flap my wings gently, hoping to get oxygen to my brain and stop myself from doing something unbelievably idiotic, like find out if Luca tastes as good as he looks. When the smoke detector squawks, the sharp, bleating alarm is the answer to a prayer I didn't bother to make.

Luca jumps up, unscrewing the device and taking the battery out, grumbling under his breath the entire time. I leave the dressing room before I'm tempted to say something I can't take back.

After my shift ends, I push through the heavy back door of the club, more than ready to go home and wind down. The door slams shut behind me, a satisfyingly solid sound marking the end of an exhausting day.

Once I get home, I'll make some food, then—my skin prickles, little electric shocks shooting from the arches of my feet to the tips of my fingers. Someone is watching.

Rolling my shoulders back, I pretend not to notice and walk confidently toward the alley where I parked my motorcycle. As tired as I am, I can hold my own if someone tries their luck.

Luca's warning rolls around in my head, and I sigh internally. If whoever the stare belongs to wants a fight, they'll have to throw the first punch.

Dominant fist curled around my keys, my wings are already stowed away, making me look as human as the people going about their business behind the magical distraction wards. Absorbing them into my skin is a skill that took me years to master. If I'm honest, it's never gotten easier. I tell people I leave them out at the club because the tips are better—and they are— but the truth is my wings hate to be hidden.

It used to be one of the many things that made him furious with me.

The skin of my shoulder blades itches beneath my leather jacket. Wearing the protective clothes over my simple nylon shorts and crop top is the safest way to travel on a bike. But it's stifling until I can get some speed going and feel the proverbial wind in my hair.

"Hey, baby doll." I stiffen at the smarmy voice behind me. "Did it hurt when you fell from heaven?" Only my exhaustion keeps me from rolling my eyes at the universe's most unoriginal pickup line.

"No," I mutter. "Because some of us know how to stick the landing."

His responding chuckle is oily. It makes the hairs on the back of my neck stand on end, yet I refuse to give him the satisfaction of turning around.

Guys try this all the time after close. Ninety-nine times out of a hundred, they skulk back into the shadows once they realize I have no intention of entertaining their bullshit. He'll take the hint. Eventually.

"What's the hurry, sweet thing? Do I make you nervous?"

*Oh fuck no.* This guy clearly needs to be taught a lesson. It's all I can do to keep my feet moving along the pockmarked asphalt toward my bike. I tighten my grip on my keys, maintaining the same unhurried pace. Damn Luca for getting in my head and making me second-guess my stab first, ask questions later philosophy.

My instincts go haywire a heartbeat before rough hands shove me into the grimy wall of the alley. I catch myself before my nose can connect and shake my head. *That's it. No more chances.* Planting one heel against the concrete wall, I use the momentum to flip backward and drive my other foot into the guy's face.

He yowls, and I smile as I recognize him. Quarter Guy is back for more, and I kicked him right in his injured mouth with the combined force of about five human men. I may not believe in divine intervention of any kind, but I can certainly get behind a little poetic justice.

*Pucker up, asshole. Karma wants to give you a kiss.* I'm considering how painful his lesson should be when he pulls a long, shiny knife from his denim jacket, dark eyes swirling with rage as he advances on me.

"Do you even know who I am?" he snarls. "You're lucky to have my attention."

I examine my nails, painted a cheerful shade of citrus and filed into the almond shape I prefer, then lift my gaze to my attacker's. Gray eyes brimming with entitlement, he has hulking, brutish features. A mixture of oversized and squashed, they sit unevenly above a harsh, square chin that's dripping blood.

I snort a laugh. "You know, now that you mention it, you do look familiar. I think my friend carved your face in a beginner's art class we took together. We were only five at the time, so it slipped my mind at first. It wasn't her best work."

For a second he freezes, probably trying to process my insult with his pea-sized brain. Kindly, I tap my foot a few times and give him a second to work it out.

This burly idiot has demon written all over him, the big, dumb kind we see often here on the Fringes. The rage in his eyes and the complete lack of stealth give him away. He'll be stronger than most supernaturals, but no match for me.

"You won't be laughing when I carve your face up," he says.

I wince. That comeback was embarrassing. Maybe I should give him another chance to think of something better. I open my mouth, then the air shifts against my back. The magic in my body hums in warning as it senses a real predator.

Blockhead looks up, over my shoulder, and glares. "Hey asshole—" the rest of the insult dies on his tongue.

His eyes calcify first, the shiny slate orbs turning dry and dull. Next, all color leaves his skin, the ruddy flesh transforming into lifeless, ashy stone. His hand reaches for me, the knife-tip glinting in the moonlight. He doesn't manage more than an inch before he's frozen in place, completely petrified.

"Seriously?" I complain, groaning and whirling around, being extra careful to keep my gaze locked on our feet. "I had it handled. I was giving him a second to come up with some better last words."

"He pulled a knife on you, Celine." Luca stumbles over the first syllable of my name, making it sound more like a hiss than a word. I take that as a verbal cue for me to keep my head down.

"Amazingly enough, I did notice that," I deadpan sarcastically. "Have you stowed the rock peepers, or do I need to give you a minute?"

He sighs. "I'm good."

Raising my head, I catch the tail end of Luca's eyes shifting back from unfamiliar reptilian yellow slits to the warm, whiskey-tinted hazel I'm used to. "At the risk of sounding ungrateful, what are we supposed to do with this monolith you made?" I thump my fist against the demon's frozen face. He looks better this way. I wish I could let him know that his final form is a definite improvement. "I bet it weighs a ton."

"I have a really strong friend," Luca says with a shrug.

I groan. "I was afraid you were going to say that." I slump against the statue and examine the knife clutched in its stone fingers. "Go get the push broom and watch for stragglers."

Luca nods, his jaw clenched as he disappears around the corner. While there's no one else around right now, that could change at any moment. Even though it's three o'clock in the morning, this city isn't known for its regular sleep schedule. Privacy of any kind is at a premium.

I'll have to act fast. After I check in all directions, I hoist the stone demon off the pavement and hurl it at the alley wall with all my strength. It hits with a deafening crack, the force doing exactly what I intended and breaking the statue into enough pieces that it isn't immediately recognizable. Quickly, I stomp on the rest, imagining the chunks as foot-sized bubble wrap.

As I pulverize the evidence, the first trickle of worry hits me.

We're a fringe community, which means we typically make and enforce our own code of conduct. An unspoken social agreement between supernaturals from half a dozen realms to do exactly two things: never alert the humans to our presence on Earth and keep the ruling enclave the fuck out of Las Vegas.

That usually isn't hard to do. Headquartered hundreds of miles away in Colorado, our regional enclave rarely makes an appearance here. The only time I've heard of it happening is when someone important dies. If the demon was trying to intimidate me, we're in the clear. If not . . . *Fuck,* I should have tested him.

Luca sprints around the corner. With a broom in one hand, a dustpan in the other, and an industrial-sized trash bag clenched between his teeth, he looks crazed. He spits the trash bag out, and it flutters to the ground at my feet. "What the fuck, Celine? That sounded like a bomb going off."

"I'm strong, not stealthy," I snap, gathering up the knife, clothes, and wallet that fell from the demon's pocket when I broke him apart, then pointing at the remaining chunks. "Stop bitching about my methods and sweep him up before someone comes to find out what made the noise."

Thankfully, Luca doesn't argue, cleaning up the powdery remains with the efficiency of a skilled bartender who's been handling unusual spills for years. Within sixty seconds, only a few fragments are left. They blend in with the assorted dirt, cigarette butts, and broken glass littering the ground.

I squat and hold the dustpan level so Luca can get the remaining bits, wheezing as his brisk work with the broom sends a cloud of dust directly into my face.

"Gross." I cough, shooting him a dirty look. "You got him in my hair."

Luca's lips curl into a boyish smile. He swings the full garbage bag over his shoulder, casting a lumpy shadow on the wall—a demented version of the humans' Santa Claus legend. "Nothing a shower won't fix," he says, eyes glittering with mischief.

*He killed someone for me.* I cross my arms to hide my shiver.

"Goodnight, Luca."

"You're welcome, Celine."

Pivoting, I toss a wave over my shoulder and hurry to my bike, frustration replacing the odd flash of desire for Luca.

He's got a lot of nerve—telling me to be more careful in the dressing room, then turning around and using his rarest ability in the middle of the fucking road. A lot of people would love to hear that the Fang's sexy bartender is a near-mythical shifter. He risked exposing his basilisk in a situation I had completely under control.

I stuff the wallet, clothes, and knife in my top case, then straddle my bike, sliding my helmet over my hair before pushing the kickstand back with my heel. The roar of the engine and the familiar vibration against my thighs settle the worst of my worry.

My shoulder blades are itching like crazy.

I'll get rid of the rest of the evidence, but Luca and I aren't done talking about this.

I navigate the tight alley slowly until I'm out on a main road, then open my bike up as much as possible. Living among the humans means I have to keep my wings hidden most of the time. The closest I get to flying around here is on the back of my bike.

Since my place is only five minutes away, I'm usually bummed that its proximity to the Fang doesn't give me a chance to let loose. Tonight though, with anxiety turning me inside out, I just want to get home and let my wings down.

# TWO

## CELINE

Since tossing the demon's body—Roscoe, if the ID I found in his wallet isn't a fake—everything has settled back to normal around the club . . . except my friendship with Luca. We've been orbiting each other awkwardly all afternoon, and the more we avoid creating conflict, the more it happens.

After an hour of bickering, Luca corners me behind the bar, reaching around me for a rag to buff out the water streaks on the cocktail glasses. Watching him polish them settles some of my tension, although I don't know why he bothers. No one comes in here for pristine glassware.

"Do you think you could make it through this shift without having a meltdown?" he mutters, his breath fluttering the red strands of hair I carefully curled between yawns after dragging myself out of bed.

"It depends on how you define a meltdown," I say, bumping

him to the side with my hip. "I'm not the one who fossilized a demon in the middle of the street."

"Gods," Luca huffs. "Keep your voice down." I shift my weight, unsettled by his angry tone. We've never argued this way before. Not on opposing sides, at least.

"Can we not do this tonight?" I ask, my shoulders drooping. I barely slept at all after disposing of the clothes and ID. Since I couldn't burn it, I tossed the knife in a dumpster near the outskirts of the city, miles outside of my normal route to work.

The glass in Luca's hand clinks against the wooden bar top as he puts it down and gives me his full and undivided attention. "What's wrong?" he demands. "You never back down from a fight."

I narrow my eyes at him, a surge of awareness running through me.

Luca is mouthwateringly sexy, easygoing, and he never forgets to add extra tequila to my drinks. That makes him the only kind of man I can tolerate on a regular basis. He's also monstrously deadly and has as many reasons as I do to stay under the enclave's radar. Why did he throw away years of careful hiding to protect me? Sure, we watch each other's backs, but in the six years we've worked together at the club, we've never put ourselves directly at risk for one another before. My magic is desperate to know why he disrupted our balance.

"Nothing," I mumble, feeling out of sorts beneath his scrutiny. "I don't know, Luca, I didn't sleep well."

"Hot date?" His tone is oddly brittle, although I can tell he's trying to get back to our normal friendly teasing.

"And when exactly would I have had time for that?" I flick a clump of uneven body glitter off the swell of my right breast, then meet his eyes defiantly. "After I helped dispose of the body or before I crawled into bed with a hard, dripping hunk of *ice*?"

His gaze flickers to my forehead, but the red mark is long gone thanks to ice and my advanced angelic healing. Luca grins as if my joke fixed everything between us, his white teeth gleaming in the dim light of the closed strip club. "When you put it like that—"

"And while we're on the subject, I'm annoyed that strippers have a reputation for getting laid often and well," I interrupt, a faint throbbing building at the base of my skull. "I can't even remember the last time I had a good time on my back unless I provided it myself."

"Preach," Imani says, walking up with Ada and Brandy to join us. "My love life is drier than this desert." I glance at Luca, but he's perfectly at ease. Choking on my frustration, I smile at the girls. The time before open is sacred. Luca and I will have to hash this out later.

"I'll be sure to make a public service announcement," Luca says, pretending to scribble notes on a wrinkled napkin with his finger. "Fewer tips, more orgasms for my dancers."

"No need to make any announcements for me. I do all right," Ada teases, her dimples winking before she bends to tighten up an intricately laced pair of heels. We all take a collective look are her mile-long legs and waist-length platinum hair and exchange grins.

"Anything I say right now will get me sent straight to HR," Luca says, earning himself a chorus of boos.

"Aren't you the Human Resources department?" I ask.

"That's right." He snaps his fingers. "I am. Make sure to submit all complaints between eight in the morning and four in the afternoon for prompt service."

"We're closed then," Brandy points out.

"Exactly," he says.

The playful ribbing continues as we get ready for the early crowd, then open our doors to a trickle of bored regulars. It's not too bad for a Thursday afternoon, especially when I manage to land an aerial move I've been working on for weeks.

An hour later, a shy, gentle wolf shifter who's scared to death of me drums up the courage to ask for a personal dance, then tips me a hundred bucks after keeping his hands to himself. All in all, it's shaping up to be a much better day than yesterday . . . until he saunters in. *Gods. Is it dark already?*

"Can I get a dance, angel?"

I tilt my head up—way up—to meet Alistair's eyes. Hair the color of a midnight thunderstorm teases the sharp angles of his face. His lips are ridiculously plump for someone known for sucking the life out of anyone who crosses him.

There's not an official hierarchy in the Fringes, but if there were, Alistair would be at the top of it. A curator of information, he's the guy lurking in the shadows that you go to for help when you're in over your head, but only if you've exhausted every other option.

"I'm too tired." I shrug, not bothering to give him a more diplomatic answer, and barely avoiding telling an outright lie.

He narrows his cool blue eyes. "And yet . . . I could have sworn I just saw you bouncing with abandon astride a flea-bitten simpleton."

The contrary part of me is glad he knows I'm brushing him off. He's been coming around the club a lot over the past few months, watching me like a hawk. Alistair is hot, but he's trouble with a capital T, and I don't want to add any complications to my life.

I run my fingers up his chest, feeling the solid thump of his heart. "I'd rather lie down with dogs than end up a forgotten blood donor," I whisper, smiling as I hear his sharp inhale. Playing with this particular vampire isn't smart, but I can't help myself.

"You sell yourself short, angel," Alistair purrs. "If I were lucky enough to taste your blood, I wouldn't expect to think of anything else ever again." Half threat, half come-on, a thrill races up my spine. Was that a compliment?

My cheeks heat, and Alistair's eyes flicker to the pulse throbbing near the base of my throat. He wants me; that's obvious, but getting tangled up with Alistair would get people talking, and I don't want to draw any more attention to myself. Even if the sex would be explosive, I never go back for seconds, and he's too high profile to scratch my itch.

"You're on deck, babe." Imani brushes past me, and I take the opportunity to make my exit, doing my best to zone out during my next dance. The cool glide of the metal pole usually feels soothing when paired with the hot blast of the stage lights, but I'm too aware of Alistair's eyes on me to truly relax.

I botch my dismount, barely managing to avoid a rolled ankle in the process. Godsdammit, I've got to either get a grip or get laid. This is getting ridiculous.

As I leave the stage to a smattering of catcalls and cheers, I kick myself for taunting him. Alistair loves a challenge, has the reputation to prove it, and his loyalty is for sale to the highest bidder. I would be better off convincing him I'm boring and brainless than provoking his mercurial interest by flirting with him.

It's too bad I've never been good at hiding the truth.

# THREE

## LUCA

I try not to look at her. It doesn't help. My body is aware of hers at all times, like I've added a Celine-specific sense to my already overtaxed nervous system.

Even now, surrounded by a clusterfuck of stimulants, I'm aware of her in a way that drives me wild. She's in the hallway, disrupting the club's natural rhythm of catcalls, bass guitar, and heavy breathing by pacing back and forth.

*Pull yourself together, asshole.* I suck in more air, soaking up the familiar smell of beer and pheromones that lives in the air of the Fang.

Celine is getting tired of my shit. I can tell. And she's right to be frustrated. She's acting normal. I'm the one dangling on the edge of ruining everything. What she doesn't know is it's not even my fault.

I've always been attracted to her—anyone with eyes would be

—but I'm cold-blooded, and I've never had any trouble shoving my desire for Celine into the neat little compartment where it belongs. Until now. Because my basilisk has decided she's ours, and it refuses to understand the metric fuckton of reasons why she would never agree to that.

"Can I get a Blood Tide? On the rocks." My eyes flick up to Alistair's face reluctantly, and my basilisk coils angrily in my chest, sensing a rival. I've got no problem with the guy, but I see how often he comes around to watch Celine.

"Sure thing," I say. Smiling like a dumbass, I drop down to the cooler where I store the blood. Vampires aren't sociable, so I didn't start stocking it until Alistair became a regular. Human, witch, or bunny-rabbit shifter—he's never been picky about the blood type and tips enough to offset the cost. Plus, I wasn't about to risk alienating someone with his reputation.

"Business is good," Alistair observes while I add blood and tequila to the shaker, running the rim of his glass through cinnamon and cayenne pepper as he studies me. He's usually better at small talk than this. If he's uninterested in having a conversation, though, why is he bothering?

"Yeah," I agree, refusing to be rude no matter how much his presence annoys me. I'm a professional. I can handle a little misplaced jealously without turning into a monster. "The girls have worked hard. They deserve the steady cash."

"Some more than others," Alistair murmurs.

My eyes rise slowly from where I'm cutting a piece of celery to garnish his drink. He's not focused on me or the stage. His head is cocked toward the hallway instead. He's listening to Celine pace, too. I'd bet a week's tips on it.

My fangs stab painfully past my gums, venom rushing through my glands. When cold pressure pounds against my retinas, I glare down at the bar top so intensely that I feel like I'm drilling holes in the scarred wood. *Pull yourself together, you jealous fuck.*

Shifting my full focus to the drink I'm making, I recite the ingredients in my head to distract my basilisk from its territorial rage. Measure. *Chill.* Shake. *Relax.* Pour. *Don't kill him.*

The monster inside me settles sullenly, but remains homicidally pissed off about the fact that I'm preparing a drink for its newfound nemesis. I snatch my water bottle out from under the bar, taking a deep swig, then swish it around in my mouth until the bitter taste of my venom is gone. My fangs retract.

That was way too close. I've got to get better control of myself. *So what if he wants her?* That's good for business. People are wary of Alistair because he's known for being merciless when cheated or wronged—not because he's an indiscriminate killer.

"Fascinating," Alistair murmurs, his voice low. It's barely a whisper in the crowded strip club. If my senses weren't focused on him, I wouldn't have heard him at all. "You're a mystery, Luca Saratelli," he says, this time at a normal volume.

I try to scoff, but the dismissive sound comes out strangled, as if I'm choking on my own spit. I don't want to be a mystery for him to solve. I want to be like wallpaper in a rich person's house —bland, simple, and easy to walk past without noticing. He's watching us too closely already, and no good can come from being on his radar.

More venom hits my taste buds, deadly to everyone but me. My mouth is coated with it. Swallowing as much as I can, I beg my basilisk to take a back seat and let me handle this. Reluctantly, it curls further inside me, and I look up at Alistair.

He's intensely focused, his piercing blue eyes inspecting every inch of my body he can see. I have the strangest sensation that he's trying to peer beneath my skin to see how I'm put together.

"You're bleeding," Alistair says. With a movement too quick to track, his right hand darts out, his thumb grazing my bottom lip. He comes away with a drop of my blood. Before I can stop him, he sucks his finger into his mouth, eyes flaring bright red.

"Fascinating," he repeats, his shoulders twitching three times before settling back to normal.

Internally, I wince. That's my venom at work. He's lucky he didn't ingest more of it and earn himself a painful end. It would have served him right for tasting my blood without asking nicely first.

I slam his finished drink down on the counter too hard, the cherry tomato rolling off its toothpick and landing between us. Purple lights paint the bruised fruit a deep crimson instead of its normal, cheery red.

"That's my bad, man," I say, blinking at the tomato and refusing to meet Alistair's eyes. I reach for my garnish tray. "Let me get you another one."

"No need." Alistair chuckles. "If you can keep a secret, Luca, I'll come clean. I'm allergic to tomatoes."

I frown at him. I've made Alistair this drink dozens of times since I started working at the club, and he's never once mentioned a tomato allergy. It's dark as fuck in here. What if he'd accidentally swallowed one of the seeds, then dropped dead in front of the bar?

"Are you crazy?" I sputter, annoyed that I might have accidentally killed him any number of times. That would have been a huge mess. Alistair gives off a quiet, watchful intensity, but I've never thought he was unbalanced before now.

He takes a sip of the cocktail and grins at me. "You make such a lovely drink, I didn't have the heart to tell you. Plus, I enjoy a little danger." His eyes dip to my mouth, then he pivots and heads back to his table before I can make sense of what happened.

If I didn't know better, I would say he was flirting with me. Shaking my head, I flush the rest of the venom from my mouth and get back to work. Alistair lives and operates a business on the Fringes, so he can't be completely sane. I'll keep that in mind for the next time he shows up and pays a little too much attention.

"Enough of this shit, Luca. You're coming home with me after work," Celine says in a low, determined growl. I picture her creamy thighs wrapped around my head, then shudder, knocking over an entire pitcher of beer while I'm at it.

"Mother*fucker*," I hiss, soaking up as much of the spill as I can with a towel I keep stashed back here for emergencies. It's almost time for last call, and the crowd is thinning.

"Why are you so jumpy?" Celine ducks behind the bar with me, pulling another towel from the stack and mopping at the yeasty puddle. The downy feathers of her right wing graze my wrist and goosebumps spread like wildfire up my arm.

"I don't know," I snap. My voice sounds whiny even to me. I toss the damp towels into the bin beneath the bar and sigh heavily.

Celine's face falls, and she glances at her feet. "Luca, I know I can be bitchy, but I thought you didn't mind," she whispers. "Is there something I need to apologize for? I'm happy to say sorry, you'll just have to convince me I'm wrong first or it will get stuck on the way out."

My lips twitch, but I hide my smile, not wanting to interrupt the most adorable ramble I've ever heard.

Celine looks up, lifting her chin to the stubborn tilt I'm used to. Her fingers curl around my bicep, brown eyes aggressive even while she's being sincere. "You don't even need to come up with a good argument," she says. "If I focus hard on my intent, I'll probably be genuinely sorry just because you're upset with me. Say the word. I'll apologize right now to get us back to normal."

I shake my head, confused, the scream of the electric guitar in the background pulling my focus. I'm trying to understand what Celine is saying to me, but my head keeps repeating the part where she ordered me in no uncertain terms to come home with her.

"I'm sorry," I sputter, grinning at her to distract from the fact that I'm a shit listener. "But I don't have a fucking clue what you're talking about."

Celine squints up at my face, her eyebrows pulling together. *Great.* I've made her suspicious. "Are you on something?" she asks, scanning the bar like she's expecting to find a bowl full of colorful, unlabeled pills in place of the limes.

I wave my hand at the stragglers scattered around the room. "No, just a busy night. Why am I coming home with you, and why are you trying to apologize?"

Celine plants her hands on her hips. "You're coming home with me so we can kiss and make up. I'm not sure why I need to apologize; I was trying to cover my bases—"

"—to get us back to normal," I finish her thought, frustration churning in my belly. It feels a lot like the venom I flushed out of my mouth when Alistair was here.

"Exactly." Celine nods, then opens the drawer between us and starts poking through the corkscrews and spare bottle openers. "Although, if you're stoned or something, I take everything back. We can't binge watch trash TV and drink our weight in boxed wine if there's a chance I have to babysit you through a bad trip."

I grip her hips in both hands, nudging her away from my stuff before she can do any more damage. Letting Celine organize is asking for trouble. "I'm not high but quit touching my shit! If you mess up my system, you will have something to apologize for." My eye twitches as I see she's already lined everything in the junk drawer up in order of size.

"Your system sucks," Celine drawls, trying to sneak one hand back in the drawer.

I grab her wrist, pulling her away from the temptation. "That's only because you don't get it."

"You can't know how wrong you are," she insists. "If I took a poll of everyone in the Naked Fang tonight, the only thing they would all agree on is that your system makes no sense."

I shrug. "Then they're idiots."

"All of them?" Celine surveys the clientele, then sighs. "Okay, maybe most of them are, but your system inflicts actual trauma on me."

"Sure it does." I smirk, unable to stop my lips from twitching. "You know what happens when a fish is out of water?"

"Painfully gradual asphyxiation?" She taps her foot on the ground, raising one eyebrow in a clear sign that I should get the fuck on with my point.

"Yeah, but I'm getting the feeling that some of this"—I wave my hand at where she's now adjusting the space between the clean glasses—"is what happens when an angel is out of heaven. You know, separated from god and all that."

Celine gags, shooting me a look of pure disgust. "First, the celestial realm is not heaven, second, there is no god there, and third, I don't know why you would want to risk antagonizing me by peddling propaganda when I was going to let you pick the show."

I ignore her rant, opening my drawer back up and mixing everything up deliberately. "Okay, so there's nothing at all to the rumors that angels love order and tend to be a bit—"

"Choose your next words carefully, snake boy."

"*Particular* about things. Because if it's all bullshit, nothing I'm doing will bother you in the slightest, right?"

Her jaw clenches as I shut the drawer about halfway, then kneel to untie my left shoe. I leave the string dangling and drag my eyes up her endlessly long legs. She's wearing thigh-high stockings—my favorites—and I don't have a ruler handy, but I'd bet my life's savings they are sitting symmetrically on her perfect legs. From my knees, I grin up at her then curl my fingers under the right stocking, pulling it down a smidge. Then I wait her out, watching the angry flush spread down her neck.

"You're doing so good," I tease.

"Fuck you," Celine hisses, batting my hand away, adjusting the fabric jerkily, then slamming the drawer shut to hide the mess. I'm laughing my ass off by the time she squats in front of me and roughly double knots my sneaker. "You don't get to pick the show anymore."

We're close enough that I can count the individual shades of red in her hair. Hidden by the bar, it feels like we're in our own little world, and I can't ignore the angry rise and fall of her chest. Gods or no gods, Celine is the sexiest woman I've ever seen. There's no denying that. But the racing of my heart has nothing to do with her appearance. *Get ahold of yourself, dude.*

"Shit," Imani purrs, dragging the syllable out. "We need to spin the spotlight this way. You two are putting on a way better show than Brandy right now." Her raspy chuckle breaks us both out of the moment, and my only consolation is that Celine is as annoyed by the interruption as I am.

"Worry about yourself," she snaps, standing up to glare at her friend eye to eye.

"Why should I, when it's more fun to worry about you?" Imani teases. "Luca, I need a fresh pitcher for table twelve."

"Got it." I lurch unsteadily to my feet and call myself every kind of dumbass I can think of. Celine saunters backstage, and I refuse to watch her leave. Instead, I spend the rest of the shift lecturing my basilisk about lying low.

By the time I'm at her place, sprawling on the couch in comfortable sweats, it's content to let me do my thing. I can only hope it doesn't change its mind.

Celine steps around the couch, rolling her neck in a circle until it cracks, then hands me a beer. She settles on the couch beside me, carefully balancing her own full glass of wine.

My tension eases, and I snag a greasy slice of pizza from the box on the table, folding it in on itself and devouring a third in one bite. Celine's eyes flicker over to me, only drifting to her own plate once she's satisfied I'm not about to anoint her furniture with red sauce and bacon bits. I may tease her about her angelic need for order, but I would never disrespect her home.

We eat mostly in silence, wired after the night at the club. It takes a lot of energy to work in a place like the Naked Fang. Supernatural clientele isn't easily satisfied in general, and the ones who live and work on the Fringes are more difficult than most.

Celine finishes eating first, cleaning her fingers meticulously with a napkin before grabbing the remote and selecting an island dating show with an entire cast of bisexuals. True to her promise, she doesn't ask for any input from me. After a couple of episodes of nonstop on-screen drama, she turns the volume down to background noise and looks at me.

"We need to talk about it," she says firmly. I'm almost positive she's referring to the dead demon and not my inconvenient attraction to her, but my heart skips a beat, anyway. My basilisk raises its head with interest.

"I'm not sure what there is to talk about," I say with a shrug. "He's dead and disposed of. No one's come to find him yet, and if they do, we know how to keep our mouths closed."

Celine hugs a throw pillow to her chest, her wings pulled tightly together. "I looked at his ID before I burned it; his name was Roscoe Daemyn—the most obvious alias I've ever seen. Isn't one of the three enclave leaders a demon, too? What if they send someone to ask questions?"

I snort, trying to sound more confident than I am. "When have they ever bothered to poke their noses in our business?" I ask. "Everyone knows they're happy living like kings in that cushy compound in Colorado. No one is going to come slum it with us because some low-level demon went missing."

"You're right," she says. "But the last thing we need is a bunch of supernatural cops sniffing around."

"Even if they do, no one will volunteer information to them," I assure her. "You and I are hardly the only ones keeping a low profile around here. Although, if you want to hide better, you'll keep your wings tucked all the time." I make the suggestion, then dip my head as I realize how much I hate my own idea.

Celine shoves one fluffy wing out, blocking my view of the TV entirely. I smirk at her and shake my head. "I guess I should take that as a no?"

"I won't hide them at the Fang." She folds her arms over her chest, pressing her lips into a tight line. "I've warped myself enough to blend in here, but some things are sacred, Luca. My wings . . . I won't allow them to be taken from me."

My heart pounds in my chest. We never talk about her past, but the careful way she dances around the details tells me enough. I want to pull Celine into my arms and tell her no one will ever hurt her again. Instead, I bite my tongue and nod, then focus back on the show.

My basilisk rattles angrily in the back of my chest for the rest of the night.

# FOUR

## CIPRIAN

Washing my face. Taking a nap. Eating a sandwich . . . all three are better ways to spend my time than playing hide and seek with the dumbest excuse for a demon on this entire planet. But Dad insisted, so like the good little soldier I absolutely am not, I find myself once again marching to the beat of his drum. I could hate myself for it, but I don't have the energy.

I take the ramp off the interstate a little too fast, tires squealing as I turn left without braking, then continue making my list. I could scare the shit out of my brother, organize my sweatpants by cotton percentage, or even befriend a feral raccoon and have more fun than I will hunting Roscoe down.

Dad is a menace these days—has been ever since Callum fucked off to his cabin in the woods with Gideon, leaving me behind to deal with him alone. No matter how many times I tell

Dad the supernatural community in our territory is thriving, the stick remains planted firmly up his ass.

Being a part of the enclave is a headache for me most days. We aren't the strictest ruling body, not by a long shot, but Dad and Joshua have taken their inherited power and run with it. They believe the lead by example method works best. Who am I to burst their bubble and tell them about all the underground shit happening beneath their noses?

I hit a pothole and hold my breath until I'm sure I didn't give myself a flat. Changing a tire in the baking sun is the last thing I want to do, grosser even than looking for Roscoe around the Fringes.

The supernaturals here get away with a lot, there's no doubt about that. The fringe nickname is twofold, because they live the most enmeshed with humans, with limited magic-warded businesses of their own, and they're also on the edge of two enclave territories.

The California enclave, headquartered in Los Angeles, is technically closer but they wouldn't dream of crossing into our space, which also includes Colorado, Wyoming, and parts of Utah. Since we're too far away to do much governing ourselves, Las Vegas is one step away from a lawless wasteland on the best of days.

I've heard it's a good time, but I'm annoyed to be here. Mainly because Dad wants me to lay the hammer down, and that's never been my style.

But here I am, and here I'll be until I figure out who decided to fuck around and find out with Roscoe, Dad's pet guard and the most stereotypical ravoc demon I've ever met. He didn't come home from his latest bender, and Dad is pissed.

Since Callum is tied up, and people love to forget that Dimitri Casanell has a second son, I've been drafted. The undeniably good-looking and pathologically forgotten enclave heir, looking for parking in one of the few streets in Las Vegas that's all super-natural.

Sighing, I street park my car near the ratty walkup I'm supposed to bunk at while undercover. It's a dump. Climbing out of my SUV, I stretch my arms over my head, then drag my suit-case out of the back seat, reminding myself again that I won't be here long.

None of my new neighbors are hanging around outside, but I feel eyes tracking my movements from multiple locations. Good for them. I'm an unknown. They should be nosy.

I climb the rusty stairs, ignoring the concerning groaning and swaying each step brings, and do my best to appear confident, but not too confident.

Weakness will make me a target here as quickly as strength. The best I can hope for is to ride the middle, find Roscoe, and drag his ass home before someone steals my car. I'm tempted to toss a nightmare illusion over the SUV to make it look like a piece of shit, but with people watching . . . No, it's better to leave them wondering than show them what I'm capable of.

Forcing the key into the warped, tarnished lock, I use a voice command to ask my phone for a list of scary movies playing in the area, then shove. Even unlocked, the door stays wedged shut. It takes me three tries to realize I have to lift up on the handle while pushing to get the damn thing to budge.

It swings open, and I step inside, closing the door behind me and tossing my suitcase on the bed. It bounces, making a metallic sound that shouldn't ever come from a mattress. A quick inven-tory of the apartment takes me about one minute total and confirms that the odds of me making it home without needing a tetanus booster are near to nonexistent.

Oh well, I'll feel better after I've snacked on some fear. Locking the door behind me, I head to the nearest movie theater. Heads are rolling within five minutes of the opening credits, and the drunk bachelor party in front of me gets so scared by the poorly written slasher film that I'm easily able to top off my magic reserves.

I leave the theater hoping that my luck is looking up.

It takes five hours for me to change my mind. There's no sign of Roscoe at any of the spots his friends say he hangs out at when visiting Vegas, including his hotel room.

The only place left on my list to check is a supernatural strip club called the Naked Fang, a name that's about as subtle as a bare ass to the face. Groaning, I push my way through the door, the tingle of magic raking over my skin as I enter. If I was human, the repelling ward would give me an irresistible urge to turn around and go back to where I came from. If I glanced back, it would likely show me a blank wall or something. Since I'm not, it feels like getting tickled by a stranger. Icky, but hardly life threatening.

As soon as I clear the ward, the thumping bass hits me hard enough to rearrange my organs. Again, with the subtlety. I laugh, then pause to adjust to the noise and get my bearings. It only takes a couple of seconds to grab a table close enough to the stage to blend in, but not so far back that I look cheap.

Roscoe is nowhere in sight, but I forget all about that ugly motherfucker when I spot the most beautiful woman I've ever seen.

Flaming red hair falls in loose curls down her back, each strand grazing alabaster skin. She's tall for a woman, or at least above average, and her curves dip and roll in all the right places. And her wings. Gods, her wings are ridiculously fluffy and glaringly feminine. I want to snuggle up against them and take a nap.

*There's an angel in our territory?* I've never seen one before in person, but those wings are a dead giveaway. What's less clear is how we managed to miss hearing about her arrival, and why in all the many realms she picked the Vegas Fringes to settle down.

From everything I've heard, the celestial realm is a cushy place to live. Most angels don't choose to leave, at least not voluntarily. Those rumors are where Earth's fallen angel legend comes from.

Angelic and demonic lore is laughable. We aren't even from the same realm, but humans love to cast us in this never-ending cosmic battle between good and evil. My genetic heritage doesn't make me any more psycho than the redhead—my kind just lost the public relations' battle before radios existed. If all angels look like her, there's no wonder.

The angel dips and grinds on the pole, and when she spins upside down while holding on with only her thighs, I'm reluctantly impressed. Also, a little worried. Will those fluffy wings help her if she falls?

Her song ends, and I stay glued to my seat, hoping she'll come my way.

"Can I get you something?" I'm so busy imagining how her voice sounds that the deep baritone interruption ruins my daydream. I blink at the stranger. Dressed in all black with a towel tucked into his belt loop, his hazel eyes are framed by thick, dark lashes. There's a ring in the left side of his full bottom lip, and he chews on it as he waits for me to answer.

*Holy shit.* Is every employee in this place stupid hot? Why haven't I been here before? I lean forward in my seat and give the guy my most winning smile.

"Thank you for asking. What do you have on draft?" He rattles off the standard options, but I can't help myself. "Surprise me with your favorite," I say, tilting my head to study his reaction.

He freezes, from the line of his chiseled jaw to the top of his messy brown hair, and peers down at me like I've grown another head. Eventually, he pulls it together and nods, pivoting with a half-smile and muttering 'another one' under his breath.

Since that makes no sense, I think nothing of it and lean back in my chair. This mission is looking up, and I'm starting to hope Roscoe is hard to find.

---

The angel takes the stage three more times, and I can't keep my eyes off her. It's embarrassing. She's far from the only gorgeous woman here, but I'm locked in. Working the floor, she weaves between the tables, talking to anyone who waves her down.

I watch from the corner of my eye, enjoying how she prowls through the room as if she's confident in every inch of herself. A queen among men and she knows it.

One big shifter calls to her, his eyes yellow and glassy from too much cheap beer. I stiffen, not liking the look of him. I'm not here to make trouble, though, I'm here to squash it. Tense, I stay in my seat and watch her talk to him. She's careful to maintain space between them, but when she turns to leave, he grabs her arm and yanks her forcibly into his lap.

I shove to my feet, about to do exactly what I swore I wouldn't. Except there's no need.

The angel plants both hands on the shifter's chest and shoves, sending him crashing backward as she stands. His wooden chair skids about eight feet before tipping over and throwing him in the floor on his back. His arms and legs flail like an oversized beetle, then he jumps to his feet with a roar, patches of fur popping up on his burly arms.

The ferocious look in his yellow eyes promises violence, but the angel grins, her perfectly even teeth winking in the flashing club lights.

I sit back down. Something tells me I'm about to get a far better show than the one happening on the stage, and maybe a snack too. Already, I feel a few tasty wisps of fear curling up around me. None of them are coming from the angel.

"Bitch," the shifter roars, his voice distorted by rage.

She laughs, shaking her head as she adjusts the complex web of straps crisscrossing her torso. "Now it'll take two apologies, Rex. Do you want to go for three?"

"You shoved me in the floor," he complains, glancing at his buddies for help. None of them are willing to meet his eyes.

"I did," she says. "And I'll do it again if you put your hands on me without permission. You know the rules, Rex. You all do." She stares pointedly at the scraggly crew loosely grouped around him, propping her hands on her hips.

"Sorry, Celine," one mutters, bright red spots staining his cheeks.

"It's the second pitcher," another adds. "You know he wouldn't hurt a fly before the beer takes over."

"What's done is done," she says, pushing her hair back over her shoulders. "You're all through for tonight, but Rex can come back once he's ready to give me those apologies."

"That's not fair!" The mountain known as Rex growls again, slurring his words as he takes a step toward the angel. This time, his crew steps in, dragging him out of the club and telling him to shut up as he loudly gripes.

The angel—they called her Celine—scans the room with that sassy smile firmly in place. "Sorry for the drama, folks! Anyone else hoping to pick a fight with me? If so, step right up."

She holds her fists up and the crowd chuckles. Raw panic rushes through me at the idea of these guys attacking her. She's practically daring one of them to try. I know a performance when I see it, but my heart is in my throat.

Celine sashays out of the main room and another dancer takes the stage, but my attention is on the hall now. From her fluffy ass wings to her giant brass balls, the angel is too interesting to ignore.

After a few minutes, she comes back, ducking behind the bar

to talk to the hot guy with the lip ring. I can't hear what they're saying, and pure nosiness drives me to my feet. I skulk casually up to the bar, wrapping myself in enough nightmare magic to stay unnoticed unless someone looks specifically for me.

"Did you serve him two pitchers or not?" Celine demands, her voice raspy as she confronts the bartender.

"Of course not, let me see your arm." He reaches for her, his hazel eyes wide with concern.

She shrugs out of his grasp. "It's nothing."

"You always say that," he groans. "I'm getting tired of hearing it."

"Would you rather I be seriously hurt instead?" Her hands land on her hips. I wince at the fire in her eyes, and . . . are her wings smoking?

"Oh, fuck off, Celine, you know what I mean. You can't keep going this way; someone is going to take it too far." I don't even know her, but I agree with him. Her strength is challenging, and for some supernaturals, well, let's just say they might have a hard time not testing the limits.

"They wouldn't if somebody didn't over serve the angry lightweights," she snaps.

"I swear, I didn't. I gave Rex one pitcher and reminded him of the limit. There's no way he got another one unless . . ." His eyes narrow, then he shuts them all together and groans.

"Unless what?"

"Chico," he hisses. "That friendly fucker bought a pitcher while I was slammed. I didn't notice where he took it."

Celine blinks up at him, unimpressed. "Rookie mistake, Luca. Chico hates beer."

"I know. Fuck. I'm sorry," he whispers. "I got distracted."

"By what?"

"This dude . . . You know what, never mind, this is all my fault." He drags a towel over the bar top, his movements jerky. *Is he talking about me?* That's exciting. I smile and lean closer, limiting my movements to keep anyone from noticing ripples in my nightmare.

Celine puts her hand on his arm, then drops it back to her side awkwardly. "It's okay, Luca."

"No, it isn't," he says, his voice brimming with tamped down frustration. "It will bruise."

"And then it will heal. There's no harm done." Her tone softens, and I'm a little disappointed in her for going easy on the sexy bartender. In her defense, he is ridiculously good-looking, but I'd rather watch her rake him over the coals.

"You coming over for another binge tonight?"

"Probably not."

"Come on," she whines. "Don't get sulky on me now. How will we ever know if Ashley Y. and the roided-up personal trainer bone if we don't keep watching?"

Luca grimaces. "Do we even want to see that? You know his ballsack is shriveled up like a clump of sun-dried raisins. Ashley Y. is going to be seriously disappointed when she sees the cost of those muscles."

"Yeah, and then she will console herself by sitting on Brianna's face."

Celine leans toward Luca as she talks, and I wonder if she notices how his eyes soak up her every move. Their conversation makes no sense to me at all, but I want to be in the middle of all that unresolved tension, stirring them both up until they snap.

Slipping back to my table, I unravel the nightmare and wedge a hundred-dollar bill under my empty glass as I plot. If I spin this right to Dad, maybe I can turn this business into pleasure. I deserve a vacation, don't I? Nodding to myself, I leave the club, not bothering to ask a single person if they've seen Roscoe.

# FIVE

## CELINE

Sitting up in my tub, I dig through my bowl of bath bombs and select a lavender one. My favorite scent after a long shift. I drop it into the water and watch it fizzle, inhaling deeply as I lean back against the curve of my cramped tub. *Relax, dammit.*

My body doesn't listen. I groan in frustration and drop beneath the water, blowing bubbles with my nose until I'm forced to come up for air.

I've got an itch, and it has nothing to do with my dry spell or keeping my wings tucked in public. This is a warning itch, a prickling across my palms as I hover over the edge of something unknown and outside of my control. I hate it.

Moving here at twenty and leaving everything I knew behind was supposed to give me a fresh start. Fewer resources, hence the cramped tub, but also something I couldn't earn in a million years back home: freedom.

The itch . . . It reminds me of how I felt before he lashed out. I shake my head to clear the dread and remind myself he's not here. I'm free of him. Safe. We both got what we wanted when I left, and even if he tries to bring me back, I'm strong enough to resist.

I'm powerful now. I don't hide anymore. And if anyone has a problem with that, I'll show them exactly how dangerous an angel can be.

I clench my fists and give up on the idea of fully relaxing. So what if I'm considering all the ways I can kill in less than thirty seconds? That's doing more to relax me tonight than the lavender.

I'm wasting time dwelling on old, misplaced worries, anyway. If bath time is doomed to introspection, I'd be much better off figuring out how I'm going to handle the Luca situation. I'm feeling way too friendly toward him recently. It's clearly annoying him, because his behavior is all over the place.

I offered to apologize to get us back on track, something that's easier said than done given my specific radiant gift, but Luca won't take me up on it. Whether that means he doesn't hold my behavior against me or if he's decided to keep things normal at work is anyone's best guess.

Fuck. I sit up with a splash. What if I made him uncomfortable when I invited him over to watch trash TV? I mean, we work at a strip club, and he sees my tits almost daily, but that's business. Does Luca feel harassed?

Before I can freak myself out more, I decide to ask him. Luca loves to overthink, but I prefer to be proactive. I've always believed that awkwardness is the figment of an anxious imagination. If you approach things head on, you'd be surprised by how many weird conversations become straightforward.

Drying my hands on a towel, I grab my phone and pull up our message thread.

CELINE

Do I make you uncomfortable? Sexually? If so,
you can tell me, and I'll clean up my act. You're
my friend, and I would never want to do
anything to make you feel unsafe.

LUCA

I don't know what to say.

Shit, I knew it. I'm out of line.

Hang on. I'm processing. You've got to give me
a minute.

I wait a minute, then watch the ticking hands on my phone's digital clock move around the circle a second time. I know he didn't mean the minute literally, but I wish he did. That would make this hang time easier to take. I squirm around in the tub, my stomach doing its best to escape and float away to dissolve next to the fizzing bath bomb.

LUCA

Okay, let's clarify some things. First, you've
never made me feel unsafe. I'm not sure you
even could if we're being honest.

I re-read his message, then scoff. He's a little too confident in his own abilities. I'm scary when I want to be. Luca just hasn't seen it.

LUCA

Second, you don't make me uncomfortable. If
you ever did something I didn't like, I would
tell you.

My stomach settles slightly, but my head picks up the slack. Luca isn't denying his discomfort, only that I'm the cause of it. So, what's his problem?

LUCA

And before you demand to know more, that's something for me to deal with, not you. You can't fix everything by bulldozing it.

CELINE

Are you sure? It's worked okay for me so far.

That's debatable, but there's no reason to dredge up ancient history. In my experience, if you have bones buried in the backyard, you shouldn't fucking dig. I type a follow-up message before he can call me out.

CELINE

Binge our show tomorrow?

LUCA

Only if you go for a run with me first.

Ugh. Fine.

I put my phone down and prop one leg on the edge of the tub. The water is a little too hot, but I'll make do. We're in the desert. It would be wasteful to drain it all and start again. *Maybe I should keep a thermometer in here, for precision.*

The itch returns, directly between my shoulder blades this time, and I wince. If things are fine with Luca, why won't it go away? I'm going to have to wait to find out.

Groaning, I stand up, giving up on my bath and wrapping the towel around my body. Not knowing is the worst, because even without answers, one fact remains absolute: when I itch, a scratch always follows, and only time will tell how deep it goes.

We start our regular five-mile route, and my itching gets better about half a mile in. Thank goodness. Exercise always makes me feel more in control, and I'm glad Luca suggested this.

The route is flat, matching the rest of the city, but there are mountains all around us, jagged, hulking, and red—especially imposing with the morning sun at their back. Cacti dot the edges of the trail, the scraggly desert brush around them adding to the harsh, unforgiving vista, like stout and squat soldiers, outshone by their heartier, spikier neighbors.

Out and back, this trail is secluded, and one of the rare places in the area with a decent amount of shade. Even still, Luca and I are both pouring sweat by the time we turn around at the halfway point.

Since there isn't room to run side by side, he's slightly ahead of me, his shirtless, tanned back muscles bunching rhythmically with each stride. I look my fill, relying on my angelic reflexes to keep me from tripping over roots and rocks. It's a little creepy, but I tell myself I'm not ogling my friend, I'm admiring him. Like art. I can appreciate a good-looking sculpture, too. That doesn't mean I want to ride it.

But what if Luca used all that sweaty stamina to wear me out? My brain short-circuits as I picture it. My heart races in a way that has nothing to do with the run or the heat and everything to do with the images in my mind. I shake my head to clear the dirty train of thought before it can travel too far off the tracks, then slam directly into Luca's back.

He grunts, throwing his right hand out to catch me before I fall. I'm about to yell at him for stopping with no warning when I see what made him do it.

A child, no more than seven or eight, sits on the trail ahead of us, her blonde curls tangled and matted to her head with sweat. Her small face is pink and scrunched up from crying, and as she spots us, unmistakable terror flashes through her eyes.

I go completely still, shocked and horrified. Luca and I only turned around a couple of minutes ago, and she wasn't sitting here when we passed this spot the first time.

"Should we call the cops?" I whisper, searching for any sign of how the child might have ended up here.

At the sound of my voice, she stumbles to her feet, turning to run away from us.

Gasping, blood drains from my face as I take in the tiny, perfect wings on her back. *Impossible.*

"No," Luca groans. "I don't think we should involve any humans."

My itch returns. It's exponentially worse. I open my mouth and force the words out anyway. "Don't run. We won't hurt you. I swear it on my wings." I say the words in the common angelic dialect, my lips forming syllables they haven't attempted in years. While my kind have dozens of languages, many specific to individual bloodlines, the common tongue is used universally for communication between the different echelons.

If she's an angel; she'll stop. I hope she doesn't.

When she turns, her tear-streaked face lined with hope, a pit the size of this planet forms in my stomach. Then she scowls, looking me up and down skeptically. *"Mat ndaa?"* she demands, pointing at my plain tank top.

Despite my dread, my lips curl into a smile. She's a smart girl to demand proof before trusting a stranger. I fight the urge to chuckle, then weep. *How in the many fucked up realms did she end up here?*

I hold my finger up, then show her my back, pulling my tank top and sports bra out of the way enough that my wings can spread without damaging my clothes. She gasps, and I flap them a few times, enjoying the stretch before pulling them into my body and dropping my clothes back into place.

*"Nish thatsha,"* she murmurs, awe in her voice.

I wince. Turning back to face her, I take in the renewed fear in her eyes as she looks at me and repeat that we won't hurt her. She considers that for a moment but doesn't come any closer.

Luca shifts his weight uncomfortably, snapping a twig beneath his feet. "Celine . . ."

"Everything is okay," I say, not entirely sure who I'm reassuring more at this point, me, the little girl, or Luca. The itch is devouring my entire body, like millions of microscopic bugs are sprinting up and down my skin all at once. I'm desperate to know who is responsible for this so I can take my frustrations out on them.

I ask the child how she got here, keeping my tone gentle. Her mouth opens, but she doesn't answer. I ask again and get the same response, but this time a wrinkle appears on her brow as she looks around the park in confusion. Switching gears, I ask what her name is and watch the wrinkle smooth out.

"Anika," she whispers.

I smile. "It's nice to meet you, Anika. I'm Celine. Where are your parents?"

Her face crumples again, and big tears leak from the corners of her wide blue eyes. *"Di sibme, snisekh. Kong nikhat,"* she wails, pointing to her thin chest as she sobs.

My shoulders stiffen. Anika blames her parents' death on a plague and claims she's immune, but I've never known sickness to spread in the celestial realm. Granted, my common tongue is rusty. I only remember the word plague from history books.

Voices echo in the distance, and I exchange a worried glance with Luca. We may not know how this young angel ended up here, but we can't leave her to be discovered by humans. If we don't get her out of sight, those wings will raise a whole lot of unwanted questions for the supernatural community living among them.

Holding out my hand, I ask her to come with me. She backs up a step.

The voices get louder.

Anika backs up again, eyeing Luca suspiciously. We could grab her, but then she would scream. Fuck. *Fuck.* She's left me with no other choice.

Closing my eyes, I send my magic out, infusing it directly into my words as I promise to keep her safe. It shoots out from my heart, eager to be summoned. I haven't used it since—No, now isn't the time to think about that.

Anika gasps as golden runes appear on every inch of my exposed skin, then reaches for me with both hands. Luca . . . Shit, I'm not brave enough to see what he thinks.

The voices are almost on top of us.

We've got to go.

Scooping Anika up, I head for the car, half jogging in my hurry to get to safety. Gods. I feel terribly exposed, like the runes burned my skin off instead of labeling me for what I am. Burying my tension, I reach the parking lot and wrench the car door open, sliding Anika into the back seat.

As her head lolls to the side, I realize with shock that she somehow trusted me enough to fall asleep on my shoulder. My stomach churns, nausea building steadily until it competes with the itch. Ignoring both, I buckle her seatbelt and close the door, unexpected tears welling up in my eyes.

Luca grabs my arm, and it's all I can do not to vomit. "Deep breaths, Celine," he urges me, walking around to the passenger side and opening my door. "I've got you."

I drop heavily into the seat, my fingers running mechanically over the upholstery. Luca opens a water bottle and presses it into my hand. I take a grateful sip, jolting as a few drops fall on my legs.

"You must have a lot of questions," I say, glancing at Luca's tight jaw from the corner of my eye. His hands are working the leather of the steering wheel like he might be able to squeeze out the answers he wants that way.

"That can wait." He sighs. "We need to decide what to do with her. What did she say?"

"She doesn't know how she got here." I look over my shoulder to make sure she's still asleep. "Her name is Anika, and she's an orphan. She said her parents died in a plague." I frown, confused by the story she told me.

"What about that is hitting you weird?" Luca asks, correctly reading my expression.

"The plague part," I admit. "I've never heard of any sicknesses running rampant in the celestial realm. Not in my lifetime at least. People catch things, but it's usually minor or knocked out by a quick visit to the healers."

Luca considers that, looking in the rearview at the sleeping kid. "She's young, though. Chances are she doesn't know what she's talking about, especially if she's been through something traumatic."

He's right . . . But her fear. My itch. "What are we going to do with her?" I ask.

"Harry might take her," Luca says. "Last I talked to her; she was fostering a few orphans already. The language barrier might be an issue, though."

"Not for long," I murmur, remembering the shape and size of the wings poking out from Anika's back. "She's *nish misha*." At Luca's questioning glance, I squirm in my seat. *He deserves some answers.*

"Not all angels are the same," I explain. "Genetically or magically. Her classification is *misha*, an echelon known for their intelligence. Most work in science, research, and higher education. They aren't typically gifted with much magic, but they make up for it by thinking circles around the rest of us."

"So what?" Luca cranks the car and heads toward Harry's home. "You're saying she'll pick up English in a few months?"

"Days," I say.

"*Nish*," he murmurs. "If that means tier or class . . . She said that word to you along with something else."

I grit my teeth. Of course he picked up on that. Luca is smart. If I tell him more, am I putting us both at risk? He's not giving me much wiggle room either way and combined with my difficulty with lying . . .

"Yes, she recognized my type," I whisper, dropping my forehead against the cool glass of the car window.

I feel Luca's eyes on me. He lets the conversation drop when I don't immediately volunteer more information. "It's going to be okay," he says instead, the promise empty given how little we know. I appreciate the gesture anyway.

Luca street parks near Harry's house, thrumming his fingers anxiously against the steering wheel. "I'll go explain. Do you want to stay with Anika in case she wakes up?"

I nod, releasing all the air from my mouth and metaphorically sliding into my big girl pants. It helps to remind myself we would have done the same thing if Anika was a demon or a shifter. Harry is the only one around here I know personally who takes in supernatural strays.

Luca gets out, shutting his door firmly behind him. Anika bolts upright, her eyes panicked until they land on me.

"Celine," she says my name, the word heavily accented. The way she says it . . . Like the voices of my childhood. The visceral reminder of home makes the hairs on the back of my neck stand on end.

I'm rattled, but I can't let this shake me. I'll process, then execute a plan. Hopefully one that involves beating someone's ass for dumping a helpless kid in the woods of a foreign realm.

I turn in my seat, smiling gently, but authentically at Anika.

This kid is smart. Magic or no magic, she'll recognize bullshit. Without sugar coating it, I walk her through where we are and why we had to leave quickly. She listens without interrupting, her serious blue eyes calculating.

When I finish, Anika blinks a few times. *"Shmi?"* she asks, then retracts her wings.

"Yes, that will help, especially when you're not in Harriet's home." I say it first in the common tongue, then repeat the same sentence in English. Her eyes light up, and I watch her lips moving silently around the unfamiliar new words.

My heart throbs, pride and regret warring for dominance. She's far too pragmatic for a child her age.

I explain that Harry is a harpy, a species Anika tells me with excitement she's read about. My smile widens as she wiggles in the backseat, pressing her nose to the glass. Her mind may belong to a tiny scholar, but her body is that of an impatient child, eager to see something cool in person.

Anika quickly loses interest in looking out the window and starts spitting rapid-fire questions my way. From the climate to the economy, she grills me without mercy. I do my best to answer in both languages, but within five minutes, I'm forced to accept that I don't know jack shit about anything. She reaches the same conclusion, the curiosity in her eyes turning to pity. She's wondering how I managed to survive this long. *Same, kid, same.*

If only Luca would hurry up and put us both out of our misery.

When he finally comes back, I'm more exhausted than if I ran ten miles after working a double shift at the club. Luca knocks gently on Anika's window, and she climbs primly out of the back seat. She bows to him, then does the same to Harry.

"Hello, Harry," she says in English, pointing at herself. "Anika."

The striking harpy beams at her, waves at me, then takes

Anika by the hand and leads her into the house. Anika skips along at her side, only glancing once over her shoulder at me.

*Has she already learned not to count on anyone?* I scrub my hand over my face, slumping in my seat as Luca climbs in. Once Harry and Anika disappear inside, I thump my head repeatedly against the headrest, groaning until I feel better.

"What?" Luca asks, suppressed laughter in his voice.

"Why haven't you ever told me I'm an idiot?" I demand.

"Because you aren't?"

I take in his confused expression and giggle, then shake my head. "It's worse than I thought. We're both stupid, that's why we've never noticed."

"You need a drink. Or a nap."

"I'd be better off reading a book on electricity," I say.

"Now you're making no sense." Luca shakes his head. "Why the fuck would you do that?"

As he drives back to my place, I tell him about all the questions Anika asked, and we make up outlandish responses to them the entire way. For a few minutes, our laughter distracts me from the itch.

# SIX

## LUCA

*Stay calm. Don't push too hard. Be supportive.* I lecture myself sternly as I fold the clean towels at the Fang while listening absently to the dancers chat before open.

I'm doing my best to be chill, but Celine's skin turned into the fucking Rosetta Stone! I can't help but have questions about that. Questions I refuse to ask because I know she doesn't want to talk about it. If she did, she would have barreled in headfirst as soon as we were alone in the car.

I try not to let it sting that she doesn't trust me with this.

Celine owes me nothing. Not her present and certainly not her past. I only hope she trusts me enough to ask for help if whatever put the shadows in her eyes becomes a problem for her future. I'll turn it to stone, then she can grind it to dust.

"They blurred his dangly bits, so we couldn't confirm if they were shriveled or not," Celine says as she meticulously contours her face. I shake my head and add a towel to my stack. When the girls shoot the shit, I'm never quite sure what's going to come out of their mouths, but it's nice to see Celine relax.

"If you watch the international version, it won't be censored," Imani says, her lips curled into the amused disgust she always shows whenever man parts are up for discussion.

Celine perks up, and I grimace. "Not sure I need to see more."

"But we've recently learned we don't know anything about science," Celine argues. "This could be helpful."

I pretend to consider that, then shake my head. "Nope. I'm comfortable maintaining a certain level of ignorance."

"You and every guy I've ever gone to bed with," Imani teases.

I groan as all of them laugh at me. "You can't blame me for every bad sex experience you've ever had with a man," I complain. "Some of us take the time to learn."

"Can confirm," Ada says, winking at me as she pencils in her eyebrows. "Luca knows what he's doing."

They cheer at that, demanding I tell them about my secrets in graphic detail. I shake my head and focus back on the remaining tasks in front of me. I've got to fill out these inventory forms and send them off. The booze won't restock itself. I've been practically running this place since the owner retired two years ago.

Celine sits silently, her mouth hanging slightly open as she applies her eye makeup. Her hand is solid as a rock as she paints dark lines above her eyelashes. Since I'm watching her closely, I notice her eyes flicker over to Ada before focusing back on her own mirror.

Ada and I slept together a few times after she moved to Vegas and before she started working at the club. It's common knowledge around here, and it's never made things weird.

Part of me can't help hoping Celine didn't like the reminder. That's toxic. I know that, but I've never claimed to be a nice guy.

Shit, I live in the Fringes for a reason, wear combat boots most days, and have no interest in becoming more civilized than I already am.

Glancing at my watch, I clear my throat, because gentleman or not, I'm a damn good manager and punctual as fuck. "Thirty-minute warning," I call out, rolling my eyes at the chorus of groans they throw my way.

"We've got a big-ass clock right there, Luca," Brandy whines, pointing at the wall with a turquoise nail covered in rhinestones.

"And yet you still manage to lose track of time," I say. "Make it make sense."

"I'm worth the wait," she grumbles.

"Yeah, you are, but imagine the tips you'd get if you were on time." I wink at her and leave the room with my stack of clean towels so they can finish getting ready. I've got a bar to prep.

***

Alistair is back. He grins a fang-baring smile at me when I serve him his Blood Tide without a tomato, seeming strangely pleased that I'm not actively trying to kill him.

I shake my head, keeping a close eye on the other complication breathing down my neck tonight: the flirty blond demon.

"She's incredible," he says as Celine pulls off an aerial maneuver that used to scare me to death every time she practiced it.

I grunt in agreement. "Wait until you see the next part."

The demon focuses on her dance, audibly sucking in air as Celine flips backward off the pole and uses her wings to flutter gracefully to the stage.

"Damn!" He whistles, shaking his head. "Do you know if she dates demons?"

I imagine biting his head off and feeding it to him, then shrug and smile blandly instead. "Who Celine dates is her business," I say.

I could tell him the last demon who showed interest in her could successfully cosplay as the sand in the desert right about now, but I don't bother. If he finds out the hard way, that's his problem.

Celine's song ends, and unease tingles at the base of my spine. She always comes to the bar for her post-dance water. I love the ritual, but I wish she would skip it tonight. The demon's black eyes are far too interested, and Alistair is only a little better. Like clockwork, though, she heads my way, crossing the room in a handful of determined strides. Internally, I sigh, bending over to get her a fresh, cold water bottle from the mini fridge.

"Thanks," she says, taking the bottle from my hand and drinking half of it in one long swallow. Her throat bobs in the club lights, and I'm momentarily transfixed.

"Nice move," the demon says to her, gulping as she turns his way. "The backflip, I mean."

Celine dips her chin in response but doesn't add anything to encourage him or the conversation. A petty sense of satisfaction rises inside me as his face falls.

"Amazing as always, angel," Alistair says, wedging himself between Celine and the stranger, then leaning over the bar. "Can I get another round?"

I nod and begin making his drink. My good mood returns as Celine sidesteps Alistair and shoots him a peeved look. He grins at her, flashing fang.

"Personal space, Alistair," Celine mutters.

"Inviting me into yours? I accept." The smug fuck winks, and I shake my head at his antics and remind myself not to overreact. I've never heard of him hurting someone for no reason, but he's got a hell of a reputation around here, and you can never be too careful.

"In your dreams," Celine purrs, cocking her hip.

Alistair closes his eyes and smiles a crooked grin that spells nothing but trouble. "Only every single night, love."

Celine laughs out loud, her real laugh, throaty and loud. "Alistair, you never miss a beat."

"I try not to, angel." He turns to face the demon. "I don't believe we've been introduced yet. I'm Alistair."

"Ciprian . . . Nice to meet you." *Did I imagine that pause after he said his name?* Oh well, he wouldn't be the only one using an alias in this club. It's not like I give a shit.

They size each other up, and Celine looks at me and rolls her eyes conspiratorially. I bite my bottom lip, chewing on the ring there to keep my mouth shut.

"Harry tells me there's a new mouth to feed," Alistair says, drawing my attention back to him in a flash. Celine's calm amusement fades, and the look she levels at him is far from friendly.

"Why do you care?" she demands, her wings glowing like banked embers. I eye the smoke detector nervously, then shoot her a warning look.

"Simply making conversation." Alistair holds his hands out, palms up. "I stop by from time to time to make sure she has everything she needs." *That's surprising, and oddly nice for a guy with Alistair's reputation.*

I hand him his finished drink, giving Celine a moment to get her anger under control. "I'm sure Harry appreciates your help," I tell him.

"It's the least I can do." Alistair takes a sip. "If more of us had had someone like Harry watching out for us at that age . . ."

"Cheers to Harry." I pour a shot of tequila and clink the glass against Alistair's larger cup, then down it. I don't make it a habit of drinking on the job, but in a strip club surrounded by unpredictable supernaturals, sometimes you need to take the edge off.

"I'm curious to hear how a woman ended up with the name

Harry," Ciprian says, his black eyes glittering as he studies the three of us nosily.

"That's a long story," I lie without blinking. It isn't. Her name is Harriet, and she used to dance here at the club, but that's none of his godsdamn business. A regular stumbles to the corner and waves me over. "Duty calls," I grunt, passing Celine another bottle of water, then shifting further down the bar.

I spend the next few hours mixing drinks and convincing the clientele I have to cut off not to punch me in the face. By the time the crowd thins, I'm dead on my feet, and my face hurts from smiling.

"You're a master manipulator, man," Ciprian says, his voice slurring around the trickier syllables. He hasn't left the bar all night, watching mostly in silence. It's been so long since he spoke, I didn't realize how buzzed he was.

"Am I?" I ask, knowing enough about handling drunk people to avoid turning a conversation into an argument.

"Yeah." He hiccups loudly. "It's fucking amazing to watch."

"Thanks, I think." I laugh, shaking my head as the house lights bounce off his blond hair. It practically glows in the dark.

"No, seriously." Ciprian picks up one of the discarded cocktail skewers and twists a straw paper around it. "You and the redhead both wrap them around your fingers, but your methods are completely different from hers. She's fire—they can't resist the heat, even if they know she'll burn them, and you, you're that green gel that gets slathered on after to soothe the sting. Total power couple."

"We aren't together," I blurt, then imagine turning my own dumb ass to stone for being incredibly stupid. He's interested in her. That's obvious, and I practically gave him verbal permission to go for it.

"Hmm," Ciprian says.

"What's that supposed to mean?" *Fuck me, why am I antago-*

*nizing him?* This whole conversation is ridiculous. He might not even remember it tomorrow. But after the day I've had . . . it bothers me that this drunk stranger noticed our dynamic so easily. I feel almost bruised by it.

"Just trying to figure out who you're lying to, me or yourself," Ciprian drawls.

I narrow my eyes at him, and my basilisk stirs. "I'm closing your tab," I snap. "You're cut off for tonight." My tone is abrasive as fuck. I wait for him to push back, but he doesn't.

"I understand," Ciprian says, climbing off his stool too gracefully for someone who has downed as many drinks as he has. "Before I go, have you seen this guy? He was supposed to meet me here a few days ago, but I haven't been able to get in touch with him."

I glance at his phone screen as he holds it out. Pain explodes in my gums. My fangs descend, and it's only years of practice keeping my mouth shut that prevents me from visibly reacting. There, clear as day on his smudged phone screen, is the demon I turned to stone for Celine. Reacting on autopilot, I shake my head.

"Doesn't look familiar," I say. "Sorry about that."

"Thanks anyway." Ciprian takes off with a friendly wave, but again, I notice a slight hesitation. If he doesn't believe me . . . I'll have to kill him, too. For his sake, I hope he forgets all about his friend.

# SEVEN

## CELINE

My whole body itches.

Anika's appearance, Ciprian asking Luca about the dead demon. It's getting to me. If I don't do something to distract myself, I'm going to stab someone.

"Let's go to the fight tonight," I say, unzipping my thigh-high boots and tossing Imani my most winning smile. We've been rehearsing a new duet routine, and it's starting to come together.

She thinks about it, her eyebrows arched, shaking her head when I pout. "Fine," she groans. "It's not my first choice for a night off, but why the hell not?"

"That's the spirit." I check the mirror and adjust my high ponytail until it sits evenly on the crown of my head, then point at her. "But you can't use your magic to fuck with the fighters."

Imani frowns. "But that's the most fun part. Why else would I want to watch sweaty, shirtless dudes writhe around in a cage?"

"They hit each other. A lot."

"That's true," Imani says. "I guess it has its moments."

I rub my hands together, getting more excited about a real night out the more I think about it. "I'll buy you a beer and kidney punch anyone who tries to feel you up in the crowd."

"Oh baby," she coos. "Talk dirty to me."

We both laugh, and I check the time on my phone. If we stop rehearsing and relax awhile, we'll have plenty of time to get ready and be there in time for the bigger fights.

"Meet me there at nine?" I ask.

Imani nods. "It's a date."

"Damn," I crow, dragging the word out as Imani giggles and spins, then blows me a slow-motion kiss. She's wearing the hell out of her black mini dress, fishnet tights making her long legs appear endless. With her corkscrew curls blown out into an afro and her lips painted a deep magenta, she's holding up traffic. I laugh out loud as one guy walks directly into a parked car while staring at her.

"You're going to end the night satisfied," I say.

Imani smiles, a hint of her siren nature peeking through. "Yeah, that's the plan. Especially if you won't let me play with the fighters."

"Something tells me you'll make do." I chuckle, linking my arm with hers, and pull her down the street in the direction of the warehouse. There's a slight stiffness in her normally fluid gait that wasn't there when we rehearsed earlier. It adds another itch to my growing collection. "Imani . . . You'd tell me if it was getting bad again, wouldn't you?"

She inhales. The sound is weary. It belongs on someone far older and more jaded than my beautiful best friend. "The nightmares are back," she admits. "It's been hard to handle the soaks, but I'll manage."

I tighten my grip on her arm, anger stirring in my bones. It takes a lot to make a siren afraid of water. If I could get my hands on the people who drove Imani to flee to a literal desert climate, I'd be happy to provide them with some payback phobias, free of charge.

"You'll let me know if I can help," I say, my tone making it clear this isn't optional.

Imani rolls her eyes. "Yeah, you can punch the water in my bathtub to your heart's content."

"Can I kick it, too?"

"Don't be ridiculous," she says. "That would make too big of a splash. I want my deposit back if I decide to move."

We turn the corner, and the wide, dented door of the Mouth of Hell comes into view. It's old, battered, and easy to overlook most days. Tonight, though—with a line of supernaturals forming outside—there's no missing it. Unless you're a human who wandered onto this street by mistake . . . then all you'd see is a filthy wall before being overcome by an urge to turn around.

My heart rate picks up, but it's excitement, not fear. The supernatural fight club is rough. The kind of place you don't step into unless you can handle yourself, which makes it wildly popular in a fringe community like ours, where it's every creature for themselves. I doubt the enclave would approve, but since they haven't bothered to shut it down, business is booming.

"It's packed," we say in unison. Imani sounds as if someone just told her she has six days left to live, and I sound like I won the lottery. We look at each other and giggle.

Imani rolls her shoulders back, tilting her chin up. "You owe me for this."

"Anything you want," I promise, unlinking our arms and

guiding her slim fingers to the waist of my leather pants. "Hold on tight; you're in for a bumpy ride." *This is my favorite part.*

With a devious smile on my face, I carve a path through the crowd, creating space for us to pass through with a few dozen well-placed elbows. Skipping the line entirely, we make it inside with only a handful of curses and glares thrown our way. All of which fade to sappy, besotted grins when the idiots catch sight of Imani.

The Mouth of Hell used to be an abandoned warehouse—now it's the most notable Vegas fringe destination I know. Every time we come, the magic and showmanship get more impressive while maintaining the grungy charm it's known for.

Exhibit one: the stacks. Made of splintery piles of pallets, haphazardly lashed together by gods know what, the stacks poke up from around the dusty warehouse floor like termite mounds in the desert. They give spectators a good vantage point and a better opportunity to brawl over the best ones.

I stop by my favorite, annoyed when I see two drunken shifters are already sitting there. "Our seats are taken," I groan, my shoulders slumping. I could yank them off, but—

"Hey boys, do you mind if we borrow those seats? I can't see a thing." Imani's voice is coaxing, melodic, and utterly mesmerizing.

The pair of shifters practically climb over each other in their hurry to get down. When one trips and falls flat on his face, I almost feel sorry for him. The other blinks at Imani with wide-eyed adoration. "You're the most beautiful woman I've ever seen," he declares.

"That's correct," I say. "Thank you for vacating our seats." I pat him on the shoulder with a cheery grin, then step over his friend's prone body to leap up on the stack. It lurches to the right but doesn't collapse. That's why it's my favorite.

"Fucking rickety ass, piece of—"

"Hey, it never lets us fall," I interrupt Imani's rant to defend the makeshift platform and give her a hand up.

Perching on one of the crates, she primly crosses her legs. She has to raise her voice to be heard over the grungy rock music pumping into the warehouse from the speakers lining the walls. "With all the magic in here, you'd think we could get some better seating."

"Permanent spells are expensive." I shrug. "And there's room up here for me to let out my wings."

Imani whips her head around. "Are you sure you should? With that kid popping up out of the blue and Luca seeing your runes . . . Maybe you should keep a low profile."

"But . . ." I scowl, the itch capturing my attention again. "I hate that plan."

"It's not forever, Celine." Imani pats my arm. "Only until we know which direction to aim you."

"You make me sound like a weapon." I grin, cheered by the thought, and check out the caged ring in the center of the floor. "They've made it bigger since the last time we came. The support beams are level now too."

"If you say so," Imani grumbles. Hovering off the ground, the ring is surrounded by a metal cage. Similar to the platform we're sitting on, it looks unsafe, but I can practically taste the enchantments woven into it from here.

"Do you miss it?" Imani asks, drawing my attention away from the cage. I consider pretending not to know what she means, then shrug. I don't keep secrets from her. Not anymore.

When I got a job at the Fang six years ago, I had no clue how to dance. Imani taught me, patiently ignoring my prickly attitude and slipping past my barriers so gradually I didn't realize it was happening until it was too late to push her out. I worry about the risk, but I can admit to myself that I would be lost without her.

"Only on the days that end with y," I sigh.

"Celine."

"I wanted to come out tonight to get my mind off everything," I say, gesturing to the bloodthirsty crowd and grinning when a guy gets tired of trying to push his way through the bodies and howls like a beast. "Even I can admit it would be a horrible idea for the angry-but-fuckable angel to paint a bigger target on her back by fighting in public."

"That makes me sad, babe." Imani's tone is soft, but matter-of-fact. No minimizing my emotions or giving me solutions we both know are a waste of time.

I shrug, flexing my shoulder blades and ignoring the complaints from my pinned wings. "I've lived more than long enough to learn life isn't fair."

"You're only twenty-seven." Imani laughs, then sobers. "I would give you fair if I could," she vows.

My heart clenches, and I squeeze her hand. "And I love you for it. Now, quit being sweet and scope the crowd out. Is there anyone here you want me to play wingwoman for?"

"That was a horrible pun." Imani groans, bumping her shoulder against mine. Despite her whining, she accepts my subject change with a knowing smirk, then scans the sea of people. Her eyes stop on a tall woman with a simple braid and an intricate tattoo sleeve. "Have I hit on her before?" she asks.

"I don't think so." I squint to get a better look at the sexy blonde. "Do you want to go over?"

Imani grins and pushes to her feet, shooting me a wink. "No help needed. I seem to remember you owing me a beer, though."

"Oh, she's cocky," I say.

"Thirsty," she corrects me.

"Yeah, yeah. I'm on it. Race you to see who's back first?"

"These things shouldn't be rushed, babe."

Rolling my eyes, I hop off the platform and muscle my way through the crowd to the bar. One guy grabs my ass, and I break three of his fingers. His scream of pain throws some attention my way, but what am I supposed to do? Low profile can't mean doormat, at least not for me.

I pay for my beer and Imani's, surprised to find our platform unoccupied when I get back. Hopping up, I use the height advantage to find her. She's got a drink in one hand, the other buried in the blonde's hair. Their lips are tightly fused.

Raising both beers to her, I clink the glass bottles together and take a sip. With Imani busy, I can get a closer view of the action. We can always meet up later, but with the way their hands are wandering, I don't see that happening. I fire off a text letting her know where I'm going in case she needs to find me.

Abandoning the platform, I head toward the ring. It's harder to get through this section of the crowd. They're actively trying to hold their spots, but I'm determined. I'm also not above using flirtation and violence to get my way. Most people move if they think it will earn them an orgasm or keep them from ending their night with a fractured toe.

Eventually, I've made it to the base of the cage. I was right—it's much bigger, but I misjudged the height. At 5'8", I don't often feel short, but I'm right below eye level of the floor of the new ring. I'll have to crane my neck if I want to see anything but feet.

I turn around and consider my odds of making it back to my usual platform without getting into a fight. The crowd is shoulder to shoulder now, screaming for violence. I groan under my breath. I'm better off staying put. A salmon can only swim upstream so many times before she gets bloody.

Alistair appears suddenly on my right, knocking a smaller guy flat on his ass in the process. He scrambles to his feet, glancing left and right. His hands curl into fists, but he seems too unsure about who knocked him over to risk starting something.

"Do you need a lift, angel?" Alistair asks, his voice awfully calm for someone who just sliced through the crowd like a machete. His dark hair hangs loose tonight, curling around his ears and neck.

My lips twitch at his audacity. Alistair is plenty tall enough to see over the cage floor. I do my best not to hold that against him.

"Amazing how you managed to pop up next to me in a crowd this big," I drawl. "I don't think I'm going to ask how you managed it."

"Smart lady." Alistair grins, his fangs poking roguishly over his lower lip. "Why question fate when you could thank her for her blessings instead?"

I shake my head, refusing to be charmed by his dubious pickup lines, then crane my neck as the bell rings. I'm determined to see as much of the fight as possible. It only takes thirty seconds for me to realize I can't see shit. I can hear the punches, but all I can see is a flash here and there of hairy toes and burly calves. I grit my teeth.

"Just this once," I huff, draining the rest of my beer and starting in on the one I bought for Imani.

"What was that, Celine?" Alistair jostles into me as the crowd presses forward. He bares his fangs at the guy behind us, his eyes flashing blood red. The stranger stumbles over himself to back away.

I shudder, steadying Alistair with a hand on his arm. Those eyes . . . I'm acutely aware of the leashed violence behind them. I should be afraid of him. I'm not. Maybe I'm losing it, but being with Alistair is exciting. The surrounding colors are brighter, the grunts from the fight louder. Shit, my beer even tastes colder. *I feel alive.*

"You can lift me," I say loudly, drawing his intense red gaze to me. I study the ruby orbs with interest until they fade back to the cozy blue denim I'm used to.

"With pleasure," Alistair says, bending too quickly for me to track the movement. His hands grip my waist, my vision warps, and I find myself perched on his shoulders a fraction of a second later. He was so graceful about it, I didn't even spill my drink.

Blinking, I grin as one fighter lands a haymaker on the other's chin. *This. This is exactly what I wanted.* Since I can be generous when the situation calls for it, I pass what's left of Imani's beer to Alistair as payment for the ride. He takes a swig, his grip on my calf firm.

With a perfect view of the action, I lose myself in the fight as the shifters exchange brutal blows in both their human and animal forms. When the bear's partial shift takes too long, the wolf takes the opportunity to bite him, gouging deeply into his flank. The wolf comes away with a mouthful of flesh that he slings at the side of the cage, splattering blood on me and a couple of other spectators in the process.

I laugh, rattling the cage with both hands and screaming for the wolf to press his advantage. He does. The fight doesn't last long after that. The wolf is simply too fast for the bear to keep up with. The bigger shifter taps out before he can end up with a hole in his throat, and the emcee shouts that there will be a half hour break between fights.

Alistair reaches up to help me, his fingers grazing my inner thigh and sending a bolt of awareness through my body. I bat his hands away, grabbing the cage in front of me and using it to climb down. Once I'm on the ground, I spin triumphantly, a wide smile on my face.

"That was a great fight," I say, my heart pounding as I relive the best moments. Alistair stares at me, his expression oddly tight. I raise my eyebrows. "What, no quip?"

He shakes his head. "You look even lovelier with a blood-splattered face than I could have imagined."

I bring my fingers up to my cheeks, and sure enough, I feel drying blood smeared there. I wince, but Alistair is already reaching out with a linen handkerchief that looks like something straight out of a Regency movie. Dropping my hand, I allow him to clean my face. His touch is confident. Thorough. His blue eyes dip to my lips as he finishes, a faint pink tinge crowding the edges.

"There," he says. "Flawless once more."

And for the life of me, I can't help myself—I swallow his charm, hook, line, and sinker. My stomach buzzes as a hundred butterflies take flight. *Just this once.* I repeat my earlier promise to myself and smile up at him. *Just this once.*

# EIGHT

## CELINE

The summer rolls in mercilessly. Beams of sunlight penetrate every inch of the city. No air conditioning unit or magical cooling charm in existence can keep up with the dry heat that hovers over the pavement. It gyrates in hazy, horizontal ribbons, the texture visible in a way it shouldn't be without eating a special mushroom or two first.

Today, Imani and I are rehearsing in the empty club. We've been keeping this weekly routine going for years, and that's comforting to me, extreme temperatures or not.

Climbing to the top of the pole, I let myself roll down slowly as I test out different holds.

Heat makes a lot of people sluggish. Not me. I feel alive, like I could outrun sweat itself if I tried. My dance routines have gotten faster and more aggressive. My tips reflect the extra effort, which is a good thing, because I'm giving as much money as I can to

Harry. I tell myself it doesn't matter. I don't even need magic to know I'm lying.

Anika popping up on the trail changed things for me.

My itch hasn't stopped, and I can't pinpoint the cause to save my life. Ciprian is gone, so it seems Luca was worried about nothing there. His departure being as sudden as his arrival doesn't surprise me. He's exactly like all the visitors who slink in and out of our lives here at the club. The Naked Fang is a vacation from reality, and by extension, we are too.

"I need a break," Imani gasps, her face twisting as she bends over. Her breathing is labored, and I frown as I drop to the floor and study her more closely.

"This is more than the heat," I guess, hoping I'm wrong. When she doesn't correct me, my belly churns. "Imani, you can't keep doing this to yourself."

"I-I can't fucking do it," she admits, anguish coating her voice.

"Then *we'll* do it," I say, gritting my teeth. "Together."

"I can't let you risk it." Imani lifts her head, her wide eyes tormented. "We could drown."

"Hey, listen to me." I infuse magic into my words. "I will not let that happen. I swear it."

Imani stares at me, scanning the runes covering my skin before clenching her jaw. "If you don't mind—"

"Bitch, don't insult me," I snap, and her lips curl up into a reluctant smile. They're chapped at the corners, and I kick myself for not noticing sooner. Imani has been pushing herself to rehearse with me and suffering the entire time.

Hurrying to the storage room, I yank the big tub away from the wall. It's here for the wet and wild events we put on from time to time, but we haven't used it in a while. With one hand, I drag it out of the room and down the hall, stopping behind the bar.

Under the counter, there's a thick, coiled hose, the nozzle resting in a bracket above the sink. I yank it out harshly, the mechanical whine abrasive in my ears as I force it to uncurl, then turn the water on to fill the tub.

Imani eyes it with dread, hands shaking at her sides. "You know, I'm feeling better—"

"It's too late for that," I say. It sounds harsh, but I'm mad at myself. I should have seen how badly she was struggling sooner.

"Your wings are smoking," Imani whispers. When I see she's right, I hiss and close my eyes. "If you're pissed, we can always do this later."

"I'm pissed at myself."

"You didn't do anything wrong."

"Except be a completely oblivious, selfish bitch."

Imani snorts. "Give me a little more credit, Celine. I'm covert, you know? Mysterious and all that."

My glare tells her exactly what I think of that bullshit. "We promised each other," I murmur.

Her face falls. "I remember."

"Do you?" I demand, swallowing around the lump in my throat. "Because the best-friend-approved list of acceptable ways to self-destruct includes banging hot losers, overspending during sales, and drinking until you forget. You know what's explicitly forbidden? Letting yourself desiccate because of baggage you never asked to carry."

"Celine," she says, her voice gentle.

"No," I shout, dropping the end of the hose in the tub and standing upright. "We don't let them win, right? You swore that to me! You fucking promised." My wings erupt in flames, and I scream at the ceiling, trying to expel my rage before I set off the smoke detector again.

"C-Celine." The fear in Imani's voice grounds me. My flames extinguish with a series of cascading sizzle sounds. Without my anger, crushing sadness is all that remains.

Imani didn't ask to be afraid of water—she needs it to live.

That was done to her, against her will, over and over again, poisoning her against the very thing that should bring her the most joy.

The drips fall before I can even attempt to regulate my emotions.

"Your wings are crying, babe." Imani sniffles, her voice stuffy.

"I know." I groan, shaking them out as they sag from the weight of the water. Droplets fly everywhere, and Imani takes a step back. I pretend I don't notice. "I'll have to mop this shit up later or Luca will murder me," I say.

"Yeah, right," she scoffs. "Is it close?"

"It's getting there." The big aluminum tub is about halfway full of tepid water. I look up at Imani and smile. "You should come over here and let me know when you think it's ready."

It's a transparent attempt to desensitize her. I'm not an idiot. I know how full the tub needs to be, but I'm not going to shove her in and hold her there until she gets the soak her siren needs. That's a choice Imani has to make on her own.

She approaches the tub like she's marching to her execution. It might seem ridiculous to some, but knowing what she's been through, I find it far more surprising that Imani manages to face the water at all.

"You're strong," I remind her.

"No, I'm not." Imani hangs her head. "If I was strong, I wouldn't fear a few inches of water in a glorified bucket. If I was strong, I wouldn't need my best friend to get in the fucking bathtub with me. If I was strong, I would have fought and won, not run away to another realm and moved to the least wet place I could find." By the time she finishes, her shoulders are heaving, silent sobs racking her body.

I go to her side, grabbing her fisted hands in mine. "Stop it, Imani," I insist. "Don't talk about yourself that way or I'll have to yell at you."

"You are yelling at me," she says, smiling through her tears.

"Fuck!" I force my voice to soften. "Is this better?"

"Eh. You're still yelling; just at a lower volume."

"Then try to ignore my tone," I say, letting my magic back out to ensure she knows what I say next is the absolute truth.

"When I look at you, I don't see someone who ran away. I see someone who forged her own path and created a new life for herself in a place she'd never been before. It took courage to start over here, and it takes courage to soak in this stupid tub, but you will do it, because you're the strongest person I know."

Imani wipes a tear from my cheek, her amber eyes glistening with tears of her own. "Okay, okay. I believe you, Celine." She closes her eyes. When she opens them again, they're fierce with determination. "Let's get in this stupid tub, then."

I nod, reaching over to cut the water off, and step in. Imani follows my lead, flinching when her bare feet and calves disappear beneath the surface. Slowly, I sit, easing myself down so the water rises gradually up her legs instead of all at once. It laps at her knees. They shake. I wait. Imani takes a deep breath, then sinks down to join me, letting the air out of her lungs in one great big puff.

I grab her hands again, locking our fingers together.

"You won't let anything bad happen?" Imani asks. Her voice is shaky, but the water is doing its job. Color is already returning to her cheeks.

"Never," I promise. "I figured room temperature water was best."

She nods, the movement jerky but not panicked.

"You're doing amazing," I assure her. "Deep breaths. In and out."

Imani's lips twitch. "If you keep talking me through it, I'm going to get the wrong idea," she teases.

I roll my eyes, then drop until only my head is poking out of the water. Imani matches my position, her eyes wide. "Good girl," I joke. "I knew you could take it all."

"I'm scared to ask what the hell I walked in on." Luca's voice startles us both. "But please don't stop on my account."

"Just cooling off," I say, giving Imani's hands a reassuring squeeze. "Our rehearsal got sweaty."

"Mmhmm," Luca says, not sounding like he believes my flimsy excuse one bit. "Gods! Why is the entire floor soaked?"

"I'll clean it up," I snap. "Go away. You're ruining the vibe."

"Actually, listening to the two of y'all bitch is a great distraction," Imani says. I roll my eyes, encouraged by how much stronger her voice sounds.

Head poking over the top of the bar, Luca studies us both, fully clothed in the tub, his eyes stopping on Imani's tear-stained cheeks. "You okay?" he asks her, his voice a low growl that makes a shiver roll down my spine.

"I'm fine." Imani sighs, then shudders. "Or I will be soon. I'm going under, Celine."

"Fuck yeah, you are." I sit up, wrapping my hands around hers again. "I swear on my life that you will come up again. Squeeze my hands twice when you're ready."

She nods, the whites of her eyes flashing as she scans the room. "What if you can't get me out?" It's a completely illogical question, but logic has nothing to do with it.

"Then Luca will flip the whole tub over," I tell her.

Imani looks over at him, and he nods grimly. "Whatever you need."

"Okay," she whispers, dropping backward until she's completely submerged. As soon as the tip of her nose goes under, her skin glows amber. I drop our joined hands beneath the water as hers relax in mine.

"It's gotten worse," Luca says, his voice tense. "I didn't notice."

"Neither did I."

"It's not your fault."

"I know that."

"Yeah, but do you believe it?"

"Don't psychoanalyze me, Luca." I ease my head back against the narrow lip of the tub, making sure not to jostle Imani or lose my grip on her hands. If the raw patches of skin on her joints are any indication, she's been putting this off for way too long. "Why are you here, anyway?"

"Sal wants me to send him the inventory reports again."

I turn my head. "What? Why?"

"You know how he is." Luca shrugs, but from the tense set of his shoulders, he's not thrilled.

"If he wants things his way, he can drag his ass in here and crunch the numbers himself," I sputter. "I'm guessing he didn't offer you overtime."

"I'm salaried now."

"Yeah, I bet." I scoff. "He gets away with requiring you to do more while paying you less. Cheap bitch."

"Careful, you never know when he's listening."

"I hope he is," I snarl. "I've got quite a few things to say to him."

Luca chuckles. "Your justice complex is showing. Focus on Imani for now, I'll be okay for a bit longer without my guardian angel."

"I'm not a guardian," I insist, craning my head when I hear the familiar sound of sloshing water. "Are you mopping? I said I would clean it up."

"Give it a rest, Celine. You don't have to do everything. Imani is my friend, too."

"I made that mess," I mutter.

Luca chuckles. "Mood wing malfunction?"

"They function as they were intended."

"Uh huh," Luca says, cleaning up quietly.

After he mops up the excess water and dries the floor with a towel, he disappears to the back room. When he returns a few minutes later, his hair is damp at the temples with sweat. A ripple of awareness shoots through me. Luca is sexy. And important to me. How did I let this happen?

"You okay?" he asks, looking me over, a furrow in his brow.

I nod, the lump returning to my throat unexpectedly. There's nothing wrong, but I don't think my wings are finished leaking for the day.

"Are you sure?" Luca narrows his eyes, clearly not believing me.

I open my mouth to speak, although I'm not sure if I'm going to tell him to get lost or come back to my place to hold me while I sob. Then Imani squeezes my hands twice and nothing else matters. I pull her up and brush the water droplets off her face.

"Here," Luca says, handing her a clean, dry towel. She buries her face in the fabric for a few seconds, then drops it to face us.

"Okay?" I ask, amazed by how much healthier she looks. Her dark skin is glowing, although the magical amber light has faded to a more natural level.

Imani nods, relief obvious in every line of her body. She leans forward, bending her neck toward me, and I mirror her until our foreheads touch. "Thank you," she whispers.

"Same time next week?" I ask, only half kidding. She can't keep doing this, and we both know it.

"I'll let you know." She stands, her water-logged clothes dripping into the tub. "This was a good start." Wrapping the towel around herself, Imani gets out, but she isn't in a desperate hurry to dry off. I've never seen anyone be so effortlessly beautiful while soaking wet.

"Do you want me to come home with you?" I ask, doing my best to make my voice nonchalant. From Imani's eye roll, I don't succeed.

"I'm good alone," she says. "See you both tomorrow?"

"Sure thing." I smile and Luca nods.

Imani disappears into the dressing room where we all keep a spare outfit or two stored, and I contemplate how I can keep checking in on her without being a nag.

"Up," Luca says, holding a second towel out for me. "You look like a prune."

I pretend to be offended while knowing he's absolutely right. Imani may be twice as gorgeous after an hour underwater, but I feel like a drowned rat. Standing, I cringe as the cold, soggy clothes stick to my skin. My nipples are hard as glass, poking through my paper-thin shirt. Disgusted, I yank the wet fabric off, throw it in the tub, then snatch the towel from Luca.

"You're cold," he says, his jaw tightly clenched.

I smirk at him, perversely pleased he noticed at all. Friend or not, when my nipples are out, I want them to be admired. "What gave me away?" I ask innocently.

"The shivering," he deadpans.

With as much dignity as I can muster, I step out of the tub and wrap the towel around myself. "That was rude," I say, shooting him a glare.

Luca smirks at me. "You already know you have nice tits."

"Yeah, but I don't mind hearing about it every once in a while."

"Seriously?" He snorts, and I raise my chin and begin to walk away. "Celine . . . wait. You want the truth?"

I plant my hands on my hips and stare him down. "Obviously."

"You have the most perfect tits I've ever seen in my entire godsdamn life. A man could be jobless and broke and happily occupy himself solely with your tits all day, every day. Is that what you want to hear?"

My mouth goes dry, and I shift my weight as Luca's husky

tone runs through my body like an electric current. "You don't have to sound mad about it." I smile as I replay his angry compliment.

"Don't I?" he demands.

I raise my eyebrows. "I can't imagine why."

"They aren't my tits to play with, are they?" Luca asks. "I get to be a little pissed about that."

I laugh out loud, then leave the room before I tell him something stupid . . . like all he has to do is ask.

# NINE

ENCLAVE EDICT #3:
CONTACT THE ENCLAVE FOR CONFLICT RESOLUTION.

## CIPRIAN

Dad drags me home for an important meeting, then doesn't say a damn word that applies to me. He could have at least had someone create a portal to make things easier on me, but of course that's too much trouble. I drove ten hours, and for what? To nod off in the conference room? I swear he gets off on making everyone jump when he says to.

Swallowing a yawn, I thrum my fingers against my knee while he drones on.

Callum and Gideon showing up with Sheena in tow has thrown him for a loop. Yet, I can already see the dollar signs in his eyes as he calculates what her appearance is worth to the enclave. How embarrassing. I keep my mouth shut.

Sheena has her work cut out for her if she wants to be part of this family. She could always take off—I would help her if she asked—but I hope she decides we're worth it. With the way she's falling for my brother and Gideon, I'm almost hopeful.

"Why do you look weird?" Callum whispers, his expression suspicious.

I roll my eyes. I think I might cease to exist if my brother didn't expect the worst of me. He conveniently forgets that he was the one who left me behind. "Be quiet," I drawl. "Can't you see I'm trying to listen to Dad?"

My voice is dripping with sarcasm, but Callum's face hardens anyway, as if he can't even tell when I'm bullshitting anymore. Whatever. That's his problem. I won't spoon feed him.

I yawn again, glancing at my phone as it vibrates in my lap.

SHEENA

Tell me more about the wings.

CIPRIAN

Gods. I was drunk. I never should have mentioned her to you.

Am I doing this wrong? The bestie thing.

How am I supposed to know? I don't get why you want to hear about my drama anyway after what happened at dinner last night.

Your parents are a lot.

Ugh... don't mention it. Seriously, please don't mention it.

Callum loves you.

I snort, and Cal shoots me another narrow-eyed stare. His girlfriend has some serious blinders on if she thinks our sibling relationship is salvageable, but who am I to burst her bubble?

CIPRIAN

Sure he does.

Nothing will come of the wings. She's incredibly
hot but radiates trouble.

It would be messy. Like a bomb going off.

SHEENA

The perfect fit.

Honestly, Ciprian, you're describing yourself.

Plus, she's got a roster of hot dicks orbiting her
like she's the sun.

Hot dicks you say?

Damn girl! Don't you have enough?

Yeah, but you could use a few.

Unless I read that wrong.

She didn't, but I'm going to make her sweat that one out.
Leaving her on read, I swallow my grin and glance up at Dad. He's
still rambling. Gideon's head droops, a few curls falling over his
eyes. They do nothing to disguise the fact that he's nodding off. I
kick him in the shin, then focus on my phone.

SHEENA

Okay, I'm sorry. Don't be mad, I was abducted
when I was sixteen. It probably stunted my
development.

CIPRIAN

You were right. I'm an equal opportunity taste
tester.

Then eat up.

You're filthy.

Sheena might be on to something, though. Celine is magnetic. Luca is mouthwatering. And Alistair—damn, Alistair is a tall, dark, and handsome drink made entirely of juicy secrets. They could be the key to learning what happened to Roscoe and how things work on the Fringes. I just can't let them know I'm part of the enclave.

"Ciprian, are you even listening to me?" Dad demands. I raise my chin, making sure my bland expression is firmly in place. "After your drunken display at dinner last night, I'm half a mind to send you back to Las Vegas to start the Roscoe investigation over from scratch."

I widen my eyes and activate faux contrition mode. "You're right," I say. "I fucked—I mean, messed up. Give me a chance to fix it, Dad. I won't let you down again."

His chest swells, and he shoots Callum a barbed, superior smirk. My brother should realize what I'm doing and take notes about the best ways to get around our father, but his expression sours and he slumps back in his chair instead. I sigh. I can lead a horse to fucking water, but I can't make him drink, can I?

"Very well," Dad says. "You'll go back to Vegas and stay there until you can successfully bring back information worth having. Roscoe wouldn't have deserted the enclave. Someone killed him, and I want them dealt with. We've let the Fringes get away with way too much, but I'm drawing the line at murder. It's high time they remember who runs this territory, don't you think, Joshua?"

"Of course," Joshua says easily, but his brown eyes are sharp. After a quick study of my face, he winks at me, then changes the subject.

I feel a rush of affection for him. Gideon may be his only child, but he and Sarah raised me as much as Dad and Mom, if not more, and they are a lot harder to manipulate. Joshua knows I want to go to Vegas, and he's suspicious, but he's no snitch.

Plus, he's beyond excited about Gideon and Callum coming

home. He never wanted them to move out, and Sheena's security issues are a golden opportunity for him to herd the prodigal chicks—I mean enclave heirs—back into the nest.

I toss him a half-smile. *I see you, too, Joshua Therion.* One hurdle cleared, I go over my game plan. As long as I can avoid getting caught by Sarah, I'll be home free.

Three days after I planted the first seeds, Dad sends me back to Vegas.

I'm more than ready to put the compound in the rearview mirror. Do any of them realize that my shoulders shoot up to my fucking ears every time I drive through the gate? Would they care if they did?

Sheena and I are on good terms, and I want to be there for her during this mess, but being surrounded by nosy, opinionated supernaturals wears me down. They watched me grow up. There isn't a skeleton in my closet that hasn't been paraded around this compound for inspection. Add in two and a half decades of preconceived notions about how I'll behave, and I have no choice but to play the role I've been cast in.

I'm getting tired of it. The lovable fuckup. Dad's last hope for a nightmare demon legacy. It's tragic, really. He wanted the perfect heir but had to squish his spare into the mold instead. Joke's on him, though. I'm happy to play the part when it suits me, but I'm Ciprian Casanell, and I'm no one's perfect progeny.

Dropping my head against the steering wheel, I breathe in through my nose. This pattern of thoughts is as familiar to me as the back of my hand. It always makes me feel worse, but I don't know how to put it to bed without crawling in beside it. And why does everything need to be good for me, anyway? I don't drink scotch for my fucking health.

I turn the radio on and try to get lost in the music. For this job, I need to forget about my enclave responsibilities and blend in. Fringe Ciprian should be sexy and caustic, a good time, but not too good. I need to ride that razor-thin line they always balance on, never showing too much interest in anyone while remaining aware of every move they make.

By the time I step back into my temporary home, I've purged the worst of my mood by scream singing punk rock until my throat hurts. There's no point in having fast healing if you don't take advantage of it during the important moments, right?

"Right," I answer myself out loud, loneliness creeping over me.

I'm talking to myself a lot these days. Thank the gods I'm a great conversationalist. Locking the door behind me, I collapse face first on the bed for a nap. After a couple of hours dead to the world, I get a whiff of myself, then stumble to the shower, feeling almost cheerful.

Next, I grab some food, then head over to the strip club to snoop. Four days away should have smoothed over any feathers I ruffled by asking about Roscoe. As I approach the now familiar building, a smile takes over my face. I'm about to see Celine, and I bet she looks fucking—

I trip over something in the dark and barely lift my hands in time to avoid face planting into the concrete wall. Poking the lumpy thing with my toe, I jump back as it whimpers.

"Umm, sorry," I mutter, squinting at the little face blinking up at me. Shit, it's a kid. Outside a strip club. That's weird as fuck.

The child blinks a few times, but there's no awareness in his eyes. He tips over and goes back to sleep, his mouth falling open against the pavement. *What the fuck is going on here?* He's a bit young to be drunk, and I don't see any sign of injury. Bending over, I gingerly put two fingers on the child's neck, relieved to find his pulse is strong and steady.

I sigh, my fun plans for the night vanishing like smoke. I'm going to have to get help inside and draw unwanted attention to myself in the process. I'm not even sure what the kid is. I can sense he isn't human, but beyond that, his kind isn't immediately obvious. Definitely not a demon or a shifter . . .

Groaning, I open the door and shoulder my way through the crowd. It's Friday night, and the Naked Fang is more crowded than I've ever seen it. Luca is behind the bar, his hair falling in his eyes as he fills a pitcher with beer. The tattered tank top he's wearing should make him look like he left his fashion game in the '90s, but grunge suits him perfectly.

I wait my turn impatiently, noting with satisfaction the recognition that flares in his eyes when he spots me. "What can I get for you?" Luca asks.

I shake my head. "You don't have anything back there strong enough for this. I need to show you something."

Luca sighs, then rolls his eyes. "That was a terrible line."

"I'm not talking about my cock, man," I say, wincing. "In fact, don't even think about my cock during this conversation, please. There's a kid passed out in the alley."

He frowns at me. "We don't serve underage here."

"No, you're not hearing me." I raise my voice over the rising thump of the bass. "There's a literal child outside. I tripped over it. Him," I correct myself.

Luca's stare sharpens. He studies me, then glances over my shoulder in the direction of the back rooms. "Fuck, okay. Show me."

I lead him out the door, feeling eyes on me the entire way. I glance back, but there are way too many people in this club to know who's watching. Part of me hopes the kid took off, but he's right where I left him, curled up in a tight ball on the hard ground. "See," I say, pointing to the child. "I told you."

Luca shoots me a disgruntled look, then runs his fingers

through his hair. "Not this again. *Shit*." I frown, but before I can ask him to explain what he means, he focuses back on me. "Can you tell what he is?"

I shake my head. "Not a demon. That's for sure."

"You didn't see wings, did you?"

His cagey tone catches my interest, and I cock my head to the side. "No wings." Angels aren't the only winged supernaturals, but given Luca's connections . . . Only a dumbass would miss the obvious logical leap. "You think he's an angel?"

Luca stiffens. "I have no idea what he is. Watch him for a second, would you? I'll be right back."

"What?" I snap. "Don't leave me with him."

Luca ignores me, disappearing into the club without a backward glance. I eye the child suspiciously, but he's sound asleep.

I count to sixty four times before the door opens again with a metallic whine. Luca steps through, followed by Celine. She has a green, silky robe tossed over her shoulders and belted at the waist. This outfit is somehow hotter than the lingerie I imagined earlier. Celine glances at me with narrowed eyes, then peers at the boy.

"What is it?" I ask while Luca grunts impatiently.

Celine levels us both with a frustrated glare. "*He* is a child," she says.

"No shit," I scoff. "But what kind? There's no way that energy is human."

Celine ignores me, giving Luca a nod. He scrubs his hand over the stubble on his jaw and digs a cell phone out of his pants. My temper surges. I hate being ignored.

"Don't do that," I hiss. Both of them lift their heads. "I found him. Don't you think I deserve to know what he is too?"

"No," Celine says shortly.

"Why not?" I demand, advancing a step toward her.

"Because I don't trust you."

"Because I'm a demon?" I crowd her, matching her glare with

one of my own. Never in a million years would I lay a hand on her, but I'm curious to see what she'll do if I push her too far. And I'm not going to let them carry this child off without knowing what they're going to do with it—fuck—*him.* "That's pretty rude, if you ask me."

She lifts her chin defiantly, then groans as her wings shoot out of her back, shredding the back of the colorful robe like tissue paper. "First, I didn't ask you. Second, it's not because you're a demon; it's because you're a stranger. Third, you owe me a new robe, you dick."

I listen to her rant with half my focus, the other half watching with fascination as smoke drifts up from her wings. Curious, I reach for the closest feathers to me, and sure enough, they're radiating heat. Right before my fingers connect, she slaps my hand away. The feather I was about to touch bursts into flames.

"Holy shit! You've got hot wings," I exclaim. It's an idiotic thing to say, but I can't help myself. They're fucking cool.

Luca groans, then the kid's eyes snap open. He takes one good look at the fireball that Celine has become, scrambles to his feet, and starts speaking in tongues.

# TEN

## LUCA

All these loose kids are stressing me out.

Seriously, I've spent my entire adult life carefully avoiding adding to the supernatural population on Earth, yet I still end up surrounded by children. What's the point of wearing a condom every time when toddlers are falling from the fucking sky?

This new one is losing his shit, babbling a mile a minute with his eyes locked on Celine. If there was any doubt about his celestial heritage, the angelic mumbo jumbo pouring from his mouth erases it.

I desperately want his appearance outside the club to be a coincidence. It's too bad I don't believe in those. To make matters worse, Ciprian is standing smack dab in the middle of the mess, his mouth hanging open as if he's never heard anyone speak a different language before.

"Stop groaning," Celine says to me, jabbing her elbow into my ribs.

I step to the side before I can end up singed. "Only if you stop burning," I toss back, wiping sweat from my forehead with the back of my hand. "You look like a godsdamn comet."

"Guys, the kid is singing now." Ciprian snaps his fingers to get our attention, and I realize with dismay that he's right. It's not a very good song, more like a chant a group of cultists would perform while dancing around a roaring fire.

I focus on Celine's flaming wings and groan again.

"I mean it, Luca. Cut that shit out," Celine growls, then switches languages. Her next words are firm but gentle. Coaxing. The chanting cuts off, she puts her wing fire out, and I force myself to stop groaning.

As Celine talks to the child, I keep an eye on the demon. Ciprian's black eyes are difficult to read in the darkness of the alley, but he appears unbothered by this chaos. Too unbothered.

"How did you say you found him again?" I ask.

"Tripped over him," Ciprian says, then laughs as he notices my face. "Oh my gods, you suspect me. That's amazing. What exactly do you suspect me of? Angel delivery?"

"Hush, demon," Celine demands, her brown eyes flickering between us with obvious annoyance. "Luca, make yourself useful and call Harry."

Ciprian backs against the wall and makes a childish show of zipping his lips. I give him a warning frown, then wince when I see what time it is. Harry will be asleep by now, but this can't wait. She answers after a few rings. Our conversation is quick.

When I hang up, I'm surprised to see Ciprian leaning against the wall in silence. He's watching Celine talk to the child with rapt attention, although I don't get the impression he has any more idea what she's saying than I do. Since I'm watching closely, I see when he perks up, cocking his head to the side.

"I know I'm supposed to shut up, but am I right in guessing that you want to keep this quiet?" He gestures around us, and I nod, confused about why he's asking. We're being as efficient as we can. It's not like Celine or I can turn back time or make the kid disappear.

"Got it," he says, before looking at Celine. "Please stop talking for a second, then."

She turns to glare at him, but Ciprian's eyes go unfocused, his cheekbones sharpening? It could be a trick of the shadows. I squint, then hear voices and freeze. Two regulars are walking down the alley toward us. I rack my mind for an excuse to make, but they walk by without even glancing our way. The door to the Fang opens and closes behind them.

Ciprian's eyes come back into focus, and he winks at me, then mimes throwing a key away.

It's all I can do not to groan again.

"Did he just . . . ?" Celine asks.

I bite my tongue and shrug, because honestly, I have no idea. "Harry is sending her niece over to pick the kid up. She'll be here in five minutes."

"Shavai," Celine says. "His name is Shavai."

The boy perks up, a half-smile spreading across his face as he stares adoringly up at Celine. *Get in line, kid.* I swallow my annoyance and my questions, fully aware that Ciprian is absorbing every second of this awkward situation like a sponge.

After Harry's niece picks Shavai up, the three of us walk back into the club. Ciprian doesn't say a word about what he saw. Instead, he orders a drink from me, tips 50 percent, then saunters over to the ATM. I watch him go, then look at Celine with my eyebrows raised.

"I know," she whispers. "It's getting strange, Luca. Nothing makes sense anymore, and I'm late for a date with the pole."

She rushes away before I can respond, and I risk another groan.

"Tough night?" Alistair asks, popping up in front of the bar out of nowhere.

"Not now, dude." I begin making his usual, ignoring how his curious gaze digs into the side of my face. "I mean it. No probing questions disguised as small talk or compliments that are thinly veiled attempts to dig up dirt. Unless you want me to add pureed tomato to your next Blood Tide, you'll let me work without adding one more thing to my plate." I inhale deeply and give him a look that tells him I mean business.

Alistair leans over the bar, crossing his arms. "I'm not sure if that impassioned speech was a cry for help or a death threat, but I enjoyed it regardless. Tell me, Luca, would you really serve me pureed tomato?"

I point at him with the index finger of my right hand while mixing his drink with my left. "See? That's the exact kind of question I'm talking about. Leading as fuck."

"Was it?" Alistair raises one eyebrow, and I notice it has a thin scar through the arch. "I fear I've forgotten how to make friendly conversation, then."

I chuckle drily, the sound frayed as Celine takes the stage and draws every eye her way. Despite his late arrival on a busy night, Ciprian somehow scored a seat directly in front of the pole. He's smiling up at her like she hung the moon and stars.

The music starts. He passes her money. She strikes a pose. He passes her money. She takes a fucking breath. He passes her more money. I narrow my eyes at him, my suspicion growing in direct proportion to the stack of cash on the stage.

"I suppose if I deny pumping you for information it would only make me more guilty in your eyes," Alistair says, sounding genuinely disappointed as he pulls my attention from Ciprian and Celine.

I sigh. "You haven't done anything wrong, Alistair. It's been a . . ." I wave my hands, at a loss about how to navigate the conversation away from all the landmines.

"Tough night," he repeats. I nod. Ciprian passes Celine more money, and my face twists. Alistair follows the direction of my glare. "I see the cheeky demon is back."

"Yup," I hiss. "And I—"

"Fucking hate that," Alistair finishes my thought. His annoyance feeds my jealousy.

"Yeah, part of me does hate it," I admit. Alistair watches me thoughtfully as I finish his drink and hand it to him. "Sans tomatoes. Sorry for the threat; it won't happen again."

"What threat?" he asks, his lips twitching as he backs away from the bar. I shake my head, then snort as he walks to the stage and bullies someone out of the seat next to the demon. Alistair pulls out his wallet, and soon his pile of cash rivals Ciprian's.

Their competition over her is obnoxious. Embarrassing even. But at least they aren't cheap about it. If their pockets are this deep, Celine can treat me to lunch tomorrow. We'll make fun of their attempts to get her attention, and maybe, just maybe, my basilisk will be pacified enough to avoid turning them both to stone.

# ELEVEN

## CELINE

Money piles up on the stage, and I can't decide if I want to throw my ass back harder or smack them both in the face. If Alistair and Ciprian keep this up, I'm going to need a broom to collect my haul.

The bridge of my song hits, and I climb to the top of the pole. Flipping upside down, I grip with my legs, then untie my top. It flutters to the ground, and the audience goes wild. My lips curl up into a smile, and I let myself slowly drop.

More cash hits the stage, most of it coming from the two idiots who are currently having some kind of dick-measuring contest. They might as well whip them out. I'll be happy to settle it for them.

I shouldn't encourage this kind of behavior, but who am I kidding? I love it.

With about a minute left in the song, I decide to wipe those smug grins off their faces. My regulars know I avoid up close and personal floor work. That doesn't mean I'm not good at it. I can bump and grind with the best of them, and tonight I want to.

My hands touch the stage, and I push off, doing a slow-motion handstand before dropping directly in front of the shit starters. I'm only a few inches away. Close enough to see Alistair's fangs digging into his bottom lip and the subtle differences between the black of Ciprian's pupils and the black of his irises.

Rolling onto my back, I use my wings to rake the cash to the sides, thrusting and rolling my hips and tits in time to the beat. An angel, spread out like a sacrifice for a vampire and demon's dark enjoyment. Even I think it's hot.

Gone are the cocky grins I spotted from the top of the pole. Alistair's eyes burn pure red, flitting wildly between my neck, tits, and lips. The frantic indecision over where he wants to look most is cute. Ciprian freezes. He doesn't blink or breathe as he watches me, his gaze caressing my skin as if he doesn't want to miss a second of what I'm doing.

I finish in a backbend, panting under the stage lights as the song fades into my longer transition track. *Good call.* It's going to take some time to collect all this cash. I rake it up as gracefully as I can, smiling when wisps of Brandy's green magic shoot out to help me, curling subtly out from behind the curtain leading off stage.

Stack in hand, I wink at the two troublemakers, collect my top, then walk off the stage. After tying the fabric back in place, I deal with the good-natured teasing from the other girls in the dressing room, tuck the cash in my locker, and head to the bar for my post-dance ritual.

Luca hands me a water bottle, the right corner of his mouth curling into a devilish smirk. "I told you," he says, his gaze dipping briefly to my chest. "The most perfect tits out there. Now, two guys are happily broke."

I laugh, my wings fluttering happily behind me. After the stress of finding the kid in the alley, I needed to let loose and regain some control. Dancing isn't for everyone, but I love the rush, and the outlet it gives me to release all the things life forces me to bottle up.

"I just did that," I say, a little surprised that I broke one of my guidelines on a whim.

Luca chuckles. "Yeah, you did. They're going to rub themselves raw for years thinking about that dance."

"Gross." I snort, glancing over at Ciprian and Alistair. They're still sitting side by side. Talking nonstop, they're completely ignoring Imani's performance. I frown, about to get pissed off, until I realize they've both continued to tip even though they aren't watching.

"This is strange, right?" I ask Luca, pointing to the unholy pairing. "What's your take on it?"

Luca shrugs, polishing a glass absentmindedly. "I think it's going to get messy, but it's nothing we can't handle." He smiles at me, like it's a foregone conclusion that we'll deal with it together, and my heart skips a beat. Wandering to the dressing room, I let him get back to work, wondering if he's right. Not about the mess, but if we can handle it.

---

Unnaturally sharp teeth graze my skin. Blood pumps hot and fast through my veins, and my heart pounds as arousal hums low in my belly.

I'm dancing on stage, lying on my back, writhing in front of Alistair and Ciprian, but there's no one else around this time. And they're making the most of it.

Ciprian kisses my ankle, his pouty lips tracing a tantalizing path up my leg. Alistair latches onto my neck, his touch wild, rough, and barely short of painful.

Instead of shoving them both off, I spread my legs, giving Ciprian room to crawl between them. He groans into my thigh, then nuzzles the soft skin there almost tenderly. It's not what I want, so I bury my fingers in his platinum hair. It's as soft as silk, and I could play with it for hours if I didn't have a different goal in mind. Determined, I yank on the strands, forcing his head where I want it.

Ciprian grins against the damp fabric of my panties. "Patience, Celine."

Alistair's fangs scrape against my neck, the pressure just short of breaking the skin, and I gasp. "Pay attention to me," he purrs before devouring my mouth.

His lips are distracting—exactly as he intended them to be—but Ciprian isn't going down without a fight; he's just going down on me. I grin as determined fingers slide my thong to the side, then a tongue grazes my clit.

"Delicious," Ciprian says. His lips and tongue form the words against my bare pussy, and it makes me shudder. "You can have this whenever you want. All you have to do is ask."

I'm getting it right now, so why would I need to ask? Alistair's lips make me forget, tormenting my neck until I'm practically bucking off the stage, desperate to get closer.

"Are you going to bite me or not?" I demand, like that's not a reckless, dangerous thing to ask. Alistair is notorious for using his bite to punish, not to please. Do I have that much trust in him?

His fangs pierce the thin skin above my right breast. There's a sharp sting, which is quickly replaced by an overwhelming number of sensations. It's as if my entire body is experiencing euphoria at the same time, every nerve ending singing with pleasure.

I scream, my muscles contracting then relaxing as the mother of all orgasms tears through me. My body arches, the mirror image of my dance for them at the club, except wait . . . Aren't we at the club? How did I end up in my bed?

Reality slowly penetrates the fog of my brain as the familiar surroundings of my apartment come into focus. I blink groggily as the sun peeks around my curtains. The aftershocks of my orgasm send another tingle through my body, and I stretch, relieved and disappointed to find myself alone in my room.

My body is relaxed. I toss the covers back, glancing at my chest to confirm that it was all a dirty dream and not an actual threesome with two guys I have no business letting into my bed.

I could be mad at my subconscious, but that sounds like a waste of time to me. If dreaming about Alistair and Ciprian can get me off, I'm getting the benefits without any risks. I'll subscribe to these dreams anytime; just show me where to sign.

Grinning, I glance at the clock and see it's a little after noon. I'm off today, and so is Luca. We have plans to go check on the orphans and make sure they're settling in. Harry has it under control, but I don't want them to feel abandoned by the only adult angel in the Fringes. I also want to ask a few more questions, maybe jog their nonexistent memories of traveling here.

I scratch my arm gently, trying to banish the itch. It doesn't work. Until I know why someone is dropping angels around my neighborhood, I'm going to be on edge. I covered my tracks, so there's no way—

A knock, if you can call it that, interrupts me mid-thought. Two lazy thumps, like the person doing the knocking is only half awake at best.

"Coffee." Luca's pitiful voice comes down the hall, husky and low. "Hurry."

"I'm naked—give me a second," I say, yanking my dresser drawer open and grabbing a neatly folded T-shirt from the stack.

"Don't care, let me in," he whines.

I roll my eyes and unlock the door, throwing it open with my head only halfway through the hole of the oversized shirt. Luca yanks it into place for me, then stumbles to the kitchen to fumble around with the coffee pot.

"I don't know why we couldn't go see the kids at a more reasonable time," he grumbles, shaking the bag of coffee beans, then shooting me a dirty glare. "You're almost out."

"I'll add it to the list." I study Luca as he grinds up the beans, then starts the machine. "You didn't have to come with me, you know. I only mentioned it last night because I thought you might want to." I open the fridge to grab the bottle of creamer. From the weight of it, I'll need to add that to my grocery list as well.

"Acting like a mistreated mother hen is an interesting choice when you're not wearing a scrap of underwear," Luca says.

I level him with my most serious scowl. "You can't tell if I'm wearing underwear or not."

"Trust me, I can." Luca inhales, his eyes flashing. "Must have been a good morning." With horror, I remember my dream orgasm and bite my lip. The way I see it, I have two options: be embarrassed or attack. It's an easy choice.

"Hey," I snap. "A girl is entitled to as many wet dreams as she wants."

Luca blinks at me. "I never said she wasn't."

"And you're in my apartment, where I can wear as much or as little as I please."

"Again," Luca sighs. "I don't care about nudity."

"It's rude to draw attention to a perfectly natural, healthy bodily function," I insist, crossing my arms over my chest.

"I didn't . . ." Luca groans, then rakes his hand over his face, muttering something under his breath. The coffee pot beeps, and he looks at it like a life preserver he swam six miles through shark-infested waters to reach. He pours himself a cup and takes a massive gulp of the scorching liquid before inhaling deeply.

I tap my foot impatiently.

"Celine," he begins. "Let me be clear about something. You can be as naked and as horny as you want to be, whenever and wherever you want. If you feel like rubbing one out in front of the MGM Grand, I'll distract the cops until you're done. But if you don't want me to know your pussy is dripping wet, maybe wear pants next time. Can you pass me the creamer, please?"

I try to hold on to my irritation, but I can't. From Luca's stubble-covered chin and his rumpled hair to the frustrated grimace on his handsome face, the whole situation is hilarious. A giggle escapes my mouth.

I hand him the creamer, and he dumps it into his mug with a shake of his head and another ragged breath. "Must have been one hell of a dream."

"Luca!" I bat him with my hand, and he grins.

"I can't tease you about it? What if I promise to let you make fun of me if I pop a boner?"

I blink at him as my brain provides a detailed rendering of what that might look like, then raise my eyebrows. "Please," I scoff. "You're trying to tell me that there's any context in which you would be okay with me laughing at your dick?"

He holds his hands up. "Woah, woah, woah—I said make fun of me, not it."

"What if it's funny, though?"

"It isn't."

"I mean, we can't be sure," I tease. "I might find it hilarious."

"Celine," Luca rasps. "If you ever see my dick, I promise you won't be laughing."

I want to give him shit, because that line is too cocky—literally. But the half-lidded heat in his eyes . . . Shit, there's something unbearably hot about the grumbly intensity he's throwing my way. And he's right. It's not funny at all.

I leave the kitchen to get dressed, breaking the tension

between us in the process while yelling at myself silently about how to behave.

Fifteen minutes later, I grab my keys from the table by the door. Luca doesn't try to argue. He pulls my spare helmet off the hook and follows me outside, settling his hands confidently on my hips as he climbs on my bike behind me. My skin hums beneath his fingers, even through my clothes.

During the drive to Harry's, I lecture myself repeatedly about my dirty thoughts. I'm acting like a teenage boy who just discovered how good his palm feels, not a grown angel who is perfectly capable of handling her body's needs on her own.

Luca is off-limits. I work with him, and more importantly than that, I like him. A lot. I can't screw that up for a quick fuck. His quiet intensity in my kitchen drifts back into my mind, and I'm forced to consider that while the two of us fucking might be a lot of things, quick probably isn't one of them.

I punch the throttle harder and shift my focus to the road, where it should be.

Parking near Harry's house, I tug my helmet off. Luca shifts behind me, and I look over my shoulder to see him leaning back as far as he can, his tanned face turned up toward the sun. His lips are curled into a contented smile, little lines crinkling the corners of his eyes in a way that makes me want to trace my fingers over them.

"Are you sure you're not a cat?" I ask, trying to return to our normal teasing so I'll feel less off balance.

Luca cracks one eye open, showing me a horizontally slit pupil. "Reptiles like to sun, too."

"Redheads don't," I say, climbing off my bike and removing my hips from the temptation of his hands while I'm at it. My body is way too comfortable pressed against his. Boundaries. That's what I need. Some plain and simple rules to follow.

Luca ambles along by my side, his face lifted to the sun. Now that he's had his coffee, his laid-back personality is in full effect. I usually aspire to his level of calmness. Right now, though, it's getting on my nerves.

"You're too chill," I complain, flinching as my joke comes out sounding waspish.

"Only enjoying the weather," Luca responds mildly, then sighs, tossing his arm over my shoulders. "It's going to be okay, Celine."

"How can you know that?" I stop a few feet short of Harry's front door and face him. "Two kids, both angels, pop up right by me. I want it to be random, but I'm not that stupid."

"I don't think it's random," Luca admits.

"Then why aren't you freaking out?"

"Because I've decided that whoever is doing this, and whatever their motives are, don't matter. They don't stand a chance against us."

My heart stutters painfully in my chest, and I shuffle uncomfortably as the itching gets worse. "Luca, I don't want you getting tangled up in this. If it involves someone from my past, it could be dangerous. You could be targeted."

"I don't care," he says simply, putting both hands on my shoulders until his warmth seeps into my skin. It's blazing hot outside, but I'm chilled by this conversation.

"You should care," I tell him, tension building behind my temples. "You're stepping directly into the crosshairs of an unknown mess. You should care about that very much."

Luca's relaxed expression fades. "I'm exactly where I want to be," he says, his voice immovable. "Watching your back."

I imagine shoving him with all my strength. I'm strong, but even in my head, he doesn't budge. It terrifies me.

"You're ridiculous," I hiss, my wings clocking my turmoil and demanding to be set free. I refuse them. "You'll get yourself killed, Luca. Heroes always do."

He sighs, then wraps his arms around me tightly, whispering in my ear. "I never said anything about being a hero. That's not my goal. But a friend? Someone you can count on? That's who I want to be, risk or not. If someone comes for you, they'll have to go through me, too."

I shudder, sinking into his hug even though his words make my fear ten times worse. I've been attacked before. Plenty of times. I always come up swinging, and I always recover physically, but if Luca stands in the way and gets hurt because of me? Fuck, that's my worst nightmare.

# TWELVE

## CIPRIAN

My new plan is going great.

Grinning, I wash my hair under the lukewarm stream of water trickling out of the showerhead. This apartment may not be growing on me, but the supernatural community here on the Fringes isn't half bad.

Alistair is the perfect example. Like half the people I've met at the Naked Fang, he's panting after Celine. Relatable, honestly, but he's far more interesting than the others. There's an undercurrent of ruthlessness behind his bored stare. He talks without saying anything, and it makes you want to open up. The rush I got knowing I might reveal something critical to him while we talked last night was the most fun I've had in ages.

At this point, I'm almost positive Roscoe is dead. I'll figure out who did it and kill them, but in the meantime there's plenty of other things going on for me to poke my nose into.

The mysterious appearance of the kid, for example. My instincts are screaming that Celine and Luca know more than they shared with me. I picture Luca's piercing stare and Celine's pursed lips. They will be difficult to crack, but fuck, do I want to try.

Even thinking about the two of them makes me hard. Groaning, I drop my hand to my growing erection, then stop. I should up the stakes. No coming until I've gained Celine's trust and can do it inside her—preferably after driving her over the edge until she's too hoarse to scream anymore.

I bite my lip, uncurling my fingers and bracing my hand on the side of the shower. My hard dick stares up at me angrily, and I laugh. It's used to getting its way. This self-imposed celibacy isn't going to be easy.

"It'll be worth it," I say out loud, soaping the rest of my body, then cursing as the water goes ice cold. "Motherfucking cheap-ass plumbing." Since I'm not a hardcore masochist, I finish my shower as quickly as possible and wrap the threadbare towel around my waist.

Hot water shouldn't be a luxury. The heat of my annoyance keeps me warm as I dry my hair with a hand towel I find stuffed in the back of the cabinet under the sink. The air conditioning unit kicks on, rattling angrily from its perch in the window. I salute it for its service and dress as quickly as possible, shoving my feet into my sneakers.

I sit on the couch to tie my shoelaces, and a roach scurries out from under the ancient piece of furniture.

"Fuck!" I squawk and stomp my untied sneaker at the intruder. It dodges, showing more athleticism than half the shifters on the enclave's payroll. "Surrender now," I tell the roach, grimacing as it wobbles across the floor, its segmented, turd-colored carapace reflecting the light from the single hanging bulb.

"It's on, bitch," I whisper.

Legs bent, I stalk my enemy into the crusty, attached kitchenette, lifting my foot slowly to avoid spooking it. Only when I'm looming over it like a made-for-TV kaiju do I drive my foot down —there's no way it will be able to avoid me this time. Sharp and slick as a switchblade, four slender wings shoot out. I gape in horror as the asshole takes flight, then begins executing aerial maneuvers with the skill of a fighter pilot.

"Gods! Shit, *fuck!*" I duck as it dive-bombs my face, then do what any apex predator with millions of years of evolution on his side would do in this situation: I get the fuck out.

Grabbing my keys, I push through my front door, lifting it an inch to get it latched. The sun slaps me in the face, and I soak it in for a second as my heart rate slows. This doesn't make me a coward. I've got bigger game to hunt, anyway.

This barely functioning, roach-infested apartment is a long way from where I grew up. Our wing of the compound—pretentiously named the Hall of Nightmares by Mom—is sterile enough to do surgery in. Gleaming marble surfaces offset by cold, rigid artwork that would be happy to make you bleed if you gave it half a chance.

My every need was met—as long as it didn't involve emotions. That I had to get next door. Callum and I got used to borrowing empathy from our shifter neighbors, like humans asking for a cup of sugar.

It wasn't a terrible way to grow up. My parents love us, despite what Callum has convinced himself of. They handled his manifestation badly; I'll give my brother that. But Cal got to leave and create his own life with his best friend. A life that's never had room for me. Not when I have to carry Dad's legacy on my fucking back.

I swallow my anger and shake my head. Much like a roach roommate, no one enjoys a bitter bitch, and Callum deserves to be happy. He's been starving his incubus for years, as if there's something shameful about a good, hard orgasm. Thankfully, his self-hatred is Sheena's problem now. I'm tired of worrying about him.

I slide my sunglasses on, squinting in the blinding sunlight even with their protection. Since it's early afternoon, I've got time to ask around about Roscoe again and see if I can uncover anything.

For the next few hours, I retrace my steps, finding the same dead ends. Frustrated with my lack of progress, I head to the grocery store. While I'm filling my shopping cart, I bump into one of the dancers from the Naked Fang. I can't remember her name, but witch magic clings to her like a thick perfume. The perky witch giggles when she spots me.

"I'm surprised you can afford that," she says, pointing to my cart. "Given how much money you dropped at the club last night."

I smile, shrugging bashfully, as if I'm embarrassed about dropping a grand on Celine's dance. I'm not. It was a fucking good dance. "I got carried away, I guess," I mumble.

"I'll say." The dancer giggles again.

With her tan face scrubbed free of makeup, she looks innocent in a way that's wildly at odds with some of the moves I saw her do at the club. Gods, women are amazing like that. I'd love to see Celine running errands on a random day off.

The witch tosses some produce into her basket, then glances back up at me. "When can we expect you back at the club? I'm sure I don't have to tell you; you were a big hit."

"Oh, you're too sweet." I grin. "I'll get back there soon." Lifting my head sharply, I raise my eyebrows to indicate I'm processing a new, exciting thought. "I'm actually trying to find a buddy of mine. He was supposed to meet me at the club a few weeks back, but he never showed."

"Is he as generous as you?" she asks, winking at me mischievously.

"You might know better than I do," I admit. "He loves to hang out there."

Curiosity sparks in her eyes. "What's his name? I know all the regulars."

"Roscoe. He's a big demon, looks like his mom dropped him on his head a time or two," I joke, chuckling when she laughs too.

"I remember him. You two share similar tastes. He's obsessed with Celine, or he was." She pauses, her smile fading. A wisp of fear trickles out of her, and her next smile is forced. "He hasn't been in for a few weeks. The last time I saw him, he threw a coin at her on stage."

"Dick move," I say reflexively, and mean it.

The dancer's smile smooths out around the edges, and her stream of fear cuts off. "I'm sure he thought it was funny, but the rest of us agree with you." She reaches to her left to grab a pack of assorted nuts from the display. "Anyway, it was good seeing you. Don't be a stranger."

I accept her dismissal, waving to her, and then finish my shopping.

Her story isn't exactly a smoking gun, except Luca didn't mention any of this to me when I asked him about Roscoe. *Did they kill Roscoe over a quarter?*

Luca's loyalty to Celine seems unshakable, so it's possible. Having seen them around each other, I'm starting to believe there's nothing in the world he wouldn't do for her. Lying to me would be second nature to him.

I respect that, but unfortunately it makes my job harder. Earning Celine's trust while pumping her for information will be all but impossible, and if she ever finds out who I really am . . . Shit, let's hope I'm as good at lying as Luca.

---

Even though I'm itching to go back to the club and follow up on the lead, I wait three days, plotting my public persona.

The witch from the grocery store did more than give me a tip; she also reminded me it's not normal for an average demon in the Fringes to drop a grand in one night.

Reminder one: appear less rich. I'm not going to rip holes in my shirts, but I do need to act aware of my spending in a way I haven't had to before. Tipping Celine a thousand dollars was a good time I shouldn't repeat. At least not for a while.

When I approach the club this time, I don't trip over a strange child. *Thank the gods.* I hope the little boy is okay, but that's as far as our interaction will go. One day, when he's famous for inventing a new, weird genre of music or something, he can thank me in his memoir.

Hot wind gusts through the alley, tousling my hair as I open the door and step inside. Combined with the wave of magic from the human-repelling ward, it's a creepy sensory experience. I shake it off, glancing around the club, and do my best to see it through new eyes.

The Naked Fang is dimly lit, with spotlights beaming down from the ceiling. A long, narrow catwalk-like stage runs nearly the entire length of the room, with a pole planted in the center. Chairs line the stage, and there are tables clustered at irregular intervals around the room. Three walls are flanked by booths, and the bar is tucked against the fourth. A hallway, easy to miss, leads to the bathroom and employee-only areas.

The Goldilocks of strip clubs, the Naked Fang is neither too grimy nor too glamorous.

*Where would Roscoe sit?* He strikes me as a table guy. I can picture him sprawled in one of the empty ones, a stupid smirk on his face as he throws a coin at the stage. Anger rises, but I let it go. I don't need to respect the bastard to find out what happened to him.

Making my way to the bar on autopilot, I fantasize about the living nightmare I'll trap Roscoe in if I find him alive. Part of me hopes he's somewhere holed up like the weasel he is. That way, I'll be able to pay him back for disrespecting Celine and wasting the enclave's time.

"Back again?" Luca's deep voice hits me, and I toss him a friendly smile.

He doesn't smile back. Instead, I get the distinct impression he's sizing me up. I grin wider, then peek deliberately over the bar at his crotch. If he wants to compare equipment, I'm ready when he is.

"I couldn't stay away," I say in my most obnoxious chipper voice, swallowing my laughter when he grinds his teeth.

"You zoned out when you walked in," Luca observes, adjusting a row of clean glasses as if my answer doesn't matter to him in the slightest. He's fishing. I love it.

"Troubled mind," I say, putting on the saddest face I can manage. "Lots of kids who grew up in a chaotic home environment space out from time to time. It's my burden to bear." That's true and something I likely have in common with the average fringe demon.

"Right." He shakes his head.

"Can I get my usual?" I ask.

Luca quirks one dark eyebrow, the metal of his lip ring glinting as the flashing lights swivel around the room before focusing back on the stage. "You have a usual?"

"Of course! Don't you know it?" I pretend to be shocked.

"Enlighten me."

I lean over the bar, unable to resist ruffling his feathers. "It's where I come in thirsty, and you . . ." I pause dramatically, letting my gaze rake over his body before stopping on his mouth. "Give me what I didn't know I needed and leave me wanting more."

Luca stares back at me, his gaze intense. The tension between us is so thick it could probably bear weight—like, support the second story of a house if it had to. I lick my lips, drawn in deeper than I intended to be. The movement shatters whatever temporary hold I had over Luca as quickly as glass hitting concrete. His hazel eyes dart away.

"Coming right up," Luca says. The words are friendly enough . . . standard bartender shit. Except the jerky way he moves behind the bar is miles from the casual confidence he usually wears as a second skin.

If I were someone else, I'd let him regroup. But I'm me, so I keep watching him closely instead, grinning when he knocks over a tray of sliced limes and curses.

"Am I making you uncomfortable?" I ask, adopting an innocent expression.

Luca looks up, scowling fiercely. "You know exactly what you're doing."

"And what is that?" I prop my chin on my hand.

"Flirting. With me. Outrageously." He licks his lips, mirroring my earlier move in a deliberately sarcastic way. It's sexy as hell, and my stomach flips.

"Luca, if you think this flirting is outrageous, your previous partners haven't been doing it right," I say, scrambling to regain my internal equilibrium to avoid slipping up.

"See?" Luca shakes his head. "That's exactly what I'm talking about!" He plops an orange drink on the bar in front of me with so much force that some of it sloshes over the rim and trickles down the side. I bend over, licking the spill up slowly.

"Delicious." I draw the word out, my voice husky, then pick

the drink up and sip from the straw with a deliberately loud gurgle. "What were you saying?"

"Unbelievable," he mutters.

I wink at him, and Luca throws his head back and laughs out loud. Despite my manufactured flirting, I'm struck by the sound. In all our interactions, I've never seen him let go, even for a moment. It's addicting, and I want more of it.

Luca is the kind of classically good-looking guy who ends up memorialized in art, no matter which century or realm he's born in. The fact that he's got this sexy grunge thing going on makes him more attractive. Perfection with a lived-in appeal.

No wonder Celine watches him when she thinks he isn't paying attention. If the two of them weren't so in denial, they would have ridden off into the sunset together way before I wandered into town. That's their mistake. I have no problem making a mess to get what I want.

# THIRTEEN

## CELINE

This fucking guy . . . He's hitting on Luca. I watch from the hallway, agitation making my wings flutter. They're heavier than usual tonight. "Damn that demon," I mutter.

"You could always piss on him or something." Imani leans against the wall next to me, her lips curving into that annoying smile she gets when she thinks she knows something.

"What?" I snap, irritated that I got caught spying.

"You heard me." She gently nudges my right wing lower to get a better view of the bar. "What I haven't figured out yet is which one you're more jealous of. You could always piss on them both to be safe."

"That's gross," I murmur, only half listening to her.

"I guess you could always lick them," she teases. "Or suck them . . . off."

Sputtering, I crane my head to gawk at her, then smack her in the face with my wing when she laughs out loud. "Dammit, Imani, I'll drown you."

She covers her mouth and gasps. "I should pretend that upset me. What kind of friend tosses her bestie's trauma in her face?"

"The kind who squares up to fight that trauma every day by her side," I deadpan, giving her a deliberately invasive once-over.

"Oh, stop it, I soaked this morning."

"Fully submerged?"

"Head and all," she groans. "It sucked."

"Good." I nod with satisfaction.

"Wow." Imani tsks. "Some best friend—saying my pain is good."

I roll my eyes. "This from the best friend deliberately misunderstanding me."

"Babe, I understand you perfectly, which is why I let you focus on me while you collected yourself." She tips her chin toward the bar where Luca and Ciprian are laughing, their heads almost as close together as ours. "You need to decide what you want. This thing with Luca is fun to tease you about, but I don't want it to blow up in your face."

I open my mouth to deny everything, then close it again. I can't bullshit her or myself. Not when I'm lurking in the hallway like a creep.

"You could come clean and tell him how you feel," Imani suggests.

I wince. "That sounds—"

"Smart."

"Dangerous."

Imani sighs. "Why would it be dangerous? You know who Luca is—your emotions are safe with him."

"Do I?" I wonder out loud, thinking about Luca with what I hope is pragmatism and not rose-colored glasses.

He killed for me, but that doesn't mean his loyalty is ever-lasting. He could get sick of me. Affection—love even—can warp into something insidious if everyone involved isn't on guard. I've seen it happen, and I'm not interested in repeating the cycle.

"Of course you do," Imani scoffs. "The real question mark for me is how you feel about the demon."

"I feel nothing for Ciprian," I say quickly. My eyebrows shoot to my hairline when my gut twists uncomfortably. *That was almost a lie.*

Imani rolls her bottom lip between her teeth, then shrugs. "That may be true, but I would be way more convinced if you weren't that quick with your answer. You can't deny there's a spark."

"He's hot," I acknowledge, seeing no reason to deny the obvious.

"You think a lot of people are hot," she says, laughing. "I've never seen you stalk them during your break before."

"Fuck you," I hiss, pushing off the wall and brushing past her as I prowl down the hall.

Laughing again, Imani follows me into the dressing room, where a handful of other dancers are either getting ready for their next sets or taking a break.

"What's funny?" Brandy asks, pausing to glance at us as she slides into a pair of uncomfortable-looking fishnet tights.

"Imani is delusional," I say, crossing my arms. "She thinks I'm in the market for a man." A chorus of boos are the response I get, and I shoot Imani a triumphant grin.

She rolls her eyes and settles in at her makeup station. "Because that's exactly what I said."

"What about the rich, blond one?" Brandy asks, yanking the fishnets up the rest of the way, then grinning. "He knows that Roscoe creep—the one with the coins—so that's a red flag, but you could put that smart mouth of his to good work." She winks at me.

"What?" I frown. "Ciprian asked you about that guy? When?"

"I bumped into him at the grocery store, of all places—gods bless it. We got to chatting. It was nice, but he didn't flirt with me once or try to look down my shirt, which was kind of refreshing. I think he's smitten with you, honestly, Celine. And those eyes of his are—"

"But he asked you about Roscoe?" I interrupt her chatter as delicately as I can. Brandy is a gem, and I'd do almost anything for her, but she can't tell a story efficiently to save her life.

"Yeah." She nods, a bright smile splitting her face. "I had barely finished picking out my avocados. You know they've been bad for weeks. Not a decent one to be found, but I managed to get four nearly perfect ones. Then I saw him."

I grit my teeth, alarm bells ringing in my head. "And he randomly asked you about Quarter Guy?"

"Now that you mention it, it was kind of odd. I didn't think much of it at the time. I told him how Roscoe threw that coin at you, and he thought that was a dick move. Which shows good sense on his part. Honestly, who wants to be friends with the kind of weirdo that throws change at strippers?"

"No one," I say, letting the subject drop before I can draw more attention to the situation. I don't think anyone in this room is a snitch, but I won't burden them with my secret either.

The skin between my shoulder blades itches ferociously. That's twice now that Ciprian has mentioned Roscoe. For a close friend, that might be expected, but for an acquaintance in the Fringes . . . it's a major red flag. The money he dropped on my dance, the obvious flirting with Luca at the bar tonight. *Is he on to us?*

I don't make it a habit of asking questions about the supernaturals around me. Most don't welcome that kind of interest. Maybe demons are more loyal to each other than I realize. Ciprian doesn't strike me as the same type as Roscoe, but they don't go around labeling themselves, so I can't be sure.

With my suspicions activated, my conversation in the hall with Imani seems silly. Ciprian is nothing to me but a threat wrapped up in pretty packaging. If he suspects we were involved in Roscoe's disappearance, I'll have to handle that.

*Dammit, Luca.* This is trouble we don't need. It was a knee-jerk reaction to turn the demon to stone, but he was watching out for me. Now it's my turn to return the favor, I need to figure out the best way to do it without tipping Ciprian off.

Is it too much to ask for one quiet night? By the time Imani and I take the stage to debut the duet we've been working on, I'm pissed.

"This is going to be fun," Imani whispers, her hand dipping to my hip as we spin around each other, never far apart, but never quite as close as our feral audience wants us to be. "Go easy on me, babe."

I nod and settle my energy before lifting her by the waist. Imani arches slowly—curling her legs until her body forms a near perfect circle in the air. The crowd claps, a few of the wolf-whistles loud enough to drown out our music. I soak up their collective surprise with satisfaction. My strength is deceptive, and there's no one in the Fang more flexible than Imani.

Waiting for the beat to drop, I tighten my grip on her hips in warning, then toss her up and to the side. She flutters like a ribbon in the wind, catching the pole with one hand as I leap up to join her, curling my body around the chilled metal.

This routine takes skill and concentration, so I wall off my frustration and focus on the music. Rotating and grinding on the pole, we push ourselves to put on the best show possible, skin brushing skin in a sensual dance that requires equal parts grace and athleticism.

When it comes time for our final move, I climb aggressively to the top of the pole, holding on with my thighs and dropping backward. With my wrists crossed, I grasp Imani's ankles, making sure my hold is firm, then squeeze her three times to let her know I'm ready. We've only tried this move twice in rehearsals, swearing to each other that we'll do an easier finish if either one of us isn't feeling it. If Imani isn't sure, she won't let go of the pole.

But she's as into it as I am, because she throws herself into a reverse dive, trusting me to keep her from falling eight feet face first. Raw adrenaline explodes in my veins like gasoline poured over an open flame. My thighs tighten, tremble, then lock around the pole, supporting both of our weight.

We spin as one, my wings flaring proudly under the lights. Imani stretches one arm toward the crowd and tucks the other gracefully over her head. The momentum of our spinning keeps her body outstretched, an arrow in flight as we rotate.

By the time we've spun from the top of the pole to the bottom, all I can hear are cheers. Imani plants both hands on the stage, doing a controlled back handspring as I release her ankles and follow suit.

The adrenaline rush that hits me is better than drugs. Better than sex. Imani and I brought them to their feet. These aren't the catcalls of the chronically horny—this is genuine admiration. Earned. Demanded. Delivered.

With my head held high, I collect the money with Imani, my face split in a fierce smile. Freedom is this moment, doing exactly what I want with my friend at my side. If I could bottle it, I would.

---

The euphoric triumph doesn't last.

Barely twelve hours later, I find another abandoned angel

steps from my apartment. This one is bleeding profusely; one small vestigial wing nearly severed from his back.

A shadow blots out the sun, and I hear the flapping of much larger, operational wings. Sprinting around the corner, my own sprout from my back, ready, eager, and willing to fly. I can catch this bastard, I know it. I'll drag them from the sky and show them exactly what happens when you mess around in the Fringes.

I crouch, muscles bunching as they prepare to launch me into the air—the motion both familiar and forgotten at the same time. A horn blares. My back spasms. If I fly, I'll be spotted and put far more lives at risk than my own.

The child whimpers. The sound pulls me away from the chase more quickly than anything else could have. I carry him inside my apartment, smothering every dangerous emotion inside me until the only thing left is my desire to help.

I call Harry. She calls for a healer. I pay without complaint.

Ladonis might lose the wing anyway.

In the aftermath, Luca drives him to Harry's home, and I wash the blood from the sidewalk, then scrub the red streaks from my kitchen counter until it glistens.

Bile rises in my throat as I remember the pitiful cries.

I cradled Ladonis to my chest while the witch examined the damage, reassuring him in the common tongue as best I could. After his wing was bandaged, I asked him who had attacked him. He didn't know. I asked how he ended up outside my apartment. He couldn't remember.

Now that they're gone, the silence in my apartment is absolute. My chest is so tight I can barely breathe.

It's time to face the facts: Harry is running out of room. She has been taking in stray supernatural kids the enclave can't be bothered to help for years, and while her heart may be big enough to love every abandoned child in the universe, her house isn't.

We need another solution.

I can't shake the suspicion that these kids are being used to taunt me. The question is how? No one from my home realm knows I'm here. In fact, most of them believe I'm dead, tragically floating in the everlasting beyond at my mother's side.

I drop to the couch and cover my face with my hands as I think.

All three of the young angels dropped here are from different classes. None share my echelon, but that's not surprising. If they did, I would recognize them. There aren't a lot of *nish thatsha* bloodlines to begin with, and father made sure I knew them all.

A plague. Angels with unexplained injuries and memory loss. None of it makes sense to me. What's happening in the celestial realm—and more importantly, how am I supposed to keep it from bleeding into Vegas?

Two thumps sound on my door. I lift my head, then shuffle over to let Luca in. I try to hide my devastation from him, but I don't have the energy.

Luca comes in, kicking my door shut behind him. "That was bad."

I sigh as he flips the deadbolt. "Something tells me basic locks won't stop whoever's doing this."

"You think it's deliberate?" He nudges me back to the couch.

I drop with a huff. "You were born here," I say. "Besides me, have you ever met another angel?"

Luca shakes his head.

"That's your answer," I mutter.

"We could always call the enclave," he suggests. "They suck, but they do have connections. The angel appearances could be happening all over. Maybe you're the coincidence and not the kids."

I consider that, a flicker of hope springing to life in my chest. It dies before it can fully form. "Then why are they always close to me?" I ask.

Luca shrugs, sinking into the couch by my side. He stretches his arm over the back, fingertips grazing my wing. I'm too numb to even consider arching into his touch.

"I don't have the answers, Celine, but you, me, and Harry can't figure this out on our own," he says. "I hate to say it, but we need to spread the word."

I frown. "Do people ever do that?" Gossip thrives in the Fringes, but it's all basic bullshit. People don't volunteer important information in our world. Especially not for free.

"No, but what choice do we have? Harry is out of room, and these kids aren't exactly fountains of information."

Luca's words ring in my ears as the uncomfortable truth that they are. With a groan, I lean back against the couch. He's right, and as much as I hate to admit it, my full-body itch won't let me sit this out.

"Fuck it," I tell him. "You've convinced me to bring in backup, but we can't plaster it on a billboard. We should only discuss it with someone who can help."

"Alistair already knows."

"Yeah," I grumble. "That was Harry's choice. What's your point?"

Luca rolls his head to the side, his lashes thick and dark around his hazel eyes. "He could involve himself more," he says. "And no one's information is better."

"Alistair doesn't do shit for free," I remind him. "Everyone knows that."

"He would do it . . . for you." Luca raises his eyebrows, making it impossible for me to misunderstand his meaning.

I glower at him. "Thanks for that. Until this moment, no one has ever confused me for a hooker. Congratulations, Luca, you've now gone where no man has gone before."

"Oh, shut up," he snaps. "I'm suggesting you ask him for a

favor not fuck him. Good to know that's where your head went, though."

I open my mouth to shut him down, then close it as an idea takes form. I roll it around in my head, the feathers in my wings perking up as I consider the pros and cons. The more I think about it, the more I believe it might be the solution to both our problems—the angels and Ciprian's nosy ass.

Luca sighs deeply, then closes his eyes and whispers, "You're about to make things more complicated, aren't you?" I stare at him silently until he opens his eyes. "Please, Celine. Tell me you're going to ask the guy for a simple favor."

I keep my mouth shut for two good reasons: one, lying to him outright would knock me on my ass; and two, Luca doesn't want the truth.

# FOURTEEN

## CELINE

I think all the gods in the universe are out to get me.

It's been seven work nights since I made my plan to recruit Alistair. Seven nights of perfect outfits and zero fanged appearances. It's almost like he's doing it on purpose.

My impatience takes on a life of its own.

Dressed in crimson red silk, tonight's one-piece hugs my body in ribbons of varying widths. The range makes it hard to achieve anything close to symmetry, but I'm managing it . . . carefully. And I look damn good. With lipstick a shade darker than my lingerie, I'm confident Alistair won't be able to deny me anything while I'm wearing this. If he shows up.

When he saunters through the door, his long, lean body moves with the sensual grace of liquid smoke. I smile to myself and beg my heart to do its thing at a slower, less embarrassing rate.

I'm the bait, the Fang is the cage, and now it's time to lock the door. Lips curled in a sensual smirk; I give all the regulars extra attention and ignore him entirely.

My skin tingles, and I sense him coming a second before he speaks.

"Have you been looking for me, angel?" *How did he know?*

I lift my head, mouth falling open in a pantomime of surprise. "Have you been away?" It's the easiest way to dodge a lie while preserving my dignity.

Alistair claps his hand over his heart as if I've wounded him, his blue eyes twinkling. "I must have been mistaken," he purrs, dipping his head in an old-world bow. "Since I've done nothing since the last time we met but think of you."

"You're a charmer." I bat my eyelashes at him.

He tilts his head to the side and studies me for a full minute before dropping into a seat and spreading his long legs wide. "Are you doing personal dances tonight?"

*Step one: done.* I nod, stepping up to him and dropping into his lap. Since Alistair is a big guy, I have plenty of room to work. I brush my face against his neck, shuddering as his stubble grazes my exposed skin, then sink into the dance and let the music lead me.

Alistair keeps his hands respectfully at his sides, and I notice for the first time how long and tapered his fingers are. He has clean, neatly trimmed nails—not a hint of blood to be seen. I wonder how often they end the night as spotless as they started it.

When I sense eyes on me, it's easy to spot the voyeurs. Ciprian sits in his now-customary spot at the bar, attached to Luca like a barnacle. I'm sure they're having a great time gossiping, but with the way they're both staring at me, I'm dancing for three.

"Why were you looking for me, Celine?" Alistair asks again, leaning back in the chair.

"Who says I was?" I deflect to avoid lying. Leaning forward, I slide my body up his chest to whisper in his ear. "I could use your help, though. Are you up for a deal tonight?"

Alistair grins, the tips of his fangs barely showing. "Always," he murmurs. "I love a negotiation that kicks off before the stakes are even laid."

"I bet you do," I tease, then drop some of my seductive act to update him on the new orphaned angels. Keeping my lips near his ear, I mention Luca's theory that the same thing might be happening in other fringe communities. I pause when Alistair catches my chin in his hand. He slowly lifts my head, his brow furrowed.

It's the first time he's touched me since the dance began.

"Angel, you don't need a deal to get my help with that. I'm more than happy to assist Harry and put your mind at ease." He sounds almost hurt, and I frown. Doesn't he realize I don't want to owe him?

"There's more." I hear my own breathy voice absently, then dart a glance at the bar. Since he's not an idiot, Alistair catches on immediately. His blue eyes take on a steely glint.

"Which one do you want to make jealous, then?"

Spinning, I arch my back and return my mouth to his ear, sharing my suspicions about Ciprian's shady motives while avoiding explaining why I want to control the narrative. Alistair listens carefully, his grin snapping back into place and growing until his wickedly sharp fangs are poised mere inches above my exposed neck.

"I'll do it," he says. "But we'll need a cover for why I'm around." His lips graze the shell of my ear, and I shiver. I'm prepared for this. What I'm not prepared for is the tightening of my nipples as my body gets the wrong idea about what's going on here. This dance is supposed to turn Alistair on—not me.

"Date me," I say, wincing at how demanding that sounds. "As the cover."

Alistair holds my gaze, a sliver of red rimming the edge of his irises. He's going to say no or laugh or dump me out of his lap. I can't believe I thought this was a good—

"When do we start?"

"Now." Blinking, I drop my weight fully onto his thighs. "Procrastination is for the dead."

Alistair stands languidly, and my body goes with him. Slowly, he sets me down, never freeing me from the intense eye contact.

Once my feet are planted, he steps back and adjusts the straps crisscrossing my throat. I glance down, prepared to fix whatever he messed up, then freeze as I take in the even lines. Before I can process that, he drops his hand, twines our fingers together loosely, then pulls me straight toward the bar.

Their eyes burn me, but I force myself to focus on Alistair. It's not hard, especially when his hand in mine is doing all kinds of ridiculous things to my nervous system.

Only when we reach the bar, do I look up at them. Luca's hazel eyes are wary but unsurprised. Ciprian's expression . . . Shit, I can't get a read on it at all. It's blank, his thoughts buried beneath so many layers of smoke and mirrors that I don't have a prayer of uncovering the real ones.

"You finally got that dance you've been after. Congrats," Luca says to Alistair, handing me a bottle of water with a question in his eyes. He wants to know what game I'm playing, but he'll have to wait. I can't spoil it yet, not when his reaction is what I'm counting on to sell this.

"I did indeed," Alistair says, smiling at me fondly. "I'm glad we don't have to hide anymore. My angel finally decided to make our relationship public, and I couldn't be happier."

Luca makes a strange choking sound. I don't dare check on him.

"Secret love . . . How exciting," Ciprian drawls.

I snuggle into Alistair's side, wrapping my arms around his

waist. "Sneaking around was hot," I say. "But I can't keep my hands to myself any longer."

Ciprian leans forward, bracing his elbows on the bar, and his deep black eyes settle on me with a focus meant to unnerve. I smile widely at him instead, knowing the next words out of his mouth with be another attempt to unsettle me. *Bring it on.*

"Tell me if I'm being too forward," he says. "But I've always been curious to know if a vampire's bite is as . . . pleasurable as rumor says."

I freeze—not because his question is out of line, which it certainly fucking is—but because I have absolutely no idea how to answer it. I've only been bitten in a dream. It was euphoric then and based entirely on the dirty rumors Ciprian is referring to and not reality. This is a test, and if I answer wrong . . .

"I don't kiss and tell," I murmur, patting Ciprian on the cheek as I walk away, towing Alistair behind me like a barge. I stop in the hall and pivot, inhaling sharply as I notice how close he is to me. "Okay, we might need to share some information to make this believable. That was too close."

Alistair bends until his nose grazes my neck. "Why talk about it when I could show you?"

# FIFTEEN

## ALISTAIR

Thank the gods. All of them. Every single deviant troublemaker who lords over the realms with their capricious favor and hedonistic meddling. I'll worship them all diligently for the rest of my miserable life if it means I get a taste of the angel.

Life on the Fringes is crowded with monsters, yet the real beast devouring us all is loneliness. It sunk its teeth into me long before I moved here and hasn't let up. Somehow, though, Celine appears immune to it. She has Luca, her friends at the club, and a fire that seems unquenchable.

I want that. I want her.

Watching her started as a way to pass the time, but quickly spiraled into something of an obsession for me. I make a living trading information, but I've never coveted anyone's secrets like I covet hers.

Celine wants to use me as cover, bait, and ally? Done. It gives me the opportunity to return the favor. Forget the wind beneath her wings, I'll be the rug beneath her feet if she gives me an opening. Then maybe I'll finally be able to make sense of this pull she has over me.

Her breath catches as I tease her about my bite, and my instincts hum. She's not against it. No, this ferocious creature, sent from the heavens to tempt me, is curious.

I don't mix business and pleasure. Ever. But I would make an exception for her.

"Would you like that?" I whisper calmly, thanking the gods for my vampire traits. On the inside, I'm trembling with excitement, completely primed to cock this entire thing up. But on the outside, I'm nature's biggest tease.

"Alistair, I'm at work," Celine protests.

I'm glad one of us remembered. Touching her is all I can think about. Rolling my bottom lip into my mouth, I imagine sinking my teeth into her neck and driving her mad with pleasure. My fangs throb.

Sex is sex. Biting is punishment. And blood . . . well, blood is food. By choice, I've never mixed the three, but Celine doesn't know that. I lick my fangs. I could do it now, in this hallway. But if someone walked by . . . Fiery rage consumes me, then turns to ice in my veins.

I can never lose control with her. I know that. That side of me is too dangerous, too cruel, too exacting to let anywhere near her. *Could she be as immune to my darkness as she is to the loneliness?* I hope to never find out.

Instead of sinking my fangs into the throbbing pulse at her neck, I pull her hand to my lips and kiss her knuckles. "I'm happy to answer any questions you have about my kind, angel, but in the interest of time, let's say you greatly enjoy my bite and all the benefits it provides."

Her pupils blow wide, devouring the rich brown of her irises as she processes my words. "How long has our illicit tryst been going on?" I ask, watching with delight as the color rises under her cheeks.

Regaining her confidence quickly, Celine pops one hip to the side and leans into me, dragging her index finger up my chest. "Let's say three months to be safe." Her finger reaches its destination—my mouth—and traces the edges of my lips. "And before you get any ideas, keep those fangs to yourself, Alistair. I'm fine with a reasonable level of touching to make this believable, but nothing over the top."

She pulls her hand back and examines her crimson nails. I'm tempted to ask her to clarify what she considers a reasonable level of touching, but I stop myself before I can make such a foolish mistake.

Over the pounding bass and whistling crowd, I hear footsteps coming our way. For the ruse and the fun of it, I spin Celine around and press her against the wall, entwining our fingers beside her head. "Trust me, angel?"

She freezes. I wait, as her heart beats once, twice, three times. "For now," she whispers.

I'll take it. Inhaling her delicious scent, I scatter kisses along her shoulder and neck. When she tilts her head to the side to give me more room, I smile against her skin.

A throat clears. "I hate to interrupt, but I need to get in there." Luca doesn't sound sorry at all. He sounds like he's chewing on gravel, and the only new information I get from his words is that the wall I pressed Celine against is actually a door.

I laugh. "My apologies, friend. I got carried away."

Celine blinks, glancing over my shoulder at Luca, then shoves me away roughly. I stumble to the other side of the hall, and my cock stiffens at how easily she moves me. *Gods . . . Let her be this rough with me all the time.*

"He's insatiable," she says, her voice husky, but missing the annoyance I suspect she was going for.

"I bet he is." Luca drops both hands to her hips to nudge her away from the door. The move is possessive and practiced. He's marking his territory. "If you don't mind," he mutters.

Celine narrows her eyes, her jaw clenching. "I don't love your tone," she says, following Luca into what appears to be a storage room. I trail after them and close the door behind us.

"Yeah? I don't love watching you get humped in the hallway while I'm trying to do my job." Luca shrugs. Celine's mouth drops open, then her wings begin to smoke ominously. "No. Nope. Absolutely not. Celine, I swear to the gods, if you set the fucking smoke alarm off again, I will lose my shit."

"You're an asshole," she snarls. "This was your idea!"

Already, I'm less bored. Grinning, I sit on one of the nearby crates to watch them square off. This is the most entertainment I've had in ages. Neither of them even glance at me.

"Umm, no the fuck it wasn't," Luca scoffs. "I suggested you ask him for a fucking favor, not let him gnaw on your fucking neck while you grind on his fucking thigh."

My, my, that's an excessive number of F-bombs. He must be quite upset.

The silence that follows is more than tense.

Celine's eyes shoot daggers at Luca as he digs around in a crate of liquor and refuses to look at her. The longer he ignores her, the more her wings glow. The snowy white feathers transform into a mesmerizing blend of reds, oranges, and yellows—burning embers brought to life. Standing, I pop the smoke alarm off the wall and remove the battery . . . just in case.

"You're not the boss of me, Luca," Celine says, her voice dropping to a poisonous, seething whisper. "You might be my manager here, but I decide who gnaws on my neck. I decide who gets to touch me. And I certainly decide who I fuck."

Luca rises from his crouching position, a bottle of whiskey clenched in one hand and a bottle of vodka in the other. When he spins and glares at her, her wings erupt into flames, perfectly matching her fiery red hair. Gods. She's magnificent.

"Celine—"

"And let me tell you something else, you judgy prick. If I want to fuck him"—She points at me angrily—"then I'll fuck him. And it's none of your damn business."

"Please do," I interject. "Whenever and however you want."

"Stay out of this," she snaps. I nod agreeably and shut my mouth, happy to watch the fireworks from the sidelines.

Luca closes his eyes and takes several deep breaths. "You're right," he finally says. "It is your business. Sorry I bothered you."

His tone is flat. Celine's wings droop in response, the flames burning out. I squint, intrigued, as particles of ice gather on the feathers instead. If Luca notices the change, he doesn't mention it. Instead, he steps carefully around Celine, keeping his hands to himself as he leaves the supply room.

That upsets her. I frown and point at the door. "Do you want me to drag him back? I'm happy to encourage him to issue a better apology. Perhaps on his knees . . ."

"No," Celine says, shaking her head as if she's trying to erase whatever's inside it. "Things with Luca are—"

"Complicated," I finish her sentence, smiling to assure her that nothing about what happened bothered me.

"Not really," she insists. "We're friends and coworkers. That's it. Disagreements happen. It doesn't mean anything." She winces visibly as she speaks, her eyes fluttering closed.

"I'm not arguing with you, angel," I say softly, deciding to back away before I scare her off. "I will inquire about the orphans right away. In the meantime, don't hesitate to call me if you need me for anything else."

I reattach the smoke detector, then kiss her knuckles before she can protest. Her eyes are far away. Whatever is going on in her head is bothering her a lot more than she's willing to admit. I don't want to leave her in this supply room with that crushed expression on her beautiful face, but I trust my instincts. Every one of them tells me if I push too fast, she'll retreat.

So I leave the Fang for the night, the moon winking at me as I walk the dark streets. While I enjoy the coolness of the night air on my face, it makes me long fiercely for the sun. I haven't felt its warmth since I was turned. It's hard to think about with any clarity.

Vampires aren't the same as the other supernaturals living as refugees on Earth. We can be turned or born, and while human lore loves to paint us as immortal, that's not actually true. I live, age, and die, just more slowly than your average homo sapiens. Unfortunately, that bit about the sun being our Achilles' heel is true. Cliché as it is, I miss it.

Pushing my melancholy away, I increase my pace while remaining hidden in the shadows. There will be plenty of time to be moody later. Right now, I have a promise to keep.

# SIXTEEN

## CELINE

I open my eyes and yawn, throwing back the covers reluctantly. Despite feeling as though there's glue on the insides of my eyelids, I wake naturally—no two-thump knock on the door for an alarm. I don't expect one, but I'm disappointed.

Luca can sulk if he wants. I won't trip over myself to fix things; not this time. Our argument made me sick to my stomach, and I spent the rest of my shift getting the silent treatment. At first, I felt bad about it, but I've realized this is a Luca issue.

He needs to figure out why seeing me with Alistair made him angry. We aren't dating. We've never dated—never even kissed.

Luca doesn't get to stomp around playing the part of a jealous ex or overprotective big brother. The only person being misled in this situation is Ciprian, and that's entirely by design. Alistair knows the score, and I do too. Luca needs to get on board. I won't dance around his mood swings any longer.

After a long shower, I settle on the couch, armed with a moisturizing face mask and every intention of spending my afternoon relaxing. I'll watch a half hour of TV, then reorganize my pantry. I already have a system in place, but the most critical part of any successful system is maintenance. If I'm still in the mood after I finish that, I'll deep clean the kitchen.

Now that I've thought about it, I'm itching to sort. Grabbing the remote, I hover over the show Luca and I have been watching, before grumbling and picking something else. If he doesn't pull his head out of his ass soon, I'll finish it without him.

I only make it fifteen minutes before washing the face mask off and diving into the pantry.

My shelves are organized and labeled, with all the canned foods and dry goods lined up alphabetically. Starting with almonds and applesauce, I check the expiration dates, tossing the few out-of-date products in a garbage bag. Another pile takes shape, made up of the items I doubt I can eat before they go bad. Those will go to Harry's since she has a pile of mouths to feed.

The faces of the little angels run through my mind as I work. Stress over this impossible situation replaces my chill, transforming my wings until they're as rigid and sharp as knives. *Calm down,* I tell myself. It doesn't help.

As I pivot to add a can of green beans to Harry's stack, my left wing rakes a bag of rice off the shelf, slicing it open. Grains scatter all over the floor, peppering my bare feet in the process.

"Motherfucker," I snarl, forcing myself to chill out when the feather-shaped blades begin to smoke. Setting all my food on fire is the last thing I need.

It takes three minutes and thirty-seven seconds of deep breathing to get my temper under control enough to sweep up the spilled rice. *Get ahold of yourself, Celine.*

My wings have always been frustrating. No matter how calm I act on the surface, they broadcast my real feelings. If I'm relaxed, they're soft, white, and fluffy. If I'm not . . . Well, stand back and watch out.

Because of my wings, I learned how to defend my emotions at a young age. Both the *nish misha* and *nish salum* wanted to study me. Father refused, screaming for days that no lowly academic or healer would get their hands on his daughter. It's one of the few decent things he's ever done for me.

If I'm the only one who isn't curious about why my wings are the way they are, it's because I already know. They are truth made physical and a defense mechanism rolled into one.

Almost all of my negative emotions manifest as weapons. They've kept me safe when I had nothing and no one else. Anger creates fire, and stress and anxiety generate the knives, which lash out even while they defend me—just ask the bag of rice.

Sadness sucks the most. Unless I want someone to slip and fall, the dripping is useless. Thankfully, my body knows better than to let me grieve unless I'm able to do it safely. It's the emotion I hate the most. It reminds me of too many bad memories.

Running a damp rag over the newly organized shelves, I recite all the magical characteristics I've seen angels exhibit: mold, echo, limit—all radiant powers that are confusing until you see them in action. It's common to develop gifts in my echelon, but I've never met anyone with wings like mine.

When the feathers finally stop switching between normal and stressed, I let out a relieved sigh and rock back on my heels.

I've got a bag full of things to take over to Harry's, and I've hopefully worked through the worst of my tension in the pantry. I don't have enough time left to deep clean the kitchen, but that means I have something to look forward to.

When I throw myself on the couch again, I'm able to relax.

After dinner, I load the groceries into my backpack and head out. It's early enough that Harry won't be asleep and late enough I won't have to deal with traffic, although my bike makes navigating the city easy, even on a bad day.

Since I texted her earlier, Harry is expecting me. I'm not surprised to see her head poke out the door the second I park.

"Anything but beets," she says, waving me inside. "I'll take anything but beets."

"Good to know." I chuckle, patting the backpack. "I don't think there are any beets here, but you'll find plenty of peas and corn. The version of me who buys the groceries is healthier than the one who eats them. Too many aspirations, too little willpower."

"Damn, I would love to get that on a T-shirt." Harry wraps me in a warm hug. It feels like a mom hug. I sink into her, letting out a deep sigh. Harry shakes her head and leans back to study my face. "Honey, if your day is that bad, you should throw it back."

"I'm not in the mood to dance today," I tease.

"Not your ass! Gods, have you never gone fishing?" Harry laughs when I shake my head. "If the day is bad, toss it back and try again."

I shrug. "How would I do that? Do harpies have a secret power I've never heard of?"

"Loads of them probably." She winks, her lips stretching into a wide grin. "But resetting the day isn't a magical power—it's a mental one."

I groan. "Count me out then. I'll push through."

"Suit yourself." Harry takes the backpack from me, grunting under the weight. I smirk and help her hoist it onto the counter. Together we unpack it while talking about the kids. As I predicted, Anika is already conversational in English. She's been translating for the newcomers to make their transition easier.

"They're out back," Harry says, tilting her head in the direction of her cramped urban patio. Seeing my raised eyebrows, she smiles. "It's not much, but a powerful witch I knew back in the day spelled it for me as a favor. They have more room to play and exercise than it seems."

I wrap my arm around her shoulders, squeezing gently. "You're amazing, Harry."

"I'm happy to do it," she sighs. "But we aren't swimming in other options around here. If you're not a demon, shifter, or fae, you've got to figure things out yourself. I've had the chance to be a lot of things in my life. These kids deserve the same—better even."

I nod, meeting Harry's eyes reluctantly. "I can't help thinking . . ." I sigh, then rip the bandage off. "That these kids are connected to me somehow. I'm the only angel around."

"So what?" Harry taps her nails against the kitchen counter, the ink-black, hardened tips a sign of her nature that's impossible to disguise.

I blink at her, confused. "I mean—"

"Did you kill their parents, leave them all alone in the world, then drop them here in the desert to be food for the vultures?"

"Of course not, but—"

"But nothing," Harry insists. "There's plenty of blame to go around without borrowing some that doesn't belong to you."

"I guess I hadn't thought of it like that," I admit, my forehead scrunching as I consider what she's saying. Can it be that simple? I didn't cause the problem myself, therefore I shouldn't feel bad about it?

"That doesn't mean you bury your head in the sand, Celine. You can do right by these kids—which you are—without drowning in misplaced guilt."

"When did you get this smart?" I ask, studying Harry as if I'll find her secrets written somewhere on her skin like mine are.

"Hmm." She laughs. "Somewhere between fleeing the

monster realm, shacking up with a wraith, and shaking my ass on stage at the Fang."

"We miss you there," I say, wiggling my eyebrows. "No one can match your moves."

Harry sighs, and a twinkle lights up her eyes. "I know that's right. Dancing is about more than having a good body you're willing to show off. It's about personality—the meaner the better."

I grin. "Mean, you say? That's it—I'm telling the other girls you said I'm the best."

"Better to let the tips do the talking." Harry winks at me, then dips her head toward the back door. "They'd love it if you said hi before you go."

I nod, then head to the patio. With my hand on the doorknob, I watch them through the window. Angels from three different echelons playing in a harpy's backyard. In the celestial realm, they may as well have lived on different planets. Now, after a few days on Earth, they're moving as a unit—the universe's cutest miniature support system.

Tears well up in my eyes, although I'm not sad. This emotion is far more complicated than that. Even my wings can't make sense of it. Harry pats my back and remains silent. Blinking back the unwanted feelings, I open the door, smiling as the kids spot me and rush over.

Ladonis's wing is bandaged and connected to his shoulders by an intricate splint. I'm relieved to notice that he doesn't seem to be in pain anymore. Hope and surprise strike me back-to-back when he grabs my hand in his smaller one and pulls me down to sit on the ground.

For half an hour, I chatter to them in the common tongue, hearing about the animals they've seen. Anika may be the youngest, but she's clearly their leader. My lips twitch as she corrects the boys' descriptions of a squirrel. None of their argu-ments get heated, and from the long-suffering expressions on their faces, they've already accepted her need to ensure that only correct information gets transmitted.

By the time I go inside to leave, my stress has completely melted away. I slide the empty backpack over my shoulders, zip my leather jacket, hug Harry goodbye, and climb on my bike feeling lighter than I have in days.

The kids are okay. They may be orphans, but they'll grow up better than I did, and that's the best I can do.

# SEVENTEEN

## LUCA

My hands shake as I try to unlock the club, the obvious sign of weakness infuriating me.

Never in my life have I been this at odds with the monster inside me. While I knew Celine was planning some kind of stunt with Alistair, nothing prepared my basilisk for the sight of the vampire wrapped around her.

*She isn't ours.* I repeat the thought four times, hoping it will penetrate the cloud of rage. It doesn't. The basilisk is furious, doubly so because I'm not making any effort to fix things.

Like a dozen snakes writhing behind my ribcage, the low rattle in my chest isn't something other people can hear, but it's unnerving to experience firsthand. Gnawing at my sanity, the rattle has ruined two nights of sleep, making it even harder to control my basilisk.

If I'm not careful, the next person to piss me off will pay with their life. I imagine turning a mostly innocent patron to stone for ordering a pisco sour, and the trembling in my hands gets worse. I drop the keys, and my vision shifts—cold and imprecise, colors fade as my basilisk eyes take over.

*No. Fuck. Losing her. Claim. Ours. CLAIM HER.*

"You don't control me," I hiss, gritting the words between my descending fangs before hauling back and punching the concrete wall. The sharp pain of my knuckles splitting sends enough of a shock through my body for my mind to regain a sliver of control.

I lose it again when someone grabs my shoulder.

Spinning, I seize my attacker and shove them against the wall.

"It's okay," Celine wheezes. "It's me." She braces her hands on my chest, and through the haze of my rage, I see her eyes squeezed shut. A horror beyond anything me or my basilisk have ever felt consumes me.

"Oh gods. Celine, I'm so—*fuck*," I sputter, releasing her to stagger backward. "I could have killed you." I cover my face with my hands, muffling my voice. With a heartbroken hiss, my basilisk retreats to a corner of my chest. Its shame is all-consuming, and I slump under the weight.

"Shh, I'm okay," Celine whispers. "I could tell something was wrong. I said your name a few times, but you were out of it. Don't worry, I closed my eyes before I touched you."

"That makes it worse," I moan, tugging violently on my hair. "Do you know how dangerous it is to remove your sight and trust me not to hurt you? I could have snapped your neck." I crowd her against the wall, illustrating my point by carefully wrapping my fingers around her throat.

Celine swallows against my palm. "Give me some credit," she scoffs. "I was trying to help, but I have no issue kicking your ass with my eyes closed."

I hear her. I do. But seeing my fingers wrapped around her neck is doing something to me. My stomach flips, and I tighten my grip experimentally, carefully avoiding putting any pressure on the front of her neck.

"Careful, Luca," she whispers. "Unless you want a firsthand demonstration of my fighting skills, you should think twice about what you do with those fingers next."

My breath catches, and I flinch—it's the opposite of a sexy noise. Why do I sound like I'm choking on a powdered donut? I clear my throat desperately . . . Celine can't talk about my fingers that way and expect my imagination not to supply a long and filthy list of things I could do with them.

She laughs, as if I'm not fighting a fucking war with myself in front of her. "Okay. Okay. I didn't think about how that would sound," she says. "It was supposed to be more threat, less innuendo."

"I took it as both." I attempt a joke, but my voice is too husky to be playful. Celine drops her head against the wall and crosses one ankle over the other, pretending she doesn't have a care in the world.

With her eyes closed, I can look at her as much as I want.

Flame-red hair secured in a sexy messy bun, she's not wearing any makeup yet. Her crop top and cutoff shorts hug her curves like they were made for her, but I don't love the idea of her riding with only her combat boots for protection. I glance around, noticing her bag and leather jacket lying on the ground a few feet away. Did she drop them to check on me?

She's everything, and I almost hurt her. I can't forget that.

Groaning, I dip my forehead to hers, prop my left forearm on the wall, and steal her air like any of that can fix what I did. The least I can give her is an explanation.

"I'm sorry," I rasp. "My basilisk and I were having a disagreement. It's making things hard for me, but I want—no, I need you to know I would rather die than hurt you."

Celine lifts her hand, then freezes, holding it next to my face as if she isn't sure whether she's allowed to touch me. I want to scream. *Please. Touch me.* I would do anything to have her skin against mine.

"Luca, I need to see you. Can I open my eyes?"

A shiver racks my body. I don't trust myself yet. I'm too on edge. To be safe, I close mine. "Yeah, go for it," I mutter. Losing our vision makes my basilisk nervous, but it's prepared to put up with it in exchange for having Celine close.

"You didn't hurt me," she insists. Her fingers graze my jaw, then travel up my cheek to bury in my hair. I shudder as her fingernails rake over my scalp. "I'm not scared of your basilisk, Luca. And I'm certainly not scared of you."

"I'm not myself right now," I argue, more terrified than ever that she's not taking this seriously.

"Have you been body-snatched?" Celine asks sarcastically. "Because you look like Luca." Her fingers tighten in my hair. "You feel like Luca." She buries her nose in my neck. "You smell like Luca."

"But my basilisk—"

"Is still you. You're still yourself when it's in the driver's seat," Celine declares. "You don't trust it. I do. But ask yourself this: Does it want to hurt me?"

My forehead furrows, and she smooths the wrinkle out. Meanwhile, my basilisk rattles in my chest, shoving angrily against my control. It's furious it can't tell Celine it would never hurt a hair on her head.

"No!" I hiss. "It doesn't want to hurt you, but accidents happen."

"I know," Celine assures me. "That's why I closed my eyes.

Seriously, though, how can you function if you don't trust half of yourself? I know I can't fully understand shifter dynamics, but would it kill you to compromise?"

I snort. "I don't think this bastard knows the meaning of that word."

"Which is hilarious, since again . . . it is you." Celine laughs, and I imagine closing the last inch between us and tasting the lips that consume my dreams. "Why is it pissed at you anyway?"

I want to answer, I really do, but how can I make her understand without telling her about all the nasty, possessive thoughts she stars in? If I tell Celine that my basilisk never agreed to the friend zone, and that it's only behaved this long because no one else was poaching in territory it considers ours . . . she'll break me in half.

"It's not modern," I mutter pathetically. "And it causes friction."

My basilisk grumbles, not caring that it makes us come across barbaric and flatly refusing to accept that Celine would never be interested in signing up for a possessive relationship.

She considers my pathetic response, then drops a smacking kiss to my cheek. "You don't have to answer; it's not my business."

"No," I grunt, panicking as she pulls back and I lose her touch. "That's not it. I just don't know how to answer." I wince, wishing desperately that I could see her face, and knowing I can't tell her the truth. She'll turn her back on me if I come clean, and I wouldn't survive that.

My basilisk can continue its obsession, but I have free will. I'm the one who chooses our actions. "I won't let it control me," I tell her. "That's important to me, Celine. More important than I can ever say."

She hums thoughtfully. "Then open your eyes."

Her statement is firm and straightforward—so dependably

decisive, so unmistakably Celine—that a smile curls up the edges of my lips. "That easily?" I ask.

"Yeah," she says. "At least, I think it is."

When she says it that way, I believe her despite my fears. Opening my eyes, I blink a few times to adjust to the blinding sun, then focus on her face. Celine's skin may seem like lifeless alabaster, but I've never seen anyone so vibrant. She is living, dancing, fighting, cursing perfection.

Her pink lips are grinning mischievously. "There he is."

My gaze dips, transfixed by her mouth, hungry to discover how it would move against mine. An inch—that's all it would take. *We can't.* Because if I taste her, that's it. I'll become as immovable as the people I turn to stone. Forever hers, even if she doesn't want me.

I step back, the movement as painful as forcing a thorn out of my skin. She's embedded in me. I allowed that, encouraged it even, and now I'm paying the price.

"You didn't give me a chance to explain the situation with Alistair," she says, holding eye contact while wiping her face free of expression. My stomach churns.

"There's no need," I mutter. "It's not my business."

"Dammit, Luca, that's what I'm trying to tell you," she snaps, her brown eyes sparking. "It is your business." My heart leaps into my throat. Is she claiming me?

"I didn't want to worry you before, but Ciprian keeps asking questions about Roscoe." Celine crosses her arms over her chest.

My heart sinks to my gut as I realize what she meant. Of course, she wasn't claiming me. Why do I do this to myself? "And how does Alistair make that better?" I ask.

"By providing an alibi," Celine explains, glancing around to make sure the alley is still abandoned. "He's more powerful and influential around here than some cocky demon. If Ciprian makes accusations, Alistair can add weight to our story."

Rocking back on my heels, I consider her scheme. It's fucking risky. Alistair is crafty, and I highly doubt he would agree to help us out of the goodness of his heart. "Are you going to tell him what actually happened?"

Celine purses her lips. "Not unless I have to. He wants me—you were right about that. I can use it as leverage."

"Playing with him is risky." I groan. "What if he decides he doesn't appreciate your game?"

Celine pulls her bottom lip between her teeth. "Then I'll end it."

"Do you want him?" I ask boldly—even though I have no right—terrified of her answer.

"I don't know," Celine says, then grimaces.

I hold my basilisk back, telling it we aren't about to hunt Alistair down and eliminate him. It pushes back, and a growl comes out of my mouth despite my best efforts to stay calm.

"Please try to remember that you like Alistair," Celine says.

I scoff. "Like is a strong word. If he steps one toe over the line; you let me know. One tomato is all it would take."

"I have no idea what that means." Celine scrunches up her nose and points to the door. "Can we go inside now? I'm only wearing face sunscreen. My shoulders are going to burn if we stand around out here shooting the shit for much longer."

I shake my head. "Literally, no part of this conversation could be classified as 'shooting the shit.'"

"Whatever, dude. Pick your keys up and open the door."

I groan. I hate it when she calls me stupid, bro nicknames. "I'm not your dude," I insist.

"No, you're the guy trapping me under a corrosive ball of gas that could turn my skin into boiling candle wax. You're my murderer," she says. "Is that better?"

I roll my eyes and grab my keys from the ground where they

fell, scooping up her bag and jacket while I'm at it. "You're being melodramatic."

"Until the day I die," she teases, dropping into a sarcastic bow. "Which will likely be today if you can't get the door open."

Snorting a laugh, I unlock the club door with no issues this time. My hands are solid as a rock, and I realize they haven't shaken once since Celine touched me.

# EIGHTEEN

## ALISTAIR

I arrive at the Naked Fang, nearly tripping over my feet in my eagerness to see Celine. The pull toward her is undeniable.

My eyes dart around the club, but Celine isn't in the main room, so I head for the bar, studying Luca as I go. I know the second he spots me, because his face loses all expression. *How far can I push him before he laces my drink with marinara sauce?*

Celine and Luca are a package deal. I know that, but they have to reach that conclusion on their own. Since they're both stubborn and I'm an expert in curating alliances, it falls on me to steer them in the right direction. If everything goes according to plan, Luca will thank me for my generous spirit . . . just probably not tonight.

"The usual?" he asks. The question sounds like the crack of a whip.

I nod. "If you have the time."

He grinds his teeth, and I swallow my amusement. "You're angry with me," I observe.

Luca rattles the shaker ferociously, then slams it on the bar, his blank face replaced by a glower. "I don't know why you would think that."

I hide another smile; his jealousy is entertaining. "It could be the vicious way you're preparing my drink," I say. "Or maybe it's that I've rarely seen your handsome face marred by such a horrific scowl."

The scowl deepens, yellow flickering in his eyes—a clear warning. I glance down; half convinced the basilisk powers he doesn't know I know about will turn me to stone before I get that "thanks."

"I can't control my face," he snaps.

"That's scary," I tease. "Should I fear for my life?"

"I won't hurt you." Luca pours my drink into the glass. "Not here at least," he clarifies.

I sigh, take the Blood Tide from him cautiously, then meet his eyes while considering how to calm him. Being frank with anyone makes my skin crawl, but we won't get anywhere if his basilisk is running the show.

"Luca, I'm not trying to take her from you," I begin.

"You couldn't if you tried," he snarls, then rakes a hand over his face. "Fucking *fuck*. What I meant to say is that she's not mine. She's also not a piece of rope to be tugged back and forth between us."

I nod, fully in agreement with the spirit of that statement, except I wouldn't mind passing Celine back and forth before working together to drive her wild. "I've never understood that ridiculous human game. Fighting over a piece of rope is a waste of energy for everyone involved." *Please, Luca, read between the lines.*

His eyes flicker, and I sip my drink calmly.

I sense Celine coming before I see her. She comes to a stop next to me at the bar, and I wrap my arm around her waist and inhale deeply. Her scent is lovely.

"I've missed you, angel," I say, kissing her temple. I sense her surprise, but she doesn't show it. Celine has been part of the fringe community long enough to perfect her poker face. "I have some information for you."

The second part is only for her ears. She smiles widely up at me. "I've missed you, too."

Ciprian wedges himself in on my other side. "If it isn't the happy couple," he says.

"I'll tell you later," I whisper in Celine's ear, grinning when she shoots Ciprian an annoyed look.

"As I was saying, *Alistair,* I'm dying for some alone time." She's making a dig at Ciprian, but it sounds like a promise to me, anyway. Goosebumps creep up my arms.

"Can I get a drink, Luca?" Ciprian asks confidently, ignoring Celine and me, even though he should feel put in his place. I'm not sure anything makes him uncomfortable.

Luca smirks, then shakes his head—as if he isn't sure why he finds it funny. "Coming right up."

"He didn't order anything," Celine says.

Ciprian shrugs. "Luca never leaves me thirsty."

Red splotches pop up on Luca's olive-toned cheeks, and I raise my eyebrows when he focuses entirely on the drink he's making and doesn't threaten to throttle the troublemaker.

I'm a simple drinker. I prefer to order the same thing every time rather than branching out and ending up with an unpleasant surprise. Whatever Luca is making is the opposite of simple. By the time I watch him add gin, honey, and a sprig of something green to the shaker, I'm lost. From the way Celine stiffens at my side, she notices too.

Luca coats the rim of a martini glass in sugar, and Ciprian nudges my shoulder. "He knows all about my sweet tooth," he says.

At that, Luca rolls his eyes, but there's no real annoyance behind the gesture. "For my most high-maintenance customer," he mutters.

Ciprian puts one hand on his heart and grins. "Thank you," he says. "For the drink and the compliment."

I can't help myself—I chuckle. He's quick-witted, I'll give him that. Like the night we showered Celine in tips together, I find myself surprised to enjoy Ciprian's company.

His humor is sharp and practiced. I suspect that he cultivated his ability to laugh in situations that would have made most people cry. It's an assumption, but I've built a profitable business around my ability to read people.

"I think someone offed Roscoe," Ciprian says conversationally, sipping his drink and glancing between the three of us. Celine freezes against my side, and I raise one eyebrow. There's much more to Ciprian than meets the eye.

"I don't know who that is, but what makes you think someone killed him?" I ask.

Ciprian shrugs. "Can't find him, and his voicemail is full."

"That's not much to go on," I point out.

"Could be drugs," Celine suggests. "I didn't talk to him much, but he struck me as kind of off. Why do you care, anyway?"

Ciprian considers that, nursing his drink like we aren't talking about a possible murder. "He's a dick, but he's useful for business."

"And what is that business?" Luca demands. The question itself, combined with his tone, shocks me. It's way too direct. Not at all how things are handled on the Fringes. Celine's wings twitch, grazing my back.

"My boss wouldn't want me to share that," Ciprian says, his black eyes sharp as he studies Luca over the bar. "But if you stumble over a dead demon, let me know."

Celine hums, the sound noncommittal. Tilting my head to the side, I face Ciprian and smile. "Of course. While we aren't known for our transparency here on the Fringes, murder would be the exception."

Luca grunts, and my senses tingle.

His stubborn antagonism. Her tense avoidance. There's more to this than Celine told me when we struck our deal. Normally, this would infuriate me . . . but for some reason, the only thing I can think about is fixing this for both of them.

Gently, I tow Celine away from the bar, concerned her wings will give her away if I let this interrogation continue. "I'm on my break," she whispers.

Nodding, I go to the storage room, pulling her inside and closing the door behind us. "You approached me for an alibi." I face Celine, and she shuffles under my scrutiny.

"Alistair, I can explain . . ."

"You mistake me, angel. If you killed him—"

"It wasn't like that, I swear," she sputters, taking a step toward me. I watch with fascination as the feathers of her wings take on the most fascinating shape, hundreds of blades shooting out from her back. "Roscoe followed me after work and wouldn't take no for an answer. He pulled a knife on me. There was no other option."

"Celine, let me speak, please," I say firmly.

She backs away from me, glancing at the door. I frown. One step turns into eight. Her spine hits the wall, and her wings make a sound like wind chimes clinking in the wind. I freeze. My reputation demands fear from everyone else, but I don't want it from her. It's fundamentally wrong.

I clear my throat. "I don't care who you killed or why. I pulled you in here to discuss how we fix it, not to berate you." I approach her slowly. "Our relationship may be fake, but for now I'm your boyfriend, and that means I have your back. Do I need to dispose of a body, angel?"

The silence is loud. The sounds from the noisy club filter through the closed door, but we're alone in here. Celine stares at me blankly. Then something changes. She pushes off the wall, and we collide, her lips fusing to mine.

I've imagined this moment a million times, and my body takes over, locking us into the hottest kiss of my life. Celine buries her hands in my hair, pulling my head where she wants it. I groan into her mouth, our tongues tangling. Her lips are impossibly soft, but her touch is rough. Just as I hoped.

"Dammit, Alistair," she groans.

I trail kisses up and down her neck, feeling immense satisfaction as her pulse races beneath my lips. "Don't worry, angel. Let me please you."

Celine pulls back, her face serious. "I don't want to lead you on."

"You could lead me to the monster realm with a bell around my neck and a slab of raw meat tied to my back and I would still follow wherever you lead," I say blandly, kissing her perfect lips again.

"See, that's what I'm talking about: I don't want to hurt you." She sighs, then yanks my head back to hers. Grunting, I lift her off the ground to erase our height difference, shivering at how tightly she wraps her legs around my waist.

"You've warned me," I say, surging into the wall with my vampire speed. "Now fucking hurt me, angel. I'm at your disposal."

"That sounds toxic." She bites my bottom lip, and her right

nipple slips free from her lingerie. We both glance at it. "Play with me, Alistair," she demands.

Her order goes straight to my cock. I drop my head to tongue her nipple, licking softly, then rolling the tip between my teeth, determined to get an idea of what she prefers. Celine arches into me, her sweet gasp of pleasure music to my ears.

"Might I suggest a new deal, angel?" I graze my fangs carefully over the swell of her breast, soaking up the hungry little grunt she makes in response. "Friends with benefits."

"We aren't friends," she argues, yanking my mouth back to her nipple. "Don't be gentle, I won't break." Taking her for her word, I nibble the tip, then pinch the other one with no warning. Celine squeals and bites the side of my neck.

"I think we are friends, angel," I say, grinding my cock into her pussy until I find an angle that makes her breath catch. "Gods, your tits are bloody amazing."

She chuckles. The sound morphs into a moan as I increase my rocking motion, using the wall as leverage. "I don't want more friends, Alistair. I want regular, leg-shaking orgasms. What I want is a reliable dildo."

I pause, processing that, then roll my hips. Even if her terms aren't the most favorable I've ever negotiated, I'm too invested to walk away from this deal. "One reliable dildo coming right up," I whisper. "I'll even clean myself off after so you don't have to make the difficult choice between tossing me in the dishwasher or lathering me up by hand."

Celine growls and yanks my head back to lock eyes with me. "Stop being nice. I'm taking advantage of you, and you're letting it happen."

"I know." I grin at her. "You're doing a magnificent job."

She kisses me again, and I devour her—long, slow, thorough kisses, the kind that require coordinated timing and careful execution. I kiss her the way I've fantasized about since the first time I saw her put a rowdy patron in his place, my free hand playing with her nipple.

"I-I-I need," she moans.

"I know," I grunt, dropping my right hand between us and locking my gaze on hers. Her eyes are half-lidded, the warm brown consumed by her blown pupils. She leans forward and tries to kiss me again, but I shake my head. "Stay like this, please. All I want is your eyes on mine."

Because we're staring at each other, I get to experience the delicious rush of her reaction when I slip two fingers inside her and roll her clit firmly under my thumb. I want to play with her body for hours, but her break won't last forever.

Celine clenches around me, her eyes glazed with pleasure. "Harder," she says.

I give her exactly what she wants. Adding a third finger, I curl them until a string of unintelligible sounds leave her mouth.

When she gasps my name desperately, I lose it, adding a hint of vampire speed to my movements. Celine breaks beautifully, her eyes rolling back as her mouth falls open in a silent scream. She goes limp in my arms, panting wildly. I've never been this close to coming in my pants.

I carry her to a liquor crate and fix her outfit. There's a smudge of eyeliner under her right eye. I wipe it away, making sure both sides are even. Celine's upper thighs are damp. I unbutton my shirt, then use it to clean her up, knowing she won't want to dance with even a hair out of place. When I check her face again, I find her watching me with an intense expression.

"What about you?" she asks, dipping her chin to my obvious erection.

With a grin, I put my shirt back on, wearing the damp spot on the front with pride. "The best thing about a dildo is that it will never demand you return the favor," I say.

Celine laughs and hops off the crate. She surprises me when

she rocks up on her toes to kiss my cheek, then walks to the door without a word, only turning to look at me when her hand is on the knob.

"Find me at the fight tomorrow," she says. "We'll have some fun, then talk after."

She slips out, and the smell of her on my shirt holds my attention for the rest of the night.

# NINETEEN

## CELINE

Street parked outside my apartment, I wait for Luca and let my mind drift to the tall, dark, and handsome complication I've added to my life. Alistair is good with his hands, I'll give him that, but can I really treat him like a dildo?

My long-dormant libido cracked one eye open last night and loved what it saw. Dildo or not, leaving Alistair in the dusty storage room without returning the favor didn't sit right with me. By the time I got home, I had discovered an uncomfortable truth: I wanted him inside me, rocking my world.

His little speech about fixing the Roscoe problem knocked over every one of my defenses. So much so that I feel bad for letting him think I killed the demon. I can't expose Luca, though. Bringing Alistair in to help is my risk and mine alone.

Plus, if I'm trusting him with a murder confession, letting him get me off a few times is the least of it. From the way he kissed me to the way he fixed my clothes after; Alistair's sincerity was blazing hot. I wish I hadn't enjoyed it so much. Either way, it won't stop me from ending our agreement when the time comes.

"Whatever you're thinking about must be a doozy," Luca says, whistling softly through his teeth.

I glance at my phone. "You're late."

He frowns. "No, I'm not. I'm exactly on time."

"Which might as well be late."

Luca rolls his eyes. "It's good not to get your way all the time; keeps you grounded in reality."

"I have wings," I remind him. "The time I spend on the ground is my choice." And to avoid scaring the humans, but that doesn't fit into my argument.

"I'm . . . You know what? Fuck it," he grunts. "I'm too tired to argue with you."

Craning my neck, I study the dark circles under his eyes. They're angry-basilisk bad. "It won't let you sleep?" I ask, relieved he didn't bail on watching the fight tonight. I'm not scared to be alone with Alistair, but his intensity can be overwhelming.

Luca sighs, then climbs onto the bike behind me and drops his chin to my shoulder. "Basilisks are stubborn bastards."

"Sounds like someone I know." I hand him my spare helmet, waiting until he puts it on to say, "Alistair knows, by the way."

Luca grips my hips in shock. I crank the bike, rev the engine, and take off before he can respond. I meant to continue the teasing tone of our conversation, but I've misjudged things—because the longer we drive, the more his body trembles. By the time I find parking near the Mouth of Hell, I'm cursing myself for dropping it on him without an explanation.

Once I plant the kickstand, I rip my helmet off and cut the engine. "Everything is fine," I assure him. "I didn't tell him you were involved."

Luca swings off the bike and tosses me his helmet. "That

doesn't make it better, Celine. Actually, that's worse." He takes off toward the crowded entrance, leaving me to stuff the helmets into the top case and scurry after him.

"Hey!" I curse when my raised voice draws some curious looks. "Godsdammit, Luca. Slow down."

I plow into his back when he stops abruptly. Spinning to face me, he grabs my shoulders. "What were you thinking?" Luca demands.

"Chill out," I whisper angrily, shoving his hands off. "I didn't volunteer the information. Alistair figured it out after Ciprian's little interrogation."

"Fuck." Luca groans.

"Exactly, and panicking won't make it better," I say, sagging as I realize how unfair I'm being. Luca is struggling, and I made things worse. "I'm sorry I dropped it on you. That was a shitty thing to do."

Luca closes his eyes, takes a few deep breaths, then grabs my hand and pulls me toward the warehouse. "I'll get over it," he mutters, walking through the open door. "But I won't sit on that splintery tower of garbage."

I huff, then hide my smile. The stacks aren't my favorite place to perch during a fight anymore, but telling him how much I enjoyed the view from Alistair's shoulders is a terrible idea.

"Was he good to you last night?" Luca's question shocks me, and I snap my head up. There's a dark shadow in his hazel eyes, but we were discreet—there's no way he knows what happened in the storage room.

"I don't know what you mean," I lie automatically, then wince from the sharp sting that shoots up my spine.

Luca narrows his eyes. "What the fuck was that?"

"I can't lie," I groan, knowing it's way past time to come clean about this.

"What?" His jaw drops.

"I mean, I can, but it hurts like hell," I explain, then glance around to make sure no one is listening in. As usual, the Mouth of Hell is packed. Everyone is way more interested in getting a good spot than eavesdropping on us, though.

Luca shoves a drunk guy away from him then looks at me, his eyes wide. "The runes," he says. "While you were talking to Anika and Imani . . . They showed up when you were making promises."

"Built in proof of sincerity," I confirm his theory, then shrug, not surprised he made that connection quickly. "I'd rather not talk more about it here."

"Of course," he says. "I shouldn't have asked you something that personal, anyway."

I roll my shoulders, trying to make the uncomfortable tingle go away. It's been a while since I tried to lie, and my magic wasn't a fan.

"Can you scratch my back?" I ask him. "The itching is awful."

Luca steps around me, his fingers searching out the spot where my wings usually are. He scratches my back with the perfect amount of pressure, and his warmth seeps through my tank top, luring me into an almost-relaxed state.

All around us, people are drinking, talking, and jostling past, but it feels as if we're the only ones here. "I hate that you lied to me, Celine," Luca whispers, his voice low.

"I didn't like it either," I mutter, sagging into his touch. "Maybe you shouldn't ask questions you don't want the answer to."

I turn to face him, and he winces. "That good, huh? Wait, don't answer that. Gods, I'm doing my own damage now."

I laugh, playfully shoving his chest. "You like Alistair," I remind him. "Which is good, because I forgot to mention it when I invited you, but he's meeting us here."

"You invited me on your date?" Instead of being mad, Luca's lips curl into a devious smirk.

"It's not a date," I correct him. "But I figured you wouldn't want me discussing the . . . incident without backup." He nods, and I hold my finger up to keep him from interrupting. "Luca, this doesn't mean I'm going to do what you say. I'm not interested in being bossed around. I can promise to communicate with you better, though—no more surprises."

"That's a pity. Surprises can be hot, angel." Alistair materializes by my side so smoothly that I'm reluctantly impressed. "You brought a friend." He smiles at Luca, and the expression is strangely genuine. I don't know how to take that—I expected him to be annoyed.

"Alistair," Luca says, clearing his throat.

"Can we skip the death threats and go straight to the part where I swear on the sun I won't betray her?"

Luca glares, obviously annoyed by Alistair's interruption. "That's cool, but I'm not a fucking astrologer. Is this you trying to tell me your sign or some shit?"

"I haven't seen the sun in almost two decades, Luca," Alistair says quietly. "I dream of it every night and long for it every day. I'm swearing on the sun to show you how serious I am."

The skin on my arms pebbles from Alistair's quiet intensity. I elbow Luca hard to get him to play nice, then elbow him again to show I mean business. He groans and covers his side protectively. "Shit, Celine, how was I supposed to know it was an emotional thing? He sounded like a crystal mommy."

"He's very sorry," I say to Alistair, who barely manages to hide his grin.

"I'm sure his ribs are, at least." Alistair offers me his arm, then glances at Luca. "I'm a Scorpio, by the way."

I chuckle, linking one arm with his and preparing to cut a path through the crowd with the other. I don't get the chance, because Luca slides into that space, effectively sandwiching me between them. No one gives us any trouble, and by the time we're in the pit, I feel cheated out of my full fight night experience.

"I'll let you sock someone on the way out," Luca promises as he sees my scowl. He bends to my level and narrows his eyes at the floor of the ring. "They changed the cage. How the fuck will you see?"

"We can lift her once the fight starts," Alistair says, casually including Luca in the plan, then winking at me.

Luca shrugs. "Okay, I'll get us some drinks if you two hold my spot." I smirk, and he scoffs. "Don't hurt anyone, killer."

He gets swallowed up by the mass of bodies, and I turn to Alistair.

"What are you up to?" I demand.

He blinks at me, his baby-blue eyes wide and innocent. "I'm sorry, angel. I thought you might want to add to your collection."

"I don't collect things. I hate clutter. What are you even—" I choke, my words catching in my throat as one possible meaning flickers through my mind. Surely . . . he can't mean that.

Alistair winks. "Every woman needs more than one dildo, angel."

I plant my palms on his chest with every intention of sending him barreling into the sea of bodies, but Alistair catches my hands and laughs at my expression.

The crowd roars as the fighters enter the cage, and it saves me from coming up with a response. I can't stop thinking about it, though. By the time Luca gets back and the bell rings, the idea has wormed its way into my brain.

The flying fists help me forget for a while how messy the consequences of my actions are becoming. Alistair and Luca take turns as my chair, passing me between them like a rag doll every couple of rounds. They never once put me down. I enjoy it too much.

Rattling the cage, I jeer and taunt the shifter, cheering

loudly for the smaller witch. He's a new fighter, raw and untested, but he's got style. With some training, he could be a formidable opponent. If that happens, I'll pick a new underdog to root for.

The fight ends, and I climb to the floor before either of them can manhandle me. "That was a good fight," I say. "The kid witch will get him next time. Did you see how he was adapting to the moves?"

"Yeah, he was fast." Luca grins.

"Are you ready to leave, angel?" Alistair scans the rowdy crowd, his eyes flickering pink as a burly guy jostles him. That's when I realize everyone is a lot drunker now than when we first got here.

I nod, bending over to grab our empty bottles off the ground. Someone slaps my ass. Pissed, I spin to teach them some manners, but Alistair and Luca already have the guy pinned to the support beam under the cage. His feet dangle, the toes of his sneakers scrambling for purchase on the stained concrete. His face turns an interesting shade of purple.

"Any last words?" Alistair snarls. Luca's arms are visibly trembling. As much as I would love to beat this guy's ass, there are way too many bloodthirsty eyes on us. I need to deescalate this.

I slide my hands slowly onto their shoulders, careful not to startle them. "I'm fine, guys," I assure them. "Seriously. Let him go; he's learned his lesson."

Luca hisses, and the sound is more reptile than man. *Shit. Shit. Shit.* Going on instinct, I trail my fingers up his neck until I can thread them through his thick, silky hair, and massage his scalp. "I'm fine," I tell him again. "I promise you. Don't let some idiot ruin our night."

Luca closes his eyes, grits his teeth, then wrenches his hand away from the guy's throat. "I need to get out of here," he says, his voice barely recognizable around his fangs.

"Go," Alistair says. "I'll take care of him after our angel gets that hit in that you promised her."

Luca carves a violent path through the crowd, and half of my attention goes with him. Wanting to get this over and done with, I study the pathetic creep and consider whether I should go easy on him. His eyes are unfocused but darting around wildly. He's not so drunk that he's unaware of how much danger he's in.

Keeping most of my strength leashed, I punch him directly in the nose. The bridge caves in, crunching beneath my fist. He howls, wailing like I smashed every bone in his face. I wiggle my own nose—his is much too flat now to do anything but gush blood, then step back, disgusted. I barely hit the handsy punk. How was I supposed to know he was made of papier-mâché?

"Let this serve as your reminder of what happens when you touch things that aren't yours," I say, spinning on my heel to follow Luca out, using my elbows as javelins.

By the time I make it outside and find Luca, his eyes are hazel again, but his pupils remain slitted. His basilisk is watching me. I can sense it, and it's almost soothing. Luca's monster side is a kill first, ask questions later kind of guy, but it won't let anyone get the drop on us.

"Are you good?" I ask.

Luca nods, his jaw locked with tension. He grabs my hand for inspection, and I shake my head when I see how much blood got on my fingers. "If I taught the witch how to throw a punch, he could have won that fight," I observe, trying to lighten the mood.

"No doubt," Luca says. his voice returning to the low rumble I'm used to.

"What do you think Alistair will do to the guy?" I ask, heading toward my bike.

"Nothing much. I simply sat him down for a polite discussion about the appropriate ways to treat a lady."

I shake my head as Alistair once against materializes beside me. "You were only a minute behind me," I say. "It couldn't have been much of a discussion."

Alistair sighs mournfully. "Unfortunately, he passed out before I could finish my speech."

Luca laughs, and the sound makes me smile. It eases the persistent itch from my wings demanding release.

Alistair's blue eyes sparkle as he scans the people milling around on the street. "Shall we go back to your place for that conversation, love?"

Gasoline poured over an open flame, his words bring all my filthy thoughts roaring back to the surface. Except this time, my adrenaline is pounding from the punch, and I have a new sexy memory to add to my montage: Alistair and Luca defending my honor like a couple of medieval knights.

"Sure," I tell him, irritated by the breathy sound of my own voice. No matter how sternly I lecture myself, I can't block the visuals my mind provides me with.

"Are you okay?" Luca asks, his easy smile fading at whatever he sees on my face.

"Of course." I grab both helmets, handing him his, then shove mine over my head so I can blush in peace. "Follow us there," I tell Alistair, straddling my bike and cranking it.

It's not until we're on the road, heat radiating up my sides from Luca's hands on my hips, that I accept how much trouble I'm in.

# TWENTY

## LUCA

With my hands melded to Celine's curves, my mind races faster than her bike. My basilisk rattles in my chest, a low-grade buzz—not of rage, but excitement.

It wants her touch. I need her friendship. Can I risk one to get the other? Celine is everything to me, but my basilisk wants more and isn't willing to compromise any longer.

We pull up outside her apartment. Peeling my hands off her hips takes major effort.

"You're quiet," she says.

I take my helmet off and raise my eyebrows. "We've been on the road."

Celine shrugs. "Your energy is loud, though."

I sigh. She's right; I don't know why I'm arguing about it. "I'm processing," I say.

"Okay."

"You'll have to be patient," I add.

"I can do that."

"Can you?" I raise my eyebrows. Celine shoves my chest playfully, and I pull her into a headlock, then bring her hand up to my mouth. "Don't give up on me," I whisper against her knuckles.

She pulls free of my hold, her expression fierce. "Never."

"How touching." Alistair's ghostly drawl glides through the air, and Celine rounds on him.

"Stop doing that," she insists. "It's creepy."

"You wound me." He dips his head, but doesn't bother hiding his grin.

Celine opens her mouth, then shuts it, shaking her head and marching toward her apartment. We follow her up the internal staircase and down the hall, stopping outside the familiar corner unit. She unlocks the door, three different locks clinking as she works.

When we step inside, she locks them all back while I try to see Celine's place through Alistair's eyes. As always, it's meticulously clean and organized. Every framed piece of art, while inexpensive, hangs evenly on her light green walls. It's warm, welcoming, and the exact opposite of my dull, boring bachelor pad.

Her attached kitchen is spotless, with one lonely plate rinsed and stacked in a dish organizer beside the sink. Even the tassels on the floor mat are stretched in the same direction, and I can picture her nudging them into place with her toes whenever they get out of line.

"Can I get either of you something to drink?" Celine asks, twisting her hands together before she realizes what she's doing and drops them to her sides. Her nervousness disorients me.

"I'm good," I say.

Alistair, meanwhile, is busy examining the art on the walls like he expects to discover a secret Monet. "Nothing for me, angel."

Celine mutters something, but my hearing isn't strong enough to catch it. Alistair's lips twitch, and I feel a sting of jealousy that he got a piece of her I didn't. *Cut that shit out.* She isn't a bone to fight over.

Determined not to be weird, I stride to the couch, drop to my usual spot, and clear my throat. "If we're doing the whole transparency thing, you should know I killed the demon, Alistair. Celine had nothing to do with it."

"Luca," she hisses. Air blows by my ear a second before the throw pillow smacks me in the face with the force of a brick. My head rocks to the side, and I see stars.

"You don't get to make dangerous decisions to protect me," I tell her, refusing to budge even if it means she beats me to death with her pillows.

"Because that isn't exactly what you did when you did the— you know what." She opens her eyes comically wide, then blinks slowly.

It's ridiculous. I can only hope that's not how I actually look when I turn someone to stone. That's embarrassing. "Gods, that was awful," I blurt. "If you're going to act it out, don't forget to sweep the asshole up."

Celine swats me with the pillow again, this time on the other side of my head.

Alistair sinks gracefully onto the couch at my side. "Fascinating."

"Don't call us fascinating," I snap. "You sound like a sunburned tourist visiting an aquarium for the first time. We aren't fish."

Alistair, typically the patron saint of calm and collected, chokes on his laughter. "It's hardly a criticism, Luca. I've just never seen two people more determined to be hostile and selfless at the same time."

"I'm not selfless," Celine insists, her voice strained.

I chuckle. Of course she takes offense at that part, but doesn't care if she seems hostile.

"Look, Alistair," I say, trying to bring us back to the point. "Celine didn't do anything wrong. She happened to be hot as fuck while in the path of a dick."

"Way to make me come across like some quivering damsel in distress." She glares at me, malicious intent in her eyes. This time, when she swings the pillow my way, I snatch it from her hand and sit on it.

"I never said you were quivering. The prick pulled a knife on you, and I stepped in. I would do it again—stop glaring at me. We've been over this," I remind her. "And I won't apologize for doing what needed to be done."

"And now Ciprian is sniffing around," she huffs, tossing her hands up in the air. "I'm going to change into something I can let my wings out in. Don't talk about anything important until I get back."

She walks down the hall, hips swaying, and we both watch her go.

"The issue isn't Ciprian's nosiness," Alistair says once her bedroom door closes. "But the fact that he's using it as an excuse to breathe down her neck. And yours."

I shake my head. "I don't know about the second part. He flirts, but he's trying to get the upper hand. Unbalance me."

"Hmm, you could be right, but the way he watches you—"

"Is nosy," I cut in.

"I was going to say hungry."

"I'm not on the menu," I insist, my cheeks heating. "At least not *his* menu."

"There's no reason to be flustered," Alistair says calmly. "You need to be honest about his intentions. They're far more primal than a murder investigation."

I groan, dropping my head against the back of the couch. "What the fuck am I supposed to do about that?"

Alistair laughs. "Have you tried being less appealing? Together, the two of you present the most tempting challenge I've ever seen. If he's having trouble ignoring his instincts . . ." He shrugs. "I'm not surprised he's using flirtation as a way to get close."

"Before either of you suggests I make myself uglier to get him to lose interest, I won't do it," Celine says, padding into the room in cozy sweats and fuzzy pink socks. "I need the tips right now to help Harry." Her wings poke out of the slits she cut in the back. She's so cute, I want to pull her into my lap and keep her there forever.

Gods, that's pathetic.

"You're beautiful no matter what," Alistair says, tilting his head to the side for maximum charm. Celine and I roll our eyes.

"You two are eerily in sync," he observes.

"Luca copies me." Celine squeezes onto the couch between us and pokes me in the ribs before turning her attention to Alistair. "What have you learned about the orphans?"

"Do you want it hard or gentle?"

Celine blinks, then sits up straight. "Hard."

Alistair nods, replacing his playful expression with a more serious one. "Luca was partially right; it's not only here. Orphaned angels with bizarre stories have been popping up around Nevada, but they've all been isolated instances, so no one put it together." He pulls his phone out, leaning over to show us a map he's pinned dots on.

Celine stiffens at my side. The map shows eighteen markers, with a cluster centered in Vegas. "There's something weird about these locations . . ." I bend over Celine to get a closer look, then jerk away as her wings slice right through the skin of my arm. Fuck. They're in knife mode, and I didn't even realize.

"Celine," I whisper, ignoring the cuts. "It's okay, we'll figure it out. I swear, no one will hurt those angels or you."

"N-no, you don't see. You don't get it!" She shoots up from the couch, and I barely dodge another swipe from her wings.

Alistair reaches for her. I hold him back by pressing my bleeding arm against his waist. "Don't touch her right now. Those wings will slice you to pieces."

"Neither of you sees it. This is fucked," Celine mutters, fisting her hair with frustration. Her wings spread wide, then curl, providing a metallic, razor-sharp shield around her torso as she paces. I'm not even sure she realizes it's happening.

"What don't we see, Celine?" Alistair's voice is gentle, like he's calming a wild animal. For a second, she ignores him and continues to pace, talking rapidly in a language I've never heard before. It's similar to the one she uses to communicate with Anika and the other children, but the cadence is different.

I hold my breath, a strange sense of anticipation building at the base of my spine. When Celine whirls to face us and gradually unfurls her wings, I brace for impact.

She closes her eyes, pushes her sleeves up to reveal her bare arms, then stretches them out. "The dots on the map—they're not a pattern or a coincidence," she says. "They're a message. For me." As she speaks, her skin begins to glow. I take in the small golden marks repeated all over her skin, then compare them to the dots on the map.

"Holy shit," I gasp. "I didn't notice before . . . It's the same symbol."

Celine looks at us, her eyes filled with too many emotions to name. "It's my symbol—the symbol for truth."

# TWENTY-ONE

## ALISTAIR

Celine's jaw is rigid. The feathers of her wings have morphed into knives, and she's covered in ancient-looking markings. They're beautiful. She's beautiful. A warrior ready to rain justice on her enemies.

Most of the human lore surrounding angels is wrong, but looking at Celine now, I have the urge to hit my knees and worship her.

Someone has crossed her. I don't know the details, but that much is clear. If she points me in their direction, I'll make damn sure they regret it for eternity.

"Angels aren't all the same," she says, pacing again. "We're born into one of seven different echelons—think of them as tiers. Once we mature, we're further sorted by skills and assigned roles that benefit society. The kid Ciprian found outside the bar, for example, is a guardian, the muscle of the celestial realm. He falls in the middle of the social order. I-I belong to the *nish thatsha*."

That name means nothing to me, but from the way Celine stops pacing to brace herself, this characterization is important. "Your echelon," I say carefully. "Does it have something to do with these orphans?"

"It's the smallest population," she admits. "But . . . *Thatsha* is the top tier. They rule the others, facilitating the balance continuum." She waves her hand, emphasizing *they* as if she doesn't want to be part of the structure she's explaining.

"I faked my own death and left because . . . I needed to get out." Celine points at one of the symbols glowing on her arm. "This rune is my calling card. Those dots on the map are a message to me. Someone knows I'm alive."

"How can you be sure?" I ask, my eyes flitting to Luca's trembling hands.

Celine sucks in a deep breath. "Because it means truth. It's my radiant magical gift."

I nod, considering all the information she's shared. Her theory is plausible, but I don't understand why she's so sure. I need more. I want to rule out all possible explanations before we reach a conclusion.

"Is it rare?" I ask. "They could be referencing someone else."

"It's not rare . . ." Celine raises her eyes to meet mine. "It's unique. I'm the only angel in existence with this gift." I let the information settle in, amazed by what I'm hearing.

Luca shoves to his feet, his clenched fists shaking. "And how many people know this? Is there a registry? Who the fuck would set up this creepy puzzle and use children with no memories as their messengers?"

Celine's wings curl around her body protectively, the overhead light from the living room fixture glinting off the metallic edges.

"My father," she says, her voice colder than I've ever heard it.

"I should have put it together sooner, but I didn't want to think . . ." She hangs her head, then snaps it back up. "Bottom line: This rune is a mark—for my death. I got away from him once; he's telling me he won't let it happen again."

"What the fuck does that mean?" Luca demands. "Just like that, he wants to kill his own daughter? Will he send assassins? What exactly are we up against, Celine?"

"It's not 'just like that,'" she says. "He's been trying to kill me for most of my life in one way or another. I'm telling you both because you deserve the truth, but there is no *we*. I'll handle this myself. You will both distance yourselves from me. We can stage a public falling-out or something dramatic, in case he's sent spies—"

"Slow down, angel," I beg.

"Um, more like stop right fucking now," Luca hisses. "I'm not staging a public falling-out or any other stupid shit like that. If someone shows up to kill you, I'll tear them to pieces. They'll beg me to turn them to rock before I'm done."

"I won't let you take that kind of risk," Celine says.

"You don't let me do anything." Luca grabs her shoulders. "I make my own choices. I always have, and I always will. And if you think I won't choose you every time, you've lost your gods-damn mind. I. Choose. You."

"Luca—"

"No, listen to me, Celine. Please. I will turn every single person in Nevada, human or supernatural, to stone before I let you go. We'll spend the rest of our lives building whatever we want from the dust of your enemies. You can slice me to ribbons with your wings, set me on fire a dozen times—whatever the fuck you want—but you don't get to push me away. Do you hear me?"

"I hear you," Celine whispers.

I watch, amazed, as her wings soften to down. My heart

swells, envy pulsing with every beat. Their bond—I want that. Viscerally. Not to take, but to share. Will I ever have it?

"Angel, if you don't kiss him now, I will," I say, my voice raspy.

And she does. Celine rises on her tiptoes, both hands digging into Luca's hair. She pulls his head down, and their lips meet as if they've kissed a million times before. It's not frantic or angry, although both of them are clearly dancing on the edge of their emotional limits.

My eyelids flutter as Luca moans deep in his throat. The sound is intimate, hot, and involuntarily relieved. It's the kind of sound someone makes when chronic pain finally lets go—only for a second—and their body doesn't know whether to cry or scream.

"You're a fool," Celine whispers angrily. Despite her words, her grip on his hair is tight, as if she's worried he will do exactly as she demanded and leave her behind.

"Shut up and kiss me," Luca says.

Celine pulls back an inch. "But this is risky. Our friendship—"

"Will be fine." He kisses her, harder this time. "A few kisses and orgasms won't break us, Celine. I won't give you up."

"This possessiveness . . ."

"You fucking love it," Luca grunts, dipping his hands to the backs of her thighs and walking her backward toward the couch. They tumble next to me, Celine's fiery hair slapping my thigh.

"Alistair . . ." she whispers, sounding unsure.

I avoid eye contact in case Luca decides to get a head start on turning the supernatural population in Las Vegas into a mausoleum paved in poker chips or something. "I can give you privacy tonight," I say. "But I have no intention of stepping to the side. If you want me, of course."

I leave the question open-ended. Luca and Celine were slow to admit their feelings, but I've always known I can't have one without the other. If they reject me now . . . Dread, raw and primal, tears through me as I wait for their answer.

I want them, want what they have even more, but nothing is worse than being permitted to stay somewhere while knowing you're not wanted. I won't force my presence on anyone.

"I want you, Alistair," Celine says, her words decisive, as if she's tying a bow. There's satisfaction and weight behind each one, and when I look at her, I see the truth rune littered across every inch of her beautiful skin.

"Thank the gods." I run my thumb across her bottom lip. It's swollen from Luca's kisses. The realization sends my blood rushing south. She's so alive.

From his spot on top of Celine, I feel Luca's eyes rake over me. Tension builds between us. My attraction to Celine was immediate. Luca snuck up on me. I meet his eyes, and the heat between us goes from a simmer to a boil.

His fingers wind into my hair, tugging my head forcefully. When his lips meet mine, I can taste his confusion, and I smile into the kiss. Luca prides himself on self-control, but he's still a shifter. He wasn't sure if he wanted to kiss me, so he's giving it a try—and he's giving it all he's got, too competitive to settle for a boring kiss.

I nip at his lip, using my vampire speed to move until Celine is sandwiched between us, straddling his lap. Connecting our lips again, I grin as Luca gasps into my mouth. Celine kisses along his neck, and we feast on him together until his breathing grows loud and ragged in the quiet of her living room.

"Your fangs," he groans.

"Your lip ring," I toss back, running the tip of one fang over the black metal hoop. He shudders. I give him a softer kiss and pull back. "Well? What's the verdict? You don't have to spare my feelings; I'm a big boy."

"I'm hard as a rock," Luca says with a shrug. His voice is matter-of-fact, as if he's telling me the odds of sunshine in the desert. I chuckle. The urge to make them both mine is overriding every other thought and instinct.

"I cannot take all the credit for that," I remind him. "Not while you have the most flawless creature in all the realms straddling your cock." I smile as Celine giggles into his neck, then deliberately grinds on his lap.

"True, but I don't think I'd mind you doing the same."

"Good to know," I murmur, imagining it vividly as I run my fingers along the tip of one of Celine's wings. She trembles beneath my touch. *Gods, if they turn me down now . . .*

"Do you want me to stay or give you a night to yourselves?" I ask, desperate to play this right.

This moment between Luca and Celine has been building for a long time. I want them both, but they need time alone together, as I will want my own private moments.

"I've never had two men at once," Celine says, shuddering.

"Neither have I," I say drily. "But you can have us both another night if you'd prefer it. I won't rush you, angel." I glance at Luca to make sure he understands I'm including him in that statement too.

His hazel eyes morph, the pupils shifting to horizontal, reptilian slits as he sizes me up. "Are you trying to talk yourself out of a good time, Alistair, or are you scared you won't measure up?" There's enough bravado in his taunt that I don't take offense.

Kissing up Celine's neck, I taste her lips for the first time since the storeroom, sinking into her mouth like I belong there before pulling back. "If you're sure, take us to your bed, angel."

# TWENTY-TWO

## CELINE

This is happening. It's really happening. I'm about to go from a months-long solo tour to a full-on group act. My heart pounds in my chest, my wings arching toward Alistair in an embarrassingly desperate way. *Maybe you should take your show on the road.* I tell my brain to shut up. It doesn't.

It's a terrible idea to jump into bed with not one but two men I know. At least if they were strangers, I could toss them out after and never see them again. But if this goes poorly, I'll have to clean up a mess. *If this goes poorly, you'll be dead.*

The unhelpful thought projects across my mind—neon-sign-on-a-marquee style—complete with a halo of flashing lights. I imagine ripping it down, then bashing it to pieces, and I feel slightly better.

"I was going to keep stroking your wings, but it seems they're otherwise occupied. Did I do something wrong?"

Alistair's voice pulls me out of my head and back to the three-some I'm about to have. Because I'm definitely about to have a threesome. If some assassin slits my throat tomorrow, I don't want to drown in my own blood while regretting all the threesomes I didn't have. I'd much rather relive my best orgasms.

"I've never seen them do this," Luca says, laughter in his voice. "Her face is blank, but her wings are flipping through settings quicker than I can track."

*Shit. He's right.* I close my eyes, focus on making my turbulent emotions settle, then clear my throat. "My wings aren't a massage chair, Luca. They don't have settings."

"If you say so." Luca pulls me up from the couch. "Now will you please treat me like a chair? I don't know if I have settings either, but I'm happy to show you all my moves and let you decide which ones you enjoy the most."

The ridiculous joke does exactly what he intended, pulling me out of my head and back into the moment. "Are you asking me to sit on your face or telling me?" I ask.

"Whichever one makes you the most inclined to do it . . . Obviously."

I kiss his grinning mouth, grab Alistair's hand, then drag them down the short hallway to my room. I changed the sheets yester-day. If this is as good as I expect it to be, I'll be changing them again tomorrow too. Undecided about the lighting, I flip the over-heads on, then off again. Luca turns both lamps on instead, raising his eyebrows at me in question. I nod, then take a beat to look at him.

I'm about to fuck my friend. This changes everything, no matter what he says. I wait for the realization to turn me off or freak me out, but it doesn't happen.

Luca pulls his lip ring into his mouth, a nervous habit he does when he's unsure of himself, and I melt. Imani was right. I trust him. With this and everything else.

Alistair waits patiently at his side by the bed, bending his head as Luca whispers something in his ear. I strain to hear, but can't make out a single word. When they both focus on me, it's all I can do not to squirm. I'm confident in myself, but seeing the dirty promises in their eyes is almost too much honesty. They can both lie. Why don't they bother hiding how badly they want me?

"Undress her," Alistair orders.

"Like I don't know how to strip myself," I mutter sarcastically, irritated by the wave of vulnerability. It's true, though. They've already seen most of my body in a setting that's far from romantic. *How special can it really be for them?*

In a flash, I find myself boxed in, tall, warm stacks of muscle surrounding me on all sides.

"I love to watch you take your clothes off," Luca says.

"But we'll handle it this time, if that's all right with you." Alistair's voice is more growl than anything else, and I shiver, nodding like a puppet.

I expect them to yank my clothes off. But they don't. Luca's hand on my waist drifts under my sweatshirt, his thumb stroking my lower belly infuriatingly slow. Alistair zeros back in on my wings, his fingers exploring the feathers confidently until I'm shaking with desire.

Wanting to touch them too, I wrap my arms around their shoulders, tilting my head back to kiss Alistair. His lips are confident against mine, but his hands never stop petting my wings. When his fingers narrow in on a specific feather, rubbing both edges at once, I moan.

He echoes the sound at a lower octave—as if I'm the one driving him crazy—then repeats the motion. Luca, meanwhile, seems to be mapping my torso with his fingers like a cartographer. Their simple touches set me on fire . . . My eyes drift closed, and I float in the sensations. No one rushes me. Would they really be content giving me this simple pleasure all night?

When my left arm loses its support and drops, I find Luca on his knees in front of me. His hazel eyes are achingly familiar, the horizontally slitted pupils the only hint that he's not as calm as he appears. It silences the last flicker of anxiety in my body. *He's mine.*

My shoulders sag, and my face softens. Luca looks up at me, his expression filled with wonder, his hands several shades darker against the pale skin of my stomach. He tightens his grip possessively.

I roll my hips toward him in a slow, blatantly sexual invitation, and it's all the encouragement he needs. Without blinking, Luca dips his fingers beneath the waistband of my sweats and pulls them to my ankles. I didn't bother with underwear when I changed clothes after the fight, and his groan as he comes face-to-face with my bare pussy is music to my ears.

"Alistair," he hisses. His gaze crawls up my body impatiently, and he narrows his eyes at the vampire who seems content to spend the whole night playing with my wings. Even though I want him to keep touching them, my urgency is building too. I need to come. Badly.

"Yes, yes, okay." Alistair's voice is raspier than I'm used to, and another wave of arousal rolls over me. Individually, they're each a walking wet dream. Together—gods, I'm a confident woman— but the truth is I might not survive this.

A second of concentration is all it takes to pull my wings in. Alistair frowns like I've taken away his favorite toy.

"I'll put them back," I promise him, already feeling the frustrated itch on my back. "Just take off my shirt."

"Rushing me. Both of you," Alistair mutters. "I should have known you two would be impatient." The dark rumble makes me shudder, his intensity rolling over my skin.

I smile, prepared to give him a smartass response, but Luca

chooses this moment to bury his tongue inside me. My legs buckle. After all the relatively innocent touching, I'm not ready for the sudden onslaught of pleasure.

Alistair holds me upright, pulling my sweatshirt over my head in a flash. Relieved beyond belief, my wings explode out of my back, stretching wide to demand his touch.

Luca licks me enthusiastically, a filthy noise coming from low in his throat. "So good, baby," he groans. The term of endearment hits me hard. I hate it when strangers at the club call me baby, but when Luca does it . . .

Grinding onto his tongue, I bury my face in Alistair's chest and bite down.

"Gods," Alistair groans. "On the bed, Luca."

The command is sharp, and Luca's eyes narrow, his tongue licking a lazy stripe over my clit as he considers whether he wants to follow orders. He does it again, and I whine, losing interest in their power plays. If someone doesn't get me off soon . . .

As if he can read my mind, Luca surges to his feet, stripping in record time and throwing himself on my bed. The headboard slams against the wall, cracking against the plaster.

*That's going to be an issue.* I toss that thought away and focus on what's important: Luca's perfect body. Every inch is beautiful —all the way down to his massive, hard, *pierced* cock. He grips it in his hand and gives it a rough stroke. I look him over, taking in the long, lean muscles decorated with a handful of gray scale tattoos.

"Luca," I say, my voice a breathy whisper. "You're gorgeous."

Alistair uses the fingers of one hand to stroke my wings, toying with my nipple with the other. "Let him lick you," he suggests. "He deserves it, doesn't he?" When I don't immediately respond, he rolls my nipple between his fingers roughly, sending a spike of pleasure through my nerve endings.

"Please, baby," Luca begs, moving his hand up and down his cock faster.

I climb onto the bed and straddle his face, planning to hover there and tease him a little.

Luca doesn't give me a chance. He grabs my hips with both hands, yanking me to his mouth, then adjusting me until he has me right where he wants me.

His tongue lashes my clit with the perfect pressure. Arousal boils inside me. The pleasure is so intense I almost want to hide from it. Knowing it's Luca's face I'm riding makes everything hotter, and the sounds he makes . . . *Fuck me.*

Luca eats my pussy like someone who's been shipwrecked for a year, then rescued and handed a cheesecake with no fork. His grunts and groans are accompanied by indecent, wet licking sounds. For a guy who isn't usually emotive, I'm surprised by how vocal he is with his tongue buried inside me.

The bed dips, and Alistair's hands join Luca's on my hips as I ride his face. Seeing four hands on my body is more than I can take. I stiffen between them, my orgasm rolling through me violently as my entire nervous system focuses on the explosion of ecstasy between my legs. I jerk in their grip, moaning as my pleasure reaches its peak, then slowly fades, leaving my body pleasantly limp.

Luca kisses my inner thigh, a satisfied smirk on his face that makes him look more like a smug fox than a mythical monster shifter. When I get ahold of him, that smirk will be nowhere in sight.

Scooting back, I glance over my shoulder at Alistair and tilt my chin back. He follows my unspoken command and kisses me until I'm dizzy.

"I want to ride him while I suck you off," I say definitively, then nibble on his bottom lip. "I also want you to bite me."

Alistair's face goes from horny to feral in a flash. His blue eyes turn blood red, and my heart races. This isn't Alistair the crafty, strategic information gatherer; this is Alistair the predator—and I'm the prey.

Knowing it will drive him crazy, I turn my back on him and focus my attention on Luca. Alistair snarls, and the hairs on the back of my neck prickle. I ignore him. Instead, I rub my sensitive clit on Luca's dick, letting it dip inside me briefly before pulling it back out.

"Pierced cock?" I purr. "How did you manage to keep that a secret?"

Luca grits his teeth. "How and when would I have brought that up, Celine?" I watch, fascinated, as his Adam's apple bobs. "Hey buddy, I know you're getting ready for work right now, but do you want to see my dick?"

I chuckle, taking him inside me a couple of inches to get used to the scrape of the metal. "I mean, given that you got it pierced, you could have led with that," I tease, dropping another inch.

He gasps. "I thought about it, but there were two problems."

"And what were those?" I tighten my inner muscles around him, grinning as a drop of sweat rolls down his temple.

"Because if I told you, I would have had to either show it to you soft—which I would never do for obvious reasons . . ." His hips jerk up, seating his dick further inside me. "Or it would have gotten hard while you were looking at it, like it does every time I think about you."

"Oh please," I scoff, planting my hands on his chest. "You do not get hard every time you think about me. I would have noticed."

"Why do you think I wear such tight pants?" he grunts.

"Enough," Alistair snaps. "Quit playing around and fuck him properly." His low, rumbling growls are straight out of my dirtiest fantasies. Before I can push him further, he drives me down on Luca's cock until he's buried to the hilt.

Luca and I both groan, but I get no opportunity to adjust because Alistair has apparently decided we can't be trusted with this. *I've pushed him as far as he's willing to be pushed.* It's the last sensible thought I have because Alistair has decided to drive.

Using his vampire speed, he lifts and pushes me down on Luca's cock until my eyes roll back. Luca and I both start making noises I've never heard before. They are beyond filthy, and this is rougher than rough. I should be scared, but it's exactly what I want.

The drag of Luca's piercing against the magical spot inside me is relentless and agonizing. I try to hang on to his chest, my nails digging vivid half-moons into his pecs as I gush all over him. I wail as I come, but Alistair doesn't stop. Up. Down. Up. Down.

"Oh fuck. Oh gods. You feel amazing. Baby. Please. More. Yes, fuck."

Luca is babbling, but I'm impressed he can verbalize anything right now. Especially since I've been reduced to a disturbing rotation of animalistic grunts and groans. When the motion abruptly stops, my limp arms can barely keep me upright.

"I'm sorry. Shit," Alistair whispers, his grip on my hips loosening. "I got carried away."

"Don't stop!" Luca and I shout in unison—and it's a good thing, too, because my voice sounds more wail than anything else. There's a short pause as Alistair's hands gently graze my breasts from behind, before one snakes up to wrap around my neck while the other dips between my legs.

"Are you sure you can handle it?" He rubs my clit in a teasing, barely there circle, and I twitch in his hold. Alistair's smoky confidence is back. My nipples harden until they almost hurt.

With trembling hands, Luca lifts his fingers to my tits,

caressing them reverently, his eyes never leaving mine. "She can take it," he says. "Celine wants everything we've got."

It's half praise, half taunt, and I clench my jaw to keep from moaning as Alistair's caresses speed up. Faster and faster he rubs me until I'm riding Luca's cock as hard as I physically can. Without Alistair's freakish speed, I can't recreate the same intensity.

He knows; he's waiting for me to beg for it. Sometime in the future I'll refuse him and hold back until we both lose our minds, but not tonight. Tonight, I know exactly what I want and how I'm going to get it.

"You must be tired, Alistair," I taunt him. "It's okay to have speed and no stamina, though. Luca and I won't judge you for it."

His grip on my neck tightens, and he uses that hold to add some force to my rhythm. It's a warning. My blood sings with excitement. This entire situation is dangerous. Alistair could snap my neck while Luca is balls deep inside me, not to mention the fact that the hazel in my friend's eyes is long gone. If his basilisk slips up, I'll be turned to stone.

There's no pretending I'm not fucking two monsters and putting my life in their hands while I'm at it. At this rate, my father may not even need assassins to take me out.

*They won't hurt you.* The thought is so firmly entrenched in my head, an excavator couldn't pry it loose. It's the truth. Magical gift or not, I know I'm safe with them.

My next orgasm hits me fast and rides me hard. As my pussy contracts around Luca's cock, his eyes drop closed. He's trying his absolute hardest not to come.

"Look at her," Alistair demands. "Don't skip a second of this view."

Luca's eyes snap open, rolling up and down my body until I feel his gaze like a physical touch. They eventually land on my face, a flicker of intensity eclipsing the pleasure in his expression. I refuse to name what it means, but it's hopelessly hot.

It traps me. I can't see anything else. Not when Alistair starts pushing me up and down again, fucking me on Luca's dick so thoroughly I'm not sure I'll ever recover.

When a smaller orgasm crashes over me, Luca follows me over the edge, grunting, his eyes flashing between warm hazel and fierce yellow. I smile, bending at the waist to kiss his lips.

"Shit, baby, I didn't even think about protection," Luca says. His hand cups my face as he looks down with a focused intensity and watches his cum drip out of me.

"I've got birth control covered," I tell him.

After moving here, I got a human implant, since I wasn't sure how sleeping with different supernaturals would affect my fertility. The witch healer who gave it to me believed it would work, although I was the first angel she had met. It's not a guarantee, but I'm reasonably confident I won't be popping out any winged monsters any time soon.

Luca smirks at me, his abs bunching deliciously as he sits us both up. "Are you thinking what I'm thinking?" he whispers.

"That we should tag team a vampire?"

He stares over my shoulder. "You read my mind."

Turning, I get my first good look at Alistair's body. He's not as tan as Luca, but he's not as pale as I am either. Lethal, lean lines of muscle stretch across his frame, his height obvious even while kneeling on the bed. His hair is so dark it's blue black in the dim lighting of my bedroom. Tied back in a short ponytail, I imagine grabbing it for leverage while I fuck him.

With eyes like blood, Alistair stares back, and there's no pretending he's not a vampire. Crawling toward him, I grin when he goes impossible still. Luca groans at the view.

"May I?" I ask, my lips moving against the tight skin of

Alistair's torso. The ridges of his muscles bunch, and I kiss lower, tugging the elastic of his boxer briefs between my teeth.

Alistair clears his throat. "I say this with every fiber of sincerity in my being, angel, but you have permission to do anything and everything you want to me—now and until the world ends."

"Smart guy," Luca says.

My mouth curls into a smile, and I wink. "I'd better get started then."

# TWENTY-THREE

## LUCA

My basilisk is smug, and I can't even blame it. Now that I've jumped the fence surrounding the friend zone, I can't imagine going back. It's the scared side of the fence. The lonely side of the fence. Fuck that side of the fence.

Friend-zoned Luca never made out with dangerous vampires for fun. And he certainly didn't get to reach out and shove his own cum back into the most perfect pussy in the universe to watch it drip out again.

Celine glances over her shoulder and shakes her head when she sees where I'm looking. When she swats me with her right wing, I roll with the movement until I'm leaning back against her padded headboard.

This will be a test for me. By the time the night ends we'll all know if I can watch the woman I've wanted for years touch someone else. If it goes badly—No, I can't murder Alistair. That would piss Celine off, and I would regret it. Probably.

*Don't kill him*, I remind my basilisk as we watch Celine peel Alistair's underwear off. He has a nice cock—big, slightly curved, with no unexpected surprises. I wonder what it tastes like. On this side of the fence, I get to find out. But for now, I'm going to watch Celine ruin him, knowing it's my cum running down her thighs.

When she grabs him around the hips and hurls him toward me, I have to admit I'm surprised. Her aim is good, though, and Alistair lands with his back against the headboard beside me.

Playful light dances in Celine's eyes. She crawls between Alistair's legs, dropping to lick the underside of his dick. Bent over, she supports herself with one hand, gathers her wild hair up with the other, then makes eye contact with me.

"Do you mind helping me out?" She flips the end of her hair in my direction, and I take the hint, holding the silky red strands up for her so she can focus on Alistair. "Luca controls the pace this time," she says, shooting him a devious smile.

Alistair groans, but I waste no time easing her head down. Never one to hesitate once she decides, Celine swallows him like it's her job. Gripping the sheets, Alistair's breathing breaks down and turns to gasping pants, and I can tell he's doing everything he can not to fuck her mouth.

Experimentally, I gently push her head down, watching as she takes his entire length—it has to be in her throat at this point— then swallows. Gods, that's hot. Tugging on her hair, I give her time to suck in some air. This is going to be the best blow job ever.

From my vantage point, I use Alistair's reactions against him, never letting him reach the point of no return. He's got a hell of a poker face, but a muscle in his neck gives him away every time he gets close to coming.

Because I'm watching him closely, I see firsthand how he looks while he's getting sucked. It's . . . well, fuck, it's intimate as hell. I'm not quite ready to reverse the roles, but watching him come undone is doing something to me.

When he glances my way, his red eyes unfocused and half-crazed, I kiss him without hesitation. I can practically taste his pleasure as Celine works him over. There's no doubt that Alistair is a good kisser, even though there's nothing soft about the way his lips move against mine. I wrap my free hand around his neck so I can feel the tendon pulse without looking.

"You're pushing it," Alistair grumbles against my mouth.

I chuckle, then kiss his neck on impulse. "All that work to be mysterious, and I found your tell in thirty seconds."

"Since I rarely let my informants suck me off, it doesn't come up often." Alistair drops back against the headboard and groans as Celine ups her pace.

"I don't think she likes the idea of an informant getting you off," I say.

Alistair's eyes deepen to a vivid crimson, and his fingers leave the sheets, pulling Celine up until her swollen lips hover in front of his face. "It's yours as long as you want it, angel."

"Damn right it is," she says, twisting her hand around his cock. "Now bite me and show me what all the rumors are about. Fair warning, if this experience isn't as life-altering as—"

Alistair snaps.

He lunges as if he's starving and sinks his fangs deep into her neck.

With my hand fisted in her hair, I freeze. Her body jolts in my grip, spine bowing, heels quivering against my thighs on the bed. A strangled gasp escapes her lips. I hold my breath, waiting to see if her reckless streak has finally caught up with her. I'll petrify him if she shows even a flicker of pain.

Then she moans.

Low. Ragged. Animal.

The sound hits like a lightning strike—raw and primal, the

kind of moan that melts your spine and tightens everything below the belt. It's pleasure laid bare, and my dick, exhausted seconds ago, hears the call and sits up.

Celine's hands rise—almost as if she's sleepwalking—then claw into Alistair's hair, yanking him closer. She can't get enough. Her hips roll with each pull of his mouth, and her moaning turns to a broken wail. Within seconds, she's screaming. It starts low, then climbs higher, sharper, until I'm half-worried the windows will shatter or someone will call the cops.

I kiss her because I can't not. Because I need to taste what he's unleashing in her. And because if some neckbeard human cop shows up at the door before she comes again, I will kill him. That is not how I want to end the night.

With Celine's hair clenched in my fist, her tongue in my mouth, and Alistair fang-deep in her neck, it's the hottest thing I've ever done.

Celine's wings flare wide, sending a gust of cool air over our flushed skin, and wrap around us all in a cocoon. It's possessive. She's claiming us, and even if it's only for tonight, I will never forget how good it feels to be hers.

When she stiffens against me, I tear my eyes open, unwilling to miss even one orgasm. I want to see them all, even if I have to tape my eyelids to my forehead.

Celine twitches, her voice catching on a broken cry. Her thighs quake. For a split second, her entire body goes rigid with tension. Then it breaks. The pleasure rips through her, and I watch, mesmerized, as she rides it out. *She was born for this.*

Alistair grunts, his cock jerking as he comes. Celine sags between us, like every drop of her energy went into that orgasm. He pulls his fangs free, licks the final drop of blood from her skin, then gently lays her on the bed.

"You are the most incredible woman I've ever met," he says.

It's a line, but somehow it comes across as the sincerest thing I've ever heard.

We lay there—I'm not sure how long—just breathing.

My body cools, allowing blood to return to my brain. My thoughts are spinning. Nothing could have prepared me for what happened between us. People talk about life-altering sex all the time, but I've never bought into the hype. Sex is good. I enjoy it. But it's never been like this before. Like something I'm not willing to lose.

The intimacy, the intensity . . . What if it makes Celine retreat? I need to do whatever I can to keep that from happening. Starting now.

"I'll get the shower going," I say, kissing Celine's cheek then padding into the joined bathroom. Like everything else in her apartment, it's clean and organized, white tile sparkling under the cheap brass light fixture. I turn the water on, poking around until I find a spare set of sheets in the cabinet.

I carry them back to the bedroom and take a minute to watch Alistair. For all I know, he has crazy threesomes all the time. Curled around Celine protectively, his red eyes are fixated, not on his bite mark, but on her face. She's half asleep, or in some kind of blissed-out state, a smile on her lips that makes her look like a Renaissance painting. Alistair, though . . . Damn, he looks entranced.

Some of my tension eases. I understand that look. He's a monster. Like me. Monsters kill, but they also protect. And with the way Alistair is staring at Celine now . . . he won't hurt her. Even if I wasn't sure, my basilisk is.

"If you want to get started in the shower, I'll change the bedding," I say, knowing good and well Celine won't be a fan of waking up on dirty sheets.

Alistair nods, gathering her up in his arms and striding into the bathroom without a word. I realize I'm the only one who's spoken since his fangs entered her neck.

I make quick work of the bed, putting the dirty sheets in the hamper and making sure the edges aren't hanging over the sides. Celine wouldn't melt down if I tossed them in the corner, but I want her to be comfortable.

After remaking the bed, I join them in the bathroom. Steam curls up from the shower as I pull back the curtain and step in. It's a tight fit, but fuck, after what we were doing, who cares? Curling into Celine, I wrap my arms around her.

She hums, then turns her head to kiss me. There's a hint of uncertainty on her face as she looks up at me. "Will you stay?"

"Duh," I say, kissing her forehead, then reaching around Alistair for the shampoo. He runs a soapy washcloth over her meticulously, his eyes darting every so often to the bite on her neck.

"It will heal soon," he assures her. "My saliva facilitates fast regeneration." *To make sure he can bite her again.* That's a handy evolutionary tool. I'm not completely sure how I feel about Alistair marking her, but that's not my business.

Celine hums again. "You'll have to give me another one, then," she says.

Alistair's eyes, which had returned to blue by the time I joined them in the shower, flash red again. His lips curl into a fang-tipped smile that shouldn't be cute, but is. It's ridiculous.

"You're hogging the water," I tell him. "I'm freezing back here."

"Poor, cold-blooded baby," Celine teases, rubbing her ass against my exhausted dick. The poor thing twitches, then rises to the occasion. Such a giver.

I back away until my spine hits the cold wall of the shower. "Nope," I beg. "Leave it alone; it's done enough."

Celine and Alistair's laughter echoes around the bathroom,

and we hurry through the rest of the shower. After we're all clean and dry, I go back to the bedroom to examine the curtains. Celine's nightly routine takes time, and Alistair joins me first. I sense him watching me from the other side of the room.

"What are you doing?" he asks as I run my fingers along the edge of the fabric.

I snort. "Checking to see if these blackout curtains work so you don't get barbecued at sunrise."

Alistair surges across the room. Air brushes against my body from his speed. "You want me to stay?" he asks, his voice flat and emotionless.

"Celine does." I shrug, pushing the curtains flat against the wall then frowning when they bounce back. "And it would ruin the mood if we woke up to your crispy corpse."

He chuckles. "You're too kind."

"Yeah, I know," I say. "Grab the tape out of that middle drawer, would you?"

"Are you sure it's there? I don't want to go through her stuff."

"Yeah, everything's labeled. You'll see."

A beat later, Alistair chuckles. "She is incredibly—"

"Meticulous," Celine finishes. "Aspirational. That's what you were going to say, right?"

"You'll never know because you interrupted me," Alistair points out and tosses me the tape.

"Safer for you that way," I mutter, taping the edges of the curtains to the wall until there are no gaps, then turning to face them.

"What did you say, Luca?" Celine raises her eyebrows, rubbing excess lotion into her arms as a grin tugs at her lips.

"Nothing, baby." I tuck the tape back into the basket labeled 'adhesive' and shut the drawer before walking out of the bedroom. Alistair follows me. "You check the front door. I'll do the windows."

I hesitate. I was planning to do this all myself. Trusting him with the windows . . . that's a bigger step than kissing him.

Celine pushes past me, her oversized T-shirt grazing the tops of her thighs as she steps up to the front door to check the dead-bolts. "How about I check my own doors and my own windows to make sure my own home is secure against potential celestial assassins meant for me."

Neither of us argue, silently checking every window together instead. By the time we're done, the situation is fully in perspective—trust is earned on the Fringes.

This newborn relationship, understanding, whatever the fuck it is, is in the stumbling-around stage. We haven't grown to the point where all the limbs can function on their own yet. Until we get there, oversight is a guarantee, and that's going to chafe.

After we check the last window, I grab Celine's hand and pull her toward the bedroom, Alistair trailing behind us. "It's physically secure, but what about magic?" he asks. "We should get a witch over here to lay wards."

Celine stops by the bed, pulling the covers back to sit. "I don't have the money to pay for that."

I shoot Alistair a warning look, silently begging him not to offer her money.

His jaw tightens, but he keeps his mouth closed.

Celine scoots to the middle of the bed and secures her hair in a massive knot on top of her head. "Get in or get out," she says, her words sharp even as her shoulders sag.

After a final glance at the curtains, I climb in on the side closest to the window. The tape is holding for now, but it could come loose while we sleep. I'm not sure how fast sun burns a vampire, and I won't ask, but I'd rather Alistair sleep on the far side in case.

After a short pause, he crawls in and turns off the lamp. It's pitch black. With the curtains taped shut, the street lights can't reach us.

"You're annoyed with me," Alistair whispers, his words a statement and not a question.

Celine sighs. "No. I mean, yes, I am annoyed. Not specifically with you, though."

"It feels the same."

"I know," Celine whispers. "Can you hold me and pretend it doesn't?"

She's talking to him, but both of us scoot closer.

Alistair's arm grazes mine as we find a comfortable position. With my eyes adjusting, I can barely make out the outline of our tangled pile of limbs. It's way too soon to say it, but if this becomes a habit, Celine is going to need a bigger bed.

---

I startle awake, blinking with confusion as Alistair shoots out of the bed completely naked and darts from the room like a shadowed dart. *Is he hurt?* I glance at the window, but no direct beams of light are making it past the curtains.

Pulling my arm out from under Celine, I follow him and ease the bedroom door shut behind me, just in time to hear a pained groan. *Fuck.* No longer giving a shit about noise, I sprint into the living room and find Alistair cradling his arm to his chest. His crimson eyes are feral as he hugs the wall to avoid the light.

"I smelled blood," he snarls. "And forgot her windows aren't all sun-proofed."

I hear him, but his voice is hollow, as if it's coming through a tunnel. Dripping runes cover every surface of the walls; runes that definitely weren't there when we went to bed. Adrenaline and sleep war for control of my brain, and my fangs descend involuntarily as my arms tremble with the urge to shift.

"How the fuck?" I hiss. We were sleeping a few feet away. How did someone come into this apartment and paint runes on the wall without any of us noticing?

"Check the door," Alistair says. "I tried, but the sun . . . Luca, you've got to stay calm until we know what's going on. They could be nearby."

His words snap me out of it, and I stride to the door and check the locks. All three are still in place, but the breeze hits me a second before I see the open window. Rushing over to it, I stick my head out, blinking as my eyes adjust. There's nothing to see besides the assorted brick and stucco buildings being broiled by the morning sun.

"Anything?" Alistair asks, his voice tight.

I glance down, then step back to get a better view. "More runes on the windowsill, but these are different."

"Let me see," Celine says, her voice reaching me a second before her hand lands gently on my shoulder.

Pulling back, I step away from the window with my eyes cast down. My basilisk is mostly under control, but neither of us want to risk her. We already failed her by sleeping through a fucking home invasion.

"This rune means open," Celine says, slamming the window and latching it briskly. "It's not a *thatsha* rune, just a common one, used most often by the guardians. They have a range of minor magical abilities."

"I'm calling a witch," Alistair says.

"It won't matter." She dismisses him with a wave of her hand, and he growls. I wince as all the tense, dangerous energy in the room heats to a boiling point.

"I'll pay, Celine," Alistair insists. "I don't care about the cost. Let me help."

"No! You aren't listening to me," she snaps, balling her hands at her sides. "It won't matter because this is celestial magic. You could call ten witches and it wouldn't fucking matter. It's like trying to fix an airplane with train parts."

"I understand that," Alistair seethes. "But we could at least get a warning when someone enters your apartment, then—magic or no magic—we could kill them."

I grunt in agreement. Celine's angry stare digs into the side of my head.

"And that reminds me," she says. "No more tips at the club. I won't accept them."

"What?" Alistair sounds shocked. "Can we discuss this after the skin on my arm grows back? I'm more than happy to have a conversation about your misplaced feminism once we figure out who broke into your godsdamn apartment."

I wince and step back. He's frustrated. I am too, but Celine is going to toss him out the window if he keeps this up. Her concern over money may seem random. It makes senses to me, though. I've spent years unraveling what makes her tick.

This break-in, the orphaned angels, two guys in her bed—Celine feels out of control. She hates that, so she'll claw her balance back any way she can. If Alistair gets in her way, she'll move him, and she won't be gentle about it.

I need to get them back on task or this could escalate quickly. Running my finger through one of the runes on the wall, I clear my throat. "It's still wet," I say, breaking their tense standoff, then sniffing the red liquid. "This isn't blood."

I make eye contact with Alistair without thinking, relieved when he doesn't turn to stone. His face twists into a frustrated scowl, his injured arm hanging stiffly at his side. I can sympathize with him. Hiding my protective instincts from Celine to avoid driving her away is a concept I'm intimately familiar with.

"I smelled blood," Alistair says. "It woke me, but you're right, it's not coming from the walls."

I nod, then inhale deeply. Smell is my strongest sense, and blood gives off a metallic odor. It's stronger by the window.

Nudging Celine out of the way, I squat to take a closer look. Sure enough, there are several drops of blood on the latch, as if the intruder cut themselves while climbing in or out. I raise my eyebrows, shocked that this small amount woke Alistair up.

"Found it," I say, pointing at the latch.

Collecting a little on my finger, I bring it over to the kitchen where Alistair is hunkering in the shadowed corner. He grabs my wrist and smells my hand, then nods.

"This is the blood that woke me," he confirms. "I've never smelled it before, but if I ever smell it again, I'll recognize it."

I nod and take the opportunity to check out his injured arm. Red and angry, the skin of his forearm is already peeling. "Do you want some ice for that?" I ask, tilting my chin toward the freezer.

Alistair shakes his head, but his scowl smooths out. "I'll be fine. It's starting to heal."

I nod, then check on Celine. She's staring absently out the window; her arms and wings wrapped around herself. Sighing, I give her space to think, digging under her sink until I find the cleaning supplies I need to fix the walls.

When Alistair reaches for a rag, I grunt and pull it out of his reach. "Can you make me some coffee?" I ask, making sure to stay between him and the chemicals. If he gets even a single drop of heavy-duty cleaner in that fucking burn, he'll be in agony. It's not worth the risk.

Alistair frowns, running the fingers of his good hand through his hair. The black strands are messier than I've ever seen them. He watches Celine walk away, frustration flashing through his eyes.

"You can't push too hard," I whisper.

He groans up at the ceiling. "Would you believe me if I told you I was holding back?"

"Yeah, I believe it." My basilisk is hovering beneath the surface, rattling in my chest. Now that Celine is out of sight, it's going to steadily get worse.

By the time she comes back, dressed in ratty sweats, the kitchen smells like coffee. Celine stops in front of Alistair, staring at his burned arm. Her own twitches a few times at her side before she goes up on her tiptoes to kiss him, then disappears into the pantry.

He blinks at me, his face twisted in confusion. I choke on my laugh. No matter what happens, I have to stay on her good side. If we both get booted, there will be no one around to watch her back.

Celine reappears with a gallon of green paint in one hand and a plastic tray and brush in the other. Eyes determined, she follows behind me, silently painting after I clean the red paint off the walls. We cover the runes slowly—they're all the same— matching the ones that glow on her skin when she uses her magic. Between the cleaning products, coffee, and paint fumes, the smell is nauseating.

Alistair breaks the quiet after about half an hour has passed. "Can I stay until dusk?"

Celine's head snaps up, a smudge of green paint on her chin. "Do you think I would kick you to the curb to burn?" I swallow a groan as her wings begin to smoke.

"No?" Alistair doesn't sound convinced, and from the frustration on Celine's face and her glowing wings, she doesn't appreciate that at all. She carefully places the lid back on the paint can, then bashes it closed with her bare fist.

"Damn, baby." I wince. "You should do that with a hammer, not your hand."

"I'm fine," she shouts. "And, Alistair, since it apparently needs to be said, you can stay until dark. I asked you both to stay. I'm not going to murder you because someone is after me. What kind of person do you think I am—or does my character not matter, since I'm fuckable?"

Her wings burst into flames, the ultimate exclamation point to her rampage. Before Alistair can say a word, Celine disappears down the hall. Alistair glares at the ray of sunshine blocking his path, a crazed glint in his eye.

"Nope," I snap, pointing at him with my spray bottle of bleach. "Don't even think about it. She will cool off, and when she does, you can discuss it. Let it ride for now, Ali." The nickname slips out. Neither of us acknowledge it.

"I hate that advice," he hisses. "I need to get to her now!" He stumbles back a step, bracing against the counter, and shakes his head, surprised by his own intensity.

I take a deep breath, regretting it as soon as the bleach hits my nostrils. "Chill out and make me another cup of coffee," I tell him, hoping an occupation will make him less likely to run through a gauntlet of sunbeams.

Alistair snarls. "I'm not your fucking barista."

"The sun says you are, though," I joke. "If you make me another cup without giving me attitude, I'll see about blocking that window so you can go to her."

He stills. "You're holding me hostage."

"No," I correct him. "That big orange star is; I'm just not rushing to help. This is for your own good."

"How?"

"You were fucking everything up." I shrug. "Now sit over there and help me figure out how we're going to keep her safe."

Alistair slams my full mug of coffee on the edge of the counter, then sinks to the floor angrily. Once I'm sure he can't see me, I let myself grin. Because as mad as he is, and as stressed as Celine feels, I'm confident we can fix it.

# TWENTY-FOUR

## CIPRIAN

Dad won't stop calling and demanding results like a drill sergeant. I explain . . . again, then hang up, frustrated that I'm letting him get to me. I'm already kicking myself for pushing too hard at the Naked Fang and destroying the camaraderie I busted ass to build.

Dad is keyed up. With the witch drama going on, he sees betrayal in every corner, including the Fringes.

Callum's return isn't helping. Their tension always spills over and lands on me. Since neither of them will confront their shit with each other, I catch it on both ends. Can't lash out at the person you really want to? No problem. Trash Ciprian instead. The family fuckup won't complain about it; he's too unserious.

Sliding my cap on backward, I glance at the shitty mirror in my apartment. It's giving asshole, but that's for the best. I know what happens when I let people close. Arm's length it is.

My phone vibrates in my pocket, and I groan. If it's Dad again, I'm tossing the damn thing in the toilet. Then I think about Sheena and scramble to unlock the screen. She isn't doing great, and I'll take a million of Dad's lectures before I'll let her down.

Worry churns in my gut as a voice memo pops up. I listen to it, rubbing sunscreen on my forehead and nose as my stomach twists. She sounds awful, but I can tell she's trying to hide it. Wiping the excess sunscreen on my jeans, I type out a response.

CIPRIAN

I'm glad you got a lead. You sound like shit.

Three dots pop up, disappear, then reappear. I grip the sink with my fingers until my knuckles turn white. This whole situation makes me feel helpless.

SHEENA

I know. Callum and Gideon will find something, I'm sure.

I won't give up.

CIPRIAN

No, you fucking won't. You can't ever give up. Promise me, bestie.

Promise.

I need another promise from you while you're at it.

Hit me with it.

I hold my breath, impossibly angry at the gods, magic, all the dead elders, and anyone else I can think of. I'm not equipped for anything but a solution to this problem. Sheena gets me. I can't even entertain the thought of failure . . .

"She'll be fine," I say out loud, assuring myself in the mirror like a total loser, then typing ferociously.

CIPRIAN

If it gets worse, you tell me. You're trying to act okay. I could hear it in your fucking voice. That's fine, but don't do it with me. Give me a chance to not fuck this up.

I hit send and release the breath I'm holding. There's barely anything left to exhale. Like always, I've sucked the good out and left only scraps behind.

SHEENA

Deal.

And for the record, you won't fuck up. Not with me or Celine.

CIPRIAN

Code names, bestie. Gods, you're the opposite of covert.

I snort as she edits her previous text, replacing Celine's name with wings.

SHEENA

Hey, only one of us managed to survive on the run for eight years! I'm twice as covert as you.

The burning fear in my gut slowly cools, and I take a series of deep, shaky breaths. *Strength only. You're the nightmare. Fear is your weapon, not your weakness.*

I finish the stupid affirmation and head to the club. No more tiptoeing around. If I don't get answers or make major progress getting Celine and Luca to trust me tonight, I'm going home to help Sheena—no matter what Dad says.

The energy at the club is off; I sense it as soon I step inside. Wanting to suss things out before I try to talk to anyone, I settle at a booth in the corner and watch.

Luca spots me from the bar, his eyes narrowing, then flitting past me to dart around the club like pinballs in an old arcade. I sit up straighter. He's on edge. His normal smiles for the customers are nowhere in sight, and he barely manages them for the dancers. Something is wrong.

I've been sitting for almost an hour before I catch a glimpse of Celine. She storms out of the back hall and over to Luca, her wings shimmering as if they're made of metal. They talk briefly before she disappears again.

I keep watching.

Alistair appears a few minutes later, wearing long sleeves and a pissed off expression. He saunters over to the bar, but there's a hitch to his normal walk. After a few minutes talking to Luca, he tosses his hands up in the air. They both glance down the dark hallway. *Trouble in paradise?* Alistair is edgy and worked up, but Luca doesn't appear angry with him over it.

Celine reappears, working the floor and tossing Alistair a tense glance. He calls out for her. She walks stiffly to his side. Alistair reaches for her, then drops his hands to his sides. She shakes her head. Dejected, he hangs his. I can't hear them, but their body language says plenty.

Celine continues circulating, oblivious to Alistair's growing frenzy. A caged animal, he starts to pace, drawing more than one curious glance. I shift uncomfortably in my seat. He's losing it. Spiderweb cracks shoot up the sides of his glass a second before it shatters in his hand.

Alistair peers at the mess blankly. Luca darts to his side, his mouth moving as he picks up the shards of glass. No one looks directly at them, but I see a few patrons move further away. They're picking up on the fury and getting out of the line of fire.

The stage spotlight rotates, glancing off them both. It's gone in a flash, but not quickly enough to hide the red of Alistair's eyes. He backs away slowly, then darts from the club so quickly he's barely more than a blur.

Luca's hands fist as he watches him go. Curiosity wars with my concern, and I make a snap decision to follow Alistair. I wait for Luca to go back behind the bar, then send out enough magic to blur the surrounding air. My nightmare demon heritage comes in handy when I want to avoid notice, and something this simple only costs me a fraction of the fear I have stored.

The door slams behind me and I wince. Alistair isn't in sight, but his scent remains. I trail after him, listening carefully and keeping my distance. After about four blocks, I hear his footsteps making angry clacking sounds against the pavement.

When they cut off abruptly, I freeze, listening to the eerie silence until I question my sanity. A grunt, harsh and loud, breaks the quiet. It's followed by the clang of metal. Before I can overthink the decision, I race toward the sound, adrenaline prodding my magic until it hums eagerly inside me.

I careen around the corner, my eyes trying to make sense of the chaos. Three armed men surround Alistair. They're grunting in another language that sounds oddly familiar. Alistair's fear hits me, hot and sticky. That's when I spot the sword sticking out of his side.

This isn't right. Only cowards ambush someone three on one. They'll pay for this. I'll make sure of it—right fucking now.

Latching onto their minds, I throw my magic at them. Like a net, it covers the consciousness of all three, leaving Alistair alone. Gritting my teeth, I drag them into the depths of a nightmare they won't live to wake from.

I replace the dark concrete walls with flames ten feet high.

They scream with terror as they watch each other grow teeth as long as their forearms. It's not real, but they believe it is, and that's all that matters. I smile as they turn on each other. They always do.

They fight each other clumsily. I dart in and snap the nearest one's neck. As he falls, I take his sword and plunge it into the second attacker's heart. The third decides to take his chances with my imaginary flames, but I grab him by his hair and throw him over my knee. His spine gives way. I break his neck, and his screams cut off abruptly.

Alistair falls to his knees, and I drop the nightmare to go to him. His breath is wet and raspy, and there's blood trickling from the corner of his mouth.

"That doesn't look good," I mutter. "Don't die, man."

The sword in his belly is buried deep. I'm scared to touch it. Taking a closer look at the hilt, I notice it's engraved with markings I don't recognize. Fabric shifts behind me, and I turn and see wings shoot from the backs of two of the bodies. Those weren't there when I killed them.

Alistair fumbles with his phone, his fingers slick with blood. The asphalt is soaked with it too, the streetlight revealing the grizzly scene.

"Who can I call?" I ask, my anxiety growing by the second. I might have been too late. He's losing way too much blood, his already pale skin taking on a gray sheen.

I try to put pressure on the wound without removing the weapon. Alistair's mouth falls open, but he can't get any words out. I frown at his fangs, then jolt upright as it clicks. "Blood, you need blood, right?"

His eyes dip closed, and I curse. This is probably stupid, but I can't let him die. I told myself I wouldn't hold back tonight.

Shoving my wrist into his mouth, I pierce my skin on his fangs after he fails to bite down and do it himself. As soon as my blood hits his tongue, his eyes shoot open, the perfect match to the surrounding gore.

"Don't suck me dry," I whisper. "And tell me what to do about this fucking sword when you get a chance."

Alistair growls deep in his throat, then latches on to my wrist. A shudder runs up my spine. It's followed immediately by a zap of arousal so sharp it almost hurts. I swallow the moan that wants to escape, shocked as my battle adrenaline switches to white-hot lust in a heartbeat.

Footsteps echo around the corner as Alistair opens his mouth around my wrist. "Pull the sword out. Now. Keep pressure. More blood."

I nod, gripping the hilt of the weapon with my free hand. "Do you want me to do a countdown or—"

"Yank it out, demon," he snarls.

"What the fuck is going on?"

I ignore Luca's frantic voice and pull with all my strength, removing the sword from Alistair's gut. The sucking sound it makes as it exits his body will stick with me for a long time. It's the worst thing I've ever heard. So bad, actually, I think I'll add it to my nightmare rotation.

Alistair groans, then goes silent. Too silent. I press the tattered remains of his shirt into the wound. My panic spikes as the suction on my wrist slows.

"None of that," I snap. "You've got to suck harder, dude. You're not dying in the damn street after I jumped in to rescue you. Someone has to tell Celine how heroic I was."

"Did you kill all of these—"

"Help or shut up," I hiss at Luca.

"What do you need me to do?" His voice is solid, and it makes me feel a little calmer.

"Put pressure on the wound or take over as his blood bank. I can't do everything."

I bite my lip as another wave of desire swamps me. I don't tell Luca this, but my new fear is that I might come in my pants. I'm going to have a stern talk with my cock later for betraying me this way.

Luca kneels at my side, balling up his flannel shirt and pressing it against Alistair's stomach. It's got to be excruciating, but Alistair barely stirs.

With one hand free, I yank on his hair until his eyes snap open. "You're biting me like a baby," I taunt. "Do better or die— your choice."

Alistair growls, and with his fangs buried in my wrist, the vibration sends a disturbing combination of pain and pleasure ricocheting through my nerve endings. He grabs my forearm and holds it to his mouth, red eyes searching my face. I can't help it; I start panting and moaning like I just booked my first porno.

"Do you have a boner?"

"Why would you think that?" I demand, clinging to my dignity through sheer denial.

Luca chuckles, and the sound makes me shiver. "Because Alistair has his fangs inside you, and I've seen the effect that has on a person."

I gasp, relieved beyond relief, then laugh out loud. "Kinky. He'd get along great with my brother." Luca raises one eyebrow, and I hear myself rambling. "He's an incubus demon. His blood . . . You know what, never mind. I'm oversharing."

"What happened?" Luca asks, dipping his head toward the bodies.

"I left the bar and was walking back to my place when I heard the fight. I don't know what started it, but these three were all over him. I finished them off, but one of them had already stabbed him." All of my practice with partial truths comes in clutch, making me sound the perfect amount of innocent, surprised, and reluctantly heroic.

"Mmm."

I study Luca. His brow is furrowed, and I don't miss the tired but loaded look Alistair gives him. Irritation flares up as I realize they're hiding as much information from me as I'm hiding from them.

"I've never seen this many angels in one place," I say. I've earned the right to do some fishing. "Is Vegas some sort of celestial hot spot?"

"Mmm," Luca hums again noncommittally.

"Cool," I drawl. "I'll shut up and think about how close I am to ruining my favorite pair of jeans."

"Mmm."

"If you say 'mmm' again, I'm going to lose my shit."

"How did you kill them all without getting hurt?" Luca is prying now, not even bothering to hide his nosiness.

I laugh. "That's rich. You get to interrogate me, but won't answer any of my questions? Not happening, you broody asshole. If you're going to act secretive, I am too."

"I'm making conversation," Luca says, peaking under the blood-soaked flannel shirt. "I think it's closing up, Ali."

"Yes. I can tell." Alistair pulls back from my wrist and licks the wound slowly, his eyes darting between me and the discarded sword. "Although, I'm not sure if my prognosis would be favorable if Ciprian hadn't happened along."

"Happy to be of service." I salute him sarcastically, pretending I don't hear him subtly questioning the story of how I found him.

"I'll call in a favor and have someone come get the bodies," Alistair says, wiping his bloody phone screen on his jeans, then scowling at the dead angels.

Luca sighs. "I'm more worried about what we're going to tell Celine." He glances at me and closes his mouth.

"Why would she care?" I snap. "Are all angels related?"

Annoyed by his secrets, I push to my feet, lurching unsteadily into the wall as the world spins sickeningly.

"Woah!" Luca grabs my arm to steady me. "Take it slow, you've lost a lot of blood."

"I'd be fine if some of it would leave my dick and go somewhere useful," I groan.

Alistair chuckles. His smirk is devious as he wipes a drop of my blood from his lips, then sucks it off his finger. "My apologies," he croons.

"I hate to criticize someone who almost died, but I feel like I need to let you know that you don't sound sorry at all," I say, yawning as my knees buckle.

"Okay, that's it." Luca helps me back to the ground. "Sit down before you fall down. I'll go get my car."

"Sounds great." I yawn again, the beginnings of a reckless idea taking shape in my head as Luca jogs away. Letting my head sag, I lean into my exhaustion, focusing on the techniques I used to fall asleep as a kid after a particularly disturbing training session with Dad.

If they have a shred of honor between them, which I suspect they do despite their fringe manners, they won't leave me unconscious in the street. If they decide to kill me, well, I can only hope I come to in time to stop them. Eyes heavy, I drift off, hoping I wake up one step closer to answers.

# TWENTY-FIVE

## CELINE

I roll my fingers over my throbbing temples, an electric current of tension buzzing through me. "I'm not sure I'm hearing this right," I say.

"That's because it's fucking messy." Luca shakes his head. "Your brain is trying to reject the reality out of self-preservation."

I smack his chest, but my heart isn't in it. Not when it's way too busy beating like a drum, every instinct demanding I step up and protect them both. *This isn't the same as before. You're not helpless anymore.*

When Luca stumbled into the Fang, missing his overshirt and streaked with blood, I wanted to strip him and check every inch of his body for injuries. After he told me what happened, the guilt almost crushed me.

I need to talk to Alistair and make things right. He's in the line of fire—exactly as I feared—and it almost cost him his life. And now Ciprian is somehow involved, lying like wilted lettuce on Alistair's black leather couch, his mouth hanging open.

Luca points at the unconscious demon. "I know it's not ideal, but he saved Alistair's life. I couldn't leave him."

I groan and pace another lap around the unfamiliar room, careful not to let my wings hit the furniture. "I get that, but why are we here and not my place?"

"He doesn't belong at your place," he says, tossing his arms up. "And Alistair said it was fine to bring him here, something about wards."

I sigh, my nerves fried. "I noticed them when I came in. Like an ice bath."

"I hope it wasn't too uncomfortable for you, angel." Alistair walks in, his normally fluid walk slow and jerky.

"Are you okay?" I demand, cringing when my tone makes the question sound less concerned and more like an interrogation.

Alistair stops in front of me, the corner of his lips curling. "Nothing eight hours of rest won't fix. I'll be right as rain before you know it."

After a slight hesitation, he dips his head and kisses me. I sag with relief. He's here. He's safe. He's standing in front of me. Alistair deepens the kiss, his tongue tracing my lips, then dancing with mine. There's a raw edge to the kiss. I wrap my arms around his neck, trying my best to assure us both that he's alive.

We argued again earlier. He wanted to stay over after my shift, but my place isn't vampire-proofed yet. I need to order more blackout curtains for the living room. When he pushed for Luca to stay instead, I realized it wasn't about wanting to spend time with me at all. He wanted to assign me a babysitter. I told him to forget it. Alistair and Luca are the kind of guys who will take over if they aren't given limits—but him leaving the club upset and distracted? That's on me.

Alistair moans, and I jerk as I realize it's from pain and not pleasure. "Shit, be careful," I snap, pulling back, then wincing at my tone.

"You're cute when you're worried." He smiles widely, his fangs visible.

Luca chuckles. His laughter cuts off abruptly when he looks back at Ciprian.

"What the hell did you do to him, anyway?" I ask, shaking my head as a light snore escapes his mouth. "He has no sense of self-preservation."

"I'm not so sure about that." Alistair settles carefully in an armchair, his features tight with pain. "Before the blood loss made everything fuzzy . . . Ciprian showed up. All three of the angels freaked out, and he cut them down one by one, as if it was the simplest thing in the world."

I study Ciprian, confused by Alistair's description. It doesn't match what I'm seeing. With his platinum-blond hair falling over his eyes and his face slack with sleep, he doesn't look like a ruthless killer. He looks . . . fuck me, he looks adorable.

"We don't know what kind of demon he is, do we?" I turn to Alistair for confirmation, and he shakes his head. With a network of informants at his disposal, he's far more likely to know people's secrets than Luca or I.

"He's powerful," Alistair murmurs. "Beyond that, I can't say."

Luca lifts his head, his eyes widening. "After Ciprian found the angel outside the club, that regular walked by us and didn't glance over once."

"Are there any rumors of demons who can turn invisible?" I ask.

"Yes, although I've never seen one," Alistair says, then drops his head back against the chair. "But how would I know if I had?"

"Even if he can become invisible, that doesn't explain why we weren't noticed either," Luca says.

"It doesn't add up." I frown at Alistair. "And he offered a vein when you needed it?" In my experience, no one in the Fringes does something for nothing, especially if it involves making themselves weaker. Ciprian must have an angle.

"He did want to make sure you heard about his heroics."

My mouth drops open as I look between Alistair and Luca with disbelief. They both burst out laughing, and I roll my eyes. Ciprian stirs on the couch, but instead of waking up, he rolls over on his side, nuzzling his face against the pillow.

"Unbelievable," I mutter.

On the coffee table, his cellphone vibrates, but he doesn't wake up.

"That thing has been going off nonstop," Luca says. "It's four o'clock in the morning."

"Booty call?" Alistair asks.

I pick it up, but Ciprian must have some common sense because the phone is locked. It doesn't even show a preview of the missed messages.

"Could be a girlfriend," I say.

"With the way he's been all over you and Luca, I doubt it's a girlfriend," Alistair teases.

Luca glances away, but not before I notice the blush crawling up his cheeks.

I put the phone down and scoff. "That rarely stops anyone from walking into the club."

"That's true," Alistair agrees. "But I don't get that impression from him. It's hard to explain, but I trust my sense of people, and he doesn't strike me as disloyal."

"That's so sweet."

In sync, we whip our heads toward the couch, where Ciprian is grinning, one black eye cracked open like a bat avoiding a porch light. "For the record, I'm not . . . disloyal, that is."

"You wouldn't advertise it if you were," I point out.

"True." He smirks. "You look ravishing by the way."

"Please." I shake my head. "Your eyes are half-closed."

"I know, and I'm still amazed. Congratulations." He lifts his head and surveys his surroundings. "Cool apartment. Where are we?"

"My lair," Alistair says drily. "I brought you back here in case I get thirsty."

"That's fine, but only if someone lends a helping hand while you're latched." Ciprian laughs, then turns a smoldering leer my way. "I was a hero tonight. Did anyone mention it?"

Despite myself, I laugh—the sharp edges of my wings reverting to feathers, something I've been unable to make them do since hearing about Alistair's attack. My laugh cuts off abruptly and I look at Ciprian with new eyes. He's disarming, and it's so subtle I barely noticed it.

"A knight in shining armor," I drawl, then wink at Alistair. "Protecting his damsel in distress."

"Watch it," Alistair growls. It reminds me of how he sounded last night in my bed, and a shiver of pure sexual energy runs through me. *Pull yourself together.*

"And I didn't even get a kiss for it." Ciprian sighs dramatically. "Only a wicked case of blue balls to pair with acute anemia."

"Would you rather I made it hurt?" Alistair's low purr is too much. I shift my weight and glance away, noticing both Luca and Ciprian are affected by the obvious innuendo.

"Ask me after my platelets return to normal." Ciprian cranes his neck to focus on Luca. "Thanks for not leaving me in the street. What happened to the . . . mess?"

"Alistair's contact took care of it," Luca says. "I loaded you both in the car before he got there. No one knows you're involved. You won't have to worry about getting in trouble with the enclave."

I snort. "Like the enclave would bother sending someone here."

Ciprian laughs out loud, the sound almost manic. He's either out of it or trying to suck up to me, because my sarcasm wasn't that funny. Sinking onto the arm of Alistair's chair, I roll my eyes internally. Guys will laugh at anything if they think it will get them laid.

"Where are my manners?" Alistair murmurs, pushing to his feet. "I have guests. Let me prepare some food."

"Sit down," Luca scoffs.

"Yeah," Ciprian drags the word out. "I don't want to bring up bad memories, but I fully saw your guts, like—what time is it right now?"

"Almost five," I tell him.

"Two hours ago." Ciprian sits up, wobbling slightly, then leans back against the couch. "I'm kind of amazed you're alive."

Alistair lifts his chin defiantly. "It will take more than a sword to kill me."

"Well fuck," Ciprian gasps. "If you're going to tempt fate, you could at least keep your voice down. Next time she might send a flamethrower."

"It's time for bed," I say, shaking my head as three sets of eyes snap to me. I shiver. Teamed up, they're a lot to handle.

Alistair swallows. "Let me get you something more comfortable to wear, angel."

"I can go home," I argue. "You're not in any position to—"

"No," Alistair snaps, then clears his throat. "I mean, it's no trouble at all, love."

He hobbles out of sight, and I look at Luca. Standing behind the couch, he's staring at the back of Ciprian's head as if he'll uncover a crazy conspiracy if he keeps at it long enough. Luca only breaks the stare to silently gesture between the two of us, raising his eyebrows in an obvious question. *Godsdammit.* I haven't considered whether I want to publicly reveal . . . whatever this is. He's giving me the choice, but I need time to think. I try to communicate that with my eyes, and Luca nods.

"I can step out if you two need to talk," Ciprian says drily. "Unless Alistair was serious about me being a prisoner."

"No . . . We're not—it's fine," I sputter, surprised he caught on.

"I'm familiar with watching others have unspoken conversations." Ciprian shrugs, his voice oddly resigned. "Many bonds go deeper than words."

"That reminds me," Luca says. "Your phone has been buzzing nonstop."

With a sense of urgency I've never seen from him before, Ciprian shoots forward, unlocking his phone frantically, a deep line carved in his forehead. It gradually dissolves as he reads his messages.

"Is everything okay?" I ask, taking a step toward him instinctively. I'm unnerved by how much it bothers me to see him unsettled.

"Yeah." He tosses me a smile that doesn't reach his eyes. "A friend of mine is struggling. For a moment there, I thought . . . You know what, it doesn't matter. I'm fine. Should I take the couch?"

He doesn't look fine. I don't point that out. Ciprian saved Alistair, and he's hot, but I'm not about to poke into his business. Mainly because I don't want him poking into mine.

"That's fine," I say, realizing with a start that as long as I'm playing the role of Alistair's girlfriend, I should act more comfortable in his home. Pretending a confidence I don't feel, I walk into the attached kitchen and open the refrigerator.

Reaching around the bags of blood on the middle shelf and a box of wilting spinach, I grab a pitcher of water from the back. If Alistair isn't completely hopeless at organization, the glasses will be—there. My shoulders dip with relief as I find a random assortment of cups shoved haphazardly inside the first cabinet I open.

I pour two glasses of water, take a sip, then walk back into the living room. "Here." I press the second glass into Ciprian's hand.

He thanks me without looking up from his phone. I know he said his friend was struggling, but the girlfriend theory feels more likely, despite Alistair's gut instinct about Ciprian's loyalty. Most people are incredibly good at justifying bad behavior. We have no reason to believe this demon is any different.

Alistair shuffles back into the room, a blanket in one hand and a question in his eyes as he glances between me and Luca. I subtly shake my head.

"Luca, you can take the spare room," he says out loud. "I use it mainly as an office, but there's a daybed."

"Good with me." Luca wanders down the hall like he's been here a million times, and I feel a pinch of guilt for sending him away.

"I'm going to order some pizzas," Alistair says, raising his voice so Luca will be able to hear him.

"Sounds good," Luca calls out, his voice muffled by the sound of running water.

"Any topping requests?"

"You know what I like," I say, my lips quirking up because he actually has no idea. This will be a fun test to find out what my fake boyfriend-slash-friend-with-benefits thinks I like.

"Meat," Luca shouts.

"Same. I need to replace all the iron I let you borrow," Ciprian jokes, but his tone is too bland for it to land correctly. Whatever is on his phone is bothering him, and he's not trying to hide that from us. *How strange.*

"I left clothes on the bed for you, angel." Alistair kisses my cheek then dials a number on his phone.

I nod and head down the hall, grabbing the T-shirt and boxers off the bed. After a quick glance toward the living room to make sure no one is watching, I duck into the bathroom and close the door behind me.

Luca is shirtless, washing his face in the sink. Water trickles down his sharp cheekbones, leaving his dark eyelashes spiky. Silently, I explore the muscles of his back, my fingernails tracing a path between his shoulder blades.

I hear his sharp intake of breath before he spins and lifts me. My legs wrap around his waist, and our lips meet in a chaotic crash. "Sorry about the spare room," I whisper.

"Don't be," he mutters. "It was the safe play. Kiss me, baby."

The pet name sounds as good today as it did last night, but the surge of fear after the initial spike of pleasure ruins the effect. Luca is too important. My father will take him from me. If he knows I have something good going, there's no chance he'll rest until I lose it.

I cling to Luca as the panic sinks its teeth in. If he can sense it, he doesn't say anything, holding me tight as his lips move against mine.

"We'll figure it out," he says, pulling back and pressing his forehead against mine. "Trust me. Please."

"I do, but—"

"No buts," Luca insists. "As long as we trust each other, we've got this."

I want to believe him. Badly. But the reality is my father is dangerous. Alistair knows that firsthand. Sending those angels to kill me is Dad's way of testing the waters. He's starting small and hoping to get lucky. I still can't figure out how he found me, though.

"If only Ciprian had left one alive to question," I say.

"The whole street was a mess. I bet he didn't have time to consider that."

Luca sighs, and I kiss the corner of his mouth and slide my

legs down until my feet are planted on the tile. "He's a mystery to me," I admit. "I can't figure him out."

"You don't think he's involved, do you?"

"With my father?" He nods, and I raise my eyebrows, consider the idea for a heartbeat, then shake my head. "No way. There's no reality where Dad even talks to a demon."

"Sounds like a stand-up guy."

There's a question in that statement. A warning that I'm going to have to tell Luca everything eventually if I want to keep him. The idea is about as appealing as dancing over broken glass barefoot. I walled my past off a long time ago—for good reason. Digging it out again will be excruciating. Thankfully, I don't have to do it while hiding in Alistair's bathroom as Ciprian lounges on the couch.

"Pizza is here," Alistair calls out.

I grunt, sliding out of the clothes I left the club wearing, and step into the boxer briefs Alistair set out for me. I lift my head as Luca chuckles. "He's surprisingly soft for a vampire with his reputation."

When I look down, I see what he's talking about and melt. The T-shirt and boxers are soft and comfortable, but he's referencing the holes in the back of the shirt for my wings. Holes Alistair had to have just cut for me while recovering from an angel attack.

I pull the shirt over my head. Luca helps me adjust the material over my wings. By the time I leave the bathroom, my heart is racing.

These softer emotions put us all at risk. If I lose focus, someone could get hurt again. The weight of that settles heavily on my shoulders. I may not be alone right now, but that could change at any point. Mom's face flickers through my mind against my will, and my wings sharpen before I can wall off the pain.

That's all the warning I need.

# TWENTY-SIX

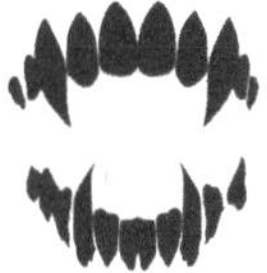



## ALISTAIR

The bumps on the ceiling resemble the surface of a distant planet, billions of light-years away for humans or one mega-expensive portal rental for me. I try to imagine how life would be there, then catch my breath until the pain in my gut passes. It's a cheap popcorn ceiling. No amount of imagination can change that.

I close my eyes, desperate for rest, but without the distraction of the bumps, the pain only gets worse. I haven't hurt this badly since I was newly turned, picking fights with supernaturals who had far more magic, strength, and common sense than I did at the time. Luckily, I survived those fights, and I'll survive this one too.

Lying in my bed with Celine's hair draped across my spare pillow, I remember the fiery burn of the sword piercing my gut. That was followed by the creeping coldness that encased my whole body as my blood spilled on the ground.

My memory of the ambush is hazy. No matter how hard I

concentrate, it's like trying to get a good look at something sunk beneath several feet of water. The edges aren't sharp, and the sounds are warbly and inconsistent—some faint, some loud enough to hurt my ears.

All I can recall with perfect clarity is the certainty that I was going to die. My thirty-second year would be my last. Within moments of the ambush, I had accepted it. The blood loss was too severe, even for me. I needed a miracle; I got a demon instead.

Ciprian saved my life and put his own at risk in the process, and I cannot figure out why. It's maddening, nearly as maddening as how close my own carelessness came to causing my death.

I wonder if meeting my end by a stranger's sword is something Mum would consider a natural cause. Not for a human, certainly, but murder is one of the most common ways a vampire dies. Perhaps if I get bored enough, I'll ask her.

The attack made one thing perfectly clear: my obsession with Celine is dangerous. She awakens every monstrous instinct I've managed to keep silenced for years. A beam of sun on my skin, I long for her even as she burns me to ash. Even if I don't survive her, I want her to be mine. I want that more than I've ever wanted anything.

Celine wears her strength like armor, but there are cracks. Moments of vulnerability. Spending time with her has shown them to me, turning what started as fascination into something more. Fixation, maybe. Possession, certainly.

Hot blood churns behind my eyes as I watch her sleep at my side, the curve of her cheeks, the way her fuller bottom lip hangs slightly open. There's no denying she's beautiful, but the groove between her arched brows is proof she's not fully at ease.

Celine would be more comfortable if Luca and I turned our backs on her.

I hate that.

My nostrils flare and my vision tunnels as I imagine leaving her to face the assassins alone. *Calm down,* I tell myself. *She's safe. She's right here in your bed.* Somehow, that makes it worse. My throat dries out, burning with rage and the unmistakable desire to drain her enemies dry. I'll kill them all. Tear their throats wide open.

In her sleep, Celine reaches for me. I clasp her hand gently in mine, careful not to wake her, and press a barely there kiss to her knuckles. My rage goes from a roaring inferno to banked embers. I blink, startled by the emotional whiplash. Why am I having this reaction?

My belly spasms as something knits back together. Gritting my teeth, I close my eyes and wait for the agony to pass. Thanks to Ciprian's blood, I'll be back to full strength soon. No scars, no lingering issues—only a vivid memory of pain. I'll carry that with me forever.

With Celine's hand clasped loosely in mine, I coax my brain to turn off, reminding it that we're in my sunproof apartment, a space protected by as much magic as money can buy. It doesn't work. I try logic next, then threats.

I'm unable to sleep until my plan to convince Celine to allow me to protect her is complete. It can't wait. My best chance is now —while her eyes soften when she thinks of my injury, and the cracks in her armor are shaped like me.

I feel no guilt for leveraging her emotions to get my way. Life on the Fringes has taught me the value of utilizing my resources, no matter how insignificant, and I never forget a lesson learned.

---

"Has anyone ever studied the cognitive effects of blood loss on vampires?" Celine tilts her head; her cheek creased from my pillow.

I smile through my pain. "I'll get right on that, angel, as soon as you agree to stay here."

My apartment is cool and dark, as always, but it's also teeming with unfamiliar sounds. A spring shifts on the couch as Ciprian rolls over, the steady puff of Luca's breathing across the hall. If I listen hard enough, I can even make out the sounds of three steadily beating hearts, disrupting the aching quiet of my normally empty home.

"I heard you the first time, Alistair." Celine's hand balls into a fist between us. "The answer is still no."

I sigh, a groan catching in my throat as I roll onto my back and the ruptured muscles in my belly protest. "Luca lives alone?"

"Yeah, why?" Celine's tone is laced with suspicion.

"No reason," I say innocently. "I'm wondering what would have happened to him if those angels had broken into his place instead of attacking me in the street."

It's not a nice thing to say, but desperate times call for desperate measures. I want to spend time visiting her bed, not her headstone.

Celine sucks in a breath, the skin around her eyes tightening. "You might remember I already raised this concern and provided a solution. You both told me to fuck off."

"The situation has changed," I admit.

"My offer stands." Celine shifts, retreating from me physically by an inch or two. It's the distance in her eyes that hurts as much as the sword in my belly. *You prepared for this, Alistair.*

"We can break up later today," she continues. "Plenty of people will be around at the club to see."

I keep my face blank, refusing to show how her words sting. She's being logical, even selfless in a way. It's not what I want. Like the air that fills her lungs or her precious motorcycle, I want to be something Celine can't live without.

"That remains the worst choice," I say bluntly. "We need to

pivot, adapt—make changes that keep us all safe. Strategize with me, Celine. Use your resources."

"You aren't a resource, Alistair." She bites the words out through clenched teeth, her hushed tone furious. "I don't know why we're discussing this. You were run through because of me. You should be running for the hills."

"I'm not up for running yet," I tease. Rolling onto my side, I reach for her, brushing my fingertips over her cheek. "But I wouldn't even if I could. Move in with me. Please."

"Surely you want your space," she tries, nibbling on her bottom lip. There's a gleam in her brown eyes. I lean closer, jealous of whatever inspired that expression.

"My space is infinitely preferable with you in it."

"I'll agree on two conditions: one, you move in with me; two, Luca also has to agree."

Victory rolls over me, frenzied and delicious. I can barely hide my delight. If she thinks Luca won't jump on this, she's lost her mind. He's going to be thrilled. The very idea that he would refuse is laughable.

I lace her fingers with mine, running my thumb over the back of her hand lazily. The tingling, aching discomfort behind my abs helps to obscure my eagerness, and I'm grateful for pain for the first time in eight hours.

"I'll sunproof today and bring in a bed for my spare room," she says.

I frown, and Celine rolls her eyes. "We need space, Alistair. There's safety in numbers, but the reality is we're all used to living alone and having things a certain way. If someone needs to cool off, I want them to be able to without being on top of each other."

I grunt, seeing the wisdom in her plan, but not loving it. On top of each other is exactly where I want to be.

"I'm going to invite Ciprian too," she says.

My frown grows.

"He killed three angels last night," she reminds me. "If my dad was watching, Ciprian could be a target now too."

I groan and bury my face in the pillow. "But they're all dead; there's no one left to—shit, the blood." In the chaos, my brain forgot something my body didn't.

"What?" Celine's voice is taut. "Tell me about the blood, Alistair."

I'm reluctant to share this detail, but keeping anything from her will erode the trust we've built. I sigh and say, "The blood of the angel on your windowsill didn't belong to any of the three who attacked me last night. Someone else is here . . ."

"And until we find them, I'm up to my wings in bossy supernatural men."

"Exactly how you like it," I joke.

Celine swats me, but her touch is unusually gentle, as if I'm made of glass. I dislike it. Rolling, I hover above her, supporting my weight with my arms. There's an aching tug in my gut, but other than that I feel fine. Another sign that Ciprian is powerful.

"You'll hurt yourself," Celine scolds, her hands grazing my skin gingerly.

"Worth it." I kiss her neck, loving how she cants her head to the side to give me better access. "You're delicious." I sigh against her throat, the warmth of her skin banishing the lingering chill from the ambush.

"No super speed," Celine orders. "In fact . . ."

She grabs me, maneuvering me onto my back until our positions are reversed—her thighs spread wide to accommodate my hips.

Annoyed, I frown.

"What's wrong?"

"Nothing."

"What?" Celine hisses. "Did I hurt you?"

"No, I . . . You'll have to do all the work on top," I complain.

Her lips twitch. "You can do all the work next time," she promises. "Today, you'll have to grin and bear it."

I nod, stifling a moan as she grinds on me. Luca and Ciprian are steps away. This apartment may be as dark as a coffin, but it's far from soundproof.

"You'll have to be quiet," I purr, grinning as her heart rate picks up. "If you were to scream, for example, they would come running."

Celine kicks her borrowed boxer briefs off, then hovers above me, wearing nothing but my T-shirt and a devious smile. "Oh, I can be quiet. The question is, can you?"

"I'll do my best, angel. No promises."

Celine pulls my shirt over my head, tossing it to the floor. Her gaze falls to my belly, a deep notch digging into the space between her eyes. My new skin is pink and angry, the edges jagged. She traces what's left of the wound with the pads of her fingers. I shudder.

"Are you really okay?" she asks. "No bullshit, Ali. I won't tell."

The nickname slips from her mouth, and my vampiric nature takes notice. It's a basic thing, but I feel claimed by the familiarity. By her concern for me too. I want all of her.

"I'm okay, Celine. I swear it." Desperate to shut my own mouth before it can ruin everything, I kiss her hard, then scrape my fangs across the graceful curve of her neck. My bite mark is fully healed, and I want to put it back. I've never drunk from a lover. Until her. Now, it's all I can think about.

"I was scared last night," Celine whispers. She runs her fingers over my stomach, my chest, and my shoulders—planting kisses of her own with lips softer than mine will ever be.

Suddenly, I'm hyperaware of my own beating heart and every place she's touching me. The admission couldn't have been easy for her. Fear is a weakness; it's a crack in her armor. Blood pumping, I dive in headfirst before she can shore it up.

"I was too," I admit, burying my hands in her tangled hair and rewarding her vulnerability with my own, even though it galls me to admit to the weakness. "I was freezing. I thought, *this is it*. I wasn't strong enough. Then Ciprian appeared. I could barely believe it."

Tears well up in Celine's eyes, and her wings droop around us until the tips graze the bedspread. "I'm sorry," she says.

"You have nothing to apologize for, angel."

I reach for the hem of the shirt I cut up for her, and she grabs my wrist. "I want to keep it on," she says, looking at the faded fabric. "Let me ride you while I wear nothing but the shirt you gave me."

"Gods," I sputter the word like a prayer, fangs throbbing as lust of all kinds short-circuits my nervous system. Celine is a vision in my shirt. I want her as I've never wanted anything, and now that I've tasted her, I fear no one else will compare.

Kicking my underwear off, I wall off the pain and slide my hands under the shirt to touch her. Her breasts are perfect in my hands, soft and warm. I roll her nipples between my fingers, pinching lightly.

"Show me what you like," I beg, desperate to please her.

Celine brings her hands up, guiding my fingers. She starts with light, teasing touches, then forces my fingers together, arching silently as she directs me to pinch her nipple harder than I would have dared on my own. Soft then hard. She's a study in contradictions.

My cock stands up, aching for relief. It can wait. I don't want this to end. Hard. Soft. I continue touching her, watching her face go slack with pleasure.

Abruptly, Celine yanks my right hand down her body, making brief detours on the sensitive skin of her stomach and the curve of her inner thigh. She stops me inches from my destination.

"Are you wet for me, angel?" I ask, so wrapped up in her, I barely remember to keep my voice down.

"Find out," she taunts, rocking confidently back on her heels until my T-shirt barely rakes the top of her thighs.

I trace the line of muscle up her leg, then explore the inner crease of her thigh. She trembles at my touch. With my eyes locked on her face, I dip the tip of my finger inside her, then retreat. "Show me," I repeat.

Celine's hand joins mine without hesitation. Straddling me here on my bed in my faded shirt, she isn't angry or untouchable. She's mine.

As if she can sense my hunger for her, Celine guides two of my fingers inside her pussy, then drags her index finger up to her clit. She uses her other hand to pull the hem of the shirt up just enough so I can watch.

"I want you to push me," she says, a hitch in her voice that I want to devour. "Almost more than I can handle."

"What about a stretch?" I ask, teasing her wet entrance with a third finger.

She nods, her chin dropping as I work all three fingers in. "That's good." She pants, increasing the pressure and speed of her finger on her clit as I stuff her full.

"What if I do this?" I curl my fingers until I feel the rougher textured spot inside her, then tap it insistently. Celine stiffens, gasps, then rubs herself harder.

"T-that's great, Ali. Don't stop."

"Never," I swear, committing the exact rhythm, angle, and depth to memory. I won't deviate from it until she comes. If the angel assassins rose from the dead and burst through the door, I don't think I could stop.

"Remember to be quiet," I whisper, "so they don't know you're riding my fingers while your tight pussy begs for more."

Celine's mouth drops open in a silent cry, and her inner

muscles spasm. Without letting her come down, I replace my fingers with my cock, shuddering as she rides me through the aftershocks.

"Yes," she hisses, the word drawn out.

I hold still even though I'm desperate to ram into her like a mindless animal. She rolls her hips, finding the perfect rhythm in no time, and I shudder. When she smiles at me, the expression is unlike any I've ever seen on her face before. It's completely unguarded. I don't know how long it will last, but for now, I'm behind her wall.

That dangerous possessiveness sinks its claws into my chest. My throat burns as if I'm gargling gasoline. The idea of claiming her forever snaps the final fraying thread of my control.

"May I?" I gasp, running my thumb over her throat, my fangs throbbing.

"Bite me," she says, bending over to press her pulse to my lips.

Heart racing, I slide my fangs in deep, pushing past skin and muscle. The second her blood hits my tongue, I groan with relief. I drink from her neck, breathless, my whole body throbbing with desire.

Celine clenches around me, panting and rewarding me with desperate mews. She brings both hands to my hair and pulls hard. I feel the sting even as her blood quenches my thirst.

My hand crawls to the back of her neck to hold her close. Her rough, unspoken demand settles the predator I keep hidden. Celine is strong, someone I can trust to keep us safe when I'm too tired to carry on alone.

"You're perfect," I whisper, taking one last drag from her vein, then pulling my fangs free. I lick the puncture wounds closed and meet her eyes. Her pupils dilate, and Celine comes again, her chest trembling against mine as she contracts around my cock.

Helpless to resist, I follow her over the edge.

Celine collapses against me, and I stroke her hair absently, ignoring the painful pull in my gut. I can smell myself on her skin, and I like it. Once our position sinks in, she stiffens. "Oh shit! I'm crushing you."

She tries to lift herself, but I tighten my arms. "A moment more, angel."

Celine stops struggling and lifts her head to meet my eyes. "Fine, but if you end up with internal bleeding, that's on you."

"Shhh." I kiss her temple.

She relaxes, but it doesn't last. As soon as her heart rate begins to speed up, I let my hands fall away from her and change my face back to its typical, bored mask.

We dress in silence, but my brain is hard at work. This pull toward her—the acute bloodlust—it isn't normal, and I think we both sense that.

If she decides to cut me off, will I be able to control myself? The question leaves me feeling even colder than last night's attack.

# TWENTY-SEVEN

## CELINE

Alarms blare, red lights flashing in every corner of my mind.

It's dangerous—feeling Alistair's skin against mine and knowing my blood is helping him heal. It makes me believe we have a chance; that I've grown strong enough to protect them. My hands shake. I ball them at my sides. I couldn't keep her safe, so what makes me think I'll have any better luck with Alistair or Luca?

Memories try to escape from the orderly boxes I've sorted them into; the locked chest clearly labeled *do not open* rattles wildly. Did she feel something similar before he lost interest in charming her and revealed the monster behind the mask? Furious with the misbehaving memories and myself, I shove the chest back in the dusty corner of my subconscious where it belongs. *I am strong enough.*

But I prefer monsters without masks. No pretense—at least they're honest about what they are. Alistair, with his deadly fangs and lethal speed, should fit into that category . . . except he holds me like I'm precious.

The tenderness in his blue eyes is far scarier than the carnal hunger in them when they're red. The bedroom walls close in more each time he glances at me.

I should back out before I'm in too deep, but . . . I need to protect him. Getting him to agree to stay with me was easier than I expected. All it took was a little resistance on my part, and then I had him. He even thinks it was his idea.

As long as Luca agrees, I'll have home advantage in what comes next. Ciprian is an unexpected complication.

"Do me a favor, angel," Alistair says, draping his arm loosely over my shoulder as we leave the bedroom. "And help me sort this assassin problem quickly. I have business I need to attend to out of state."

Frowning, I shrug his arm off. The bored drawl. Muttering about business. It's such a departure from the clingy way he held me in bed. Maybe I'm not the only one playing games. The question is, what does he hope to win?

"You can go if you need to," I say, matching his blasé tone. "I'm sure Luca is more than capable of helping me find the last angel."

Alistair smiles and nods, his fangs glinting in the dim hallway. The window shades in his apartment are so solid, there's no way of knowing that it's noon in Nevada without checking a clock first. He flips the light switch in the living room, and I blink at the sudden blinding light.

Ciprian sits bolt upright, black eyes flashing dangerously. "A warning would be nice," he growls, massaging his temples. "Fuck. My head is killing me."

"I took a lot of blood." Alistair winces. "Make sure to eat plenty of iron today."

Ciprian runs his fingers through his messy blond hair, but it doesn't help much. The top of his head is a haystack after his night on the couch.

"A steak or five coming right up," he says, yawning. "But before that, I have an intensely personal question for you." Ciprian levels Alistair with a penetrating stare, eyes narrowed, brow furrowed. Tension crawls through my veins. Personal questions are against the rules around here, especially in front of others.

Alistair rolls his shoulders back and stretches to his full height. "What?"

"Do vampires drink coffee or go straight for the vein every time?"

My unease disappears like mist in the wind. When I glance at Alistair's slack jaw, I lose what's left of my composure and giggle, only cutting the sound off when I realize how ridiculous it is to be laughing.

Alistair shakes his head, the corner of his mouth turning up. "I'll put a pot on."

"Consider your life debt paid then," Ciprian says. "Because if I don't get my caffeine fix soon, I'll be dead."

"Demonic weakness?" Alistair teases.

"For this demon, absolutely."

"Bathroom's down the hall." Alistair points as he heads for the kitchen. "In case you have any other demonic weaknesses you need to take care of."

"Demons do pee. That's correct." Ciprian stands up and stretches, his shirt pulling up to reveal a chiseled slice of stomach. "But we never poop, Celine. If anyone claims otherwise, let me know and I'll take care of them, because they're a liar."

I close my mouth to abort the laugh before it can escape. "I'll keep that in mind," I assure him as he heads toward the bathroom. "After you're done in there, though, I do have something I need to tell you."

Ciprian looks over his shoulder at me, eyes sparkling. "What a tease. I'll hurry back." He disappears down the hall, whistling cheerfully under his breath.

"Have you decided what to say to him yet?" Alistair asks.

I shrug. "The bare minimum."

"Understood." He bustles around the kitchen, and before long the smell of coffee fills the apartment. Like magic, Luca appears, his nose tilted toward the smell. Without a word to me or Alistair, he digs through the cabinets, banging the doors closed one after the other until he finds the mugs.

"Make yourself at home," Alistair drawls.

Luca grunts, then holds his borrowed mug out insistently.

"You aren't the only coffee addict here," Alistair tells him, holding the full pot out of Luca's reach.

"Cool." Luca snatches the pot from him with a snakelike strike and begins to fill his mug. "Celine?"

"Can I have a sip of yours?" I ask, keeping my tone light.

Luca looks at me, his face twisting into an expression of abject horror. "I-I mean, sure—"

"Gods, don't panic." I shake my head, not bothering to hide my grin. "Of course I want my own. Although I'm starting to wonder if you have a problem."

Another grunt is all I get in response.

"It's only a problem if you stop giving him coffee," Ciprian quips as he rejoins us, the ends of his hair damp. Even soaking wet, the strands are only a couple of shades darker than usual, candied caramel instead of icy blond.

To my surprise, Luca retrieves another mug from the cabinet without complaint and fills it up, putting it on the counter in front of Ciprian.

Shaking my head, I tug the fridge open, grateful to see creamer hiding in the back behind the bagged blood. I'm not sure how anyone can drink coffee black. If I wanted to consume liquid despair, I would go back to the celestial realm and sip on my own endless supply of tears.

The room is silent as we drink our coffee, but it's surprisingly comfortable. Especially considering the fact that we don't actually know each other all that well, except for Luca and me.

"You're edging the hell out of me with this wait, babe," Ciprian says to me, his lips curling. "I'm kind of into it, but do us both a favor and put me out of my misery."

"Are you sure?" I run my finger over the rim of my mug, dropping my tone to a husky rasp. "I'm happy to let the anticipation keep building."

I'm not sure what possessed me to say that, but his jokes make me want to join in. Some part of me wants to make him laugh when he least expects it for a change.

Ciprian groans and closes his eyes. Alistair shakes his head, but I'm pretty sure he's more amused than annoyed. Luca doesn't even bother to look up from his mug.

I clear my throat. "There's no sugarcoating it, so I won't bother. Helping Alistair last night put you at risk. They might come after you next."

Ciprian's face shows no visible reaction to my words. "I killed them all," he reminds me. "Unless there's a hell of a necromancer around, I don't see how they plan to come after me."

"There's another player," I admit, having expected this exact response. "Someone else is working with them who didn't join the ambush."

"How do you know that?" Ciprian asks, his brow furrowing.

I cross my arms over my chest, careful not to spill my coffee. "I just do."

"What exactly do you want me to do with this ridiculously

vague information? Scream bloody murder every time I see wings?"

"I'm trying to warn you," I say. "There's no need to be a jackass about it. I can tell you with complete certainty that the person behind this attack won't give up. This is a courtesy heads up, and I'm only issuing it to you at all because you put yourself at risk to save Alistair."

"Let me get this straight. A bunch of angels are hunting your boyfriend and—" Ciprian cuts himself off, narrows his eyes at me, then snaps his fingers. "Oh, I see. They aren't after the sexy vampire at all, are they? The angels are here for you."

"That's none of your business." My fingers clench around the mug.

"Like fuck it isn't," Ciprian argues. "Anything involving my life and sudden death is certainly my business."

"If you would let me finish," I say, seething at his snarky attitude, "I was going to offer to let you stay with me a few days, until all this shit settles down."

Ciprian freezes, and his mouth drops open until he's gaping at me.

"This offer is contingent on you keeping quiet and staying out of my way," I add. "And you've got about thirty seconds to make your decision, because I'm already starting to regret it."

Luca looks at me with a frown.

"You're obviously invited too," I say to him, kicking myself for not finding a way to tell him first. "Except you don't have to keep quiet or stay out of my way."

"You're going to let us shack up with your girlfriend?" Ciprian turns his attention to Alistair and voices what may be the stupidest, most irrelevant question I've ever heard. I barely hold back a snarl.

"Don't forget you'll be shacking up with me as well," Alistair drawls.

"We'll need blackout curtains," Luca mutters. He ambles back to the coffee pot, frowning when he pours what's left into his mug and it only reaches the halfway mark.

"You're good with this?" I ask him, surprised by his quick agreement.

"It's smart," he says. "If we stick together, we can watch each other's backs." Luca doesn't say *your*, but the heat in his hazel eyes as they drill into me over the rim of his coffee cup heavily implies it.

It makes me want to argue against my own plan. "Store, sunblock, work?" I ask, keeping it simple.

"I'll need to pick up some stuff from my apartment," Ciprian says. He's calm again, almost thoughtful as he traces a vein in the granite countertop. Alistair's apartment is much fancier than mine, but it's bare, dark and soulless in a way that makes me sad.

Luca nods. "Same."

I take my mug to the sink and rinse it. "We can meet at my place after."

From the corner of my eye, I see Alistair and Luca exchange a look. I ignore it. If I'm about to share my seven-hundred-square-foot apartment with them, I'm going to need a few hours to prepare mentally. This is a big change.

"Call me if you need anything," Luca says. "Please."

I soften at his demand disguised as a request. The please sounded as if it was yanked from him about as willingly as a hunk of hair between two fighting, stray cats. I can be gracious, though. Especially since I'm getting a chance to say goodbye to my alone time.

"I will," I tell him.

"Can someone drop me at the club?" Ciprian asks, smiling at me with a boyish, hopeful expression. "My car's parked nearby."

"It's on my way." Luca claps him roughly on the shoulder. "Let's go."

I walk toward the front door, trailing after them, but Alistair is too fast. He grabs me and spins me around until I'm sandwiched between him and the kitchen counter.

"No risks," he growls. "Swear it."

I draw back to tell him where he can shove his possessive bullshit, but he kisses me breathless, his tongue plunging into my mouth like it belongs there. Mine tangles with his as I do my best to tell him without words that I won't be controlled—not now, not ever.

"It's not that I'm trying to . . ." He groans as I bite his lip. "Shit, angel. I'll be stuck inside until sundown. I don't know if I can let you walk out that door if I'm not sure you'll be careful."

"I could break your arms," I offer, mostly kidding. "Then you'd have firsthand proof of how capable I am."

Alistair rolls his eyes, unfazed. "Swear that you'll watch your back."

I sigh; the weight of my past perches heavily on my throat. Unlike the locked chest of memories in my mind, my body isn't capable of forgetting. It remembers every bruise. Every night I went to bed with hunger gnawing at my belly. If Alistair knew the half of it, he'd know I'm physically incapable of not watching my back.

"I will," I say, keeping the truth simple to ensure neither of us get sucked into my past. Finger by finger, I detach his grip from the counter to leave, being careful not to bruise him in the process. "See you soon."

"The instant the sun falls and not a moment later," he promises, his brows cutting two dark, angry swaths across his face.

My lips curl. "That was almost poetic."

"There's more where that came from." His blue eyes rake over my body, heating my skin like an open flame. Shaking my head at his annoyingly distracting smolder, I join Luca and Ciprian at the front door, where they haven't made a single attempt to give us privacy.

"Go to your room," Luca orders Alistair, sounding every bit the exasperated mom. "I don't want to roast you when I open the door."

Alistair glares, then shuffles away without arguing, and I shake my head. I need to ask Luca how the fuck he does it. Sighing, I pull my wings into my skin, cool air rushing through the holes in my shirt. I'm still wearing Alistair's clothes.

"I forgot to give you your shirt back," I call out.

Alistair reappears in the arched opening in a flash, his gaze hungry. "Keep it," he insists. "It looks better on you, anyway." Before I can respond, he disappears again.

Shaking my head, I follow Luca and Ciprian out the front door, closing it firmly behind me as my vision adjusts to the bright light.

Once we're on the street, I straddle my bike and head out, enjoying the peace . . . for all of three minutes. Luca and Ciprian follow me to the store. Once I get there, Luca waits by his car until I come out with the room-darkening shades, then trails my bike home. Only when I'm inside the apartment and glaring out of my locked window, do they pull away from the scuffed, sunbaked curb.

I swallow my frustration. At least Luca didn't try to follow me inside the store. I huff, chopping the decorative pillows on my couch into submission until I feel better.

My apartment is exactly as I left it; no sign of more intruders. After scarfing down a dry sandwich with the last of my bread, I get to work preparing for company. While the sun is brightest, I hang the shades, resigning myself to an immediate future with little to no natural light.

I don't know how Alistair stands it. I guess he has no choice. I've never asked him how he became a vampire. It's not a polite question to throw at someone you barely know, but now he's been inside me in more ways than one. He knows how I taste—again, in more ways than one.

Can I ask him about his past without revealing my own? My sense of fairness nips that idea in the bud. It's too risky, and I don't need to know more about Alistair. He's good in bed, and he's decent out of it too. I should leave it at that.

Once I'm sure the shades are keeping enough light out to allow him to get around the apartment without catching fire, I blow up the air mattress and put clean sheets on it. A sigh escapes me when I realize all three of my guests are too tall to sleep comfortably in here.

My back itches.

This isn't my fault. It's not like I decided to open a bed-and-breakfast and cut costs on accommodations. They're lucky I even have a second bedroom. We can all thank my horny superintendent for insisting on the free upgrade. He wants me to thank him on my knees, which is never going to happen, but at least I have the extra space.

My grocery delivery arrives as I'm tucking the spare quilt under the bottom of the air mattress. I collect the bags of food and thank the delivery guy, then stock my pantry and refrigerator. The repetition relaxes me in a way ten million empty words never could.

When you know the truth, nothing grates more than a lie—even if it's meant as kindness.

I put Luca's favorite beer next to my seltzer water, clearing out space on the right side in case Alistair needs to store blood there. Ciprian is a wild card. I don't know what he eats or drinks. Maybe I should have grabbed some different options—*No, quit stressing about this,* I tell myself. *You aren't running a hotel.*

Toeing the fridge closed, I survey the main living area with a critical eye. It's perfect. There's nothing else to do. My shoulders sag.

Luca should be here soon. Like I thought him into existence, two familiar knocks sound on the door. I breathe a sigh of relief and throw it open.

Luca steps in with a duffle bag tossed over his shoulder, and a piece of stress I didn't realize I was carrying falls away. He's here. Safe. Not lying somewhere in a ditch. I check his clothes to be sure, but all his blood appears to be in his body where it belongs.

"Do I even want to know where your head went?"

I shrug. "Probably the same place yours went when you followed me to the store."

Luca's face softens. "Am I the first one here?"

After I nod, he drops his bag, then wraps his arms around me and kisses me. "Good. We've got to talk about hiding us from Ciprian. He doesn't strike me as a gossip. If we told him we're together, I doubt he would tell anyone. I know why we started with that story, but I don't think I'll be able to lie low while Alistair paws at you on every piece of furniture."

"He doesn't paw," I say, laughing a little, even as my shoulders tense.

"Fine," Luca admits. "Gnaw was the better word choice, but my point stands. I might accidentally kill him if he gets to sleep every night in your bed while I keep watch from the floor."

Rolling my eyes, I shove him playfully. "You're not going to be on the floor."

"Celine," he sighs. "You're deliberately missing the point. I don't want to be your dirty little secret while Alistair gets you out in the open."

*And I don't want to paint a bigger target on your back if it gets back to my dad's assassins.* I should tell Luca the truth, but something stops me, and instead I say, "But secrets are hot."

Luca stills, his face blanking as he looks at me. I sense my misstep, but it's too late to take it back. "You know what, it's fine," he mumbles. "Don't worry about it."

I reach for him, but he steps back. "Hey, I didn't mean—"

"No, you're right: secrets are hot. Where should I put my bag?"

Luca goes into my spare room without waiting on a response. I throw my head back and scream silently up at the ceiling. It's been all of five minutes, and I'm already fucking this up.

# TWENTY-EIGHT

ENCLAVE EDICT #12:
NEVER EXPOSE THE SUPERNATURAL COMMUNITY
TO HUMAN SCRUTINY.

## CIPRIAN

I zip my suitcase with difficulty as the prehistoric window unit wheezes and coughs behind me. Calling it an air conditioner is too generous. It sounds like an old man with a head cold. The ancient appliance can't get to me today, though. Neither can the shitty water pressure.

Torn between worry for Sheena and absolute amazement that my crazy plan worked, I'm far too amped to be distracted by minor inconveniences. Hoisting my suitcase off the bed, I lock the apartment behind me even though there's not a damn thing left here worth stealing.

This is the best chance I've had to uncover what happened to Roscoe. Dad would piss himself with excitement if he knew . . . so I'm not sure why I kept it from him. When I checked in after Luca dropped me off at my car, I lied and told Dad there were no updates. He lectured me for ten minutes, and I never came clean.

My stomach roils, anxiety pitching around in there. I frown, throw my suitcase in the backseat, and slam the car door harder than necessary. I've been telling a lot of lies lately. It's starting to get to me. Hiding who I really am from Celine is a necessary evil.

But if she knew the truth, she might understand.

There's another lie.

Thrumming my fingers on the steering wheel, I load the address Luca gave me into my navigation system and pull out. Celine's apartment isn't far—only a few blocks. Squinting, I ease my car past a red curb that could use a fresh coat of paint and parallel park in the only remaining space. Celine's bike is parked further down, making me pretty confident this is the right place.

Grabbing my suitcase from the backseat, I jog up the stairs, double check the number, then knock on the door and wait.

I have no reason to be guilty. Secrets are more common than slot machines around here. I'm positioning myself in Celine's home under false pretenses, but I'm not going to slit her throat. I have a job to do. That's it. Returning to the compound with another fuckup under my belt . . . I can't do it.

My heart beats a little quicker as I hear footsteps approaching. Then the door swings open and Celine's face is looking up at me.

"Hey, roomie," I say, grinning to hide my nervousness.

She shakes her head and holds the door open slightly to usher me in. "Behave," she warns.

"Me?" I sketch an imaginary circle over my head in a halo motion. "I'm always behaving."

"Behaving like what exactly?" She closes the door behind me, and I smile. Celine is quick with her comebacks. I respect that. And her home . . . I whistle as take in the neat apartment, with its careful organization and cool, inviting tones. She plants her hands on her hips and stares at me expectantly.

"What?" I ask.

"Nothing, I'm waiting for the joke."

"What joke?" Does she think I can't be serious? I'm not sure why that feels especially awful today. She wouldn't be the first.

"The one about how angels are uptight."

"Sorry to disappoint, but I don't know any of those," I say. "Are they normally knock-knock style or what?"

Celine rolls her eyes. "Please. Like you haven't heard the rumors about angels."

"I'm a demon, hot wings—we're not known for being easy breezy ourselves."

Her brow furrows, and she pushes a strand of flame-red hair behind one ear. "That nickname . . ."

"Is perfect?" I lean over and steal a whiff of her scent. It's the perfect balance of sweet and spicy, like a cardamom bun rolled in cinnamon sugar.

"It's the worst thing I've ever been called," she says frankly. "And I'm a stripper on the Fringes, so that's saying something."

I clap my hand over my heart and dip my head in a low, sarcastic bow. "Earning a superlative . . . on our first day as roommates? I'm honored."

Her lips twitch, but she pivots before I can watch the smile overtake her face and turn it from merely beautiful to breathtaking.

"I've only got one bathroom, unfortunately. You're on the couch." Celine looks around her tidy living room, and her shoulders dip. Something tells me she's imagining my dirty socks wedged between the cushions.

"I'll do my best not to make a mess," I assure her, keeping my tone serious. She seems about as uncomfortable with this as I feel when people enter my family's home.

"Luca is getting settled in the guest room, but we'll have to head to the club soon." Her phone vibrates on the kitchen counter, and she turns to glance at the screen. "I need to respond to this," she says awkwardly.

"You don't need to worry about me." I give her my most winning smile. "You'll know I'm here, but I won't be any trouble."

Celine nods crisply, then disappears down the narrow hall, hips swaying as she walks.

Gods, I want to feel her move all that sexy, sensual grace against me. A memory flies into my head of her flawless tits under the stage lights at the Naked Fang. Fuck, she's perfect. *If only—*

Luca steps out of a room halfway down the hall, eyeing me with his steady, suspicious stare. He's dressed in a ragged tank top with his biceps on display and I have to fight the urge to rile him up for the fun of it. He's more levelheaded than a lot of the shifters I'm used to, but every so often I see the familiar flash of animal instinct in his eyes. I'm dying to know what he is.

"If you get lonely in the guest room, I'll be happy to join you," I say, giving in to the urge to tease him.

Luca snorts, pointing at the door he came through. "Have you seen the size of that bed?"

I shrug, grinning as I check him out. "Who says we have to use the bed?"

"Good gods." Luca shakes his head, raising his voice to say, "Celine, I'm going to cook something for dinner."

"Okay." Her voice is muffled but easy to hear. *This is a small apartment for four adults.*

"You cook, too?" I lean against the back of Celine's couch, giving Luca my full attention. It's fun to rattle him. Even more fun than messing with my brother, but in a very different way.

Ignoring me, he pulls a bowl out of the cabinet and tosses me a menacing glare. "Stop flirting with me or I won't feed you."

"Harsh." I sigh. "But I can accept those terms. Where's the bathroom?"

Luca's head is buried in the fridge. "Through Celine's room," he says, his hazel eyes peeking over the open door. "Knock first."

"Obviously." I shoot him the bird. "What kind of asshole wouldn't knock?"

I head down the hall before he can respond. The greenish-colored walls are covered with art, each piece meticulously hung. I don't have a level handy, but I'd be willing to bet these paintings are even to a fault.

"Celine." I knock gently on her closed door. "Can I use the bathroom?"

She doesn't respond, but a second later the door swings open. I blink in surprise, absolutely fucking dumbfounded. Slathered head to toe in lotion, coconut oil, or gods know what, she looks like an entire soccer team ran a train on her.

"Don't say a word," she snarls.

"A-are you okay?" I sputter, unsure how the goop isn't getting into her eyes and blinding her.

"Can you piss already and get lost?"

Ignoring her demand, I lean closer and sniff, fascinated, a sick curiosity building in my gut. It's amazing how thoroughly she's covered in this stuff. From her bare feet to the top of her forehead —even the curves of her ears are iced. "You're a glazed donut," I say, unable to help myself.

Celine sighs. "I see you can't be mature about this. You have thirty seconds to get it all out."

"Starting now?" I blurt, eyes widening.

"Already started, you've wasted seven seconds."

"Did you have a run-in with a flock of lactose-intolerant birds?" Her lips purse tightly. "Or maybe you're thinking of trying out life as a human candle. Is your hair the wick?" I sniff her face again, inhaling the herbal smell, then shake my head. "Honestly, you should have told me to preheat the oven. You're clearly marinated and ready to roast."

"And your time is—"

"Choo choo!" I make a chugging train engine sound with the last of my breath.

"Up," Celine finishes, grabbing me by the arm and yanking me into the bedroom. "Honestly, I expected better from you."

"Damn, babe. I can't bring my best material while I'm actively in shock. In fact, do you have one of those aluminum-foil-looking blankets humans use after car wrecks lying around? I think I need to sit."

"You can sit on the toilet."

I scoff. "I don't sit when I pee."

"Not my problem," she snaps. "Tuck it in or something."

"Tuck it in?" I look down. "This monster? No can do." I run my finger through the thick layer of slime on her shoulder. She swats my hand away, leaving a snail trail along my forearm.

"It's a long-lasting magical moisturizer and pore reducer," she says. "Not that it's any of your business, but my appearance pays the bills, and witches are damn good at what they do."

"Spells?" I ask, my eyebrows rising to my hairline.

She groans. "There is more to witch magic than spells. Were you raised under a rock?"

"Close enough," I admit, picturing the stone walls of the compound I grew up in. There were witches behind those walls with me, but they weren't big on sharing trade secrets, and I never once saw one flopping around like a trout freshly plucked from the stream.

"Hurry up," Celine says. "I need to wash it off in seventy-eight seconds."

"Roughly," I joke, wondering again if she has a clock ticking in her head at all times. While fascinating to think about, that sounds exhausting. Anyone as magnetic as Celine should be able to kick her feet up and zone out when she wants to.

"Ciprian," she hisses, and I jolt into action.

It takes about thirty seconds to take care of my business. I wash my hands, then use my remaining time to poke around in her stuff. Militantly organized, the cabinet under the sink is designed for maximum efficiency. I'm most impressed by the fact that she's managed to slather herself in a magic potion without spilling a drop.

With about six seconds until my deadline, I open the door and smile at her shiny face. "I bet you'd be unbeatable in a wrestling match right now. Want to give it a try?"

"I would crush you like a grape, demon."

I shudder, not sure if I'm more scared or turned on by the unshakable confidence in her voice. "It might be worth it."

"Get out of my bathroom."

"Yes, ma'am." I salute her and leave, feeling energized by the exchange. Celine is inflexible, antagonistic, and guarded. Getting her to trust me will be about as easy as climbing a tree with no branches. I love a challenge.

As I meander toward the kitchen, I tilt one colorful abstract painting about a sixteenth of an inch to the right. Most people wouldn't notice, but Celine is exceptional. I bet she spots it as soon as she leaves her room.

"Have you seen Celine's skin lube in action?" I ask conversationally, leaning against the counter that runs about half the length of the kitchen. Luca is standing over the stove with his back to me, shoving something around with a massive spatula.

"What?" He pivots, one eyebrow lifting effortlessly.

"I know," I say. "Some kind of witchy goop for perfect skin."

"Interesting."

"It is, isn't it?"

"Not really, I was trying to get you to drop it." Luca turns back to the stove to continue herding the food around. Steam fills the air with the mouthwatering smell of rosemary, garlic, and melted butter.

"Harsh. Dinner smells good."

"Don't expect much," Luca says. "It's just one-pan chicken and veggies."

My stomach rumbles. It's pathetic, but I haven't had a home cooked meal since I came here. The idea of consuming a dinner that wasn't frozen ninety seconds before it reached my mouth is ridiculously nice. I keep that thought to myself.

My phone buzzes in my pocket, and I pull it out, seeing a text from Sheena. The tone of her message is flat. I silently curse my brother for taking so long to figure this out. With the grumpy fae getting involved, it shouldn't be this hard.

I clench my hand around the phone, wishing, ironically, that I could do more. I've offered to come back and help—ten times now—but Sheena won't let me. The feeling of helplessness won't go away, and I wonder if I would have been better off not caring. Her friendship is the best thing to happen to me in years, but if I lose it?

A chill rolls over me, even though with the stove on, it's plenty warm in here. Pushing my worries to the back of my head, I half hope they'll get lost and decompose before I'm forced to confront them again.

"Is your friend okay?"

I look up from my phone, a bolt of energy shooting through me as I find Luca's hazel eyes fixed on me. Surprise follows my unease, joined by something I can't identify. He remembered.

"Yeah, she's fine," I say. It's true, if you're free and loose with your definition of fine, but this secret isn't mine to tell. It is, however, mine to keep, and I would relive the year I turned fourteen a million times before I would betray Sheena.

"Dinner is almost ready," Luca says, turning back to the stove. "And it's mostly dark. I bet we can expect"—a brisk knock interrupts him, and he shakes his head—"Alistair to be here soon."

Shaking off my stress, I walk to the door and work my way

through the deadbolts. There are three. That's a lot, but I'd actually like to multiply it.

"It's a little toasty out here," Alistair says through the door, tension in his tone.

"You should have waited until it was dark," I call back, unlocking the final lock then swinging the door open. Alistair's face is visibly red beneath the hoodie he's wearing. "Gods, get in here, you maniac."

I step out of the way, and Alistair darts inside, letting out a deep breath once the dying rays of the setting sun can no longer reach him.

"Are you trying to broil yourself?" Celine snaps, appearing in the hall, hands on her hips, no goop in sight.

"I'm fine," Alistair insists, his tone biting enough to call him a liar without anyone else having to go to the trouble.

Luca shakes his head as he plates the food, deliberately meeting my gaze. I shake my head. *Is he trying to call me out for claiming the same?*

Alistair picks up his bag and heads to Celine's room, his fingers brushing her cheek as he passes. "Your skin is softer than rose petals," he murmurs.

I shake my head—what a corny fucking line—then laugh out loud when I see the triumphant look Celine is leveling me with.

"Choo choo," I call out as they disappear down the hall together.

"Fuck off," Celine shouts. "And don't touch my paintings again."

# TWENTY-NINE

## CELINE

Imani corners me in the dressing room, crossing her arms. "What's going on, babe?"

"Why do you think—"

"Nope," she says. "Try again and skip the bullshit this time. I'm already pissed. If you play dumb it'll only be worse for you."

"I'm trying to keep you safe," I insist.

"Thanks. I appreciate that. Now spill."

"It's complicated," I groan, tossing my makeup kit onto my station and flicking on the lights around my mirror.

Imani drops into her chair and begins pinning sections of her curls back. "It always is. Fill in the blanks for me."

"You know what I've told you about Dad," I say, then hold my breath until my wings aren't threatening to turn to knives any longer.

"Dick and a half," Imani mutters.

"Yeah, well, I didn't mention this because it didn't seem especially relevant at the time, but he wants me dead. And he knows where I am."

Imani drops the clips on her station with a clatter and slowly turns her body toward mine, leveling me with her most intense stare. "Celine . . ."

"I know. Believe me, I know. It's not great. He's been sending goons to take me out. If you see someone with wings, turn around and go the other way."

Imani slumps back in her chair, her piercing gaze so compassionate that my eyes well up with tears. "Gods, babe—are you okay?"

I shrug dismissively, then remember what she's been through, and let out the breath I've been holding. Imani's concern isn't from imagined empathy—it's from lived experience. If anyone in the Fringes can understand how I feel, it's her. Which is exactly why I can't let her get anywhere near this mess.

"There's not a mark on me," I assure her. "But I don't want him to know who I'm close to."

"You think he'd come after me?" Imani asks, raising her eyebrows. "It won't matter if he does, I'm with you no matter what."

I force a smile, feeling a pinch in my heart. Imani won't abandon me, yet six inches of water are enough to paralyze her with fear. It's funny how friendship gives us the strength to fight someone else's monsters, when even the thought of our own sends us scurrying for cover.

"He's already tried with Alistair," I tell her, desperate to make her see how serious this is. If I have to worry about her on top of everyone else . . .

Her eyebrows shoot up, then she grins. "I knew things were getting real with him."

"What? Imani, you're missing the whole entire point." I shake my head and begin applying my makeup to give me something to do with my hands. "My dad is insane."

"Yeah, I heard all that, and I'm appropriately freaked out, I promise. But Alistair hasn't stopped hanging all over you . . . even after someone tried to kill him. That's about as serious as it gets in the Fringes, babe. Like—when's the wedding?"

"Shut up." I laugh, but it comes out sounding manic. *Pull yourself together.*

Imani checks her phone, then grins. "I came in early to ambush you. We've got half an hour until the other girls get here. Spill, and leave nothing out. I want all the dirty details."

"Fine, but in exchange, I need a promise from you," I say, locking my eyes with hers. I'm willing to talk this through with her, but only if I know she'll be safe. It's the perfect opportunity to get her perspective and ensure she doesn't become a casualty to my father's cruel vendetta.

Imani sits up straighter, the humor falling away from her face. "Let's hear it."

"Until this settles, you keep your distance from me in public. I'm already losing sleep worrying about who could get hurt because of me. I can't worry about you too."

"Fine, but I have a condition of my own." She points one perfectly manicured nail at me. "You'll let me know if you need backup before it's too late. No prideful, loner fringe bullshit where you try to go it alone, then end up as desert detritus."

"Detritus? Really?" I chuckle. "Did you subscribe to one of those word-of-the-day email newsletters again?"

"Maybe." Imani levels me with an exasperated look. "Don't change the subject."

I pinch my lips together, carefully drawing on my winged eyeliner. By the time I'm done, my mouth is hanging open despite my best efforts.

"Swear it, Celine," Imani demands.

"Fuck," I mutter, putting the makeup down and facing her. "Is that necessary?"

"Yes, because I don't believe you'll do it."

"It's almost impossible for me to lie," I remind her.

"Which makes you an expert at not quite telling the complete fucking truth."

"Fine," I snap. "I swear on my honor as a *nish thatsha* that if I need backup, I will let Imani know immediately. Now, can I tell you about my new roommates?"

"Oh, gods, yes." Imani meets my eyes through the reflection in the mirror and grins. "I thought you'd never ask."

I slump in my chair, then clear my throat. "I want to start by saying that absolutely none of this is my fault . . ."

---

I dance my first set absentmindedly. Unloading on Imani left me feeling like a freshly sharpened blade. While going over things prepared me to face them, it also brought the danger back to the front of my mind. My only comfort is her reluctant promise to keep her distance until this all settles down. If only Luca and Alistair would do the same.

The club is different tonight. The lights are the same, and the smells and sounds are all pretty standard too. I can't put my finger on what's off—except the eyes feel different on my skin . . . more sinister. I give the crowd another scan. It's a mix of regulars and strangers. None of them stand out. *You're being paranoid.*

Finishing my dance, I collect my top and the loose bills scattered around the stage, telling myself to chill out while I'm at it. Acting jittery is far more likely to put me at risk than going about my normal routine.

Dad wants me dead—but he won't want a scene. Slaughtering a stripper under literal spotlights with dozens of onlookers standing by is hardly discreet. That means I'm safe here, or as safe as I ever am in the Fringes.

I imagine his minions reporting to him about my chosen profession and grin. That vein in his temple would bulge ominously, followed by the narrowing of his gray eyes. My smile fades as I let the scene play out in my mind. Since he's no longer in possession of his two favorite punching bags, Dad would find a servant to exorcise his anger on.

Familiar guilt swirls in my stomach. His actions are no one's responsibility but his own. As always, that statement feels like a lie. After all this time, I can't make myself believe it. *You make me do this,* he would shout. *Discipline—once you learn discipline, these lessons will stop.* Lies. I could sense that even then. He was lying to me. Lying to her. Lying to himself, too, I suspect.

Nerves tingling, I avoid weaving through the crowd after my set. I usually pick up good tips that way, but I can't make myself do it tonight. Not while I see the crowd as nothing but a collection of clenched fists attached to dangerous strangers.

Backstage, I tie my top back into place, adjusting the cups of the lingerie until they sit perfectly over my breasts. The curtain wobbles slightly, then Luca steps into the tight space, a water bottle in his hand. He offers it to me without a word.

Luca's kindness makes it harder to hold on to my composure. My eyes burn. Why won't my stupid memories leave me alone?

"Who's manning the bar?" I ask, trying to keep my voice even.

"It can man itself for a few minutes."

I nod. "If you want a break, I can keep an eye on it. That's no issue."

"Breathe, baby." Luca takes an exaggerated inhale, worry in his hazel eyes.

"I'm fine. I j-just—" I stutter, a lump swelling in my throat, thick and tight. It burns as if it's wrapped in barbed wire, making it hard to get the oxygen I need. I toss up my hands, at a loss for how to explain why I'm freaking out.

"Breathe," Luca says again. "Take it one breath at a time."

I match his every inhale, then drain the bottle in long, greedy chugs. Some of the water trickles from the corner of my mouth, and I wipe it away, cringing as I picture how messy I must look.

Luca takes the empty bottle from my hands, tosses it on the floor, then hauls me into his arms. His hold is tight—perfect. I sag against him, convinced he'll hold us both up if I need him to. Another shaky breath brings me his familiar, comforting scent, and slowly, my panicked thoughts fade to the background where they belong.

Lifting my chin from his chest, I study Luca's face. Concern for me is carved into every angle and curve. If my father catches even a whiff of what he means to me, I'll lose him forever. That's the reality we're living in.

Gritting my teeth, I cradle Luca's face in both hands. "You'll be careful at all times; do you hear me? I can't bear to . . . Be careful, Luca. Promise me."

"I promise." The words have barely left his lips before I'm kissing them, hungry and frantic. I should drive him away to keep him safe, but I can't. I'm too selfish, too weak. I lack the discipline to do this alone.

"Celine," he groans, then pulls back to glance at the thin black curtain blocking the crowd's view of our position. "I don't want to hide. I want Ciprian to know you're mine. I want all those horny bottom feeders out there to know it too."

I open my mouth to give him a valid excuse. It's more dangerous. It makes the target on his back twice as big. Then I focus less on what I'm going to say next and more on what Luca is saying without words: there's hurt behind his eyes.

"Is this because your basilisk wants ownership or something

else?" I ask. "Because if you're feeling territorial, you can deal with it."

He runs his fingers roughly through his hair, making his normally tousled look even messier. For once, I don't want to bring order to the chaos. Luca is perfect exactly as he is.

"No, I mean, I am territorial. There's no point lying about that, but watching you claim him while you hide me . . ." Luca won't meet my eyes, and I feel sick.

"I'm hurting you," I say, and the truth of that statement hits me square in the chest.

He sighs. "I know it's not intentional."

I swallow hard. Does intention matter when the end result is the same? Luca does everything he can to make sure no one gets the chance to hurt me, yet I'm hurting him constantly with this decision. Well-meaning or not, that's on me.

"What if we tell Ciprian so we don't have to hide while we're in my apartment?" I suggest. "He can have the spare room, and you can stay with me and Alistair."

"Yes," Luca says without a second of hesitation. He lifts me up on my tiptoes to kiss me, his tongue stroking mine before I push him back.

"You didn't let me finish." I gesture to the curtain, where the stage lights are currently shining through the dark fabric. "I still want to keep it quiet out there. I won't put you more at risk than I already have, Luca. Please try to see it my way. If someone from your past was trying to kill you, would you drag me directly into the line of fire?"

He groans. "When you put it like that—"

"I sound smart and impossible to argue with."

Luca smiles, rolling the hoop between his lips. "I wouldn't go quite that far."

I shove at his chest, but he catches my hands, pulling me into his body and trailing kisses along my neck. His touch makes me hot and needy, and I can't believe I managed to keep my hands off him for as long as I did.

"You're important to me," I tell him emphatically, admitting the only version of the truth I'm brave enough to share right now.

Luca's eyes flicker yellow, and he kisses my forehead. "You're important to me too." *Does he mean what I mean when he says that?* I refuse to ask, bending over instead to grab the discarded water bottle so he won't be able to read the question written all over my face.

"We can handle this, right?" I ask, feeling more myself than I did fifteen minutes ago, despite the butterflies knocking around in my stomach.

Luca nods, bringing my knuckles up to his lips. "No one will take what we've built, Celine. Not without a hell of a fight." He's not talking about material things but about everything else. The things in a person's life that can't be measured; things that make life worth living.

I nod, determination replacing my fears. I traded everything familiar to me in order to gain autonomy here on Earth. I chose this life. I'm exactly who I want to be. And Luca is right: no one will take that from me. If they try, I'll kill them. It's the most unvarnished truth I've confronted all day.

# THIRTY

## LUCA

My phone rings at six in the morning.

With bleary, bloodshot eyes, I squint at the screen and answer as soon as I recognize the number. "Harry? Are you okay?" The twist in my belly tightens as I hear crying in the background.

"We're safe, but someone broke in."

"Did they take anything?"

I keep my voice low, hoping not to wake anyone else. I want to be sure before I rip them out of bed, since it's only been two hours since we got home from the club. Two hours since I collapsed on the air mattress and discovered it had more in common with a rock than a bed. Two hours since I realized my feet hung off the end and decided to suck it up. It's only one night. We'll tell Ciprian tomorrow—today, now, I guess—and I'll curl up with Celine tonight.

"It's not about what they took, it's about what they left behind," Harry says. There's a strain of unease in her voice; one I've never heard from her before. "Three more angels, dropped directly into my house. I didn't even hear them come in, Luca. Anika is translating. But I don't have enough room to keep them long-term. I don't want to turn them away . . ."

"We'll find another option," I assure her, my head spinning as I push to my feet and grope around for the pants I kicked off before I crawled into bed. "Celine and I will be over soon to help." And to figure out if whoever broke into her house is connected to the piece of shit trying to kill her.

I hang up the phone, padding down the hall to Celine's room and easing the door open. Alistair is lying on his back, sound asleep. Celine is draped over his chest with her wings covering them both. My heart swells. *Fuck, they're cute.* Since they're likely to gut me for that thought, I'll have to keep it to myself.

Bending over the edge of the bed, I run my fingers up the center of Celine's back. "Baby," I whisper. "Baby, wake up." I'm about to shake her shoulder, when I find myself flying backward and slamming into the wall.

Celine pins me there, her brown eyes glazed. She's staring right through me. I grunt as my collarbone gives way under the extreme pressure of her strength.

"Celine," I gasp. "I-It's me. I won't hurt you." With no sign that she hears me at all, Celine moves her right hand to my throat and squeezes.

I hiss at the white-hot pain the pressure puts on the fractured bone. My basilisk stirs, rattling angrily in my chest, then freezes in confusion as it recognizes who's attacking us.

Celine increases the pressure, and I see spots—closing my eyes in case my instincts decide to override my brain and try to protect me.

"It's me," I wheeze. "I w-would never hurt you. Never." The

words are jagged and thin. Getting them out burns up the little air I have left.

"Angel, snap out of it." Alistair's voice is tight and threaded with tension, but the pressure on my throat eases.

I suck in a heaving lungful of oxygen as Celine's hand drops. "What's going on?" she asks.

"I didn't mean to startle you," I whisper. There's a new rasp in my voice. I crack my eyes open, but keep them on the floor as my adrenaline levels off.

Celine hisses. "Shit, Luca, I thought I was dreaming. I swear on my life I didn't mean to hurt you." With my eyes on the floor, I see her truth rune glowing on the top of her bare foot.

"You don't have to prove—" I cough, then clear my throat. "I believe you, baby, you don't have to go all billboard of truth to make me understand."

"But you came in here for a reason, Luca," Alistair prods gently, bringing the frantic conversation with Harry back to the front of my mind.

"Harry called," I tell them. "She had an unexpected delivery overnight. Three new angels abandoned . . . inside her locked house."

"But the wards," Alistair snarls. "I oversaw their installation myself."

"Angels operate on a different plane of magic," Celine whispers, her voice shattered.

"I told her we'd come help," I say. "Do you want to jump in the shower first?"

"Yeah. I can do that." Celine's foot disappears from my limited field of vision, and I glance up in time to see her run into the bathroom and close the door behind her. I wait until the water turns on, then level Alistair with a serious look.

"I need you to pop it back into place before it heals wrong," I say, pointing at my broken collarbone. There's a visible lump where the end of the bone is trying to push through my skin. Thankfully, it's dark enough in here with the blackout curtains that Celine didn't notice.

"Fuck," Alistair says, dipping his head to get a closer look. "Do you want some whiskey first?"

I consider the offer and drop my head back against the wall. This is going to hurt like a bitch, but if I drink enough to dull the pain, I won't be alert when we go to Harry's.

"No," I decide. "Let's go down the hall, though." *In case I end up whimpering . . .*

Alistair follows me out of the bedroom silently. The hallway is cool and dark, not a single thread of early morning sunlight slipping past Celine's meticulously installed blackout shades.

"I've never done this before," Alistair admits, a frown in his eyes.

"You're not inspiring a lot of confidence," I mutter, glancing at my bare chest and moving my shoulders experimentally. It fucking hurts. "I don't think the pieces are overlapping, you just need to poke them back together." I suck in a deep breath and tell myself to be tough.

"I can do it." Ciprian's voice startles me. I turn my head toward the living room, then hiss in agony from the sudden movement. His white blond hair is standing up in all directions, those eerie black eyes blending in perfectly with the gloomy surroundings.

"Look," I snap. "Someone do it before it heals wrong or Celine gets out of the shower." I need to get this over with before I lose my nerve.

Ciprian steps in front of me. He examines the break closely, then gently prods the skin around it. Alistair hovers at my side, his brows drawn tightly together as if he can't decide if he wants to shove Ciprian away or let him take over.

"Distract him, okay?" Ciprian says, his voice uncharacteristically serious when he addresses Ali.

Confusion flickers in Alistair's blue eyes—then he drops his mouth to mine, kissing me hard. His fingers graze my abs, a barely there touch that makes my skin pebble.

Shocked, it only takes me a few seconds to kiss him back. He moves his lips to the hollow beneath my ear, scattering biting kisses along the sensitive curve. It's good. Better than good. I bet it would feel even better if his fangs broke the skin.

Sharp pressure replaces my pleasure, then blinding pain sears through me. I bite the back of my own hand to keep from screaming.

"It's lined up," Ciprian says. He runs his fingertips back over the skin, careful not to put any pressure on the bone, and nods with satisfaction when it stays put. "Shifter healing should take care of the rest."

He's awfully confident about that for a demon. I tilt my head, wondering why he knows so much about shifter abilities.

"You okay?" Alistair asks. He kisses my neck with a feather-soft touch that makes me shudder, and I forget all about the puzzle that is Ciprian.

My collarbone still hurts—really damn bad, if I'm being honest—but the dull throb is manageable. I force a grin. It feels more like I'm baring my teeth. "I'll survive," I say. Glancing at Ciprian, I give him a nod. "Thanks for poking it back in."

He winks at me, charcoal sweatpants riding low on his hips. "I'm happy to 'poke it back in' any time you want." Ciprian leans against the wall and turns his mischievous gaze on Alistair. "I expected you to do a dance or tell him a joke, not leave half a dozen hickeys on his neck, but I do enjoy a surprise."

"Alistair," I hiss, bringing my hand up to my neck and poking the side he was sucking on. It's tender to the touch. What was he thinking marking me up this way?

He throws up his hands. "Give me a break! I woke up to Celine pinning you to the wall like a butterfly, then got asked to set a bone." He turns his glare on Ciprian. "And you demanded a distraction and gave me no time to think—I had to improvise."

Ciprian claps his hands on Alistair's shoulders, his face deadly serious. "If you're going to explore impact play, you need to be ready for the consequences. Kink without careful preparation is dangerous."

I laugh out loud as the expression on Alistair's face warps from outrage to complete and absolute shock. "We weren't. It was . . ." Alistair stutters, then knocks Ciprian's hands off his shoulders. "You're absolutely ridiculous. How can anyone take you seriously?"

Ciprian stiffens, his easy smile vanishing. "Don't make any sudden moves today," he says to me, ignoring Alistair. "It'll take a few days for it to heal completely."

I nod, wondering again how he knows that, then find myself more distracted by the rigid way he walks off. Ciprian just set my bone and left without asking why Celine broke it in the first place. Either he's the least curious person in the Fringes, or getting away from us was more important.

The water in the shower turns off.

"You can't go to Harry's," I say, focusing on Alistair.

He nods, running his fingers through his hair. "I know. Send updates and let Harry know I'll be by after sundown to check on her."

I overlook his demanding tone, knowing the stressful wake-up call has him on edge. It can't be easy, knowing there's shit going on but being unable to leave until dark.

"We need somewhere to take the overflow kids," I say. "Harry doesn't have enough room."

Alistair nods, standing a little taller and rolling his shoulders back. "I'll make some calls."

I dip my head toward the bedroom. "There's no reason to mention this." I point to my collarbone. "It was an accident, and I want her alert."

Alistair agrees, and I duck into the guest room to grab a change of clothes and my toothbrush. When I get back to Celine's room, the bathroom door is standing open, steam drifting out.

I walk inside, shut the door behind me, then curse silently. Alistair is in the shower, which is fine. But Celine—fuck—Celine is sitting on the closed toilet, staring blankly at the wall. Her wings are dripping water all over the tiled floor.

Before I make a conscious decision, I'm on my knees at her feet. Carefully, I take her balled-up hands in mine. "Talk to me," I urge.

Her eyes meet mine reluctantly. In comparison to her wings, they're almost painfully dry.

"Why won't he let me go?" she asks.

"Your father?"

Celine nods. "When I hit you, I was dreaming about—" She pushes to her feet. "You know what? It doesn't matter."

I stay in my hunched position, looking up at her. "That's bullshit. If you're flooding the bathroom because of it, your dream matters a lot."

Celine stares at the wall over my head. "Dad wasn't a safe person to be around," she whispers. "He used his fists to prove points."

Anger hums low in my stomach. I hate the haunted shadow in Celine's eyes, and the drips falling from her drooping wings? They're unacceptable. I prefer her fire, even when it burns everything in her path . . . including me.

I could tell her I'm sorry. I could promise to kill him for her. Neither feels right, so I remain crouched where I am, silently listening, afraid to interrupt and make things worse.

"As soon as she—I mean, as soon as I could, I left. Faked my death and used an illegal portal with the tracking magic disabled to get off realm. It's been years; I thought he'd forgotten. But no, he won't be satisfied until he's taken everything in the universe that brings me happiness. Don't you see? He can't win unless I lose, so he'll keep trying. It's his own sick, twisted form of balance."

My face contorts. Some of her word choices . . . They're specific, but I don't get the significance. I need to tread lightly. I also need to understand.

"Balance?" I ask. "Balance for what?"

"For my flaws," she whispers bitterly. "In his eyes, they're endless."

My anger builds, but I shove it down. This isn't about me or my desire to make him pay. It's about Celine. It's about erasing the agony on her face.

"Baby, I can't pretend to understand what you've been through," I say. "But I swear to you—on my basilisk's life and freedom—that I'll fight by your side until all your nightmares are dead."

There isn't a thing more important to me. My parents fled the monster realm with nothing but the clothes on their backs. They made a life for us here, all to keep me from knowing the pain of having my basilisk bound. To betray their sacrifices would be unthinkable. Almost as unthinkable as betraying Celine.

She knows how fiercely I cling to my free will. It's how we first bonded, six years ago when she wandered into the club, thick thighs, thicker accent, and the thickest guard I'd ever seen. I looked out for her then. Now, I hope she sees my words as what they are: an unbreakable vow.

Celine stares at me, the steam making a few strands of red hair stick to her temples. She pulls her bottom lip between her teeth, and my heart sinks as I read her skepticism loud and clear. *She doesn't believe me. Not fully.*

"Luca, I appreciate what you're trying to do, but you don't have to make pretty speeches," she says. "Not to me."

I shove to my feet. "I hate your doubt," I say. "If you can't take me at my word after all we've been through, then test me. Fucking test me, Celine, because I'm not leaving this room with you thinking I'm a liar."

Even though all I want to do is scream, I force myself to keep my voice low. I've noticed how she sometimes flinches when someone shouts, and the last thing I want is for her to be scared of me.

"If truth is your radiant gift, then test me. Prove to us both— now, tomorrow, and forever—that I've got your back no matter what."

There's a beat of silence. The constant dripping of her wings is a slower, gentler rainfall compared to the pressure of the shower. My raspy breaths are out of place, but there's fuck all I can do about it. I'm a live wire. I need her to ground me this time.

One by one, the runes wallpaper Celine's skin, as seamless and natural as the smattering of freckles on her lower back.

Clearing my throat, I hold her gaze, every nerve in my body singing. "I vow to you that I will fight by your side. Right or wrong, I don't care, you'll never have a reason to doubt me. If I need to storm the heavens and drag every one of your enemies to hell, I'll do it, baby—and I don't give a single solitary fuck what anyone has to say about that."

I cradle her face, ignoring how my fingers tremble. "Truth or lie?" I ask, biting my tongue to resist the urge to say more.

"Truth," Celine whispers, a flicker of shock flashing through her eyes. "You're telling the truth."

I roll mine. "I fucking told you I was."

"But why?" Her voice cracks.

Determined, I hold her stare. It's time for the ultimate truth. She won't be satisfied with less. In a perfect world, Alistair wouldn't be listening from the shower and we wouldn't be in danger, but this isn't a perfect world. It's ours.

"Isn't it obvious?" I ask her. "I'm in love with you, Celine. I always have been, and I always will be."

I let the words sit between us, the lump in my throat threatening to choke me as I wait for her response. Besides a sharp intake of breath, she doesn't say a word. Her silence hurts a hell of a lot more than my snapped collarbone.

My basilisk screams in pain, feeling the rejection acutely, then coils in the back of my chest to lick its wounds. I'm a fool. I did it. I manned up and told her my biggest secret—the only one left between us—and now I know exactly how it feels to be cannibalized by my own vulnerability.

Unable to face Celine's blank stare a second longer, I shove my pants down, yank the curtain open, and step into the shower. Alistair makes room for me, sympathy written all over his face.

Still, she says nothing.

I close my eyes, then open them again. I'm not a coward. I said something I meant, and I won't be ashamed of it.

Pressing shampoo into my hand, Alistair mouths, *Give her time.*

I nod shortly. For some reason, I'm not ashamed that he witnessed my most humiliating moment.

Alistair backs away from the spray, giving me room to lather my hair. I wince at the pain in my collarbone as I try to lift my hands to my head. Silently, he bats them away, rinsing the shampoo out himself, then working conditioner into the ends as I wash my body.

After about three minutes, I'm squeaky clean, heartbroken, and working my way toward blissfully numb. On two hours of sleep, it's the best I can manage.

Alistair audibly clears his throat. "You two be careful," he says.

"There's something going on here that we're missing. We need to quit reacting, put our heads together, and figure it out."

Celine doesn't respond, and I'm tempted to look around the curtain and make sure my declaration didn't actually scare her to death. I don't, though. I can't, at least not while I'm holding out hope that she'll yank the vinyl back herself and tell me she loves me too.

"We'll be careful," I tell Alistair. "Hopefully, whoever broke in left a clue behind, or maybe these kids have more to say."

Still nothing.

Alistair frowns, then pokes his head out of the shower. "Celine," he calls.

No answer.

"You don't think . . ." I mutter. "She wouldn't take off without me while all of this is going on?"

"I'll wring her neck if she did." Alistair looks back at me, his eyes glowing red. He shakes his head to clear them, clenching his jaw tight.

"It would be on brand for her," I say.

Turning the water off, I wrap a towel around my waist and rush into the bedroom. There's no sign of red hair or wings. Alistair surges down the hall, completely naked, not even bothering with a towel. He's barely out of sight when I hear a furious growl.

"She's gone," he snarls. "They both are."

I push my throbbing emotions aside, leaving only cold, focused determination. This isn't a crisis, but I need to find her and make sure she's okay. Knowing her hang-ups, I should have expected this, but part of me thought we were past it.

"I'll find her," I tell Alistair, noting the crazed gleam in his eyes and feeling vaguely relieved that he's stuck indoors for this one. "I'll find her. I swear."

I mean it as much as I meant what I said to Celine in the bathroom. The only difference is, Alistair believes me without magic to prove it.

# THIRTY-ONE

## CIPRIAN

I'm not exactly sure what's going on, but I've heard enough shit hit the fan over the years to recognize the sound.

So, when Celine tears past me on the couch and my gut tells me to follow, I listen to it. Slipping into my shoes, I throw on last night's shirt and run down the stairs, skidding into the street in the nick of time. She's slipping her helmet over her hair when I plant my feet in front of her bike and clear my throat.

"Going somewhere, hot wings?" I let her livid glare bounce off me like rain on an umbrella. If only I could have done the same when Alistair pushed my buttons earlier.

"Get out of my way," she says, her knuckles bone white against the handlebars.

"You know, if I'd known I'd get this little sleep while staying at your place—and not a single reason for it would be sexy—I might have turned your offer down."

Celine glances at the empty staircase that leads to her unit, anger seeping from every pore. "I don't have time for this," she snaps.

I pretend not to hear her, scratching my elbow and adopting a casual stance. "I thought no one was going around alone for now. Something about safety in numbers."

"Look, Ciprian, I'm not doing anything crazy," she says, sounding, well . . . pretty fucking crazy. "But this is my apartment. I need a little space. Some alone time."

I hear a slight waver in her voice and frown. "Makes perfect sense. Can I come with you?"

Celine stares up at the sky like she's begging a deity for patience. I'm familiar with the expression. Mom loves it.

"If you come, I wouldn't be alone," Celine argues.

"Sure you would," I say. "We would just be alone together."

"Only an extrovert could come up with something that stupid." She glances again at the stairs, then yanks the top case open and pulls out another helmet, slamming it viciously into my gut. "Get on and shut up. I mean it, Ciprian. You've got to be quiet."

"I can do that," I say. "You don't even have to take me seriously." Bile rises in the back of my throat as I repeat what Alistair said. Celine revs the engine, and I choke it down, straddling her bike and shoving the helmet on before she can hop the curb or run me over.

In the next breath, we're off. My heart leaps into my throat as she takes the curve too fast and we lose the rear tire for a heart-stopping second. We're supernatural and sturdy as fuck, but a high-speed crash would kill us both—fast healing or not.

With my hands gripping her hips, I hold on for dear life and do my best not to scream. If Celine wants quiet, that's what she'll get. Maybe it will help her drive. When we hit traffic on the freeway, I say a prayer of thanks. Am I grateful for rush hour? That's embarrassing as—fuck, my relief was premature.

She's a lane-splitter.

Every hair on my body stands up. I want to close my eyes, but I'm too godsdamn pragmatic. If a turn comes up, I'll need to lean, or leap clear of the fiery wreckage if she loses control.

A trickle of someone else's fear hits me as Celine veers around a big truck, clearing the chrome grille with only two inches to spare. I soak it in, enjoying the snack and the temporary kinship with all the other poor fucks she's scaring to death. My fear tank is nicely topped off by the time we exit—a testament to how recklessly she's driving.

While I'm scared shitless, I'm also oddly at peace. Somehow, the idea that we could end up pinned to a cactus or wrapped around a bridge abutment is freeing. It'll be my own fault, at least, since I decided to climb on the back of her bike.

I wanted to know where Celine was going, but I didn't do it for the enclave or Dad or even myself. I did it because I was worried about her. Letting her take off—alone and upset—was too much for me to stomach.

When we slow down to weave through a grid of narrower residential streets, I squint in confusion at the road signs, then laugh. We're only a couple of minutes from Celine's apartment. That death-defying, law-breaking race against our own mortality was completely and utterly pointless.

*What a woman.* I'm proud of her for putting me through the paces, although she might not have been trying to scare me at all. Pressed tightly against mine, her body is twice as relaxed as it was when we started this ride. Something tells me she needed this.

Celine parks next to Luca's car, tugs her helmet off and hangs it on the handlebars. "You don't see anything," she says. "You don't hear anything, and if you even think about asking a question—"

"You'll drive off a bridge with me tied to the front of the motorcycle."

"No. I wouldn't risk my bike like that." She blinks at me, a smile tilting the corner of her mouth up. "I'd toss you off myself."

"Got it," I say, following her to the home ahead.

Celine knocks, and a good-looking older woman opens the door. She's visibly frazzled, and her eyes narrow as she spots me. "Who is this?"

"He's with me," Celine says. My chest puffs up. After being relegated to a couch for the first time in my life, then mostly ignored by the occupants of her apartment, it's nice to be claimed. Even in this minor way.

"If you vouch for him, that's enough for me," the woman says, reaching out to shake my hand. "I'm Harry." *Ah, this is the mythical Harry I've heard so much about.*

I return the gesture, dipping my head respectfully and noticing her long dark nails. "I've heard nothing but good things," I say, deciding to risk Celine's wrath by responding. I was raised to be polite, and some instincts don't die easily.

Harry chuckles, but it's too brittle to be genuine. "Bunch of liars, all of them," she mutters, leading us into the house and closing the door.

Luca is inspecting the windows. Wide and squat, they're multi-paned and low to the ground. He's bent over when we walk in, and he doesn't turn around to greet us. I slant a glance at Celine, but she's avoiding him too. *Trouble in paradise?*

"Luca told me you would be here as soon as you could," Harry says to Celine. "Thank you for coming. It's pretty chaotic back there."

She points her strangely curved fingernail at a closed door. It's as old as the rest of the house, stained a rich cherry color and scuffed along the bottom, like it gets closed by careless, swinging feet more than gentle hands.

"Do you want me to talk to them?" Celine asks, shifting her weight and ignoring the thanks.

"If you don't mind. Anika's English is incredible—exactly as you said it would be—but some things are hard to explain because of her age."

Celine nods and visibly straightens her spine, shrugging out of her leather jacket and handing it to me. "This conversation calls for the wings," she says to no one in particular. A beat later, they pop through the holes in her shirt, fluffy, white, and ridiculously soft and sexy.

During my last text conversation with Sheena, I told her I was developing a Pavlovian reaction to feathers, and I'm starting to think the joke might've been a little too real.

"Stay here," Celine orders me.

I dip my chin, happy to follow her orders and figure out what crawled up Luca's ass and died while I'm at it. Celine and Harry step through the door to the adjoining room, giving me a glimpse of enough supernatural children to make my back sweat before they close it firmly behind them.

"Is she okay?" Luca's voice is rough. Given his cold shoulder and her hot anger, I'm convinced he's the reason Celine tore out of the apartment like her feet were on fire.

"I don't know anything," I say, shaking my head.

He sighs. "She shouldn't have brought you here."

"I'm not going to fuck up," I snap, bristling at the familiar stupid implication. Alistair and Luca don't even know my brother, Callum, but they manage to act just like him sometimes.

Luca turns away from the window, scrunching his face up. "Didn't say you would, but now you're more involved. If she took you on a joyride around Vegas, the odds that whoever is watching us saw you are high. It was a dumb risk."

"I didn't give her much choice," I admit. "She was shaken. I didn't think she should be alone."

Luca grunts. "Check the entry points."

Shaking my head at his bossy dismissal, I do as he asks and scan the other windows. Nothing is broken or split, and the wood along the sill is scarred, but with no fresh gashes. Like the door, they're well-maintained, but old. There are smudges on some of the lower panes, as if someone with tiny legs pressed their even tinier fingers against the glass while looking out.

Beyond that, it's hard to get a feel for who's been here. In addition to the thick coating of magic over the entire house, there are so many traces of different supernaturals, it's impossible to pick out anything specific.

I blow out a breath to clear my nose. "This place is one of a kind."

"Harry is one of a kind," Luca says. "And she deserves answers about how someone managed to enter her home in the middle of the night without her knowing."

Nodding, I swallow my initial suggestion. I've been here long enough to know they won't consider calling the enclave for help with anything. With how my dad and Joshua run things, I'm not surprised, but it does bother me.

A flash of something catches my eye. I bend over, shove the heavy checkered curtains aside, and pull the object free from where it's wedged in a thick crack in the floorboards.

I call for Luca, and he's at my side a heartbeat later.

"A feather."

He runs his finger along the edge, and I nod absentmindedly. It's big, about the same size as Celine's, but while hers are as white as freshly fallen snow, this one is the color of freshwater pearls. Not quite gray or white, but a cross between the two.

"This could belong to our mystery assassin," Luca says, stuffing it in his pocket.

Excited by the discovery, we search the rest of the entry points quickly and thoroughly, but there's no other sign that anyone else has been here.

The scuffed door swings open, and Celine and Harry step through, closing it behind them. I glance at Celine's wings, noting the differences in the feathers. Not the same.

"No sign of forced entry," Luca says. "And you were right, Harry—the wards didn't go off at all."

"Definitely an angel," Celine mutters, the deep groove returning to the center of her forehead. I ignore the urge to smooth it out. That's not my place. If she wants to frown, she can.

"I guess the kids didn't know anything?" Luca asks, glancing at the closed door.

"Nope," she sighs. "They can talk about growing up and their parents, but they get stuck every time I press them to tell me how they ended up here. It's like a record-scratch moment in their memory." Her frown grows, taking over her entire face.

"Trauma can cause memory loss," I say, vaguely remembering a lecture I mostly slept through during my supernatural psychology class at Starfall Academy.

"Yeah, but these reactions are too uniform. The trauma response wouldn't be identical for this many different kids."

"You suspect something," Harry says, her strange yellow eyes sharpening.

"More like someone," Celine admits. "Except some of the pieces aren't adding up. Regardless of who is doing this, though, I don't think they plan to hurt the children or you. If they wanted to, they could have last night."

Luca's phone buzzes, and he pulls it out of his pocket and clears his throat. "Alistair found a spot for the overflow kids," he says. "He's going to call you to coordinate, Harry."

Celine nods, but her eyes are far away. She studies the wall as I study her, watching as her wings subtly twitch, then sharpen into knives. As Luca talks quietly with Harry about transferring some of the kids to the new location, I notice he doesn't mention the feather I found. Since I was told in no uncertain terms to shut the fuck up, I keep it to myself.

Everyone is tight-lipped here, even among their allies. They clearly like Harry, working with her closely and trusting her to keep these kids safe—but they aren't fully transparent with her.

Lies may be optional for the enclave, but here on the Fringes they're a way of life. Withholding details is innate, almost like breathing. I don't know how anyone ever truly relaxes while knowing that everyone around them could be blowing smoke up their ass.

It's a subtle but major difference from how I was raised. The enclave has seen its fair share of betrayal, don't get me wrong. Just ask my dad about witches, then stand back and watch the vein in his forehead pulse, but information is usually readily available.

*You're a hypocrite, Ciprian Casanell.* I silence my conscience as we leave Harry's house.

The tension is so thick we may need an axe to cut through it. My shoulders clench, rising incrementally the longer the silence drags on. Luca's quiet anger is an exact match for my family's brand of rage. You would think I would be numb to it by now, but instead it's like he's pouring lemon juice in a paper cut.

"Luca," Celine begins, her voice stiff.

"Not now," he says. "You've made your feelings clear. We can discuss the break-in when we get back to your apartment."

"But—"

"I said not now." Luca doesn't raise his voice. He doesn't even look at us, but Celine flinches as if he slapped her.

I keep my mouth closed. Of all the things that aren't my business in any way, shape, or form, this is at the top of the list.

Luca wrenches his car door open. The metal complains loudly about his rough treatment. Celine watches him drive away, then heads for her bike, her wings flipping between so many settings that it's clear her head is spinning.

I hesitate before holding her leather jacket out to her. In this mood, I'm not sure I'm brave enough to climb on the back of her bike.

She snatches it from me, lips pursed. Her wings shudder but don't retract. She closes her eyes and tries again. This time, they don't move at all, shifting instead to sharp-edged blades.

Is stress the cause? At first, I thought fear triggered the knives, but I can't sense any of that from her. Besides a whiff here and there, fear isn't an emotion Celine she seems to have much of.

"Is this a supernatural neighborhood?" I ask, glancing along the street at the small but well-kept urban block. There are no front yards, only a row of squatty entryway steps flanked by rusting cast-iron railings. A handful of pots with assorted drought-resistant plants litter the stoops.

"Yeah, why?" Celine snarls, glaring at me like the trouble with her wings is my fault.

I hide my smile, unbothered by her grumpiness. "Let's take a walk," I suggest.

Ignoring me, Celine rolls her eyes and then closes them again. Her fingers curl as she concentrates, but her wings, still in blade mode, remain stubbornly in place. I suspect they're the only thing protecting me from a grisly death.

"Fine. Let's go for a fucking walk." She takes off down the street, each step echoing. With her hands balled against her thighs, her wings' gentle, rolling bounce is comically at odds with the rest of her furious march.

Again, I keep my mouth firmly shut as I match her pace. The only way I'll gain any ground with the beautiful angel is by letting her come to me. Hopefully, it won't take long. I'm not a fan of uncomfortable silences.

# THIRTY-TWO

## CELINE

Ciprian strolls along at my side like there's nothing inside his beautiful head but fluff. I don't buy it for a second, but I've made too much of a mess on my own to focus on him.

My wings clink with every step. The annoying sound is proof that my emotions are out of control. And the horror reel playing in my head . . . it's all too much. Waking up to my hand around Luca's neck. *Clink.* His face falling in the bathroom when I didn't tell him I love him. *Clink.* How he'd driven away without looking back. *Clink.*

I will my wings to disappear, then beg them when that doesn't work.

*Clink.*

Fuck. Fuck. FUCK.

I know I messed up. I should have said something—anything.

But Luca blindsided me. I had no space to process, no room to be alone. I had to get out. And damn him for making this harder than it has to be. He knows me. Knows I avoid attachment. There's no way he thought telling me how he felt wouldn't send me running.

My itch is all-consuming. Less warning, more torment. It hasn't fully gone away in weeks; there's too much going on.

I'm being hunted by my father's legion of assassins while someone deposits kids around me as if I've been cursed by a celestial stork. To top it off, I've got a basilisk shifter swearing he loves me, a surly vampire embedding himself beneath my skin, and a tagalong demon who acts more like a puppy than the sinister being he really is.

I want to scream—but I can't even do that, because it would cause a scene. I peer at the houses around us and consider letting one rip, anyway. If my wings would go away, I might risk it, but I'm too recognizable with them out.

Ciprian bends to examine a spindly cactus growing from a crack in the sidewalk, then hums softly as he continues to amble along at my side. I narrow my eyes at him. He saved Alistair, and I still can't figure out his motives.

"You have nothing to say?" I demand, fearing I may lose it if the only voice I'm subjected to is the one screaming inside my head.

"Oh, hot wings, I have plenty to say." Ciprian looks at me and winks. "But I got the impression this was a rampage ramble."

"What the fuck is a rampage ramble?" Can't he tell I have no patience for vague bullshit right now?

"You know—a walk where you purge your pissed off, frustrated, sometimes illogical thoughts all at once with no consequences. You air them out to a friend and relieve the pressure so they don't accidentally come out sideways and bite you . . . or someone else."

"You're not my friend," I point out, then stiffen as my magical core sends a stinging wave of pain along my skin. *That was a lie?* The last thing I need is a new friend. I can't even protect the ones I have. My heart beats faster in my chest, and the itch migrates to the middle of my back where I have no chance of reaching it.

"Maybe not," Ciprian says with a shrug. "But I could be today. I promise not to judge."

I let a sliver of my magic out, my runes barely visible in the bright sunlight as I test his intent. *No signs of deception.* He means it. I frown. That's so . . . strange.

I try to vanish my wings again, groaning when they stubbornly stay put. Ciprian doesn't comment. I sigh. Am I really about to confide in him? He's practically a stranger. *Or a new friend.*

"I am pissed off," I admit, kicking a chunky piece of gravel with all my strength. It flies across the street, hits the side of a house, and sends up a small cloud of dust on impact.

"Be specific," Ciprian encourages. "What's making you feel that way?"

"Fucking everything," I hiss. "These kids are popping up left and right. I can't even pick up groceries without expecting to find a winged toddler in my cart. And my dad—he's a complete and total sack of shit. I know he's trying to kill me, but the kids don't fit with his methods. It doesn't make any sense, and that pisses me off more."

Ciprian nods. "Like you're overlooking something that would bring order to the chaos."

"Yes!" I throw my hands up. "Exactly that. And everyone expects me to have an answer for the orphans. Just because we're all angels doesn't make them my problem. I left the celestial realm behind, and I'm on birth control; I don't want to adopt fifty kids."

"Of course you don't," Ciprian says with a shudder. "That's grotesque. What else?"

"I'll tell you what else," I snarl, pivoting to face him. "Alistair,

Luca, even you—you all look at me like an expensive steak you want to sink your teeth into. I'm not a hunk of meat. And it takes me time to understand my feelings. Some of us don't wake up every morning with perfect emotional clarity."

"May I point something out?" Ciprian asks.

I shoot him a warning glare, then nod shortly. "If you must."

"I think you're more comfortable with people looking at you like a piece of meat than you are when they look at you like something else."

I scoff. "You're full of shit."

Ciprian shrugs, unbothered by my hostility. "Maybe. But it seems to bother you more when they look at you like you're on a shrine rather than the dinner table."

"What's the difference?" I whisper, my wings drooping to graze the ground. "It doesn't matter if I'm on a plate or a pedestal, I'm still an object to them."

"Hmm, you could be right about that." Ciprian nudges my shoulder with his, his tone forcefully cheerful. "But you can't know for sure if you only tackle it during a rampage ramble."

"For the record, though, you're just Celine to me. Angry, more walls than a labyrinth, witty but sometimes cruel, and painfully hot. You're interesting because you aren't perfect or shitty—you're everything in between."

"Do you think I'm overreacting?" I ask, trying to make sense of his speech. It was convoluted, but not a single word rang false.

"I think you're just reacting." Ciprian nudges me again and grins. "Give them room to do the same, yeah? No one has a playbook."

"You think you're pretty smart, don't you?" I ask, trying to rile him up one last time. I feel way better, and I don't know how he managed it.

Ciprian stares at me, and a weird expression crosses his face. "I'm not smart; I'm a fuckup. I have a lot of miles of rampage rambles racked up. If there were a reward program, I'd be in platinum."

Frowning, I study him more closely. There's a tightness around his eyes that wasn't there a minute ago. I want to ask why he thinks he's a fuckup, but I don't get the chance.

The whooshing sound of flapping wings interrupts the silence.

It's been a long time since I flew, but the sound is more familiar to me than breathing. Unmistakably celestial. I stiffen, looking up, then around for something to defend myself with. "Get out of here," I bark at Ciprian, giving up on finding a good weapon. My bare hands are more than enough.

"Not a chance," he whispers. "Don't move or speak."

"Don't tell me what to—"

Ciprian claps his hand over my mouth and pushes me into the nearby retaining wall. *Fuck.* I need to prepare to fight, and I can't see anything but his shoulder. His stupidity is going to get us killed.

The flapping wings get louder until they're right on top of us. *Enough of this.* I brace to shove Ciprian out of my way, but . . . no one lands. The sound gets fainter, then disappears completely. It doesn't make sense. We're standing against a concrete wall in broad daylight. How could they have missed us?

Forcefully, I move Ciprian, but I'm too late. The sky is clear. Our winged visitor is gone.

I spin to face Ciprian, my mouth dropping open to yell. Then I close it. Open but unfocused, his eyes are bottomless, swirling pools of inky, roiling obsidian. Magic skitters along my skin, only obvious now that my battle adrenaline is fading.

"What did you do?" I ask, frustrated beyond belief. This was my chance to figure out who Dad sent to kill me. This was my chance to get answers.

"I saved your life," Ciprian says, blinking until his eyes clear. "Did you forget someone is trying to kill you?"

My wings droop. Suddenly, I don't have the energy to yell anymore. "This was my best shot to figure out what's going on, and I didn't even get a good look," I whisper. "You hid us somehow. How did you do it?"

Ciprian's onyx eyes turn hard. There's no hint of our earlier camaraderie, only impenetrable, flat darkness. "I showed him what would be true nine times out of ten: a blank, boring street. I'm sorry that messed up your plans."

"Don't do it again," I say, but my words lack their usual bite.

The Ciprian staring back at me is an enigma. I don't recognize him at all, and it makes me wonder: if there are multiple versions of him, how will I ever know which one is real?

I need to get home.

This time, when I tell my wings to retract, they obey, and I'm able to drive us back to my apartment. I don't take the long way.

By the time I unlock the stack of deadbolts on my front door, my stress is hovering at a manageable level. Ciprian trails along behind me, silently scrolling on his phone. His face is pinched.

I don't ask him what's wrong. It's not my business, and it's not how we do things out here on the Fringes. Information is currency. It wouldn't be right to demand credit on a personal account I never intend to settle.

This afternoon was an exception. A mistake. I told him too much. Learning about his magic will be my payment for those ill-thought-out moments of transparency. I don't plan to share the knowledge with anyone else unless I have to.

Ciprian has some sort of illusion power; there's no other way he could have hidden us from the angel. It's not a common skill, at least not around here, so it didn't occur to me before.

I know a couple of witches who can manage simple visual warps, but it's incredibly taxing and they have to prepare ahead of time. Brandy is one of them, but she would be laid up in bed if she tried something on the fly, and Ciprian is fine. Besides the tightness around his eyes, he couldn't look healthier.

"Do you need to take a nap?" I ask.

I promised myself I wouldn't prod, but now I'm curious about how he regenerates his energy. It's the one thing all supernatural species share. Alistair feeds on blood, and Imani soaks in water. I have no idea how demons recover their magic.

"I'm fine," Ciprian says. His tone is polite and detached. I don't like it. Somehow, it's less honest that his snark.

"Suit yourself." I lock the door behind us, my shoulders climbing to my ears. It's ridiculous. I'm more stressed walking into my own home than I was while being actively hunted by a winged assassin.

"Remember, you're everything in between," Ciprian says.

Sighing, I face him, feeling like there's an impossibly large boulder coated with itching powder strapped to my back. "What do you even mean by that?" I ask.

"If you don't forget that you're everything in between, it's easier to remember that they are too."

I frown. "You think I should ignore what happened?"

Ciprian shakes his head. "You're doing it again. You try to distill everything, to separate the salt from the water—like saltwater's too messy for you. But it's real. Just more complicated. I know you want things neat and orderly, but life doesn't work that way. You've got to embrace the mess."

A bolt of pain shoots through my jaw, and I realize I'm clenching it way too tightly. I roll it around until the cramp stops. His words ring true, even without using my gift. "Anything else, wise one?"

"Yeah, don't call me wise. It makes me feel old." Ciprian grins, a hint of the playful, sarcastic demon peeking out at me.

Rolling my eyes, I flip him off, head down the hall, and say, "In case it wasn't already clear to you, Luca and I are together."

Ciprian snorts. "Please. I've known that since the first night I stepped into the Naked Fang. Do you also want to tell me the walls in here are a cool, verdant green while you're at it? Because that's the only thing more obvious."

"It's springtime viridescence, dick-for-brains," I say, looking over my shoulder at him.

"Cool." Ciprian glances at his phone, then back up at me. "Since you've finally quit hiding Luca like a bad bald spot, can I have the spare room?"

"No," I say waspishly, then continue down the hall. My smile fades with each step.

*Embrace the mess. Embrace the mess.* I repeat Ciprian's words in my mind like a battle cry, not quite sure I know how to put them into practice. Hand on the doorknob, I release my breath and twist the cool metal. I'm not a coward, and one thing is crystal clear to me: I owe Luca and Alistair an explanation.

# THIRTY-THREE

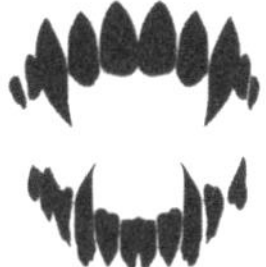



## ALISTAIR

They're back. Ear pressed to the door, I eavesdrop without shame, ready to kill Ciprian if he steps even one toe out of line. After he gives her a cryptic pep talk, I'm surprised—then thrilled—to hear Celine claim Luca.

Through it all, Luca's poker face doesn't budge. He sits stiffly in the chair by the window, the lamp casting harsh shadows in the hollows beneath his cheekbones.

I jump back as the door swings open, trying to appear casual as Celine walks in and tosses her leather jacket on the bed. She stares at it, her wings twitching.

"It's dark in here," she mutters, glancing at me and cocking one eyebrow. "I know you're deathly allergic to the sun, but I didn't realize an overhead light could take you out."

I cross the room in a flash, reaching around her to flip the light switch. "I was trying to convince Luca to nap before work. Neither of you got enough sleep last night."

"Nothing a little caffeine can't fix." She smiles at me. It doesn't reach her eyes.

*Enough of this chitchat. It's a waste of time.*

"You bolted this morning," I remind her. "We were worried."

She looks between us calmly. "I never asked you to worry."

"That's bullshit," Luca hisses, shoving to his feet. "We don't need permission to care about your well-being. Are you telling me you wouldn't give a damn if something happened to Imani? Because I know you would. Get it through your head, Celine—someone caring about you isn't a threat!"

"Yes, it is!" she screams. "That's exactly what it is. And the more you care about me, the bigger that threat becomes."

They can use the word care all they want, but we all know what they really mean.

I hold my hand up before Luca respond. We won't get anywhere if they let their anger do the talking. "And why is that, angel?" I soften my voice until it's barely more than a whisper.

"Because people who care for me pay for it," she says.

Her voice is devoid of emotion, but her wings give her away. Sharp as knives, the feathers begin to condensate—beads of water rolling down the edges before dripping onto the carpet.

For an instant, I'm transfixed by the sight. I've never seen her wings convey more than one emotion at a time, but they're clearly showing stress and pain right now . . . even as Celine does her best to hide both.

Chest heaving, with his hair sticking out in all directions, Luca grunts and scoops Celine up. He carries her to the bathroom and sets her on the bathmat, throwing the shower curtain aside to let her wings drip directly into the tub.

"You'll be upset if the carpet gets wet," he says matter-of-factly.

"And you'll die because of me." Celine grips Luca's shoulders, staring at him with bloodshot eyes. "I'm not who you think I am —I'm who he made me to be. The perfect angel you're imagining? She's not me."

"That logic is warped." Luca tucks her hair behind her ears. "You're the only fucking angel I know, and I'm pretty fucking positive I've never once thought you were perfect."

I prop my hip against the sink and smirk at them both. "You're captivating, angel, which is far more interesting than perfection."

"What can we do to make this morning not happen again?" Luca takes a step back. "All I can think about is that you'd rather die than hear me say I love you again."

"Luca," Celine sighs, fisting his shirt in her hands and yanking him back to her chest. "It's not like that, I needed to think and sort through the chaos. Everything is out of control."

He slumps, obviously disappointed but doing his best to hide it. "I can avoid adding to the things that throw you off balance."

Celine nods, then frowns. Perhaps having gotten what she wanted from him, she's now realizing she doesn't want it after all.

"I told Ciprian about us," she says. "You can move into the bedroom if you want to."

It's an olive branch. Luca is proud, and I worry he won't take it, but he proves me wrong when he dips his head and kisses her.

"Thank the gods," he groans. "I'm not sure my spine could take another night on the air mattress. I was thinking about trying to sleep standing up."

Celine smiles, and her wings stop dripping. "I want you both to know I'm trying," she whispers. "It might not be a quick fix. I'm struggling with the . . . messiness, but I want you two here where I can protect you."

I hide my smile by scrubbing my hand over my stubble. This is Celine doing exactly what I feared she couldn't: bending. That's worth celebrating. A dark shadow shifts through my mind, blotting out the joy of the reconciliation. If she tried to send me away . . . my reaction would be uncontrollable. This obsession I have with her, with them, it's not good for me, but it's too late to change course.

"Thank you, angel." I step into them and press a kiss to her neck. "We'll do our best not to make it overly difficult." And I'll control my urges. Forever, if that's what it takes. She must never be allowed to see the raging monster inside me, the one who sees only prey, weakness, and victory. I'll keep that side of myself away from her at all costs.

"Speak for yourself," Luca teases. "Now that we're all here, we need to talk about the feather."

Celine shakes her wings, flinging water into the tub. "What feather?" she asks.

Luca reaches into his pocket and pulls out a rumpled feather. At first glance, it seems to be the same as Celine's, but when I look closer, the colors are different.

"Ciprian found it at Harry's," Luca says, pressing the feather into Celine's hand. "Is it familiar?"

She turns the feather over, holding it up to the light and rolling her bottom lip between her teeth. "Many angel feathers look like this . . ."

"But it's familiar?"

Celine shakes her head. "It's not enough to go on. Even for speculation." She holds it next to her drenched wings. "There are a lot of angels with wings this color," she says again, softer this time.

"It was worth a shot." Luca throws one arm over her shoulder. "They aren't nearly as pretty as yours anyway."

Celine laughs. "White wings are the most common."

"And do most of the common white wings in the celestial realm catch fire or transform into blades?" I ask.

"No," Celine purrs, dragging her fingertips up my cheek, then fluttering her wings so flirtatiously that her intent is obvious. "Mine are one of a kind in that way."

Luca snaps his fingers, breaking the moment. "I bet they're part of your magic," he says. "You can spot lies—but your wings? They're your truth, and you have to wear it on your back."

"Amazing," Celine says drily. "I think you've landed on something there."

"Hey!" Luca laughs. "It's not like you voluntarily offer up the details. You drop breadcrumbs—stingily—then expect me to keep up."

"Stingily? Really?"

"Shut up, I'm sleep deprived," Luca says. "Take a nap with me, baby."

"Only because you asked nicely."

Celine grabs Luca's hand and leads him to the bedroom. She carefully places the feather in the drawer of her bedside table, then glances at her leather jacket. It's dangling off the end of the bed where she tossed it when she came in.

Her brown eyes narrow, then she growls. "Fuck me, I can't do it." Grabbing the jacket, she stomps into the closet, and I hear hangers rattling. When she comes back out, her face is more annoyed than it was when she went in.

"It's okay to want an orderly space, angel," I say.

"I know that." Celine shrugs. "Some demon told me to embrace the chaos, though, and I'm exploring what that's like for me."

"It's not terrible advice, but I think you'll be able to embrace uncontrollable chaos more if you keep your home the way you like it." Luca takes his shirt off, folds it neatly, then puts it on the bedside table.

He crawls into the bed, his eyes drifting closed as soon as his head hits the pillow. With his chest bare and the blanket slung low over his hips . . . I want to follow him under those covers.

Smirking, I tug the comforter down to expose his lower abs. Celine grins at me and fans her neck.

Luca cracks one eye open. "Stop eye fucking me. Both of you. I'm too tired."

"Have a good nap," I say, backing away from the bed reluctantly. "I have to touch base with some of my contacts, then check on Harry. I'll see you both at the club tonight."

Celine frowns at me. "Take the demon with you."

"You mean, your best friend, Ciprian?"

"He surprises me." Celine looks thoughtful as she snuggles into Luca's side. "Constantly."

"And that's a good thing?" I pause with my hand on the door.

"I'm not sure yet."

"Think about it while you sleep," I suggest.

Celine perks up. "Do you know a way to make dreams productive?"

"Why do you sound excited about that?" Luca groans. "Go to sleep. Dream like a normal person."

"What do normal people even dream about?" I ask, shaking my head, curious to hear what a mythical shifter such as Luca could think is normal.

"You know, sex, getting eaten by a shark . . . shit like that." He yawns, his mouth stretching wide.

"So wet dreams and nightmares? Got it." Celine stretches and her left wing smacks Luca in the face.

He sputters, his eyes snapping open as he removes feathers from his mouth. "Those things should come with a warning label."

I chuckle, strangely reluctant to leave them. But I'm not someone who naps, and I'm falling behind with my business. I need to make calls, work through my latest encryption system, and vet the additional supernatural foster homes I've uncovered.

Despite all of that, I'm almost tempted to throw off decades of precedent and crawl back into bed with Celine and Luca.

"Be safe, Ali." Luca's voice is raspy, and when I look, I find his hazel eyes locked on me.

"Of course." I smile. Then—unable to resist—I go back to the bed and pull the covers over Celine, kissing her surprised mouth. "Have a good nap."

Leaving the room quickly before I can do anything else to embarrass myself, I find Ciprian sitting on the couch. He's scrolling on his phone as a mindless sitcom plays on the TV.

"You're clearly busy." I smirk around my fangs. "But are you up for a field trip?"

"Yes," he responds without looking.

"It could be dangerous."

"Even better; I need to charge."

I tilt my head, considering him. Most supernaturals guard their magical secrets viciously. His comment, while vague, was oddly lax. There's no way Ciprian grew up in a fringe community —I'm starting to think he's just good at blending in.

Or he could be lying. I can rarely tell with him, and that unsettles me. We've basically abducted him, yet he hasn't complained once. Why would he leave his own life behind so easily?

"After sundown," I say, glancing at my watch and promising myself to pay closer attention to him tonight. If Celine has a hard time reading him and I feel the same, it's time to figure out what makes Ciprian tick. The last thing we need is to discover we're living with a bomb.

Ciprian drops into my passenger seat at dusk and slaps his thighs. "What's our dangerous mission?" he asks. "Are we settling a score? Busting someone's kneecaps for failure to remit payment?"

I laugh as I back away from the curb. "What exactly do you think I do for a living? I'm not a cheesy Mafia enforcer."

"Disappointing," Ciprian murmurs. "But you trade information, right? And you said it might be dangerous. I figured we were going to handle a client."

I shake my head. "Sorry to disappoint. We're helping Harry out."

Ciprian thrums his fingers on his knee, tossing me a nervous look. "I thought your contact was going to come get the kids."

"They weren't able to make it out," I tell him. "We're going to drop them off instead."

"Gods," he groans. "You said dangerous, not miserable. What if they cry?"

"Then we'll kill one to teach the others a lesson."

Ciprian snaps his head toward me, then whistles. "Shit, you said that without flinching. I actually believed you for a minute." He glances out the window. "How long is the drive?"

"About an hour. My contact lives near Valley of Fire." I shoot him a narrow-eyed look. "Honestly, I'm starting to worry more about being cooped up with you than the kids. Tell me something . . ."

"What?"

"Do people often complain about you during road trips?"

"That's for me to know and you to find out." Ciprian smirks out the window, his mischievous expression captured perfectly in the reflection.

I pull up outside of Harry's house as the moon rises above the shimmering Vegas skyline. Before I can even get out of the car, she comes out with three kids. The smallest child has her stubby arms wrapped tightly around her neck. Harry smiles at me, but her eyes are bright with unshed tears.

"Fuck," I mutter.

"She's a good woman." There's no hint of a joke in Ciprian's tone this time. "Let's not make this any harder on her than it has to be."

He opens his car door, climbs out, and waves his hands. Two of the kids giggle, and I watch, amazed as the toddler reaches for Ciprian, his blue eyes shining with laughter. I join them silently, not wanting to cause a distraction.

"Can I show you something cool?" Ciprian asks the kids, winking at Harry. The oldest child says something in the angelic language, and the two younger ones nod enthusiastically.

Ciprian's black eyes go unfocused, then the toddler gasps, reaching for the air in front of his face as the youngest girl giggles with the careless abandon most kids in the Fringes are missing. The older one is more subdued, but the smile that lights her face is enough to make my throat lock up.

"Wow," Harry whispers to me. "If I had his help to get them to agree to nap time, I would look five years younger."

The kids walk calmly to the car, focused on something only they can see. Once they're inside, Ciprian blinks and his eyes come back into focus.

High-pitched complaints follow, and he winces. "I don't have a clue what they're saying, but something tells me I've opened a box I won't be able to close." The skin at the corner of his eyes wrinkles slightly as he smiles, bracketing the dark circles under them.

"You're their new favorite toy." Harry pats him on the arm, then wipes at her eyes, ferociously brushing a tear away as Ciprian waves at her and walks back to the car.

"I'm sending Anika to make things easier," she tells me. "She's got the language mostly mastered. She'll be able to help the other two adjust, although I hate to lose her."

"We'll make sure she's safe," I assure her, hating that we have to separate them at all. Anger burns in my gut. If we had the resources to outfit Harry properly, maybe Anika could stay. "I'll text you as soon as they're settled."

I turn to walk away, and Harry smacks my butt hard enough to bruise. I look back at her in disbelief. "Chin up, Alistair," she orders, handing me a small bag. "Those kids are tough. They'll be fine."

"Yes, ma'am." I back away slowly, making a show out of rubbing my ass.

"Don't call me ma'am." She scowls. "It makes me sound older than I am."

I put my free hand on my heart, bowing dramatically at the waist. "I'll never do it again."

"See that you don't." Harry lifts her head defiantly, no sign of her earlier tears. "Now get out of here. Those kids need a good night's sleep, and they won't get it if you keep talking nonsense with me while that nightmare shows them gods know what."

Half listening, I nod and climb in the car. Ciprian shushes me as I slam the door, a wild terror in his eyes.

"What?" I demand.

"You'll wake them up," he whispers.

I turn to the back seat, shocked to find all three of them not only buckled in but sound asleep. I level Ciprian with a hard stare. "How did you manage that?"

He shrugs. "I'm good with kids."

"Did you knock them out?"

Ciprian rolls his eyes. "Yeah, Alistair, I smacked the shit out of three small, terrified kids to get them to shut up." He holds his fists up and throws two fake punches at me. "It worked like a charm, but I'm ready for another round if they wake up."

Shaking my head, I crank the engine and head toward the highway, glancing at my phone to put our destination in.

"You shouldn't mess with your phone while driving kids around," Ciprian says, slumping back against the seat. His jittery energy from earlier is gone. I consider teasing him about it, but sleeping children are the best-case scenario. The smart thing to do is keep my mouth shut, drive, and hope they don't wake until we get there.

"If I fall asleep, wake me up." Ciprian yawns. "I don't want to get a bad road-trip report card."

I consider asking him why he's so tired all of a sudden, but I hold off. My instincts tell me I'll learn more about Ciprian by watching him than interrogating him.

Within five minutes, he's asleep, a few strands of platinum hair falling over his closed eyes. Reckless demon. He barely knows me. I could leave him high and dry in the Valley of Fire to get eaten by coyotes if I wanted to. Smiling to myself, I wonder what Celine and Luca will think when they hear that Ciprian is a wonderful babysitter and a terrible bodyguard.

# THIRTY-FOUR

## CELINE

I wake to Luca's scent. One of his arms is tossed carelessly over my waist. The weight, the warmth . . . I'm not used to it. Maybe that's why my heart is racing. *Liar.*

Luca swears he loves me.

I can't even deny it. My magic saw the truth, and even if it hadn't, the expression on his face was proof enough. Ruthlessly honest. Stubbornly insistent. In that moment, it felt less like he was offering me his heart and more like he was tearing mine from my chest.

Nothing has scared me that badly in years. Not since I found my mom's lifeless body sprawled across the tile floor of our summer home. That sharp tug in my gut, the pinpricks of electricity racing across my skin, urging me to run.

When she died, my grief and terror were followed by an emotion that shames me to this day: relief. Relief that I could finally leave. Relief that—for the first time in my miserable life—I could be free.

Free of the soul-crushing agony of trying and failing to protect her from the man she bound herself to and refused to leave behind.

The truth is, he'd been stealing her from me for years. I lost more of her every time he laid a hand on her. But that day, he stole her permanently.

So I ran. After pressing a kiss to her cold cheek, I made a vow to her and to myself that I wouldn't let him hurt me again. She would be his last theft.

The only time I ever heard her stand up to him was when they argued about me. He complained I was stealing her attention, slapping her across the face when she told him that was how it was supposed to be. I remember watching in horror, frozen behind the curtains, as blood trickled from the corner of her mouth. She stood strong in that moment, defiant in the face of his jealous cruelty.

"My daughter is the best of us," she told him, lifting her chin. "She will do great things, with or without your support."

He made her pay for every word. And while I cowered beneath the heavy linen drapes, I learned a lesson I've never forgotten: love is dangerous.

Now, I have someone else I can't bear to lose.

Luca loves me. My mother did, too.

And look where that got her.

I slam the lid of the chest closed, trapping the memory inside and locking it up tight. I don't want to relive my past—once was more than enough.

Luca's arm shifts against my belly, his fingers rubbing gently up and down my arm. "Talk to me, baby," he whispers. "I can't take it back, and gods know I don't want to, but I won't say it again if you don't want to hear it."

His honesty is the sweetest pain.

I sigh, snuggling deeper into his chest. Here in my bedroom, surrounded by the four walls I meticulously painted the color my father hates most, I can almost convince myself things are different. That I don't have a murdered mom. A homicidal dad. And assassins haunting my every step. But my magic is cruel, even now. It won't let me forget the truth.

"I will be the death of you, Luca," I say, sorrow bleeding into my words. "Loving me will be the last thing you do, then I'll be forced to carry the weight until I can't stand it any longer."

"Hey, don't think that way. You don't know that's how it will end." Luca cradles my face in his hand. "We're stronger together, and we both deserve a happy ending."

"Happy endings aren't real," I tell him. "They're sanitized propaganda for people who can't stomach the truth. Most of the original human fairy tales were horrific. Cautionary tales, not bedtime stories."

Luca smiles against my temple. "Okay, say you're right and happy endings aren't real. If you believe that, why do you bother watching reality dating shows? Why do you make Imani soak when she'd rather give up and dry out? Face it, Celine, you may say you don't believe in happily ever after, but you search for it every single day."

He's right, and I know it. Isn't that why I left the celestial realm behind—to discover a version of myself who's happy? Overwhelmed, I press my mouth to Luca's, threading into the kiss all the things I'm not brave enough to put into words.

Luca kisses me back, and it's different this time. His lips are the same. The rough scratch of his stubble is exactly as I remember it, and the thrill remains. But now, I know how he feels about me. All the question marks floating between us are gone, banished by his honesty, for better or worse.

I don't deserve him, but I'm too selfish to let him go. If I can't give him the words he wants to hear, I'll have to show him instead: by holding him tight, pressing my skin against his, and clinging like I'll never let go.

I strip out of my clothes and toss his aside too. My movements are jerky, almost uncoordinated, and when I climb on top of him and sink until we're joined, I don't try to muffle my sigh of relief.

Luca moans softly, pressing his forehead to mine. "You feel amazing," he whispers.

I nod. The stretch of him inside me, the sharing of pleasure, the knowledge that I can trust him not to drive a knife into my back when I turn around—this is better than amazing.

Hungry for more of him, I suck in a startled breath when he surges beneath me and flips us over. Gazing up at his face, I lift my chin, and his lips find mine again.

He starts to thrust, setting a slow, steady pace that drives me wild. His dick piercing grazes the spot inside me that makes my legs turn to jelly. I nibble on the hoop in his bottom lip in retaliation, tugging until he groans my name.

"I'm sorry I panicked," I blurt, staring into his familiar hazel eyes, desperate for him to understand. Ever since I woke up to his pained expression as I pinned him to the wall, I've been hurting him. I never want to see that look on his face again.

"You don't have to apologize," Luca insists, feathering butterfly kisses along the side of my neck. "We're all haunted by something."

I plant my heels on the bed and roll my hips, creating a delicious friction I want to experience every day for the rest of my life. "You never talk about what haunts you," I say, panting as a particularly perfect thrust makes my toes curl.

"You want to discuss it now?" Luca asks, a light sheen on his forehead.

Chuckling, I gasp, then lick the salty sweat off his neck. "After."

Luca grunts and braces both hands on the headboard above me, his fingers curling around the top. He grins. The carefree expression makes my heart leap.

"What are you doing?" I ask.

"Making sure we don't knock a hole in your wall. Or break the bed."

"Why would—" My question melts into a surprised moan as he shoves into me with ten times the force, using his grip on the headboard to get better leverage.

"Your ankles," he says. "Put them to good use."

I curl my legs, walking my feet up his chest until they're both planted on his collarbones. He winces, then kisses my right ankle. "That's it, baby. Try not to be too loud . . . Or scream all you want. They're your neighbors, not mine."

I clench my pussy around his cock in punishment, enjoying the way his eyes flash yellow, his pupils narrowing to horizontal slits. "Do your worst," I taunt, a shiver of anticipation adding an edge to my pleasure.

Luca smiles. The look is monstrous. It's the last thought I have before he systematically tears me to pieces. Hard, deep thrusts; he shows me no mercy, and I refuse to ask for any.

My mouth drops open, and I breathe in the air desperately. It's heavy with sex.

"I'm going to fill you so full of my cum, it'll be dripping out of you later while you dance," Luca growls, sounding nothing like the man I know and everything like the beast inside him. "Then those assholes at the club will know they have no chance."

My pussy tightens automatically, as if it wants him to make good on that promise right now. "Yes," I hiss, driving my hips up and meeting his thrusts halfway.

The jarring motion is brutal, and so is my orgasm. It crashes into me with the force of a sucker punch to the gut, reducing me to a whimpering, quivering, panting mess only capable of gasping Luca's name.

He looks at me, and I'll remember the expression on his face until the day I die.

"Please, Celine. Can I say it?"

At first, I don't understand. Then it hits me, and the realization sends a smaller orgasm ricocheting through my body. "Yes," I gasp. "Tell me. I want to hear it."

"I love you," Luca shouts, loud enough that my neighbors will definitely hear. I like that. No, I *love* that. Knowing that someone, somewhere might overhear Luca claiming me. "Fuck, Celine, I love you so fucking much."

The tendons in his neck bulge as he thrusts into me like he would rather have a heart attack than stop. He chews on the hoop in his lip, and when Luca comes, every line of muscle and bone freezes at once. He holds himself still, then collapses on top of me as our combined panting fills my room.

I kiss his neck, having a hard time catching my breath when my whole body is jelly. That was a life-altering fuck, and I need to regain my equilibrium. I clear my throat. "So we're clear: cum dripping out of me on the pole would not be hot."

"Agree to disagree." Luca pulls back and grabs his phone off the bedside table. His focus sharpens as he reads his messages. "Alistair picked up the kids. No problems there."

"That's good." I stretch my arms above my head. "How long do we have before we need to leave?"

Luca checks the screen again and winces. "Twenty minutes."

I groan as I sit up, my muscles protesting. "Shower."

Luca drops back on his heels, his lips curling into a pout. "Spoil sport."

"Freak," I toss back.

Luca smirks, then raises one eyebrow. "Baby, you haven't seen freaky yet. I've been keeping it vanilla to avoid scaring you off."

I roll my eyes and try to power walk to the bathroom. Unfortunately, it's more of a waddle than a strut.

When something cracks behind me, I whip my head around in time to see Luca straightening a wildly crooked index finger. "What the fuck?" I say, flinching as he snaps another one back into place.

"That's the third bone you've broken today," he says, grinning at me. "I think you're dangerous, Celine."

"I already told you I'm dangerous," I remind him, collecting my hair on top of my head into the mother of all messy buns. "And I don't take credit for the fingers. Getting pulverized by the headboard was your idea."

Luca nods. "I guess you're right."

Ignoring him, I raise my eyebrows as I do the mental math. "You said three bones, but you only reset two fingers."

"Hmm?"

"What's the third bone, Luca?"

Guilt flits across his face. "Umm, well this morning, before you actually woke up, you might have maybe snapped my collarbone. Ciprian fixed it though, and it barely hurts anymore."

"What?" I shriek. "Luca. I had my heels planted against your collarbone just now. Why didn't you say something?"

He puffs out his chest. "I don't mind some pain with my pleasure."

I throw my hands up and turn on my heel, ignoring the tingle that runs through me. *Three fucking bones.* That's ridiculous. Stepping into the shower, I let the warm water soothe my sore muscles, then throw together my bag for the club.

By the time I walk into the kitchen, Luca is plating a salad. He used my favorite raspberry vinaigrette and topped it with toasted almonds. He sniffs the bottle suspiciously. "This smells like shit."

"No, it doesn't," I defend the dressing, snatch the salad from the counter, and take a massive bite. *Gods, that's good.* "Thanks."

Luca watches me eat with satisfaction. "I knew you wouldn't want something heavy before your shift, but after? After, I'm going to feed you your bodyweight in protein and carbs."

I imagine a greasy burger, and my stomach gurgles. "What will you eat?"

"You. Duh." Luca winks and presses a water bottle into my hand.

I hide my smile. Him being in my space is starting to feel good. Maybe happy endings aren't only for fairy tales and porn, after all.

# THIRTY-FIVE

## CIPRIAN

Head pounding, my magic sputters angrily as it tastes my fear while hungering for someone else's. It's pointless, like swallowing your own spit when you need a glass of water.

I shouldn't have made those nightmares to calm the children. My fear stores were already low, and I gained nothing by creating those illusions. But they were scared.

When I got out of the car, their fear hit me. I perked up, then felt sick to my stomach. Orphans dropped in an environment they don't understand . . . I saw Sheena in their faces and acted without thinking.

Now I'm the only one afraid.

Sheena isn't answering my texts. It's been more than twenty-four hours since I last heard from her. Something is wrong. I can't deny it anymore, and I need to hear her voice or I won't be able to sleep.

I glance at Alistair. We skipped the club after a pileup on the interstate made the drive back from Valley of Fire take longer than expected. Head buried in his laptop, he isn't paying any attention to me, so I make for the bathroom. It's late, about an hour before Celine and Luca get back. I have plenty of time to make a call.

Passing through Celine's bedroom, I shut the bathroom door behind me and turn the fan on. I dial Sheena's number, fingers clenching tighter and tighter around the phone as it rings and rings and rings and rings, before going to voicemail.

The acidic bubbling in my chest burns, spreading like lava in my veins. I scrub my palm over my ribcage, trying to push the worry away.

It's going to be okay; she's tough.

I call her again, my heart leaping into my throat when someone picks up.

"Ciprian? Is that you, sweetheart?"

I frown. The voice on the other end of the line is as familiar to me as my own, but it doesn't belong to my best friend. "Sarah? Why do you have Sheena's phone?"

"I'm sorry, sweetie. Someone should have called you, but everything happened so fast—we've been reeling."

"Slow down," I beg. "What happened fast? Where's Sheena?"

I listen to the rest of the call through a dull roaring in my ears. Sinking down on the closed toilet seat, I ask Sarah to keep me updated, then hang up.

Should I text Callum or Gideon? My stomach churns. Why should I reach out to them when they never consider me? I scoff, shaking my head. I would gladly swallow my pride if I thought it would help Sheena, but there's nothing I can add. There's no way my brother isn't already tearing the world apart on her behalf. He doesn't need me. He never has.

What if I never see her again?

Sheena's laughing face flashes through my mind. We fell into our friendship fast. And I admit, it started as a way to piss Callum off on my end. I didn't expect it to last. Now, though . . . she's important to me, and there's nothing I can do to help her.

The panic comes for me. I let it in, allowing the tendrils to grab hold of my organs and squeeze. My palms prickle. Cold sweat beads on my temples. Pleased with its unfettered access, the terror rips and claws at me in a way it hasn't been able to since Dad trained me to master my fear as a boy.

I deserve this. We all do, for failing her.

My breaths come quick and fast. They're coming too fast. I see spots.

The spots expand, looking more like splotches.

Shit. I've let it sink in too deep. I need to get up and go scare Alistair or something before I pass out. This was stupid.

I lurch to my feet, and the room spins. Groping for the wall to steady myself, I grab the shower curtain by mistake and fall to the floor in a pile of damp, wrinkled vinyl.

I try to get up, then fall back into a useless heap.

This is bad.

I close my eyes, trying to banish the fear, but its grip is too strong. Like vines woven through a crumbling brick wall, the panic doesn't want to let me go.

*Calm down,* I tell myself. *You'll be fine if you give yourself time to regroup.*

The door swings open. Didn't I lock it? Three sets of vivid, supernatural eyes stare at me from the tops of their blurry, blob-like bodies. I back up until my head hits the wall.

"What the fuck?" Luca demands.

"Did you hurt him, Alistair?" Celine sounds pissed. On my behalf? Probably not, she's likely upset I yanked her shower curtain down.

"Of course not," Alistair snaps "He was fine a half hour ago."

"I'm okay," I whisper, closing my eyes. Trying to focus on them is making me nauseous.

Celine scoffs. "I don't need magic to know that's a lie. You two, get out."

There's some grumbling, then I hear the door close. When I force one eye open, I see Celine crouching in front of me.

"Sorry," I mutter, embarrassment joining the fear and magical exhaustion. I don't want her to see me this way. Fuck, I don't want anyone seeing me this way.

Is having a panic attack in my crush's bathroom while trapped in a self-induced fear void my new rock bottom? I have to hope it is.

"Don't apologize to have something to say—it's a pathetic human habit," Celine says, pressing the back of her hand to my forehead. "What's wrong with you?"

To my absolute horror, a tear squeezes loose from the corner of my right eye and runs down my cheek. I feel it graze every pore. Clearly, I was wrong. I have more rocks to hit on the way down.

"My best friend is in trouble," I say. "Big trouble. She might not make it through this. I might never see her again, and there's not a godsdamn thing I can do about it. How can I accept that?"

Celine hums, then wipes my tear away—Another rock. "It's not often I see someone crying over a friend in the Fringes," she murmurs.

"That's their loss. Having a friend is . . ." I sigh, not sure how to put it into words.

" . . . One of the best parts about living." Celine finishes the thought for me. "I would kill dozens of strangers for Imani, no questions asked. If I could buy her a moment's peace, I would bleed myself dry as payment."

*Exactly.* I force my eyes open. "But it hurts."

"That's the helplessness, not the friendship." Celine runs her fingers through my hair absentmindedly, and I shudder. It's incredible, and I'm starving for her touch. "Why did you collapse? Your body seems okay."

I tense. We're treading on shaky ground with this line of questioning. I have to tell her something, though. She's too smart, and she's seen too much to be put off by half truths.

"I used too much magic," I whisper. "The kids were scared, and I pushed too hard."

"Alistair said you did something that calmed them down. It was an illusion, wasn't it? Like when you hid us from the angel earlier."

I nod, seeing no reason to hide that truth from her when she's already pieced it together.

Celine's nails scour my scalp, and I curl into her touch like a fucking sapling in search of the sun. If this is another rock on my way down, at least the edges are soft. If that's pathetic, I can't bring myself to care.

"How can I help?" she asks.

I shake my head. "I'll be fine."

"Still a lie, Ciprian."

"It's not something you can help with," I argue.

Her fingers stop moving in my hair, and I curse myself for ruining it. "Let me be the judge of that."

It's tempting, but I shouldn't tell her this. She could figure out who I am and kill me for misleading her. An enclave heir, unprotected, alone, and deep within fringe territory . . . some of the supernaturals around here would cheer if she took me out.

But I want to tell her. Fuck, I want to tell her exactly who I am. Ciprian Casanell, habitual screwup and Dimitri Casanell's last resort for a nightmare demon legacy. The one who relies on humor and wine to get the job done, single-handedly breaking through every layer of family tension and distracting them so they never once have to look in the godsdamn mirror.

If I threw all my cards on the table, would Celine still look at me like I matter?

Here, on the bathroom floor, as I sit on the wet shower curtain, my resolve slips. The pain of being overlooked by my own family is too fresh to ignore. *They didn't even call.*

"It's fear," I blurt. "I need fear to recharge my magic."

For a moment, Celine says nothing. Sprawled out and helpless, I call myself ten different kinds of stupid. She's disgusted. Or she knows who I am. Feeding on fear is an extremely specific demonic trait. If she has even a basic knowledge of my kind or enclave politics . . .

A trickle of fear hits my parched, magical core. It sinks in like the first drop of rain in the desert. And it doesn't belong to me.

Celine's hand tightens in my hair, no longer stroking, but latching on. She's using it to anchor herself.

Energy slides into me at a steady stream.

Opening my eyes, I look at her in wonder. Red hair, pin straight tonight, falls over her shoulders. Her brown eyes are wide open, but unseeing.

Her fear intensifies. The stream has a current now—strong, cold, and demanding. I lap it up.

My headache vanishes.

Her bottom lip trembles.

"That's enough, Celine," I say, hating that I'm getting better even as her eyes well up with tears.

She ignores me, gripping my hair tighter. The feathers of her wings sharpen and quiver, making a spine-chilling sound—slaughterhouse chains stirred by a summer breeze. It's too beautiful to come from fear. She's too beautiful to feed my darkness.

"I'm fine now," I tell her, rolling my muscles around until I realize it's not even a lie anymore. I'm not fully recharged, but like everything about Celine, her fear is potent.

A wave of terror hits me, fifty times the size of the last current, and she whimpers.

The sign of her distress breaks the irresistible grip her fear has over me. I roll to my knees and cradle her face, my thumb grazing her lips.

"Celine, please stop," I beg.

Her eyes are squeezed shut; eyelids creased with the force she's exerting.

Fuck it. I can't stand another second of this.

Signing my own death sentence, I press my lips to hers. My kiss is soft and gentle—everything I wish I could be for her. Not a monster who needs fear to function. I move my lips against hers and try to apologize through the kiss. For lying. For feeding off her fright. For yanking her godsdamn shower curtain down. I apologize for it all.

She gasps into my mouth, and I brace for a punch that doesn't come. The hand fisting my hair adjusts its grip, pulling me in instead of pushing me away. Then Celine kisses me back.

I drop back on my heels, giving her room to process. Maybe she doesn't realize what's happening yet. Or not. She grumbles against my mouth, then crawls forward to straddle my thighs. Our kiss turns hungry and hot. I lick into her mouth, and her tongue battles with mine.

An angel and a demon clinging to each other in a Las Vegas bathroom? I must have fallen into an alternate reality. Five minutes ago, I was at rock bottom, now my wildest dream is coming true.

"Thank you," I whisper stupidly—not even sure what the fuck I'm thanking her for.

"Shut up," Celine mutters, nipping my lower lip. "And never bring it up again."

"Deal." I drag one hand away from her face and run my fingers over the tips of her wings. They're impossibly soft, no sharp edges left. "Do you want to make out some more?"

"Obviously," Celine says, connecting our lips again.

Blood rushes to my cock, and I help her grind down on it. "Anything you want," I promise, letting the words dangle in the shared breath we're fighting over. "I'll give you anything you want."

Celine chuckles. "A demon with manners? I'm amazed."

"Have you met many of my kind who don't take no for an answer?" I growl, my fingers tightening on her hips. "Give me their names. I'll make their final minutes terrifying, I swear it."

She pulls back and I notice her brown eyes are dazed. Celine looks exactly like I do after one too many glasses of wine. I frown, then shudder as she grazes her teeth over the sensitive skin of my neck.

"Your buddy, Roscoe, actually, but . . . I took care of him, so you're a little too late to deliver the terror." Her lips continue exploring my throat, but the blood in my veins is icing over.

*I knew it.* They killed Dad's favorite guard. Everything makes complete sense. I think part of me feared this reality, and it's why I didn't push harder for answers. *Fuck.* Why would she tell me this? She has no idea what's she's done. The impossible position it puts me in.

*Think, Ciprian, think.* What are our options? There's no imme-diate answer, and Celine's lips return to mine before I can make sense of my scattered thoughts.

"Anyone else?" I ask. I'm worried her answer will be yes, but I need to know the full extent of what we're dealing with. "I'm feeling violent."

"Thanks, but I can take care of myself." Celine nibbles on my ear lobe. "I do have one request, though . . . don't ever call me hot wings again."

Groaning, I force myself to calm down and play my part. I pull back with an overdramatized mask of horror on my face. "Anything but that!"

Celine's lips twitch, then she throws her head back and giggles. The sound echoes off the bathroom walls. "I don't know how you always make me laugh," she gasps, holding her sides.

*Gods, she's stunning.* This afternoon I told her she was everything in between. I meant it then and I mean it now. I've never met anyone like her.

"You should laugh more often," I say, winking to make the comment seem lighter than it is, then rocking my hips suggestively.

Someone knocks on the door. "I don't know what the fuck is going on in there, but I've got to piss. Any chance you two could relocate?" Luca's voice is strained. He's pretending to be calm.

Celine and I lock eyes, and I notice hers are back to the sharp, focused brown I'm used to. She stands and pulls me to my feet. My dizziness is gone, thank the gods, but the memory of what brought me here in the first place weighs heavily on me.

Guilt joins the party. How could I have a moment with Celine while Sheena is in trouble? *Don't be an idiot.* It's Sheena's voice I hear in my head, and I smile. She would be furious if she knew I had a chance to kiss Celine but didn't because of her. As soon as I can, I'll tell her all about it. I won't give up hope.

"She'll make it through this. Your friend," Celine says, squeezing my hand and reminding me that she isn't the only one who spilled her guts on the bathroom floor. "Women are resilient; we have to be. And she's lucky to have a friend like you."

I squeeze back and smile. "I think I'm the lucky one."

As long as Celine keeps looking at me this way, it will be true.

# THIRTY-SIX

## ALISTAIR

A splinter of shadowed intuition digs into my mind, firmly embedding itself beyond my reach. Sleep evades me, no matter how much tossing and turning I do. My pillow is too warm, the bed too soft. I peel the covers off my right side and stick my leg out.

Now I'm cool . . . yet I remain vividly awake. It's maddening.

I use my tongue to count my teeth—thirty-two of them—as I already bloody knew there would be. I count the ceiling tiles next. There are twenty-eight. *Incredible information gathering, Ali. Exemplary.*

If I could figure out why my mind won't quiet, I could address it and sleep. But some instincts require decoding before they can be understood. Mine are screaming at me, telling me I've missed something, yet refusing to show me a clear picture.

Rolling onto my side, I study Celine and Luca in the darkness.

Celine's lips are parted, her chest rising and falling at a slow, measured pace. *Safe. She's safe.* I focus on Luca next, noticing how thick and dark his eyelashes are. Beautiful. Both of them.

My fingers curl, and my eyes heat as blood collects behind them. Vision sharpened, I can see every dip and curve with perfect clarity despite the darkness. It doesn't help me sleep. There's a puffiness under Celine's eyes, skin irritated by her tears. The bruising on Luca's neck is yellowing around the edges.

I fight the urge to tug them closer. I should have protected them both better. When Celine and I made our deal, I promised her something casual. Fascinated by the both of them and envious of their dynamic, I meant it wholeheartedly at the time . . . I just didn't realize how hard it would be to keep my word.

Vampires traditionally avoid attachments and keep to themselves. Frankly, I never expected to experience anything like the raw, possessive thirst that consumes me now. Yet here I am. Sleepless. Frenzied.

Celine and Luca would never again sleep soundly by my side if they knew how ferociously I desire them. To pursue them without restraint would be to lose them.

Celine especially isn't ready. Listening to her shut down during Luca's declaration proved it. My blood runs cold as I imagine her rejecting me. I tug the covers back over my leg. Dwelling is a waste of time, yet sleep refuses to come.

The sun rises behind the protection of the blackout shades.

My eyes are gritty and bloodshot.

Is it the family we placed the angels with in Valley of Fire? Maybe they aren't what they seem. I replay our interactions ruthlessly. Nothing stands out.

Hours pass. Celine and Luca stir. I do my best not to resent them for their rest, ransacking every nook and cranny of my brain to explain my unease.

We get up after noon, and I tell no one about my sleepless

night. My body feels like it's moving through quicksand, my nerves ground down until even the slightest stimulation jolts their frayed ends.

By the time Luca and Celine head to the club, I'm more exposed nerve than man.

Ciprian tosses me a few penetrating looks, but doesn't pry. Five minutes after sunset, he glances up from his phone and clears his throat. "I'm having a bad day too, you know. How about we go to the club and flirt with Luca until he kicks us out?"

I force a smile and nod. Dwelling at the club is better than dwelling here. At least at the Naked Fang, I'll know they're both okay.

"Off we pop," I say, bracing my hands on my thighs.

Ciprian stands and smirks at me. "Has anyone ever told you that you sound British sometimes?"

I flinch internally. Gods, my lack of sleep really is taking a toll if it's that noticeable.

"Nice catch," I mutter. "My mum is English. Blood bluer than the aristocracy, although she would disagree due to these." I tap my fangs. Technically, she considers what we are to be far more damning than a simple class demotion, but Ciprian doesn't need to know that.

"That's cool." He opens the front door and steps out onto the landing. "My mom would love to be royal."

I cock my head. There's something there . . . in his tone. I can't put my finger on it. A wry sort of amusement?

"Are you close to your family?" I ask, locking the apartment behind us and following Ciprian down the stairs. The street light shines on his face, bathing it in a sickly yellow glow. He scrubs his hand over his chin, but not before I see his frown.

"Gods, that's kind of a loaded question. Mom would tell you yes, but she's not interested in a real relationship." He sighs, then chuckles. "Here I am rambling about my mommy issues while we head to a strip club. Someone, somewhere, with a lot of letters after their name would have something to say about that."

I grunt in response as I process his words, scanning the street, rooftops, and sky for winged assassins, before facing him. "Mothers can be complicated," I admit.

Pain flickers across Ciprian's face, only to be replaced a heartbeat later by the cocky smirk he wears so well. He changes the subject smoothly. If I wasn't expecting it, I might not have noticed. And even though I'm fully aware he's steering our conversation into less turbulent waters, his chattering soothes me.

Ciprian is charming in a way many people train for years to achieve and never reach. He would be a tremendous asset to my information network. If only I trusted him.

I pull in outside the club, but it takes a while to find a parking spot. "Must be busy tonight," I say.

He mumbles something noncommittal, the first resurgence of his 'bad day' since he stopped talking about his mom. I remember him trembling on the bathroom floor last night and frown. I'm not sure flirting with Luca can fix whatever's wrong with Ciprian.

We walk silently to the club, both monitoring our surroundings carefully. The door is only about ten feet away when someone shouts.

"Hey, Casanell!"

I turn to look. A guy I've never seen before is waving excitedly at us—no, at Ciprian. The yellow glint in his eyes tells me he's a shifter. Probably drunk and confused.

We keep walking. Ciprian is moving more quickly than before. I narrow my eyes and slow down.

"Dude, wait up," the stranger shouts. "Your dad sent me. He says you haven't been answering your phone."

I stop. The splinter quivers wildly inside my brain.

"Ignore him," Ciprian mutters, reaching for the door.

I ignore him instead, turning to face the shifter. "Who did you say you were looking for?" I ask politely. "Maybe I can help."

"Ciprian Casanell," the man barks, his eyes flashing a brighter yellow as his chest puffs out. "I don't need help from fringe scum either; I'm here on enclave business. Don't even think about getting in my way."

The splinter disintegrates, and everything snaps into place.

Ciprian's careful questions. How powerful he is. The way he never quite fits in.

"Ciprian *Casanell?*" I repeat, shaking my head as my eyes burn. "I should have known. You're here for a job. Tell me, Casanell, are *we* the job?"

"Listen, Alistair, please." Ciprian grabs my upper arm. "Let me explain."

I shove his hand off. He's not who he claimed to be—I've heard all I need to hear.

"You lied to us," I hiss, shoving him back into the outer wall of the Fang. "And you betrayed Celine."

"No." Ciprian's head snaps up, anger and desperation twisting his face into something I don't recognize. "I absolutely did not."

I scoff. His audacity, to keep pretending, even now . . . It reeks of enclave entitlement. I should have recognized it for what it was the first time I saw him. My judgment is to blame for this; I let a rat into our midst. That ends tonight.

"Come on, man," the shifter whines. "Let's go back to the compound. It's gross here."

"Brendan," Ciprian snarls. "If you don't fuck off right now, I will remove your organs and feed them to my father one by one."

Brendan goes unnaturally still, one finger twitching at his side. "He'll kill me if I come back empty-handed."

Ciprian shrugs—he doesn't give a shit if that happens or not. "Sounds like you've got a choice to make," he drawls. "Stay and die tonight or crawl back to the compound and survive a few more hours."

"You're a fucking asshole," Brendan grunts. "Everyone says so." His tone is belligerent, but there's fear in his eyes as he backs away and disappears into the darkness.

The insult rolls off Ciprian as if he didn't even hear it. His black eyes are fixed on me. The heat in my veins, the burning. I want, no *need* to tear him to pieces.

That night he saved my life, he wasn't wandering around or heading home like he claimed, he was following me. If I had died, his lead would have died with me. He played us all, every step of the way, half-truth after half-truth. One calculated risk after the other.

For the first time in years, I've been completely fooled.

It cuts through the thin veneer of my control until I'm hanging on by a thread.

"You'll tell Celine the truth," I tell him, my fangs throbbing. "Then you'll crawl behind your gilded walls and leave us alone. Forever."

"Let me explain, Alistair. Please!" It disgusts me that he thinks I'm so easily tricked. I won't give him another chance to deceive me. He's been playing a game of chess and using us as the pawns. I won't forget it.

"I can't stand to look at you," I snap. "Go tell her. Now."

Ciprian flinches as if I hit him, his shoulders slumping. The begging. His dejection. It's all part of a carefully curated act. He's upset that his game is over.

The door swings wide with a sickening screech, but the cold glide of the Fang's wards does nothing to cool my rage. Noise crashes into us. It bounces off my exposed nerves like hot wax. The Fang is packed, bodies stacked from corner to corner as Celine works the pole, her routine drawing raucous hoots and hollers.

Every inch of my vision is tinged in red. I clench my teeth. The urge to paint the club in blood is difficult to ignore. Nearly impossible. We were played, and I was too blind to see what was right in front of me all along.

I blame Ciprian.

I blame myself.

I blame the enclave.

And I blame the Fringes too.

The closed-mouth mentality ends for me tonight. I'll pry if I want to, bones, teeth, secrets and all. No one deserves privacy at my expense. Here in this crowded strip club, I make a vow: to learn everything I can about the supernaturals living in this realm.

I won't be taken by surprise again.

Ciprian marches to the bar, his jaw rigid, pulse racing. If I focus, I can hear it over the music. *Thu-thump. Thu-thump. Thu-thump.* I lick my fangs, testing the sharp points. I can practically taste his blood on my tongue.

Overconfident fool that he is, he's letting me walk at his back. I could kill him before his heart finished one full pump. I reach for him, longing to feel his blood trickle down my throat again. I know how good it tastes, how warm and satisfying—Phantom pain pierces me, and I relive the indescribable agony of the angel's sword plunging to the hilt in my gut.

Ciprian tasted like my salvation that night, but he was our damnation all along. Still . . . I retract my hand. Motivations aside, my honor refuses to kill the man who saved my life. At least while his back is turned. If I end him, I'll do it while staring into his eyes.

"What's wrong?" Luca demands, wiping the sweat off his brow and ignoring the line of people clamoring for drinks. His forehead pinches as he focuses first on Ciprian, then me. "Are you both okay?"

"We need to talk," Ciprian says. His voice gets swallowed up by the din of the crowd, but we both hear him fine. "Once Celine wraps up." He glances at the stage, anguish on his face as he watches her dance. My lips curl with disgust. He's a consummate liar. Even now it looks like he truly cares for her.

Luca turns his attention to the line of people jockeying for his attention. "You assholes better order a pitcher now if you want it," he shouts. "I'm about to take my break."

Loud complaints greet that announcement, all of them yelling to be served.

Ciprian slumps onto a barstool, and I watch him like a hawk, happy to let him wallow in the anticipation. He snuck into our community, gained our trust under false pretenses, and now it's time to pay the bill for our hospitality.

The enclave has earned every bit of the derision it gets around here. Never around to help, Dimitri Casanell and Joshua Therion love to send a minion to the Fringes to enforce their authority every few months. I am surprised we warranted a visit from Casanell's heir, though. Ciprian must be out of favor with the self-proclaimed powers that be.

The cheering gets louder, signaling the end of Celine's set. Like clockwork, Luca grabs a water bottle and rounds the bar.

"Here she comes," he says, tossing me a warning look. I can only imagine how I seem to him right now. My bloodlust is teetering right below massacre level. His basilisk senses the predatory intent, and Luca the man doesn't approve. "Let's make this quick."

I scoff. He'll be singing a different tune as soon as he hears what happened. Ciprian will be lucky to walk out of here alive. I have to get a grip. Lying asshole or not, if we kill Dimitri Casanell's son, we'll pay with our lives.

"Hands to yourself, Rex, or you'll get banned again." Celine's voice pulls me out of my thoughts, and I turn my head to see her prying the bear shifter's fingers off her waist.

"I love it when you're mean to me," he says, slurring his words.

I blink, and everything turns ruby red. He reaches for her again, then my hand is around his throat, shoving his face into the bar top. His forehead hits the wood with a massive thump. Several people back away. I sense others closing in and snarl.

"Let him go, Alistair," Celine hisses, tugging on my arm.

I growl. "Not until he apologizes."

Using her full strength, Celine yanks me off the brute. "He doesn't have to apologize. Gods, what's the matter with you?"

I can't believe she's defending him. In front of all these people. "He had his hands on you," I hiss and lunge for the bear again.

Celine shoves me back, glaring up at me like I'm the problem. She tosses the stunned crowd an apologetic smile, then levels me with an icy glare. "I had it handled," she whispers.

"I'm supposed to stand by while someone paws at my girl?" I roar, my voice booming over the whispers and grumbles. *No. Don't do this.* The thought is barely a whisper inside my mind. It's no match for the anger.

"I don't belong to anyone," Celine says, steel in her voice and murder in her eyes. Every head in this bar is turned our way. She shifts uncomfortably on her feet.

"Nothing to see here." She laughs. It's the fakest sound I've ever heard.

"A little show for added value," Luca jokes. "Rex, your next pitcher is on me." He pats the surly bear on the back and hands him a napkin.

Rex glowers at me, his face warped with rage as blood drips from his nose. It smells acrid. Gamey. But it's warm and wet, and for an instant, I pray he lunges for me like he wants to. When he shakes his head and backs away, I taste my disappointment instead.

"What the *fuck* was that?" Celine says, her voice cracking.

"He was touching you," I seethe, looking to Luca for backup.

His face is carefully blank. It stings. Another betrayal.

"I'm serious, Alistair." Celine crosses her arms over her chest. She's squaring off against me, positioning herself as my enemy. "You better knock it off with the territorial bullshit or I swear—"

"You'll what, Celine?" I snap, rolling through her weaknesses until I pinpoint the quickest way to hurt her as much as she's hurting me. "Will you take your clothes off for a bunch of strangers? Oh wait, you already do that."

Her mouth drops open, and she takes a step back. Too late, I realize what I've done and reach for her, regret overpowering my anger. She shakes my hand off and wipes every trace of emotion from her face.

Ciprian shoots to his feet. "Watch how you speak to her," he says. "Don't take it out on Celine because you're pissed at me."

My fury coalesces into a flash point with him at the center, and I lunge. "You're asking for it," I snarl. "Telling me to watch my mouth when every word out of yours has been a lie."

"Woah, woah, woah." Luca muscles his way between us, wincing when his collarbone gets jostled. "You're making a scene. We need to go somewhere private."

"Fuck that," Celine says. "Alistair is obviously taking me up on my original offer, that's all."

My heart sinks, panic turning my blood to ice. The public falling-out she wanted to stage to keep me safe? I don't want that; I want her. Can't she see? I made a mistake, but this is his fault. All of this is Ciprian's fault.

Celine looks up at me, her eyes hard and unforgiving. "I have better things to do during my break than hear a bunch of dicks-with-legs fight over me like a piece of meat."

Mind at war, I stare at her, undecided. One side urges me to protect my wounded heart; the other demands I drop to my knees and beg her forgiveness.

She takes another step back.

I'm losing her.

It hurts, and I bare my fangs. When she flinches away from me, I try to stop, but the words are already pouring out of me. "Because you're such a good judge of character, aren't you, Celine? A magical truth detector who lets a liar into her midst and doesn't even notice—it's the start of a bad joke."

"What are you talking about?" Her wings spread wide and smoke ominously. "You know what, I don't even care anymore. Get out of here, Alistair. I'm not dealing with this."

Her rejection is the final straw. The third betrayal I've faced tonight, and the last.

I point at Ciprian, fury coating my insides in molten heat.

"He's enclave," I say, not bothering to keep my voice down. Gasps echo around us, and I spin to face the crowd. "A demon who feeds on fear with powers greater than most of you could imagine? It should have been obvious . . . His name is Ciprian Casanell, and his daddy wants him to come home."

Whispers break out. The onlookers stare at Ciprian, first in surprise, then with growing hostility. Flames curl up from the tips of Celine's wings, but when she turns to Ciprian, there's fear in her eyes.

"Is that true?" she asks him, her voice smaller than I've ever heard it. "Did you lie to me about everything?"

# THIRTY-SEVEN

## CELINE

He hangs his head, then lifts it and squares his shoulders. "My name is Ciprian Casanell, that's true, but I didn't—"

"Get out of here," I hiss, the truth of his admission smacking me with every syllable out of his mouth. Emotions assault me on all fronts, and I flinch away from them, bumping into someone, then lurching forward unsteadily.

I trusted Alistair with my body and my friendship, yet he called me a whore in front of dozens of our neighbors. The spiteful man in front of me is unrecognizable to me, and I wish I'd never let him past my guard. I want nothing to do with him.

As for Ciprian . . . my lack of judgment with him could get me killed, if my father doesn't get the job done first. For fuck's sake— I admitted to a murder while sitting in his lap. Alistair was right about one thing at least: I am a joke.

My wings spasm, treating us all to drips, flames, and knives. A shifter I've seen around cries out in pain as boiling water hits his face. Horrified, I back away, ignoring the panicked look on Ciprian's face.

Luca shouts at me to stop. I don't. I can't listen anymore; I've got to get the fuck out of here before I accidentally kill someone. Storming down the hall, I shove Imani's hand off my shoulder as she tries to pull me back, then wrench open the employee exit and break into a sprint.

Ciprian lied to me. That's obvious, but the question is how? I run through our interactions. The ache in my heart intensifies as I remember how he looked last night—broken, on my bathroom floor. I gave him my worst fear and made myself vulnerable.

I allowed his charm to draw me in. I should have used my magic to test every word out of his mouth, but I was too afraid to give away who I was to see the threat in front of me. He was probably laughing at me the entire time.

How long do I have before Ciprian drags me away to face the enclave?

I cling to my anger, hating the weight of my hurt. It's too heavy, even for me.

My fists clench. This is exactly why I didn't want to get involved with anyone. I chose this life—risked everything to escape the one I was born into—and now everything I've built is crumbling around me because I gave them the power to hurt me.

My wings droop lower and lower until the tips graze the dirty asphalt. Fuck. This is pathetic. I'm strong enough to snap every bone in this city, yet here I am, stumbling along these dark, deserted streets half naked with tears rolling down my cheeks. *I'm weak. They've made me this way.*

"Celine! Baby, wait!" Luca's shout is panicked. My heart throbs. What else will I learn tonight? Is Luca harboring some dark, terrible secret, too? Annoyed with myself for the self-pity, I pat my bare hips, growling when I realize I fled the club without my keys.

I stop, holding my head high and hardening my heart. *Enough is enough.* Obediently, my tears stop, and the desert heat dries the ones left on my cheeks.

So what if my almost-lover is a liar? Almost every other woman in the realms could say the same at some point in her life. And who cares if my fake boyfriend thinks I'm a slut? Men love to make their insecurities a woman's problem. The only thing that matters is what I think about myself—and I slept fucking great before my bed got crowded.

They can all kiss my ass, except for Luca, who hasn't done anything wrong that I know of. I'm going to march back to the club and tell them all—I freeze. The air rustles, and the scent of celestial magic overwhelms my senses.

They've come for me at last. I feel no dread or fear, only grim determination. That ugly scene with Alistair in the Fang revealed a lot of things, including half of my angelic secrets, but if everyone knows about my truth, I might as well use it.

A pained groan reaches me, and my feet move before I even tell them to run. I'd recognize the sound anywhere: Luca, my Luca. He came after me and probably walked right into their trap. If they hurt a hair on his head, I'll make them regret stepping foot into this realm.

Bursting around the corner, I bowl through a petrified guardian. I wince as the rough stone of his body breaks to pieces against my skin. It hurts like a bitch, but it also frees his sword. I snatch it from his crumbling fingers. He certainly doesn't need it anymore.

Luca is fighting for his life, blood dripping from his face as he defends himself against four, no, five angels. All of them are guardian tier, the tops of their heads and faces covered by armor. Luca only turned the first one to stone by knocking his helm off first—I see it laying on the ground near his feet. The others obviously noticed, and they're keeping a tight guard around their heads.

"Surrender now," I shout, testing the balance of my stolen sword before dropping into a fighting stance. It's a style typically reserved for more uneven terrain, but my six-inch heels make the flat pavement plenty hazardous.

The guardians gawk at me, then stand at attention. One bows his head. I shudder. *Weird ass sycophants.*

"I will kill you all without blinking," I snarl, advancing a step.

"Lady, we mean you no harm," the biggest one says in the common tongue.

I pause. That felt like the truth, but it can't be. "In what reality could breaking into my house, attacking my allies, and trying to assassinate me be defined as 'no harm?'"

"I swear—"

Luca takes advantage of the distraction and punches the leader in the gut. "Don't meet my eyes, baby," he shouts, then narrowly avoids being decapitated by a blow.

"Pay attention," I hiss. "I can handle myself." It's true, especially since the one I'm parrying with continues to pull his strikes and avoid . . . looking at my body? It doesn't make sense.

I use my strength to shove my opponent into the concrete wall. His head makes contact, and he falls to the ground unconscious, slumping over at an awkward angle. "These assassins are terrible."

"These four are fighting hard," Luca complains. "And I don't have a fucking weapon."

He shoves one of the soldiers back into the other three. I sneak up behind them, swinging my borrowed sword like a baseball bat and smacking the flat of the blade into their heads in rapid succession.

They collapse, but since I wasn't swinging to kill, they'll live to see another day. With the headache they'll have when they wake, though, they might wish they hadn't.

Luca drags the back of his hand over his face, smearing blood across his forehead when he grazes the split above his eyebrow. He frowns at the unconscious guardians and nudges one with his toe. "Those weren't killing blows."

"I know," I say, avoiding eye contact as I try to make sense of what happened. "Put your murder eyes away. Something about this wasn't right."

"No shit," Luca snaps. "They jumped me out of the blue."

"But they didn't try to hurt me," I point out. "Which is a pretty strange trait for an assassin."

Luca considers that. "Maybe they thought you were too hot to kill."

"That's ridiculous." I roll my eyes, my nerves too fried to engage in banter. "That one over there nearly stabbed himself while trying to avoid checking me out."

The adrenaline of the fight fades and everything else comes rushing back. I prop myself up with the sword as my energy abandons me all at once. "Ciprian played me."

"He played us," Luca says, his voice painfully gentle. "And I'm not convinced we have the full story. None of it adds up."

I frown. "He told us his name, what more do you need to know? He's enclave."

"If that's true," Luca says. "Then why are you walking around free? I heard you tell him about Roscoe last night."

"I knew you were eavesdropping." I try to muster some outrage, but I'm too tired and heartbroken to pull it off.

"I had to pee," Luca says stubbornly. "And it's a small apartment."

I shrug. "Does it even matter why I haven't been arrested? Maybe he wanted to stick around and get more dirt."

Luca touches the split on his face and examines the blood on his fingers. "From everything I've heard about the enclave, that's not how they work."

"We don't need to understand his motives," I snap, pointing at the fallen soldiers around us with my sword. "We need to deal with this mess."

"He saved Alistair, though."

"Lucky us," I snarl.

"Baby." There's enough quiet judgment in Luca's voice that a thin outline of fire spreads around my wingtips.

I groan. We're surrounded by bodies, dead, dismembered, or lights out, and my wings decide now is a good time to impersonate a road flare?

Frustrated, I toss up my hands. The sword feels a lot heavier than it did when I first grabbed it. "I don't want to talk about either of them yet," I say quietly, then turn as I hear footsteps running our way.

Imani skids around the corner in a silk robe, breathing heavily. "Celine, thank the gods you're okay." She takes in the crime scene around us, her mouth dropping open.

"I'm sorry I shoved you," I tell her. "But you need to get away from here. I'll call you after I get this cleaned up."

"Celine, listen," she begins.

"There isn't time." One of the unconscious angels groans, and Luca kicks him in the head. The sound cuts off abruptly. "Don't kill him until we know what's going on," I hiss.

"Shut up!" Imani shouts.

I stare at her, shocked. In all our years of friendship, I've never seen her lose her temper before. Not with me at least.

"I ran out here to tell you that someone is here to see you."

"Okay," I whisper, ashamed of myself for pushing her this far. "Did they mention their name?"

Imani shakes her head, her eyebrows drawing tightly together.

She shoots a worried glance at Luca. "He said . . . shit, Celine, he said he was your husband."

I'm running before she can say another word. It's all I can do not to scream into the night and never stop, because here, on the Fringes of supernatural Las Vegas, we live every moment in the darkest of valleys, even when the sun is blinding. And the truth none of us can ignore for long is this: we're never safe.

# EPILOGUE

## CIPRIAN

I leave the Naked Fang and go to a nearby bar to get blind drunk and wallow, stumbling out at last call with a numbness that can't begin to silence the angry, screaming wound inside me.

Celine hates me. Why wouldn't she? I didn't lie to her face, but what I did was worse. I tricked her, deliberately concealing my identity and my motives, embedding myself in her life like a parasite.

I want to tell her I hate myself as much as she does, but she doesn't want to hear that.

Dad's stunt almost got me killed. Alistair thought about it—I watched him weigh his options. It made me wonder who would come out on top if we fought without holding back.

If he got the drop on me, a snapped neck would be the quickest way to go, but I think I would prefer his fangs in me.

That way, I could at least imagine that I mattered to him a little while he tore me to pieces.

Luca was shocked, but he didn't offer to hear me out. No one ever does, so I'm not sure why I'm surprised. I'm not the guy who gets the benefit of the doubt, and I'll never be someone who has a loyal group of friends supporting his rights and wrongs.

My own brother always thinks the worst. Mom sees only her baby's face and nothing more when she looks at me. And Dad, well, the only thing he likes about me is the fact that his magic runs through my veins. The weight of my last name has always been heavy. Tonight, though, I'd give anything to put it down and stand on my own.

I laugh up at the sky, then burp loudly. I can metaphorically throw off my identity a million times. But it won't change who I am.

Fumbling for my phone, I dial Sheena's number to hear it ring. She can't answer, I know that, but part of me hopes she will. *Pick up, bestie. I need you.*

"Hello," Callum answers, and my heart sinks. "Ciprian, is that you?"

I sigh bitterly. "Who else would it be?" Turning down a random side street, I wander aimlessly along the Fringes. This could be the way to my shitty apartment or a path to nowhere. I won't know unless I keep walking.

"Is everything okay?" Callum asks. His voice is laced with exhaustion. I consider lying, but I've done enough of that recently, and I'm drunk enough to not care what he thinks of me.

"You didn't tell me," I say. "I was scared out of my mind for her, sick with worry. You didn't even think to send me a text."

There's a pause on the other end of the line. I think he hung up on me until I hear him release a heavy sigh. "There was nothing you could do."

"Believe me, I know." I laugh bitterly. "I'm no help. Worthless. Everyone thinks so."

"What's wrong, Ciprian?" Callum demands. "It's late."

I laugh again, then sag against a graffiti-covered building. It smells like vomit and despair. "Everything," I tell him, my voice cracking around the word. "Dad made sure of that."

"What did he do?" Callum demands, and I cock my head. His voice is angry—on my behalf for once. It drags my mind back to a simpler time, when he used to stand up for me. There were years when I counted on him. Years when I had the best big brother in all the realms. Then he left me behind.

It hurts to remember that it was ever different.

"Does it even matter?" I ask. "It's done now; there's no changing it."

Another long silence comes down the line.

I hold the phone tighter to my ear, desperate to hear his voice and be less alone.

"I'll call you as soon as there's an update on Sheena," Callum finally says, his voice choked with emotion. "And if you need someone to kick Dad's ass, Gideon is one dirty look away from removing his head from his body, anyway."

"Yeah?" I say. "Record a video for me. I'd love to see that."

"Will do. Are you coming home soon?"

I consider the irony. It's been a long time since Callum called the compound home, but I guess old habits die hard. The thought of crawling through the gates now makes my stomach churn.

"Maybe after I cool off," I say.

"Be safe," Cal orders.

"Duh." I roll my eyes at his bossiness and prepare to hang up.

"And about what you said . . ."

"What?" I ask, my voice sharper than I mean for it to be.

"That shit about being worthless? Sheena doesn't think that about you . . . and neither do I."

Callum hangs up before I can respond, and I'm oddly relieved. Two Casanells talking about their feelings together can only end in—The punch comes out of nowhere, hitting me square in the jaw. My head smacks into the filthy wall I was leaning against, and I see triple.

"Fucking enclave prick." My attacker spits at my feet.

I reach for my magic, doing my best to weave a nightmare that will send him running, but I can't concentrate. Unease sinks into my belly as he lands another blow, this one to my nose. The next hit cracks something—maybe a rib—and it comes from a different angle.

Not triple vision after all. There are three of them.

I land a few hits . . . maybe, but it isn't enough.

Everything around me spins, and the ground comes at me hard. The hits don't stop, though. If anything, they get worse. And while the first kick to my ribs hurts, I don't feel the ones that come after it. I could thank the booze for that, but I won't. If I wasn't drunk, I could use my magic to defend myself. It's another in a long line of mistakes.

All I can do is lie here and accept the fact that I'm getting the shit kicked out of me because of my last name. I'll have to wait to find out if I'm also going to die for it. The sole of a thick boot is the last thing I see before everything fades to black.

# AUTHOR'S NOTE

Don't be mad. It's Celine who doesn't believe in fairy tales . . . not me. If I don't make her work for it, will she even appreciate her happily ever after?

Shadow of Death is available now.

If you enjoyed Darkest Valley, please consider leaving a rating or review. These make such a difference for indie authors, and I love hearing from you!

**Stay up to date by signing up for my newsletter or scanning the QR code below with your phone's camera.**

# ACKNOWLEDGMENTS

*Darkest Valley* is one of those ideas that hit me in the middle of the night—I sat up like a mummy in bed and grappled for my notepad to scribble it down before I forgot:

*Angel. Mood wings. Motorcycle.*

And now, here we are.

While writing and revising the *Lost Legacy* series, these characters wormed their way into my brain and heart, demanding their own page time. Raw, flawed, and sometimes unapologetically toxic . . . they made me cringe, laugh, and cry. I hope you adore them as much as I do.

Writing can be a lonely journey, especially for an extrovert, but I'm lucky to have an amazing support system cheering me on and helping make my books better.

A special thanks to my husband, mom, and sister, who are always ready with encouragement when I need it. (Mom, you still can't read this one.)

To my editor, EJ Lounsbury—thank you for rolling up your sleeves, diving into this universe, and helping me bring it to life in a way that makes sense.

And to my beta reader team: Lisa, Madeleine, Alyssa, Krista, Sara, and Bruce. Y'all are so wonderful! I love you equally for the hype and the critiques. Celine would call me out for that lie, but I'm working on making it true.

Most of all, thank you to the readers who supported *Lost Legacy*. *Radiant Legacy* wouldn't exist without you, and I hope to keep adding to this world for a long time.

Happy reading!

# ABOUT THE AUTHOR

ALANA KAY is a romance author with a soft spot for imperfect heroes, tough heroines, and steamy love stories. She made her debut into paranormal romance in 2024 with her novel *The Last Wish* (Lost Legacy Book One) and completed the trilogy in February 2025. Alana Kay fell for romance novels in the early aughts after sneaking bodice rippers from her mom's dog-eared collection of paperbacks. A big believer in happy endings, she likes her love scenes on page, her adventures nonstop, and her magic off the rails. When she's not typing feverishly, she's either snuggling with her dog, cats, or husband in sunny Los Angeles or impulsively signing up for a sporting event she's not nearly athletic enough to commit to.

Author of the completed *Lost Legacy* and *Radiant Legacy* series. Stay tuned for the *Bad Bones* duet, coming early 2027.

*For updates, follow @AlanaKayAuthor on social media or head over to AlanaKayAuthor.com.*

# ALSO BY ALANA KAY

## LEGACY UNIVERSE

### LOST LEGACY

The Last Wish

The Last Dream

The Last Djinn

### RADIANT LEGACY

Darkest Valley

Shadow of Death

Fear No Evil

Eternal Light